Gift

LIES SLEEPING

D0626313

LIES SLEEPING

BEN AARONOVITCH

This edition first published in Great Britain in 2019 by Gollancz

First published in Great Britain in 2018 by Gollancz
an imprint of the Orion Publishing Group Ltd
Carmelite House, 50 Victoria Embankment
London EC4Y 0DZ

An Hachette UK Company

5 7 9 10 8 6

A CIP catalogue record for this book is
available from the British Library.

ISBN 978 1 473 20783 7

Typeset by Input Data Services Ltd, Somerset

Printed and bound in Great Britain by Clays Ltd, Elcograf S.p.A.

www.gollancz.co.uk

This book is dedicated to all the people whose job it is to rush into danger when everybody else is running in the other direction.

ριστος τρόπος τοῦ ἀμύνεσθαι τὸ μὴ ἐξομοιοῦσθαι

The best revenge is not to become like your enemy.

Marcus Aurelius, *Meditations*, Book 6

Prologue

Protective Marking	Restricted
FOIA Exemption	Yes
Suitable for Publication Scheme? Y/N	No
Title and Version	Operation Jennifer
Purpose	
Relevant to	
Summary	Approval to commence operation Jennifer
Author and Warrant/Pay Number	DAC Richard Folsom
Creating BOCU/Branch & Unit	SAU
Date Created	14 Nov 2014
Review Date	N/A

FOR THE ATTENTION OF THE COMMISSIONER
HARDCOPY ONLY

It is proposed that the following operations be amalgamated into OPERATION JENNIFER:

OPERATION TINKER; BROMLEY MIT – SIO DCI MAUREEN DUFFY

Murder of George Trenchard by unspecified but confirmed FALCON method. Not only has George Trenchard been linked to Martin Chorley financially (cf OP. WENTWORTH) but statements from Varvara Sidorovna Tamonina have directly implicated him in the Mulkern murder.

OPERATION WENTWORTH; CTC and SFO

Investigation into public corruption; financial fraud; attempted murder; conspiracy to cause an explosion. Martin Chorley has been linked to this case through the money trail from County Gard Holdings and its numerous subsidiaries and cut-outs. There is additional corroboration from witnesses including, again, Varvara Sidorovna Tamonina.

OPERATION CARTHORSE; DPS – SIO DI WILLIAM POLLOCK

Investigation into allegations of misconduct in public office by former Police Constable Lesley May. PC May has now been positively identified as a criminal associate of Martin Chorley.

OPERATION CARTWHEEL; BELGRAVIA MIT – SIO DCI ALEXANDER SEAWOLL

Investigation into criminal conspiracy to commit murder.

OPERATION MARIGOLD; BELGRAVIA MIT – SIO
DCI ALEXANDER SEAWOLL
See Appendix 2, 3, 4 & 9

It is the unanimous belief of the senior officers involved
in the above operations that Martin Chorley represents
a serious and immediate danger to the Queen's Peace
on a scale that could, conceivably, match that of the
7/7 bomb attacks. To this end it is their conviction that
we should effect the capture, arrest and prosecution
of Martin Chorley as soon as possible. To do this will
require an aggressively proactive intelligence led investigation. The DPS have advised that internal communi-
cations within MPS have been subverted requiring any
operation to be run on a 'need to know' basis and with
compartmentalised IT support.

As the MPS', and the UK's, lead agency on Falcon
matters I can see no alternative but to let the Special
Assessment Unit run the operation in line with their
rather, frankly, risky and unorthodox methods. It will,
at least, create a degree of plausible deniability should
matters become messily public and remains the best
chance for a positive outcome with the minimum expo-
sure to the media.

Famous last words!

1

Chiswick Poke

H is name was Richard Williams and he worked in public relations. Despite living in a nice Edwardian semi in Chiswick, his family were originally from Fulwood, Sheffield and had enough readies to send him to Birkdale School as a day boy. Thus allowing him to get both an expensive education and a home cooked meal. He'd moved to London after graduating with a creditable first from Magdalen College, Oxford. There he had met his first wife while working for a major advertising agency. Now with a second, younger, wife and a pair of daughters on the cusp of primary school he was, if I was any judge, getting ready to move out to the Thames Valley or even further west to ensure that they went to schools that were a little less 'colourful' than the ones in Chiswick. I could guess this because I knew just about everything there was to know about Richard Williams, from his school records to the last thing he bought online with his credit card. No doubt he would be horrified to hear that he'd fallen victim to the ubiquitous surveillance state, and even more horrified to learn that two police officers, me and DS 'count the stripes' Guleed, were sitting across from his house in an unmarked, but mercifully not silver, Hyundai and keeping his house under observation.

Me and Guleed were less horrified, and more bored out of our tiny little minds.

We were there because while at Oxford Richard Williams had joined a dining club called the Little Crocodiles. Nothing unusual about that; plenty of posh students and their aspirational middle-class groupies joined dining clubs, if only for the chance to get pissed and boisterous without the fear of turning up on a cheap Channel 5 documentary about the moral decline of the English working class.

Or as my dad always says: it only becomes a social problem when the working man joins in.

What made the Little Crocodiles different was their founder Professor Geoffrey Wheatcroft, DD, DPhil, FSW, and fully qualified wizard. The FSW is the give-away. It stands for Fellow of the Society of the Wise, otherwise known as The Folly – the official home of British wizardry since 1775. And if this is coming as a shock you might want to consider doing some background reading before you continue.

Geoffrey Wheatcroft thought it would be a laugh to teach some of the Little Crocodiles how to do magic – we don't know how many. A small percentage of them got really good at it, but we don't know how many of these there are, either.

What we do know is that at least two of them decided to use their magical skills to do some serious crimes. Including a couple that might just qualify as crimes against humanity – and I'm not joking about that.

Geoffrey Wheatcroft died before all this came to

light, and so managed to avoid the consequences for his actions, although I know my governor occasionally fantasises about digging up his corpse and setting fire to it. Also conveniently dead was Albert Woodville-Gentle, who we used to call Faceless Man number I. But, before he went, he helped train up Martin Chorley, who we called Faceless Man II. Trust me – it made sense at the time.

We know who Martin Chorley is, and we know what he's done. But we don't know *where* he is. Or what he's planning. And that's what's keeping us all awake at night.

The man was clever, I'll say that. He didn't count on getting busted, but he definitely had contingency plans and resources squirrelled away just in case.

We really only had two viable lines of inquiry to find Martin Chorley. One was the fact that we know he recruited former Little Crocodiles to work for him, and the other was that there were more of those that we hadn't identified. So some bright spark came up with the idea of the 'poke' strategy.

We got our analysts to locate likely candidates amongst the Little Crocodiles, then we put them under close surveillance and then we went and practised some light intimidation – the 'poke' – to spook them. That done, we sat back and waited to see if they reacted. Hopefully they might call a number or send an email or a text to an unusual contact. Even more hopefully, they might run out of their house, jump in their car and lead us somewhere tasty.

That's why me and Guleed were in the Hyundai – so

we could follow Williams if he ran for it.

'This is all your fault,' said Guleed.

'It's bound to work sooner or later,' I said.

Richard Williams was our third 'poke' and the consensus was that we'd only get another two or three attempts before Martin Chorley twigged what we were doing, or someone tried to sue us for harassment.

'There they go,' said Guleed.

I looked over and saw a battered green Vauxhall Corsa pull up outside the target house.

The house had probably cost a couple of million quid, with its two storeys plus loft conversion, red brick, and detailing on the porch roof that hinted at Arts and Crafts without actually making it over the finishing line. It was at least mercifully free of pebble-dash and fake half-timbering. They'd retained the original sash windows but installed the venetian blinds that have replaced net curtains as the genteel response to sharing your neighbourhood with other human beings. The blinds were currently open. But to avoid being bleeding obvious we were parked ten metres up the street, so the angle was too poor for us to see inside.

The burner phone I was holding pinged and a sideways smiley face appeared.

'Stand by,' I said.

We were avoiding using our police issue Airwaves as much as possible, and not just because of the danger of them being wrecked if something magical happened. The smiley face had gone out to the team covering the next road over in case somebody made a break out of the back.

Nightingale and DC David Carey got out of the Corsa and started up the path to the front door.

'Here we go,' said Guleed, and stifled a yawn.

We'd been swapping roles since we started the operation. Nightingale and Carey had been in the observation car for the last poke – in Chipping Norton. We were calling that one 'the Aga saga' because our target hadn't shut up about his kitchen, which, as far as I could tell, had been designed by the same people who'd decorated Bag-End.

'Door's open,' said Guleed, and I made a note of the time in the log.

Normally the police like to turn up nice and early, preferably around 6 a.m., because not only are people liable to be actually at home but that early in the morning they're rarely playing with a full deck. Today we were going in Sunday lunchtime because we weren't looking for shock and awe but aiming for sinister and creepy instead. Nightingale is remarkably good at that – I think it's the accent.

Richard Williams had once had a job with a company called Slick Pictures, who'd done a lot of work for a land development company that was, via a series of shell companies, wholly owned by a firm called County Gard. Which just happened to be the remote instrument by which Martin Chorley ran some of his criminal enterprises.

It was thin, but we were desperate and, at the very least, it might keep the pressure on.

Guleed fussed with her hijab, an unusually plain one for her, police issue and designed to tear away if somebody grabbed it. We were both wearing the plain clothes version of the Metvest under our jackets – just in case.

I watched a cat leap out of the next door garden and streak away down the road. Something about its frantic pace made me uneasy and I was just about to mention it to Guleed when the burner pinged again and flashed up 'aa'. We'd worked out a series of codes as part of our operational planning. The character was irrelevant – the code lay in the number of them you sent. Three characters meant stand by, one meant charge in screaming, and two meant we were to take up our prearranged 'intervention' positions.

Guleed grinned.

'That makes a change,' she said.

We climbed out into the muggy warmth of a suburban Sunday lunchtime and headed for the house. The plan was to loiter as unobtrusively as possible outside the gate and await further instructions. But we were still eight metres short of the house when it all went pear-shaped.

The first I knew of it was a burst of *vestigia* from the house, as heavy as a mallet and as sharp and as controlled as the point of a needle – Nightingale's *signare*. If it was that intense, then he must have really let rip. And the last time he did that we'd needed a JCB to sweep up the remains.

I started running and got to the gate in time to see a fountain of slates erupt over the gable roof. As the slates tumbled and cracked down the front of the house, I saw a figure in pink and blue twist and squirm onto the ridge of the roof. It was a woman, slender, black haired, pale skinned and balanced perfectly on the guttering as if auditioning for the next *Spider-Man* movie.

She swung around to look down at me, head tilted to one side. Even from that distance I could see a wash of crimson around her mouth and chin, and running down the chest of her blue Adidas sweatshirt. I didn't think it was *her* blood.

She was wearing pink tracksuit bottoms and her feet were bare.

I recognised her from the briefing as the Williams' family nanny and also, from the way her lips were pulled back to bare her teeth, from a fight I'd once had years ago in the Trocadero Centre.

Oh shit, I thought. Haven't I met your sister?

Having seen us, I assumed she was going to scarper over the roof and down into the back garden. So it was a bit of a shock when she launched herself straight at me. Now, me and Guleed are bona fide detectives with the PIP2 qualifications to prove it, so we're not really supposed to be fighting anyone. That's what we have the TSG for.

Still, our careers being what they are at the moment, we'd taken some time with Nightingale, Carey and a couple of other members of the team, discussing what to do in various scenarios. And the principal lesson was – don't close, don't grapple, don't get clever. And don't hesitate.

I went right and Guleed went left.

The nanny landed like a cat on the pavement in what I thought was clear defiance of the laws of physics. I don't care how supple you are, landing like that from three storeys up should have driven her shin bones through her knees.

Once I'd put a nice new Nissan Micra between her and me, I conjured up an *impello* and whacked it at her knees. Guleed had gone over next door's garden wall and had her baton out. I watched her tense to jump forward as the nanny went down on her face.

And then rolled over, shaking off the blow to spring onto the bonnet of the Micra, and got a second *impello* in the face for her trouble. Because I don't hesitate with my follow-ups these days. This one knocked her off the bonnet and she landed on her back, her face contorted into a silent snarl of rage.

We weren't going to get a better opportunity than that, so me and Guleed threw ourselves on top of her. I went for the legs, Guleed for the arms. She kicked me as I came forward, her bare foot smashing into my shoulder and knocking me sideways. I saw another dirty heel coming at my face and I twisted enough to take it on the shoulder again. The first kick had been numbing, but the second was agonising. Despite the pain I tried to wrap my arms around her legs and use my body mass to pin her down. But it was like wrestling with a forklift truck. I swear she lifted my whole body weight and threw me over and onto my back.

I didn't wait to get comfy. I rolled clear – straight into the gutter – and scrambled to my feet. The nanny was up, too, and facing off against Guleed, who'd kept a grip on her right arm. Even as I lurched back into the fight the nanny struck at Guleed's face with her free left hand. But Guleed pulled her head back and in one fluid motion, pivoted around and swung her baton. It made a peculiar noise – like tearing silk – and slammed across the nanny's back. The woman arched in pain and I watched as Guleed, still holding her arm, ran up the side of the Nissan Micra in a way that didn't actually look physically possible and used her whole body weight to bear the nanny face down on to the pavement.

I decided that this was my cue and jumped forward to seize the nanny's ankles. Before she could react I threw my weight backwards so that her legs were fully extended. Deprived of leverage even the strongest person can't throw someone off their legs by main strength, and with Guleed on her back we almost had her. We only had to hold her until backup arrived, but we didn't even have our cuffs out when she rippled like a snake. Guleed tried to hang on, but she was knocked flying into me. By the time we were untangled and on our feet the nanny was away.

'Where the fuck is Nightingale?' I asked.

Saving Richard Williams from bleeding out, as it transpired.

'She tried to bite his throat right out,' Carey told me later.

2

Site Report

We probably should have guessed something like that had happened when the ambulance screeched up and a pair of paramedics charged past us into the house. Me and Guleed didn't follow them because we were too busy circulating a description of the nanny and warning responding officers not to go anywhere near her until Falcon qualified officers arrived. Then we grabbed a response car so we could be properly mobile in case she was spotted.

We needn't have bothered – she'd evaporated into the summer afternoon.

Because we were the second Falcon response team, Nightingale being the first, me and Guleed ended up in a corridor at UCH guarding Richard Williams's hospital room, along with a reassuringly solid member of Protection Command in full ballistic armour and armed with an H&K MP5 sub-machine gun. Her name was Lucy and she had three children under the age of five.

'Compared to them,' she told us, 'I don't find this job stressful at all.'

You use Protection Command people for this kind of job because unlike SCO19 they're trained to do guard duty. You want a certain kind of personality who can stand around in the rain for eight hours and still be awake enough to shoot someone in the central body mass at a moment's notice.

Nightingale and Carey were still out west hunting the Pale Nanny, and Richard Williams was seriously sedated and so wasn't going to tell us anything, either. Which at least gave us a chance to write up our notes and for me to ask Guleed about the sound of ripping silk and her impossible bit of vertical parkour.

'Ripping silk?' she asked.

'Not really a sound,' I said. 'A *vestigium* – the sort of noise magic makes when you do it.'

And leaves behind in its wake as well, but I try not to overburden my colleagues with too much explanation. Not even Guleed, who I suspected knew way more than she was letting on.

'That,' she said. And smiled.

'That,' I said.

'I've been training,' she said.

'With Michael?'

Meaning Michael Cheung, the Folly's 'liaison' in Chinatown and a man whose business card listed his profession as 'Legendary Swordsman'.

'It's just like any other martial arts training. You learn the patterns, you practise – you get better.' She leant closer and tapped my shoulder. 'And you don't know if it's going to work until you try it for real.'

'Did it work?'

'I think so.'

'Can you teach me?'

She laughed.

'Michael specifically said I wasn't allowed to. No matter what you said.'

'Why not?'

'Because Nightingale called him up and told him to refuse if you asked.'

'Did he say why?'

'Because you should master at least one tradition before you move on to the next,' said Nightingale, coming up the corridor.

Carey, following behind, gave me and Guleed a grateful look – I could sympathise. Keeping up with Nightingale could be knackering. Especially when he was in one of his man-of-action moods and forgot that we weren't all about to parachute into Germany.

We had an impromptu after-action briefing in the corridor before Nightingale sent us off about our business. He was planning to stay outside Richard Williams's door in the hope that somebody else would turn up and have another go.

'She had the advantage of both me and David,' said Nightingale. 'And yet she felt that silencing Richard Williams was more important. That implies to me that he knows something Martin Chorley does not want us to find out.'

He didn't need to elaborate.

Obviously if it was worth killing Williams for, we really wanted to know what it was.

Guleed, with her sympathetic manner and better interview accreditation, was actioned to interview Richard Williams's wife Fiona. Which involved whisking her off to the pastel coloured 1980s retro calm of Belgravia's Achieving Best Evidence suite and gently prising intimate details of her life out of her while trying not traumatise her further. I was to go over the tapes later to check for Falcon material, but in the meantime I headed back to Chiswick to see if we could learn anything from their happy home.

Fiona was actually wife number two, having met Richard while interning at the company he worked for in 2011. It looked like fast work to me, since he'd only been married to his first wife for five years. They had two daughters, who we'd left in DI Miriam Stephanopoulos' office for the duration of the interview. There was a son by the earlier marriage but he lived with his mother, who'd moved back to King's Lynn after the divorce.

A POLSA team had already worked over the house looking for covert hiding places and secret stashes of shameful stuff, but had found nothing. All the computers, laptops, phones and the PlayStation 4 had been whisked off to the Operational Technology Support Unit at Dulwich to have everything stripped out. We had information analysts on the payroll for this operation and, by God, since it was coming out of the Folly budget we were going to give them something to do.

So I was basically there for the magic – which often hides in plain sight.

As a police detective – which, by the way, I had officially become just that month – I get to spend a lot of time in people's houses, often without their consent. Homes are like witnesses. They pretty much lie all the time. But, as Stephanopoulos says, the longer someone lives in a house the more intrinsically interesting the lies become. When you're police, an interesting lie can be as useful as the truth. Sometimes more so.

The ground floor had been knocked all the way through from front to back. The living room part had a faux antique leather three piece suite and a kidney-shaped glass coffee table with, amazingly, a couple of thick coffee table books on it. The small lie was in the way the seating was arranged to face the, possibly, original Arts and Craft fireplace and not the medium sized flat-screen TV.

We don't waste time on the idiot box, the room was saying. But the stack of box sets and the fact that both the remote controls, Blu-ray player and TV, were on the coffee table made it a liar. That was the small lie.

The big lie was the complete absence of mangled toys, random pieces of scribbled-on paper and half-chewed sweets along the whole length of the ground floor. There are no difficult, messy, screaming small humans living in this house. We live in a bubble of serenity.

Now I'm the son of a professional cleaner, but I'm also blessed with enough pre-school cousins to cause your average UKIP voter to relocate to Spain, and I know for a fact that there should have been way more chaos downstairs.

She might have been a homicidal creature of the night but I suspect our fugitive must have been a really good nanny. That, or she'd traumatised the kids into obedience – we were probably going to have to bring in a special child psychologist to find out. I made a note to check to see whether Guleed had asked about that during the ABE interview.

The kitchen was the kind of brushed steel monstrosity that looks more like it's designed to weaponise viruses than cook dinner. Just to be on the safe side I checked the fridge for Petri dishes – nothing. But there was a reassuring ton of healthy yogurts for tiny tots and genuinely unadulterated fruit drinks made with real fruit.

Just you wait until they start mixing with real children, I thought, and it's going to be Mars bars and crisps for all eternity.

There was blood on the grey Italian tiles and yellow evidence markers scattered across the floor and on the counter. You could see where Nightingale had pulled the nanny off Richard Williams by the spray of blood droplets running diagonally up the wall.

According to Nightingale, they'd just been settling down to a superficially pleasant but calculatingly sinister chat in the living room when Richard Williams had popped out to the kitchen to prepare coffee. Something furtive in his manner had alerted Nightingale, who'd already started after him when they heard a crash and a scream.

'I couldn't tell,' said Nightingale, 'who was doing the screaming.'

As per the agreed operational plan, Carey had moved to secure Fiona Williams and the children while Nightingale engaged whatever it was provoking the screams. In the hallway he'd found the nanny chewing on Richard Williams's neck. We think she'd been going for his throat, but he'd tried to dodge and she'd ended up taking a chunk out of his right trapezoid muscle instead. Nightingale didn't give her a chance to have a second go – smacking her in the back of the knees with an *impello* and trying to physically pin her down.

She'd turned and run at that point – sensibly, she hadn't wanted to face off against Nightingale.

But why up the stairs? Why not out the back or front doors? She could have had it away over the back fence and garden-hopped to the end of the road. Judging by the speed with which she moved, I doubt our perimeter teams would have even seen her.

There was more blood drip on the stairs and a couple of red handprints on the banister's handrail. I put my forensic booties on, as much to protect my own shoes from cross-contamination as to preserve the site, and up I went.

The first floor was more honest than the ground floor. The master bedroom had a custom built king-size bed with carved white head and footboards. The polished floor had coarse wool rugs woven with rectangular blocks of red, blue and yellow, identical to those on the ground floor. There were no visible bookshelves, which always looks weird to me, nor any books by the bed. I was pretty certain this was odd, for people who worked in a 'creative' industry, but perhaps they'd gone over to ebooks to save on space.

The walls were painted the same bland white with a hint of white as the living and dining room. It looked fresh, and when I got my nose in the dark corner be-tween the bed and skirting board I found droplets of white paint in the hard to reach places. Done recently,

and off the books, because the work hadn't registered in the official family expenditure. I'd been right.
The whole house reeked of being ready for Zoopla,
estate agents and home viewings. They'd been planning to sell and had been stripping down for the
move. I made a note to action a check of the local
charity shops – to see if they'd dumped their books
there.

There was a hardback copy of Ishiguro's *The Buried
Giant* on the side table in the en-suite bathroom, sitting
next to a neat pyramid of toilet paper rolls. The flap of
the cover had been tucked into page 15, but there was a
thin film of dust on the exposed front.

Nice try, I thought, but one of you bounced right off
it, too.

If the master bedroom hinted that the family was
moving out, the kids' bedroom said that nobody had
told the girls yet. I've been in enough rich people's
houses not to be surprised at the sheer amount of stuff
their kids have. Piles of board games and drawing kits
and kites and dolls and life-sized teddy bears. The girls
had bunk beds, an industrial sized bin full of Lego and
enough Barbies, Kens and cheap knock-offs to cast a
major stop-motion picture. It was clean but it wasn't
tidy – which was a relief, because I was beginning to
worry about what the nanny's idea of discipline might
have been.

And I'm saying that as the son of an African mother.

The bunk beds surprised me, but it turned out that
Richard Williams had grabbed the back bedroom to
serve as his home office. Again, the room had been

recently painted but you could still trace the outline of extensive bracket shelving by the filled-in screw holes. There was a small blond wood gate-leg table under the window to catch the light and various connection and charging cables, although the tech guys had had it away with the actual laptop and phone. There were a series of cardboard boxes which the POLSA team had methodically opened, leaving their contents neatly piled on the floor awaiting inspection.

Most of it looked like a decade's worth of invoices, utility bills and insurance forms – that was all going to have to go back to the Annexe. One pile caught my attention. At first I thought they were brochures or thick company prospectuses, but they were actually site reports from MOLA – Museum of London Archaeology. Slim technical documents with card covers and spiral plastic bindings – full of nice technical drawings and at least thirty pages of endnotes.

Martin Chorley had had an interest in archaeology and a romantic view of the Dark Ages – I wondered if this was a connection.

Sitting on its own was part of a film script which the POLSA team had found buried among the insurance documents. It was, I was told later, professionally formatted and had originally been held together with the metal two-hole binders popular with aspiring screenwriters. Part of the binder remained and held shreds of paper that indicated that the missing part of the script had been ripped out with some force. Leaving only the first fifteen pages. I read the title.

AGAINST THE DARK
By Richard Williams & Gabriel Tate
From a story by John Chapman

The opening scene on the next page started.

FADE IN
EXT: THE RUINS OF ROMAN LONDON – LATE
EVENING

Which was enough to have me call the Annexe and ask
for a full IIP check on Gabriel Tate and John Chapman.
Since all we had were the names and the connection to
Richard Williams they started grumbling almost immediately, but the good thing about Operation Jennifer was
that we had now had plenty of bodies to do that sort of
thing.

I went up to the loft conversion and saw there was a
hole in the roof where Nightingale had thrown the Pale
Nanny through it.

I could still feel the sharp tang of the *vestigium* and
detected a weird crispy lemon taste on my tongue
that might have been magic or the smell of bathroom
cleaner.

'She was going for the front window when I caught
up with her,' Nightingale had told me. 'There's quite a
good spell for holding people in place.' He'd held up his
hand to stop me asking. 'Next year. You will be ready to
learn it next year. And it proved less use than you might
think, given that our suspect managed to wriggle free.'

Nightingale likes to be precise in his language so

when he uses a word like wriggle he means wriggle.

'There was magic involved,' he said, when I asked for a clarification. 'I'm afraid I overreacted and used more force than I should have.'

It was a slightly less impressive throw than it looked at first. The loft conversion had a strong whiff of the Wild West about it; the plasterboard was flimsy and the rafters were widely spaced and the battens were sub-standard. I reckoned the force of the spell had done most of the material damage while our Pale Nanny had sort of ridden the force of it out onto the roof.

Quite impressive, really, and not lost on Nightingale.

He'd have followed her out, but he had to run downstairs and make sure Richard Williams didn't bleed to death.

'This one seems far more capable than the individual you encountered in Soho,' he'd said.

But who was 'this one'?

When we'd done the initial Integrated Intelligence Platform check on the Williams household her name had been listed as Alice McGovern of Leith, Scotland. When the Belgravia follow-up team finally tracked down the real Alice, she turned out to be a heroin addict currently living in Glasgow who'd sold her identity to a group of entrepreneurial information brokers. They liked using addicts because they generally tried to stay off the grid and, contrary to what people think, can live a long time without coming to the attention of the authorities.

The loft conversion had two bedrooms and a bathroom. The rear bedroom had been turned into a playroom for the children. A half-demolished canvas and bamboo Wendy house sat in the centre where light from the window pooled. There were more shelves stuffed with toys and puzzles and picture books. And a cushion nest in the corner for naps, and a pair of pink fairy costumes hanging from a hook on the back of the door.

There was a smell in the front bedroom. It reminded me of the period when I was sharing a house with half a dozen young PCs, and from student digs I've visited since. A bit of old sweat and leftovers and overstuffed swing-top bins. The Pale Nanny's queen-sized bed was unmade and, when I had a sniff, the sheets hadn't been changed for a couple of weeks. Whoever cleaned the rest of the house hadn't come into this room.

It too had been painted the same white-with-a-hint-of-bland as downstairs and furnished during a sale at Ikea. About half the Pale Nanny's clothes were draped over a straight-backed chair and matching writing desk. The rest were tumbled into drawers with no apparent organisation. The Pale Nanny had favoured tracksuit bottoms, T-shirts and hoodies in pink, sky blue and navy, and her underwear was sensible and cheap.

After the initial engagement with Nightingale she could have gone out the back door but instead she ran up the stairs. Why? Was there something in her room she wanted, something important? Something sentimental?

I checked the drawers again, but there was a stunning absence of cryptic photographs hidden inside.

I sat down on the bed and looked around the room from there.

Nothing sprang out at me, but given the way my day had gone that was probably a good thing.

3

More Pepper

'**M**aybe she went back for her phone,' said Bev. 'I'll bet you didn't think of that.'

'We didn't find a phone,' I said, although it was true I hadn't thought of that.

We were in Bev's outsized kitchen cooking pasta and random things we'd found in the fridge. I was frying onions and garlic in the bottom of a saucepan while Bev defrosted the mince by dragging it out of the freezer and glaring at it until it melted. She's done this before and it takes under a minute. My current working hypothesis is that she's scaring the water molecules into a state of excitation. I'm dying to wire up the mince and get some precise measurements, but Bev won't let me. She says it's because a goddess should retain a few mysteries, but I think she's saving it for a future PhD project. I did try to further the cause of science once by grabbing her around the waist and kissing her neck in the hope it would cause the mince to burst into flames. Sadly, this did not happen – although she did smell nice and, anyway, in science a negative result is almost as good as a positive. And however arduous kissing Beverley becomes, I am willing to persevere in the name of progress.

There was a shriek from the back garden, where Abigail and Nicky were doing something youthful and thankfully unspecified down on the riverbank. Beverley had taken both of them down to Runnymede earlier to hunt insects as part of our ongoing project to keep Abigail out of trouble during the summer holidays.

Once the mince was steaming gently Beverley broke it up with a wooden spatula and dropped it into the saucepan, where I stirred it as it browned.

'I wish we knew what the Pale Nanny was,' I said.

'You can't call her the Pale Nanny,' said Beverley, who was hunting through her cupboard for anything vaguely tomato-ish. 'The Pale Lady is a very specific person upstream and using her name casually like that is a mistake.'

Mistake has a specific meaning when Beverley says it like that. It means likely to provoke outrage and adverse consequences, and I don't mean on social media either.

'Ash called the one in Soho a "Pale Lady",' I said. Mind you, the woman in question had just thrust a metre of iron railing through his abdomen so he wasn't what you'd call a reliable witness.

Beverley found a tin of peeled plum tomatoes hidden behind a couple of jumbo tins of boiled chickpeas that I doubted anyone in this house was ever going to be hungry enough to cook.

'Wasn't she some kind of chimera?' she asked, as she rattled through a drawer for the clean tin opener. 'Isn't that what Abdul called her?'

Dr Abdul Haqq Walid was the Folly's very own part time cryptopathologist and weird specimen collector.

We'd recently ponied up to get him a qualified assistant and she, one Dr Jennifer Vaughan, had spent the last year reclassifying everything.

'Jennifer says "chimera" is not necessarily a helpful term,' I said. 'I think she's right. I think the Soho Lady and the Pale Nanny were High Fae.'

Beverley snorted. It didn't help that her and everybody else in the demi-monde couldn't agree on terminology, either.

The mince was browning nicely so I turned down the heat to stop it from burning and Bev tipped in the tomatoes and went looking for some peppers.

The good gentlemen of the Society of the Wise had plenty of theories and systems of classification for the people of the demi-monde, most of them involving a mixture of Latin, Greek and misinterpreted Darwinism. To them, *fae* basically meant anyone who was vaguely magical who hadn't gone to the right school, with the High Fae being the creatures referenced in medieval literature who dwelt in their own castles with a proper feudal set-up and an inexplicable need to marry virtuous Christian knights.

I'd been pretty certain it was all folklore, until one hot summer when I nearly got myself whisked off to fairyland – which looked suspiciously like a parallel dimension, or whatever the cosmologists are calling them these days. Bev rescued me, by the way, which is why I never argue about emptying the dishwasher.

The best general description I ever heard came from Zachary Palmer, self-styled half-fairy, who once told me that there were three basic types of people. Those who were born magical, which included most of the fae; those who acquired magic through their own agency – like me, Nightingale, all the other practitioners, and presumably aspiring legendary swordswomen like Guleed . . .

And the final group were those who had been changed by magic, often against their will. I had documented cases of children who'd brushed up against fairyland and come back with different coloured eyes and magical abilities. Then there were those who had been altered by evil practitioners into monstrous chimera, real cat-girls and tiger-boys. Like I said, I wasn't joking about the crimes against humanity.

And there was at least one person whose mind and body had been possessed by a revenant spirit, or possibly the ghost of a god, and that had left her 'changed'. But I've got to believe that biology isn't destiny, and we're more than just the puppets of our endocrine system – or else what's the fucking point?

Beverley smelt the sauce and wrinkled her nose.

'Are you sure you don't have any tomato puree at all?' I asked.

But there wasn't any, so we fell back on the time-honoured approach of throwing in peppers until it tasted like something my mum would cook.

We laid the kitchen table and called in the girls.

'Wash your hands before you come in,' yelled Beverley as Nicky and Abigail ran up.

Abigail was fifteen, short and skinny, and making a spirited attempt to make the puffball Afro if not fashionable again, then at least unavoidable. She was also, in a semi-official official way, my fellow apprentice – having taken a hastily rewritten oath in the presence of, and with the written consent of, her parents. Both of who were holding me personally responsible for her safety, which was totally fair and completely uncomfortable.

I watched as she stopped just short of the back door and held out her hands to Nicky.

Who being goddess of the River Neckinger, albeit nine years old, conjured a wobbly globe of water as big as my head in which both girls washed their hands. Then, with a flick of her fingers, the globe evaporated leaving their hands clean and dry.

Abigail caught me watching and winked.

The science teachers at school had noticed Abigail's interest in Latin and history and, fearing the loss of a star pupil to the arts, had started tempting her with the prospect of after-school classes. The consensus was that, when the time came, she was going to have her pick of unis from Oxford to Edinburgh, and Manchester to Imperial.

Personally, I thought she should stay in London where I could keep an eye on her.

'You're worried about her going to Edinburgh?' Beverley had said. 'You'd better start worrying about her going to Massachusetts.'

But did Massachusetts have as many ghosts as London, I wondered as, over dinner, Abigail asked about the latest spate of ghost sightings. She was convinced there'd been an increase in activity despite a lack of empirical evidence.

'What about Brent's horses?' asked Bev.

'I couldn't find a trace of anything,' I said.

Brent was another of Bev's sisters – her river ran through West London – although since she was only nine years old she mostly lived with her mum or her sister Fleet. I've tried asking Beverley how this growing up almost like a normal person thing works but she doesn't appear to understand the question.

Anyway Brent had complained that there were horses in her river in the spring and, finding nothing myself, I stuck Abigail on the problem. She found nothing, apart from discovering that a minor battle from the English Civil War had taken place along the A315 from where it crossed the Brent to about where the Premier Inn is – at the end of which the Parliamentarians ran for it and the Royalists looted the then small town of Brentford. Thus revealing their general intentions as to London proper which, in the words of one historian, *significantly contributed to Londoners' determination to defend the Capital.*

The Royalist cavalry had been heavily engaged and we did dig up some ghostly horsemen reports from the eighteenth century, but whatever had spooked Brent hadn't stayed for me or Abigail.

After supper it was my job to drive Abigail back home to Kentish Town. I considered driving all the way back again to spend the night with Bev, but I needed to make an early start the next morning.

Still, there was a bit of sly snogging on Beverley's doorstep as I left, with Nicky giggling and Abigail harrumphing in the background.

'You've got a big stupid smile on your face,' said Abigail when we got in the car.

'That's because I'm in love,' I said – which had the double virtue of being both true and shutting her up for the whole drive home.

4

The Society of the Wise

At the end of the eighteenth century London was well into the mad, technology-driven expansion that would only stop with the establishment of the Metropolitan Green Belt in the 1940s. Since then, developers have gnashed their teeth and looked enviously back on a time when a man armed only with his own wits and a massive inherited estate could shape the very fabric of the capital. Times like when the fifth Duke of Bedford found his country house surrounded on three sides by Regency London, and decided there was nothing for it but to dig up the old back garden and rake in a ton of cash. He enlisted the legendary architect and developer James Burton, who had a thing for elegant squares, the newfangled long windows in the French style, and vestigial balconies with wrought iron decorative railings.

The only carbuncle on the road to progress was the weird group of gentlemen who'd taken to meeting in the faux medieval tower that an earlier duke caused to be built to add some drama to his garden. These gentlemen were in the nature of a secret society, although they seemed well favoured by certain members of court – particularly Queen Charlotte.

In return for being allowed to demolish the tower, James Burton agreed to incorporate a magnificent mansion into the terrace along the southern side of the square. It would be built after the style of White's – the famous gentlemen's club – and include a demonstration room, library, dining hall, reading room, and accommodation for visiting members. The central atrium was so impressive it's thought to have inspired Sir Charles Barry in his design of the more famous Reform Club forty years later.

And so the Folly was born.

And all of this at below market cost.

So it's not for nothing that Sir Victor Casterbrook, the first properly respectable president of the Society of the Wise, was sometimes known as the pigeon plucker – although probably never to his face.

It also explains why he's the only other person with their bust on proud display in the Folly's atrium – the other being Sir Isaac Newton.

I've got a room on the second floor with a nice view of the street, bookshelves and a gas fire retrofitted into the original fireplace. In the winter you can hear the wind whistling among the chimney tops and, if you leave all four burners on overnight, you can raise the ambient temperature to just above the triple point of water. When I started my apprenticeship I lived there full time, but these days Nightingale trusts me to tie my own shoelaces so I spend half my nights at Bev's. Especially during the winter.

Bev calls the Folly my London club, using her posh voice when she does. But officially it's leased to the

Metropolitan Police and treated as a genuine nick – it's got a call sign, Zulu Foxtrot, and everything. Unfortunately we don't have a PACE compliant custody suite, otherwise we'd be able to bang suspects up and subject them to Molly's cooking until they confessed or exploded – whichever came first.

Since Operation Jennifer got underway I've fallen into the routine of waking early and doing an hour in the Folly's very own gym. True, it hasn't been refurbished since the 1940s so it's a bit short on cross-trainers, steps and the sort of hand weights that haven't been carved out of lumps of pig iron. But it does have a punchbag which smells of canvas, leather and linseed oil, and I like to pound that for a bit and pretend I'm Captain America, or at least his smarter, younger half-brother.

Next door is the only real working shower in the whole building and if I give Molly twelve hours' notice I can get ten minutes of hot water. I did suggest getting some serious Romanian redecoration done, but apparently we're not supposed to mess with the plumbing.

'Quite apart from anything else, Peter,' Nightingale had said, 'once you started who knows when you'd stop?'

After my shower I had to squeeze past the Portakabin taking up half the courtyard and up the wrought iron spiral stairs to the Tech Cave – where I keep all my technology and the last of the Star Beer. There I checked my Airwave charger and made sure that I had three burner phones on warm-up – we tended to run through them at a rate. I transferred the notes I'd made onto my stand-alone computer and printed a copy for physical collation. It was just coming up to quarter past seven as

I squeezed back out past the Portakabin and in through the back door of the Folly.

For complicated and needlessly mystical reasons you can't run modern telecommunication cables into the Folly proper. That's why my Tech Cave resides on the top floor of the coach house and why, when we needed to establish a proper on-site Inside Inquiry Office, we ended up with that Portakabin in the courtyard.

I mean, we couldn't put it downstairs in the coach house – that's where we keep the Jag, and the Ferrari, and the most haunted car in Britain.

I found Nightingale in the central atrium, watching as the Operation Jennifer personnel filtered in through the front and headed for the dining room where Molly was serving breakfast. We hadn't planned on feeding the multitude, but having this many people in the Folly had done something to Molly's brain and by the third morning she'd reopened the dining room and was presiding over breakfast and lunch plus tea and cakes in the afternoon. Somewhere there was a budget spreadsheet piling up red numbers, but that wasn't my problem – at least not yet.

'They're all so ridiculously young,' said Nightingale.

'They' were mostly Police Staff, what we're not supposed to call civilian workers any more – analysts and data entry specialists – who'd got the boot when the government decided that in the light of an increased security threat what London really needed was a smaller police force. Others were experienced officers seconded from Belgravia MIT and other specialist units, all out of uniform and all carefully selected by DI Stephanopoulos as reliable, competent and discreet.

And all signatories of the Official Secrets Act and security vetted twice – once by the Met and once by me.

Guleed wandered out of the dining room with a coffee cup in her hand, saw us and walked over.

'You know, if every nick had a canteen like this,' she said, 'morale would be ever so much higher.'

'Well, we could turn Molly's kitchens into a stand-alone business unit and go for some contracts,' I said. 'Molly gets to cook to her heart's content and we replenish some of our reserves.'

Nightingale nodded thoughtfully.

'Interesting,' he said.

'Really?' I said. 'I was just kidding.'

'Ah,' he said. 'I see.'

And headed off to the morning briefing.

Guleed flicked me on the arm.

'You've really got to learn to keep your mouth shut,' she said.

I wisely kept my counsel and went off in search of some coffee.

The visitors' lounge was a long room built just off the Folly's entrance lobby to provide an agreeable space for wives, daughters and other suitably genteel visitors to be entertained by members while making it quite clear that they weren't welcome in the Folly proper. Still, it had been nicely furnished with oak panelling, portraits of Sir Isaac Newton, Queen Charlotte, the fifth Duke of Bedford, and some quite splendid second-best upholstery.

Upon setting up Operation Jennifer we'd whipped off

the dust sheets, put most of the furniture in storage and installed the sort of institutional desks and workspaces that no modern copper feels he can work without. Or at the very least avoid. The line of tall sash windows would have provided plenty of natural sunlight if we hadn't installed modern metal blinds to stop people looking in. So we fastened LED strips along the walls and plugged them into the single wall plug in the whole room. Fortunately it was a computer-free room so we didn't risk overloading the Folly's circuitry, although people constantly complained about having nowhere to charge their phones.

The far wall had been covered in a whiteboard which was slowly filling up with a tangle of photographs, lines, personal names, company names and question marks. DCI Seawoll was looking at it when we entered.

'Fuck me, this is getting complicated,' he said.

Alexander Seawoll was as modern a copper as had ever authorised a community outreach action going forward, but you would never know it from casual acquaintance. A big man who wore a camel hair coat and handmade shoes, he was, reputedly, from Glossop – a small town just outside Manchester famous for its beautiful setting, its role in the cotton industry, and being twinned with Royston Vasey.

Minus DI Stephanopoulos and DC Carey, who were both back at Belgravia Nick, Nightingale, Guleed, Seawoll and I constituted the inner decision-making core of Operation Jennifer.

'Well, the plan was to poke people until we got a reaction,' said Guleed. 'I'd say that in that sense it was a success.'

Seawoll glared at me – not at Guleed, you notice, who was the apple of his professional eye – but at me.

'Yes, it did,' he said 'But not what you'd call fucking quietly. But I haven't seen a bunch of police analysts this happy since they brought back *Doctor Who*.'

Exposing the Pale Nanny had not only confirmed Richard Williams as an associate of Martin Chorley, but as one important enough to kill in extremis. Now the analysts could go back over their data, but give him a higher weighting. In the normally shifting world of information theory, poor Richard Williams had taken on a new solidity – which was not bad for a man who was still unconscious.

'We can't overlook the possibility that his wife is the connection,' said Seawoll, and looked at Guleed. 'Speaking of which, how did the ABE interview go?'

Guleed took out her notebook and ran through the outcome. Fiona Williams didn't know anything about her husband's contacts from his Oxford days apart from Gabriel Tate, who he had occasional drinks with.

'And co-wrote the script I found,' I said.

Guleed had already actioned an IIP report and checked our lists and found he wasn't a suspected Little Crocodile.

'He is now,' said Seawoll.

Because Fiona had been in the living room with Nightingale and Carey and hadn't witnessed the attack, we hadn't revealed anything to her beyond the fact that it had been a serious assault.

'She seemed suspiciously uninterested to me in how

her husband was injured,' said Guleed. 'I mean I'd want to know – wouldn't you?'

But Fiona Williams had accepted Guleed's explanation with what psychologists call a 'flat' response.

'She might still be in shock,' said Seawoll. 'We'll give her a day or two to recover and then you can have another pop.'

Fiona Williams had hired the nanny from an agency But when Guleed had followed up they'd denied knowing anything about Alice McGovern, aka the Pale Nanny, but whether the substitution had been made with or without the collusion of Richard Williams we wouldn't know until he woke up.

'*If* he wakes up,' I said.

'Abdul seemed confident he would,' said Nightingale.

So we were going to have to find a way to secure him against future attack. We'd discussed housing high-risk witnesses and/or suspects inside the Folly, but that had its own problems – running from PACE compliance to operational security. Ultimately, safety for the likes of Richard Williams and his family lay in us nailing Martin Chorley's feet to the floor.

'We're stuffed until he does wake up,' said Seawoll.

Neither Nightingale not Seawoll were looking particularly happy at the lack of results so far, but I kept my mouth shut because I'd noticed that Guleed had skipped over a couple of pages in her notebook and guessed that she'd saved the best for last. You don't make your way up the Met's particularly convoluted greasy pole without knowing when to use a bit of showmanship.

'There was one more thing,' she said and gave me

the barest flicker of a wink. 'Richard Williams had an unusual interest in bells.' She paused for applause – not a sausage – and went on. 'He made several trips to the Whitechapel Bell Foundry.'

'Good lord,' said Nightingale. 'I didn't realise it was still open.'

'Could it have been for his work?' asked Seawoll.

'We're checking that now, but he went to some lengths to keep it secret from the missus,' said Guleed.

The missus, perhaps because she was missus number two, had twigged that Richard was keeping secrets. And, having way less faith in his fidelity than his first wife – go figure – followed him down to Whitechapel to see what he was up to. This sort of thing is pretty common – people often draw more attention to themselves trying to hide their activities than whatever it was they were up to would. Plus sometimes the cover-up is more illegal than the thing they were covering up.

Still, if people were brighter routine police work would be much harder.

Guleed had held off contacting the bell foundry directly.

'I didn't want to risk tipping anyone off,' she said, and both Nightingale and Seawoll nodded approvingly.

'I think you two should go and have a poke around the place,' said Seawoll. 'While we finish up with Chiswick.'

He looked over at Nightingale, who gestured at me and Guleed.

'Well, what are you waiting for?' he said.

5

Two Sticks and an Apple

'I think I preferred it when they didn't get on,' said Guleed.

'They still don't,' I said. 'They're just being professional about it.'

So professional, in fact, that if you listened closely you could hear both Nightingale and Seawoll creaking under the strain. Fortunately, modern technology allows the modern minion on the go to do his prep work far away from his superiors and, bonus, get some reconnaissance in while he's at it.

Me and Guleed had ensconced ourselves in the Café Casablanca, whose window seats afforded a nice view of the front and back entrances to the Whitechapel Bell Foundry and who served coffee that was strong, hot and properly *grande*. It also served a selection of India sweets made on the premises that were doing their through smell alone, to convince me that type tes was a small price to pay.

Back in the day, or rather *rursus in di* your newly minted Romano-Brit with his eye on the main prize might wa cart full of garum from the bur inium to the brand spanking ne

– Camulodunum. To facilitate this vital trade in fermented fish guts the Roman Army thoughtfully laid one of their famously straight roads between the two cities – that this allowed for the rapid redeployment of various legions in their quest to bring the joys of under-floor heating to the benighted tribes further north was mere serendipity.

You could tell Whitechapel Road was Roman by the fact that it was straight and wide enough for bus lanes, a cycle superhighway, and a street market. It carved a line from Aldgate to the Mile End Road and beyond. It's been the East End's one-stop shop for life, death and culture since the docks drove the massive expansion of the city eastward. You can shop in the market, worship in a mosque that was once a synagogue, that was once a Huguenot church, educate yourself in the Whitechapel Library, culture yourself in the Whitechapel Gallery, live in the shadow of the sci-fi tower blocks of the City, and then die in the London Hospital.

And still get the, allegedly, best bagels in London.

And if you wanted a bell made good and proper, you went to the Whitechapel Bell Foundry, established 1570. Currently occupying the best part of a Georgian town-house and various industrial extensions out the back. It was here that they recast Big Ben after the original bell cracked.

While Guleed chased her paperwork and eyed up the halal delights of the café's menu, I spent an interesting half an hour on the phone to MOLA. They recognised the names of the site reports I'd found in Richard Wilson's office but didn't think they had anything in common beyond being digs from the last five years and all from around the city proper. Most archaeology in London these days is rescue archaeology – projects designed to preserve as much as possible from the relentless cash-driven redevelopment. It's not a new problem. Ask a medievalist about Victorian cellars or an Iron Age specialist about medieval ploughing – but take snacks, because you're going to be there for a while.

'There was one thing,' said the helpful lady at MOLA. 'At one of the sites . . . Adrian will know.'

There was much shouting to see if Adrian was around, a bit of a wait and then the man himself took the phone – he sounded like he was from the Northeast with just a threat of full-on Geordie, should the need arise.

'Is this about the thefts?' he said.

Thefts – plural.

'How many thefts have there been?' I asked.

'That depends on how you define it,' said Adrian.

Because material went missing off sites all the time, which is why important finds were collated and secured the day they were found.

Important in archaeological terms not always being the same as valuable – at least not in the fenceable sense. Archaeology came in all shapes, sizes, and apparent degrees of nickableness.

'We wouldn't have even noticed some of the thefts if they hadn't been important to the context,' said Adrian.

Context being the key concept of modern scientific archaeology, and what separates your modern professional from the fumbling archivists and swivel-eyed tomb raiders of the past. It's a religion they share with scene of crime technicians and it had been drummed into me from my first day at Hendon.

Context – where you find an object – is more important than the actual object. In policing it's whether the broken glass is on the inside or the outside. In archaeology it's whether that datable coin is found in the wall foundations or its demolition infill. You can live without the coin, but you need the dating information.

'Material was taken from about five sites,' said Adrian. 'I'll have to check the reports to be certain, but as I recall it was nearly all Roman brick.'

Apparently, the only thing the sites had in common was that they were within London and they all either had ritual significance in the Roman era or had been repurposed as church sites during the five hundred years or so following the withdrawal of the Empire from Britain.

I asked whether the thefts seemed random or whether the pattern made sense in archaeological terms.

'Whoever it was didn't just scoop things up at random, so I'd say they knew what they were looking for,' he said. 'Assuming it was the same person.'

I got a firm promise that he'd email the details to us, and warned him I might need to contact him again. He seemed moderately pleased by that.

The boys and girls back at the Annexe would soon be adding archaeologist to the mix of qualities they were looking for in an associate of Martin Chorley – see, context.

But I did wonder what the hell they wanted Roman bricks for.

'Nothing good,' said Guleed.

Both us having actioned our morning actions we finished up and popped over to find out exactly what Richard Williams had wanted a bell for.

When you arrive unexpectedly at someone's house you go in through the front door, often after making sure you've got a couple of mates waiting round the back. For a business, especially the kind that involves big trucks and heavy metal, it's always better to go in through the back. The customer-facing part of any modern business is purposely designed to be as politely unhelpful as possible. If you go in from the rear, the customer-facing staff are all facing the wrong way and everybody starts their conversation on the back foot.

Apart from us, of course.

The big gates round the back on Plumber's Row were open for a delivery, so we walked in bold as brass until someone shouted at us. We showed them our warrant cards, but they weren't impressed – they weren't going to talk to us until we were wearing hard hats and had signed in.

We did as we were told, both me and Guleed being big fans of health and safety, particularly when it's our health and safety. Plus you could feel the heat of the main furnace from five metres away. Molten copper, I learnt later, for a relatively small one ton church bell. It filled the workshop with a smell like fresh blood.

London used to be full of workshops, craftsmen and manufactories. But the industrial revolution sucked all the jobs north, where the water and the coal flowed freely and a man could wear a flat cap and fancy his whippet free from fear. Much of what made Dickensian London Dickensian was driven by that shift. What people forget is that, in the short term, the Luddites were right.

Still – policing is a service industry, so no worries there.

We were introduced to a white guy in a blue boiler suit, with burn and grease marks I noticed, who was in charge that morning. His hair was a tight mop of grey curls and his face was dark and deeply lined. I thought he might be the same age as my father, but he radiated physical strength as if decades of hard work had made a furnace of him. When he shook my hand the skin was as rough as sandpaper and his grip as deliberate as a machine tool.

Another one for Dr Walid's DNA database, I thought, if we can persuade him.

He introduced himself as Gavin Conyard.

'But you can call me Dr Conyard,' he said, and smiled.

I showed him a picture of Richard Williams and asked if he remembered him visiting the foundry.

'Ah, yes,' said Dr Conyard. 'The drinking bell.'

It turned out that Richard Williams, under his own name, had commissioned and paid for a bell – and not a small one either.

'Not the largest we've ever made,' said Dr Conyard, 'but pretty vast all the same.'

Also not the sort of thing our POLSA team would have overlooked back at the family home.

'Did he pick it up himself?' I asked. 'Or did you deliver?'

'Oh no,' he said, and pointed to the other side of the foundry. 'It's still here.'

It was sodding enormous – as tall as me and a deep rich brass colour that seemed almost red in the light from the foundry. It was, I learnt later, your classic church bell tuned to five partials to give it that full-bodied main note.

'Not that the buyer seemed particularly interested in the tone,' said Dr Conyard.

'It's beautiful,' said Guleed.

It was very plain, with no decoration around the dome. Just the crest and name of the foundry and below that an inscription in what I recognised as Greek.

δέχεσθε κῶμον εὐίου θεοῦ

'We had to get the lettering made specially,' said Dr Conyard.

'Do you know what it means?' asked Guleed.

'We asked that ourselves,' said Dr Conyard. 'It means "Prepare yourself for the roaring voice of the god of joy".'

I asked Dr Conyard whether he'd worked on it personally, and he gave me a sly grin.

'I thought you were one of them,' he said and winked.

'One of them what?' I asked, but he shook his head.

'Put your hand on it,' he said. 'Tell me what you think.'

I gingerly reached out and touched the side of the bell with my fingertips.

Nothing.

49

I nodded at Guleed to step back – just in case – then I put my palm flat against the bell and closed my eyes.

And there it was. A cool tone like the moments that follow the ringing of a bell, like the sound a finger running around a wine glass makes – if the glass was as wide as a cannon mouth and made of brass.

It was definitely a *vestigium,* but faint and subtle and deep. I thought that if I could push my way through the gaps between the tones and semitones I might find another sound on the other side. If only I could listen a little harder . . .

I snatched my hand away.

Great, I thought. It's not enough that every supernatural creature feels free to try and put the 'fluence on me, but now I've got to put up with inanimate objects trying it on as well?

But before I let go I got a whisper of the straight razor strop and a smell of blood that was all slaughterhouse and fear.

'Dr Conyard,' I said, 'I'm going to have to ask you to temporarily close this premises and evacuate all the staff.'

'What for?'

'I believe you may have inadvertently helped construct an explosive device.'

6

Centre Mass

Nightingale spent a long time with both palms pressed against the side of the bell. Long enough for the inside of my riot helmet to become slick with sweat and for the faceplate to start to fog up from my breath. I was in my full personal protection kit, including petrol bomb resistant overall, boots and helmet. I was also crouched behind a nice thick piece of steel reinforced with the greenest bit of wood I could find on short notice – a brand new garden table from the Argos across the road. The wood was to help protect me if the bell went bang in a magical way, and the metal in case it exploded physically.

Nightingale had made it clear that some demon traps could do both.

'The trapped spirit ignites the metal in some way,' he had said during an informal training session with me, Guleed and a handful of London Fire Brigade volunteers. 'I'm not sure why.'

It had something to do with the ignition point of vaporised metal, but it could be 'rather inconvenient' if you were expecting the demon trap to do something else.

Ten metres behind me was Guleed, and behind her

was a fire engine, with a full crew in search and rescue gear.

According to the literature, demon traps were invented by the Norwegians back around the seventh century to while away those long winter nights while you waited for the fjord to unfreeze so you could pop out and murder some monks. Creating them involved torturing a person to death over an extended period and trapping their ghost in a piece of metal. That energy stayed dormant until triggered and could be tuned to create a number of effects.

The Germans had refined the technique as a weapon during the Second World War. Nightingale swears blind that no British wizard ever stooped to such practice, and I admit I've never found any record to show they did. But still – you have to wonder.

Martin Chorley had either developed or discovered that you could use dogs instead of people, and that you could use demon traps like batteries to store magic. Which was a neat trick, because neither he nor any practitioner that I know actually knows what magic is. You can stick a label on it, call it *potentia* or *mana* or an interstitial boundary effect, but all that does is make you sound like you're auditioning for *Star Trek* – *TNG*, not the movies.

I checked my watch. Nightingale had been standing in front of the bell for more than two minutes. I'd warned him that there was definitely a *seducere* style effect built in, but he seemed confident he could deal with it.

At three minutes I made a considered risk assessment and decided to go grab him and pull him off. But, as I came out of hiding, Nightingale took his left hand off the bell and held it up – palm towards me.

I stopped.

And considered crawling back behind cover – which would have been the sensible thing. But before I could do that Nightingale took his right hand off the bell and beckoned me over.

'It's not a trap,' he said.

'What is it, then?'

'I have no idea whatsoever.'

Fortunately we got word that a man who might know something had woken up back at UCH. So me and Guleed bundled into the character-free Hyundai and headed over while Nightingale stayed with the bell, just in case it suddenly started ticking or something.

Lucy was back on shift when we arrived outside Richard Williams's room. He'd been put in one of the max isolation wards. Designed for ebola outbreaks and the like, it had its own atrium with a big white sink and a couple of jumbo waste bins with big biohazard symbols painted on their lids.

Lucy was positioned in the corner of the room with a clear field of fire on anyone coming in through the heavy fire door to the corridor – the square window in the door had been blacked out with a sheet of cardboard. Someone opening the door would be in Lucy's sights before they even knew she was there.

'Warrant cards,' she said as me and Guleed walked in.

We're trained not to argue with stressed people with guns – especially our own people – so we dutifully pulled the cards out of our jackets and showed her.

'Your governor's a bit scary, isn't he?' said Lucy as she checked them.

She'd obviously been given the Nightingale lecture – that explained the increase in caution.

'He's a big softy, really,' said Guleed with a straight face.

'Of course he is,' said Lucy, and settled back into her guard stance as we pushed open the inner door and went in.

Richard didn't find Lucy's presence half as reassuring as we did.

'He's going to kill me,' he said. 'There's nothing you can do to stop it.'

We gave the usual reassurances, but everybody's watched way too many films to trust our word. He was your classic amateur – your proper professional criminal would have been screaming for a brief and demanding to know by what right we were holding him against his will, but Richard had cracked before we'd stepped into the room.

We'd done the caution plus two – which is when we caution you and then rush to assure you that you aren't under arrest while we make it clear, through subtle non-verbal communication, that arrest was totally an option.

Richard seemed happy to talk, eager even, as if none of it was important any more. Looking back, perhaps that should have raised more alarm bells than it did.

We started with the basics, like did he know the current location of Martin Chorley.

Richard swore he didn't. It's not like they'd been mates. But a friend of a friend had introduced them after he'd graduated from Oxford. He just did Chorley the occasional 'favour' in return for some lucrative contracts and a bit of cash under the table.

What kind of favours? we asked.

Providing video equipment, arranging to move packages around.

'It didn't occur to you that any of this might be dodgy?' I asked.

'It didn't seem *that* dodgy,' said Richard. 'Not illegal as such.'

I wanted to press on, but we had to pause there to get names, dates and as many details of the people involved in the 'favours' as Richard would admit to. It's tedious stuff but it all goes into the great mill that is HOLMES 2, the better to grind the flour of truth and produce the wholesome bread of justice.

And then, while they're busy thinking about something else, you go down a different track.

'Who was the friend who introduced you to Martin Chorley?'

'Gabriel,' said Richard. 'Gabriel Tate. We were at Oxford together.'

The other name on the film script I'd found.

'Was he a Little Crocodile?' I asked – keeping it casual.

'No way,' said Richard. 'He was mad into Oxford Revue and OUDS.'

'OUDS?' asked Guleed.

'Oxford University Dramatic Society,' said Richard. 'He always wanted to write.'

'But you were a member of the Little Crocodiles?' I asked.

Richard sighed. I think he'd already planned to tell us everything, but old habits die hard and we suspected that all the Little Crocodiles had been sworn to secrecy. Even perhaps with a little supernatural something to seal the deal.

'Yes,' he said. 'But I didn't take the magic seriously.'

Nobody does, I thought, until it smacks them in the face.

Guleed asked if the Little Crocodiles had stayed in touch after graduation.

'God, no,' said Richard. 'We just did it for fun – well, most of us. Some people took it more seriously than others.'

We asked if he could remember the names of the ones who took it more seriously and then, because that was just as valuable, the names of the ones who didn't. The analysts in the Annexe were going to be up all night cross-referencing and some poor sod was going to find their colourful university days knocking on their door and asking for help with its inquiries.

'What's the bell for?' asked Guleed.

'The bell?' asked Richard.

Ah, I thought, not *that* keen on telling us everything.

'The bell,' said Guleed firmly.

'The bell.' Richard shifted uncomfortably in his bed. 'The bell is complicated. You saw the quotation written on the side?'

'Something in Greek,' said Guleed, who'd pioneered the use of intersectionality theory as an interview technique. Richard took the bait – no matter what the evidence, the posh ones always think they're smarter than you.

'It's from Euripides,' he said. 'He's a Greek playwright, an ancient Greek playwright, and he wrote a play called *The Bacchae* and it's a quote from it. That's why we nicknamed it "the drinking bell".' He gave us reassuring nods. 'It's about Dionysus, the god of winemaking.'

We knew this, of course. Because I'd texted Dr Postmartin, our archivist and a noted classicist, who had not only recognised the quote but also criticised the translation. He'd then given me a ten-minute lecture on Euripides, *The Bacchae* and Dionysus that was really quite soothing considering I was less than twenty metres from an unexploded magical device.

And Dionysus was the god of winemaking, fertility *and* the theatre.

I didn't miss that last little wrinkle, although looking back I possibly should have followed up a bit harder.

Dionysus had your standard Greek mythological bio – son of Zeus, mortal mother who burst into flames while pregnant, sewn into his father's thigh as a foetus, torn apart by Titans and then resurrected. Famously, his worshippers met in forests where they got pissed, laid, and tore unsuspecting small woodland animals apart. Unfortunately, anything that much fun is bound to be frowned upon by the ruling class. And so they got a stern lecture from Livy and were seriously suppressed by the Roman state.

'What's the bell for?' I asked.

'I don't know,' said Richard.

'You weren't curious?' asked Guleed.

Richard gave a startled bark of a laugh that turned into a cough. I offered him some water but he waved me off.

'Of course I was curious,' he said. 'But you didn't ask questions – at least not more than once. Not if you knew what was good for you.'

'Did Chorley say anything about the bell at all?' I asked. 'Anything that might indicate what it's for?'

'All he said was that it was a bell for ringing in the changes,' said Richard. 'To wake the nation.'

'Which nation?' asked Guleed.

'I don't think he was thinking about the French,' said Richard.

I'm sure I had a snappy comeback, but I can't remember what it was, because just then we heard Lucy challenge someone outside. Then, before I could react, there were three gunshots, astonishingly loud, a pause, and before we could react to *that*, two more.

I was out the door first, with shield spell half prepared, but it was too late.

Lucy stood in the far corner of the atrium, gunstock against her shoulder, barrel angled down to cover a figure on the floor. It was the Pale Nanny, dressed as a nurse, lying on her back gasping for breath while a dark stain welled up on the chest of her blue uniform tunic.

I dropped to my knees beside her and grabbed her hand and squeezed. Her skin felt hot, feverish, and she turned her head a fraction to stare at me. Her eyes were wide and uncomprehending.

I was vaguely aware of Guleed going for help and of Lucy keeping a clear line of fire – just in case.

You're supposed to say the casualty's name. They teach you that, to keep them focused on you, but they never say whether it actually helps. And we still didn't know her name.

'Hey,' I said. 'Hey, what's your name? You've got to have a name.'

I saw her eyes focus on my face and she looked puzzled, as if surprised to see me there.

'Is it Claire?' I said – babbling. 'Barbara? Aya? Maureen?'

People were moving around me. There was a whisper of cotton against my shoulder, voices calling back and forth, all the jargon you don't want to be hearing while in a prone position.

'Tell me your name,' I said. 'There's nothing happened that we can't sort out.'

Her lips parted and I thought she might be about to speak, but suddenly there was a blur of green and blue arms between us and, when they'd moved out of the way, she'd been intubated and masked. Her eyes still held mine for a moment and her hand squeezed one last time. Then her eyes unfocused and her grip went slack and she was gone.

Just like that.

I stayed where I was – mostly because I couldn't think of anything more sensible to do – but Guleed shook my shoulder to get my attention.

'Peter,' she said. 'Richard Williams is dead.'

7

Brand Loyalty

Supernatural creature of the night or not, this was a DSI, death or serious injury, while in contact with a member of the police force and therefore triggered a mandatory referral to the Independent Police Complaints Commission under Section 2 of the Police Reform Act 2002.

That meant it was the Department of Professional Services that arrived to secure the scene and take statements while we waited for the notoriously slow IPCC investigators to get their arses in gear. I knew a couple of the people from the DPS from my many, many visits there and they all shook their heads upon seeing me.

We all knew that this was going to be a full-on independent inquiry conducted exclusively by IPCC investigators, so we didn't try and co-ordinate our stories or anything foolish like that. It was obvious to me that Lucy had done the right thing, both legally and morally, and any attempt to put the fix in would create more problems than it solved.

Or at least that's what I told myself, while I waited to be interviewed.

The police don't like being policed any more than your average member of the public does. But I've had more experience of being investigated than most officers my age and have learnt to sit still, be polite and give short, precise answers to any questions. Do not get clever, do not volunteer information and do not offer a helpful critique of your questioner's interviewing technique – no matter how justified it might be.

One bonus is that you get to keep a copy of the interview tape so you can hone your own interviewing technique, anticipate further lines of inquiry, or auto-tune your responses while you wait for your contact to get back to you.

I did ask if there was any word on Richard Williams's cause of death. He'd just been lying there, eyes closed, mouth open, left arm limp across his chest, the other lying by his side. There was no sign of violence that me and Guleed could see and definitely nobody else in the room.

'We're still waiting on the PM,' the IPCC investigator told me, and sent me home.

The IPCC were going to want a pathologist of their own choosing to do the PM. Never mind about what they were going to make of the Pale Nanny's teeth, what were they going to make of Doctors Vaughan and Walid?

So I went back to the Folly, which has the advantage of being both home and work at the same time. Guleed went home because she has, she says, a deep and mystical understanding of the work-life balance. A concept I once tried to explain to Nightingale with the aid of the big whiteboard in the visitors' lounge. I think he grasped it in the end, and said he was all in favour as long as I understood that this in no way applied to apprentices.

'And I've had quite enough time doing nothing,' he said.

The main shift in the Annexe was just leaving as I settled into the Tech Cave to see if I couldn't tie up some loose ends. In deference to the spirit of the balance, however, I had a can of Special Brew while I was doing it.

The Annexe had already produced an IIP check of Gabriel Tate and John Chapman and had determined that both of them had left the country a year earlier. Chapman had left no forwarding address, although Border Force had a record of him boarding a flight to JFK. Gabriel Tate had been much easier to track, not least because he had a webpage advertising his brand new company in Brisbane, Australia. I fired off a formal request for assistance to Australia, who would be fast asleep. It was the middle of the day in the States so I called a contact of mine at the FBI to see if she could help.

I was going through the action list to see if there was anything I could do sitting down when I got a call from Dr Walid, who invited me to an autopsy. I said that I couldn't think of a better way to spend my evening and called Nightingale to see if he wanted to come.

'I think I'd rather stay here,' he said.

'Here' being the Whitechapel Bell Foundry, where Nightingale was keeping an eye on the bell just in case. I knew he was hoping that Martin Chorley would turn up in person to try and get his bell back. He's gone one round with Chorley already and, whatever he says, he's dead keen to go round two. And, as an operational plan, it had a certain merit. Providing collateral was kept down to – what, a two-to -three block radius?

I doubted Martin Chorley would be that stupid – I also could hear a rhythmic metallic clanking sound down the line.

'Are you forging?' I asked.

'I thought,' said Nightingale, 'that since there was all this good metal lying around, I might lay down some enchantments – just in case.'

So it was off down the Horseferry Road to the Iain West Memorial All You Can Stomach Forensic Suite, which is state of the art and a good place to impress outside pathologists who have been requested by the IPCC. Out of tact I waited until the IPCC lot had buggered off, and as a result this was my favourite kind of autopsy. The kind where the conclusions have already been drawn and the bodies have all been sewn up and covered tastefully with a sheet.

Dr Vaughan and Dr Walid were waiting for me in the space between the bodies with faint smiles that were only sinister because of the context. At least I hope it was the context. We started with the cause of death determination for Richard Williams.

'We don't have one,' said Dr Vaughan. 'For what it's worth, we can call it heart failure. But that's not particularly useful, now, is it? Just about everything is heart failure when you get down to it.'

Cause of death can be hard to determine even when the victim has a knife sticking out of their forehead, let alone with no visible wounds or gross pathology. Half a litre of Richard Williams's blood was now distributed among labs from Euston to Cambridge, but unless you know what toxin you're looking for, you can't screen for it. Besides, I could tell from the ever more sinister smiles on Dr Vaughan's and Dr Walid's faces that they had a theory – and not one that involved a neurotoxin.

'*Voila*,' said Dr Walid.

He twitched the sheet off Richard Williams's leg to reveal a large abstract tattoo – almost one of those faux Maori sleeves, but not. The lines were too angular and yet very familiar. I thought one patch looked fresher until I realised that its darkness was not fresh ink but burnt flesh.

'Burnt down to a depth of two centimetres,' said Dr Walid. 'We were just about to excise it so we could have a closer look.'

'You can watch if you like,' said Dr Vaughan.

I barely heard her because I'd just recognised the shape of the tattoo. A long upright stroke with two right-hand strokes going diagonally up.

'*G* for Gandalf,' I said.

Specifically *G* in Tolkien's imaginary Dwarvish runes or actually, as I learnt from a bit of googling, his imaginary early Elvish. I explained this to the doctors, which at least had the effect of wiping that sinister smile off their faces.

'And I suppose you're fluent in Elvish?' said Dr Vaughan, by way of retaliation.

'No,' I said. 'But *G* is what Gandalf stamps on his fireworks. Gandalf is the wizard, by the way.'

'I know who Gandalf is, thank you,' said Dr Vaughan.

'I think we can assume that this is Martin Chorley's work,' said Dr Walid.

He was right. Martin Chorley really did have a sick sense of humour. He'd once labelled a demon trap in Elvish script.

'And the rest of the tattoos?' asked Dr Vaughan.

'It's all Dwarvish iconography,' I said. 'From the films, though, not the books.'

'We're still waiting on the lab work,' said Dr Walid. 'But Jennifer here thinks there may have been metallic particles under the skin.'

'A small demon trap, I was thinking,' said Dr Vaughan. 'Or something working along the same principles. I'd like to see if your boss knows something about it.'

I said I'd set up a meeting.

'If there was a remote trigger of some kind,' I said, 'it must have quite a short range. Why else would Chorley sacrifice his killer nanny as a distraction if he didn't have to get close himself?'

Which meant someone was going to have to go back over the hospital CCTV looking for Chorley. More work for some unlucky sod in the Annexe, or perhaps lucky sod, if they had no social life and needed the overtime.

'We're calling her Charlotte Green,' said Dr Vaughan primly.

'What?'

'Well, it's a bit unfeeling to keep referring to these young women as "killer nannies" and the like,' she said. 'Whatever they did in life they're in my care now and I don't think it's too much to expect a bit of respect.'

65

'Why Green?'

'Because I didn't want to use Gamma as a category name,' she said. 'And Charlotte because she's our third Jane Doe.'

The first being the young woman with the unusual teeth who'd died at the Trocadero Centre.

'Alice Green,' said Dr Vaughan.

The second being the weird half-man, half-tiger person who'd tried to kill me on a roof in Soho and got himself shot in the head for his trouble.

'Barry Brown.'

'You've started a new classification system, haven't you?' I said.

'Well, we couldn't go on with what we had, could we?' said Dr Vaughan.

Dr Jennifer Vaughan had taken one look at the various cataloguing methodologies for the fae and come to the same conclusions I had – that they were bollocks. She'd been threatening to devise her own system ever since. Now, for solid historical reasons, I'm not comfortable with dividing people up into groups. But the medical profession cannot sleep easy until it has a category for everything.

'It's all about instilling confidence,' Dr Walid had explained once.

Apparently patients much preferred doctors who sounded like they knew what they were talking about – even when they didn't. Perhaps especially when they didn't.

'If it helps, think of it as provisional,' said Dr Vaughan.

So Brown for the chimera – the cat-girls and tiger-boys,

and God knows what else Martin Chorley's sick little brain might have come up with.

'Brown for Beta, right?'

'Just so,' said Dr Vaughan.

'And Green for Gamma.'

'Oh, he is bright, isn't he?' said Dr Vaughan to no one in particular. 'Subjects that are not the product of modification, or at least modification of their phenotype.'

'So she was born the way she is?' I said. 'How can you tell?'

'Why don't we have a look?'

She tweaked the sheet back to expose poor Charlotte Green down to her navel. The horribly familiar Y incision had been sewn up, although I noticed the cut had wiggled slightly to avoid bisecting any bullet wounds.

'We won't have the genetic results back for a week or so, but I'm willing to bet good money that we won't find any evidence of chimerism,' she said.

So no genetic manipulation at the cellular level.

I asked her how she could be so sure, which got me an approving nod from Dr Walid.

'From this,' said Dr Vaughan.

I watched, wincing, as she reached into Charlotte's mouth and pulled her tongue out to its full extent. It was at least twenty centimetres long.

'Now, as you can imagine,' said Dr Vaughan. 'You can't just a fit a tongue like that into someone's face – there's no room for it. If you detach her lower jawbone and have a good look down her throat you'll see it's substantially different from the human norm.'

Which didn't necessarily mean anything, since the

67

human norm was a spectrum that went from smaller than you'd expect to larger than you can imagine.

'Vastly different,' said Dr Walid, who's had this argument with me before. 'But very similar to Molly's. As is the dentition.'

'Molly let you look in her throat?'

'Not me,' said Dr Walid, who had never got close to Molly with so much as a tongue depressor.

'She's perfectly reasonable if you explain yourself properly,' said Dr Vaughan. 'She let me have a quick look with a bronchoscope. Admittedly, it took a little while for her to get used to it, and I did have to get a second bronchoscope after she bit through the first one.'

'Did you get a tissue sample as well?' I asked.

'Of course,' said Dr Walid. 'That's what we'll use as a comparison for genome sequencing. But at an anatomical level, the positioning of the hyoid bone and the larynx are identical between Molly and Charlotte.'

'Longer tongue, more control, and extra room to keep it in,' said Dr Vaughan.

And if Charlotte the killer nanny was the same as Molly, then the chances were that she was the same as the so-called High Fae I'd encountered in Herefordshire. We couldn't call them gammas. It made them sound like bad guys in a cheap first-person shooter – and what if they found out?

'In that case,' I said, 'can we change the surname to Greenwood?'

'Whatever for?' asked Dr Vaughan.

'Because one day we might want to share this data with them,' I said. 'And it will be slightly less embarrassing.'

8

Flat Roof Pub

So I spent the next couple of days seeing if I couldn't find where Charlotte Greenwood had come from.

Some say there is an invisible line in the world that separates the demi-monde, the world of magic, from the mundane world of everyday existence. They say that if you step over that line, however unknowingly, your world will be changed for ever. They say that once you have taken that fateful step you can never go back, never unsee what you have seen, never unknow what you have discovered.

This is of course total bollocks.

Of course you can cross back; you can move to Burnley and become a hairdresser, or to Sutton and work in IT. You can go caravanning in Wales and never see a single dragon, and go swimming in the Severn and never meet the goddess Sabrina.

Even the very strange can leave the demi-monde if they put their mind to it. There's definitely at least one bridge troll that I know of teaching PE at a comprehensive in Reading.

Those that don't choose a quiet life teaching basketball to twelve-year-olds form what we call the demi-monde, because calling it the half-world in English would lead to too many questions. It's made up of fae of all kinds, and also people who want to be fae or have been touched by the supernatural in some way, or just found this great pub with this really spooky atmosphere.

So pub crawling I went – from the Chestnut Tree at Hyde Park Corner to the Spaniards Inn in Highgate, to the *shebeen* that's run off the roof of a tower block in Hillingdon. Everywhere I went I was greeted with the glad cries and open-hearted welcome that a police officer comes to expect when trawling his suspect pool.

I did get some co-operation if only, as it was made clear, to speed me on my way.

While I was out fruitlessly outreaching the community, the Queensland Police emailed back to say that Gabriel Tate had died the previous November after being bitten by an eastern brown snake at his home in Middle Park, Brisbane. That he didn't recognise the bite for what it was, until he was too far gone, was attributed to his inexperience with Australian wildlife and it was considered an accidental death. Just to be on the safe side I requested the full file.

An email from the US regarding John Chapman just said *Call me*.

By the time I got back from Hillingdon it was past 8 p.m. in Washington DC, and so late enough to catch my US contact at home.

Leaving aside dumb luck, criminals are mainly caught by systems, not individuals. Most of these systems are officially sanctioned and come with virtual folders full of regulations and best practice, but some are complex webs of interpersonal relationships and traded favours. Where everyday policing butts up against boundaries – jurisdictional, national, ideological – the official link-ages can clog up or break down or just plain fail to exist at all. Here the informal networks take over at every level, from ordinary hard-working but newly qualified DCs to the chief constables of major forces – they are tolerated as the quickest way to get the job done.

Foreign is always tricky even when you share a common language, and so a sensible young copper looks to maintain whatever contacts might fall into his lap.

Special Agent Kimberley Reynolds was my contact at the FBI and ostensibly worked for the Office of Partner Engagement in Washington DC. She was also, as far as we both knew, the Bureau's only Special Agent currently tasked with investigating weird bollocks. She suspected there might be more, but the top brass at the Puzzle Palace had made a point of discouraging her curiosity.

We'd been very cautious about our contacts until the previous winter, when Kimberley had been forced to break agency protocol and get my help, or at least my advice, long distance. And, in the aftermath, nothing happened. Which is impressive considering the centre of a small town was effectively levelled as a consequence.

Since that contact we'd regularly exchanged in-formation, gossip and advice on the basis that if the powers-that-be didn't want us to –and we had no doubt that we were being monitored – they'd bloody well say so.

'I think we can safely assume,' Kimberley had said

during one conversation, 'that the FBI now considers you a partner it's engaging with.'

Still we didn't say anything out loud that we didn't want the NSA overhearing.

'John Chapman taught Latin at John Carroll University in Cleveland,' said Kimberley. 'That's the one that's in Ohio.'

'Taught Latin?' I asked, not liking the past tense.

'Died in an officer involved shooting last January,' said Reynolds, who'd managed to get a look at the file.

Chapman had been filling up his car at a local gas station when he was attacked by a lone figure dressed in black combats and a black or dark blue winter jacket. Police theorise that the assailant was either planning a straight mugging or a carjacking, but either way he was out of luck because a Cleveland PD cruiser pulled into the gas station forecourt just as the attack went down.

The subsequent events were confused and not helped by the fact that the police cruiser's camera was facing away from the action and the footage from the gas station's CCTV was never recovered. According to the officers' own statements they responded to what they initially perceived as an altercation, but as they were approached they were threatened by the unidentified assailant.

'This is where you might find it interesting,' said Reynolds. 'The officers' statements in the official investigation both say that the unidentified male threatened them with a long knife, "almost a sword", and in fear of their lives they opened fire.'

Emptying their Glock 17s – 17 shots each – at their target.

'I've seen panic fire before,' said Kimberley. 'And judging from the dispersion pattern those boys were strictly spray and pray.'

John Chapman had been struck three times in thigh, hip and chest and had died on the way to hospital. The unidentified assailant fled the scene and was never apprehended. The Cleveland PD's follow-up investigation was swift, comprehensive and, to Kimberley's eye, almost entirely fabricated.

'It helped that Mr Chapman lived alone with no relatives and didn't seem particularly loved at his place of work,' she said.

'No interest from the British Consulate?' I asked.

'Chapman had dual citizenship and Cleveland PD only recovered his American passport,' said Kimberley. 'I doubt it occurred to them to check further.'

'Sloppy,' I said.

'Under pressure, in my view,' said Kimberley. 'But fortunately for you the DOJ was conducting an investigation of the whole department.'

Which meant that Kimberley had access to confidential documents without all the hassle of getting warrants – or permission.

Both the officers had been long-standing veterans. During their careers neither had faced complaints for excessive force and only one had discharged his firearm at an incident while the other had not – they were both described as reliable, professional and level-headed.

And both had retired from law enforcement within six weeks of the incident.

'You think they ran into something,' I said. 'Something they didn't understand?'

'Oh, definitely.'

'Any chance of you talking to them directly?'

'Already booked on a flight.'

Kimberley was too experienced to make a move without cover – she had to have sanction from higher up. Strangely, who precisely constituted these higher-ups never arose in conversation. Obviously not worth discussing.

If this was sanctioned, then they must have been as spooked as Kimberley.

'You're that certain?' I asked.

'Thirty-four rounds, Peter,' said Kimberley. 'They hit the car eight times, two gas pumps three times each, they hit the "We're Open" sign and the support pillars either side. And the only thing they didn't hit was the mystery assailant? I know you have a low opinion of American law enforcement, but trust me when I say we teach our people to shoot straight.'

'Then be careful,' I said.

'Always am.'

I checked in the next morning to see if we knew the whereabouts of Zachary Palmer, the demi-monde's very own go-to guy for ducking and diving, bar work, fixing and general dishonesty. Due to a lucrative consultation contract with Crossrail, currently worth three hundred large a year, he didn't actually have to do any ducking and diving. That he still fiddled his change and sold dodgy goods on the Portobello Road while the money piled up in a low interest building society account seemed to wind up Seawoll no end.

'He could at least move to a Home Office priority crime,' he said. 'Something worth nicking him for. Or maybe he could buy something worth sequestrating.'

I explained that people like Zach were wired differently from most of us. Driven by a different set of priorities – even if they were as blind to their obsessions as we were to ours.

'Is that what it is?' Seawoll had said, giving me a long look. 'Well, that explains a lot.'

Zach was also costing us a fortune, because a full-time surveillance is three shifts of five running 24/7 plus overtime – a cool two and a half grand a day. And every week or so he managed to shake them anyway. As he had that morning.

We still had to pay the bloody team, by the way – police work is by the hour, not by results.

'Is he using magic to do that?' asked Guleed.

'He's just really sneaky,' I said. 'But I reckon he only makes an effort when he wants to slope off and meet Lesley – which is a good thing.'

'Because?'

'For one thing, it means if we ever find Martin Chorley we can time his arrest to when she isn't there,' I said. 'One less thing to worry about.'

There was no Goblin Market that week but Marcia, who grows underwater blow on the Regent's Canal just outside Camden Lock, mentioned that she'd heard of unusual sightings of the High Fae around Southend and Canvey Island.

'Only on moonless nights,' said Marcia, a muscular white woman in her seventies who favoured sleeveless tops that showed off her impressive tattoo collection. 'Do you want a cup of tea?'

'Yeah, thanks,' I said. 'But can we make sure it's just tea this time?'

'I've already said that was a mistake,' said Marcia. 'I got the labels mixed up.'

She ducked into the cabin to put the kettle on. Marcia's boat is one of the few remaining narrowboats still rigged for cargo, with a small cabin at the stern and a long tarpaulin-covered A-frame over the holds forward. The tarpaulin was blue, which clashed horribly with the lurid red and orange gingerbread trim of the boat itself. Marcia had bought it in 1974 when she'd mustered out of the Merchant Marine. Previous to that she'd been first mate on a tramp freighter registered out of Panama. At the bow of the boat, just behind the prow, a half metre high carved wooden statue of an orangutan sat cross-legged, palms upwards in the style of the Buddha. This mark of allegiance being why Marcia didn't pay tying up fees anywhere along the length of the canal.

That and the blow, of course. Which, while not containing any Falcon-actionable ingredients, and you can be sure we tested extensively, was potent enough for me to be missing one whole weekend. Guleed swears blind I didn't do anything too embarrassing and so far nothing has surfaced on YouTube. Occasionally she or Bev, or once even Molly, will look at me and laugh . . . but that could just be my paranoia.

I glanced inside Marcia's cabin long enough to make

sure it was Sainsbury's own label tea bags going into the mugs. Once the tea was done we did the whole 'no obligation' exchange – nobody knows whether this is really necessary, and nobody wants to be the first to find out the hard way that it is.

We sat opposite each other on the padded gunwales and chatted shit for a bit. It's good when you're running an investigation not to get tunnel vision. Sometimes spending a bit of time with the local faces can often yield better results than charging around yelling 'Just the facts, ma'am'. So it proved that afternoon, although I didn't spot the connections until much later.

'You guys haven't been stirring up the City, have you?' she asked.

We were moored off Muriel Street in Islington, just short of the west end of the Islington Tunnel, which gaped like the entrance to a dark dimension, but really just led to more Islington. Marcia had gestured down it when she spoke – so I knew when she said 'the City' she meant the City of London proper.

'What makes you say that?'

'Things have been unsettled recently.'

She refused to provide details – although she did suggest I might want to check out the Goat and Crocodile. Which turned out to be a pub in Shoreditch. When I checked the map I keep on my phone I saw that it lay squarely on the theoretical course of the Walbrook. The river that originally bisected the Roman city from north to south.

Worth a look, I thought.

*

Few buildings evoke the sinister horror of 1950s municipal architecture more strikingly than the flat roof pub. Thrown up in their thousands wherever the working class were being rehoused, it's hard to imagine that the architects were not secret teetotallers looking to make the whole pub experience as grim as possible. How else do you explain the cheap portal frame construction, the equally cheap uninsulated concrete slabs, and the flat roof with just enough parapet to ensure that damaging puddles formed with the lightest drizzle.

The Goat and Crocodile was a classic flat roof pub, and the fact that it sat squarely under the brand new concrete viaduct that linked the London Overground to the station at Shoreditch High Street marked it out from the start.

The sign looked even older than the pub, and in patches had been bleached blank by the weather. There was enough left to make out the image of a goat standing on its hind legs, head tilted upwards, jaws open as if screaming. The bleaching made it hard to see, but there was a suggestion that the goat had its forelimbs around the shoulders of figures to either side – as if it were dancing in a chorus line. There was no sign of the crocodile. The more I stared, the more I was convinced of the mad gleam in the animal's eye. The paintwork was very fine and if ever a pub sign was ripe to be restored and hung in a museum, this was it.

The interior décor of the pub, on the other hand, couldn't have been dumped in a skip fast enough. In fact, quite a lot of it looked like it had been salvaged from skips in the first place. The floor was a patchwork of different coloured lino, faded blue in one corner, scuffed brown in front of the bar. A mismatched collection of fabric-covered benches, stools and repurposed wooden kitchen chairs were clustered around chipboard tables with genuine wood-finish laminated tops. The light coming in the dirty windows was a dusty brilliance on one side of the pub and cast the other side into shadow. In those shadows I saw two figures hunched over a table playing dominoes. The pieces clacking down in a demure English style. The players seemed to be the only patrons.

The place couldn't have been more demi-monde if it had changed its name to Biers and had a sign saying *Do not ask for normality, as postmodernism often offends.*

The bar was the only solid bit of furnishing, an old-fashioned wooden pub bar with a brass foot rail that looked like it had been looted during the Blitz and cemented awkwardly into place by someone on work experience.

As I walked towards the bar I felt a strange wave of *vestigia* – the smells of burnt earth and incense, and behind them a wash of sound like an outdoor market, with shouting and calls to buy and haggling, and the sound of anvils ringing like bells.

I blinked and realised that there was a young woman waiting behind the counter. She was tiny and dressed in orange capri pants and a purple T-shirt with a scorpion printed on the front. I couldn't tell if she was mixed race or Portuguese or something like that, but she had a straight nose and hair and light brown skin.

And black eyes, and a disturbingly unwavering gaze.

'What'll it be?' she said in an old-fashioned cockney accent.

I introduced myself as Detective Constable Peter Grant – because I'm allowed to do that now.

'Yeah, you're the Starling, ain't you?' she said, and managed to work an improbable glottal stop into the word 'starling'.

I figured, if we were going to play it that way . . .

'That's me,' I said. 'So who are you, then, when you're at home?'

'Where do you think you're standing?' she said. 'From a topographical point of view?'

The answer was, well, in the shallow valley carved by the second most important river in London.

'So, you're the Walbrook?'

'You can call me Lulu,' she said.

'I know your mum. And a couple of your sisters.'

A hush fell all around me and there was a sound like wind chimes – the bottles along the back of the bar tinkling into each other.

'If you want to stay on my good side,' said Lulu, 'you might not want to be name-dropping in this pub – especially not those names.'

My mum maintains a couple of rotating feuds with the vast cloud of family and semi-family that now stretches across four generations and eleven time zones. I know for a fact that one Aunty Kadi hasn't spoken to another Aunty Kadi for six years, although, just to confuse people, she gets on fine with a third Aunty Kadi. Which is why most introductions in my family start, 'This is your Aunty Kadi who lives in Peckham and married my half-brother from Lunghi, but is not the Aunty Kadi who said that thing about me which was totally not true'. Not all my aunties are called Kadi – some of them are called Ayesha, and one of them, on my dad's side, is called Bob. The upshot of this is I'm well skilled at keeping my head down in the face of intra-familial wrangling.

'Fair enough,' I said and, because I thought it might be a spectacularly bad idea to ask for a drink, I asked whether the High Fae came into the pub.

Lulu gave me a crooked smile.

'High Fae?' she asked.

'You know,' I said. 'The gentry, elves, those posh gits with extradimensional castles, stone spears and unicorns.'

'You mean them what step between worlds?'

'Could be.'

'Who walk on paths unseen and wax and wane with the moon?'

'Them sort of people,' I said. 'Yeah.'

'Not in here, squire,' she said. 'I run a respectable pub.'

Later that evening, when I got Beverley alone in the big bath at her house, I asked about Walbrook.

'She doesn't mix with us,' she said, leaning forward while I soaped her back.

'Why not?

'Don't know,' she said. 'If she doesn't want to mix with us we can't exactly ask her why, can we?'

'You don't seem very curious about what she's like.'

'I am curious, but . . .' She shifted and a wave of cool water from the other end of the bath sloshed over me.

'It's like the back of your head. Apart from after your yearly haircut, do you ever look at the back of your head?'

'That makes no sense at all,' I said, and used my toes to open the hot tap.

'I suppose not,' said Beverley, and leant back against my chest. She had her locks all tied up on the crown of her head and they brushed my face, smelling of lemons and clean damp hair. 'Some things we do are never going to make sense to you. They barely make sense to us half the time.'

'What does your mum say?'

'She says, "When you are older these things will be clearer. Now go away and stop bothering me with all these questions".'

'Helpful,' I said, and managed to get the hot tap off before the bath overflowed.

There was a pause.

'If I tell you something can you keep it a secret?'

'Sure.'

'Nah, nah, nah, you said that too quickly,' she said. 'I mean really secret. You don't tell nobody, not your boss, not your mum, not Toby, not nobody.'

'Yeah, OK.'

'Swear on your mum's life.'

'Not my mum's life.'

'Yes, on your mum's life.'

'I swear on Mum's life I won't tell nobody,' I said.

'I don't think Walbrook comes from my mum at all,' said Beverley. 'I think she's way older than that.'

'Older than Father Thames?'

'Nobody's that old.'

82

9

Two Plus Two

Unlike most of the Folly's cases, Operation Jennifer was a full-on major investigation with a full-on inside inquiry room stuffed with analysts and data entry specialists and lorded over by a case manager. The case manager keeps track of what goes into HOLMES and what comes out. It is their job to keep an investigation on the rails even when the senior officers have all been sidetracked by an unfortunate fatal shooting.

Stephanopoulos used to do this job for Seawoll and our case manager, Sergeant Franklin Wainscrow, had been picked on her say-so. So it's not surprising that when we came in on Friday morning fresh lines of inquiry were waiting on our desks in the visitors' lounge.

David Carey had been busy at the bell foundry, and while we were failing to save Richard Williams he'd been conducting a properly thorough interview with Dr Conyard. One of the questions he'd asked was – had Richard Williams supplied any special instructions or materials for the construction of the bell? Turns out that Richard had provided several sacks of aggregate for use in making the mould. One of the analysts had spotted this, linked it to the brick thefts and pushed it back to Wainscrow, who generated an action for Carey, which he fobbed off on to me over breakfast by pretending to need my advice. The cheeky sod.

'You'd be amazed to know what they use to make the moulds,' said Carey. 'Not just the clay and the loam, which I get by the way, but manure?'

'What kind of manure?' asked Guleed, who was having an omelette with toasted crumpets.

'What?'

'What kind of manure – horse, cow . . . human?'

'I didn't think to ask,' said Carey. 'I'm not sure it's relevant to this particular line of inquiry.' He poked at his kippers a bit and sighed. 'Anyway – one of the analysts wanted to know whether it was possible the aggregate had come from the bricks stolen from those archaeological sites.'

I paused with a forkful of kedgeree halfway to my mouth and kicked myself for not thinking of that myself.

'Yeah,' I said. 'That would be interesting.'

'Lucky for you,' said Carey, 'there was enough of the mould left to get samples.'

'And?'

Carey frowned down at his plate, shook his head and reached for his tea.

'We'll know when we get the results. Two weeks to a month, depending.'

'Depending on what?' I asked.

'Just depending,' he said, and pushed his plate away.

'Are you OK?' asked Guleed.

Carey shook his head.

'Not really,' he said. 'No offence, Peter, but when this case is done I'm going back to my nice horrible murders.' He shook his head. 'I used to think that a six-week floater was horrible, but the shit you deal with . . . Fuck.'

Toby, who had an instinct for abandoned breakfasts, materialised beside Carey's chair and gave him the big eye special. Carey did a quick scan to make sure Molly wasn't watching and put his plate on the floor under the table.

'She hates it when you put the plates on the floor,' I said.

'Gets them clean though, don't it?' said Carey, retrieving his suddenly gleaming plate. He looked at me. 'I reckoned that since you were already in with the archaeologists you'd want to take that over that line of inquiry.'

See what I mean? The sly sod.

I had another round of IPCC interviews where I got the distinct impression that they wanted rid of this case as fast as possible. Contrary to what you might think the IPCC, being understaffed and poorly resourced, try to avoid being assigned cases. Which is probably why the Police Federation tries to dump as many on them as they can – the better to educate them about the nature of most complaints. Still, even with my Federation rep glaring at them, the interviews took up most of the day.

After which I headed back to the Whitechapel Bell Foundry to spell Nightingale, who was practically camping in their foundry room and no doubt swapping manly stories about hitting pieces of metal together.

While he went back to the Folly I sat guard in the corner of the furnace room, partly because of its good lines of sight but mostly because it was the only place I could get a decent Wi-Fi signal.

Given that all three named authors had died suspicious deaths, I had another look at the PDF of the script fragment I'd found in Richard Williams's home office.

Judging by the surviving fifteen pages, *Against the Dark* was a historical horror or supernatural mystery. It started with a simple Saxon herder being stalked through the ruins of Londinium by an unseen horror before being horribly killed. We then cut to our hero, a chiselled, devil-may-care adventurer who tells the first person he meets that he's from Ireland, presumably so they could cast an American, before neatly talking himself into a fight. He's only saved at the last minute by the arrival of his companion, a blackamoor, whose dark skin confuses the Saxons long enough for a messenger from the king to rescue them. Although I ran out of script one page into their audience with the king, you didn't have to be a master of TV tropes to see where the story was going.

I didn't think it was very good. But it wasn't so bad that you'd kill the writers.

I like the Dark Ages, Martin Chorley had said when he was monologuing in the basement of One Hyde Park. *When a man could make himself a myth.*

Or, more precisely, the Post-Roman period. Or, if you like your history fast and loose, the Age of Arthur.

You get a lot of stuff like this in an investigation – things that look suggestive but could just be coincidences. Which happen more often than people think they do.

Yet ... three people were dead – all of them suspiciously close together.

Bev, who'd been doing lab work down the road at Queen Mary's, turned up with takeaway, which passed the time until Nightingale returned and I drove her back to SW20 and spent the night at her place.

I woke up at six in the morning to find that Nicky had arrived and had wormed herself into the covers between me and Bev. She smelt faintly of diesel oil and left mud stains on the duvet cover.

'How did you get in?' I asked.

'Uncle Max let me in,' she said, meaning Maksim, the former Russian mobster who'd forgone crime in favour of being Beverley's one and only acolyte/handyman.

Bev had reacted to Nicky's intrusion by muttering, rolling over and going back to sleep.

'I thought you were staying with Effra?'

'Was,' said Nicky. 'But she won't be awake for ages.'

'Does she know you're here?' I asked, and Nicky gave a little uncaring shrug.

'Want to play water balloons in the garden?' she asked.

'Is there any chance of you letting me go back to sleep?'

Nicky solemnly shook her head.

'Fine,' I said. 'Just as soon as I've left a message for Effra.' Flinging magical water balloons around was as good a practice session as Nightingale could ask for. 'And I've had some coffee.'

'Can I have pancakes?' asked Nicky.

*

Saturday I had off but I had to head back to the Folly Sunday morning. Now that I was properly PIP2 qualified, Nightingale felt I would have time to concentrate a bit upon my magical studies. Since he was still guarding the drinking bell, that meant Latin and Greek and two hours on the firing range alternating between perforating cardboard cut-outs and fending off paintballs.

Since the police staff mostly work office hours, the Folly had started to feel a bit empty on the weekends. Sometimes the only sound was Toby barking or Molly humming a happy little tune as she tenderised a steak or beat a carpet to death. The place, at least, has thick walls to keep the heat out, and the magical library on the second floor gets a good cross breeze if you open the right windows. Abigail might be outpacing me, but my Latin's got to the point where I just need a dictionary for the vocab. Cicero wouldn't approve of my writing style, but at least I pronounce his name with a hard *C*.

Unlike the clergy of the Middle Ages, who were halfway to speaking Italian by the end of the fourteenth century. As soon as I went looking for the Post-Roman period I found some eighteenth-century references to Roger Bacon, old Doctor Marvellous himself. His Latin was remarkably good, so it's just a pity that he wrote what I was looking for in Greek. For extra confusion it was called the *Opus Arcanum,* which is Latin. I've never really got the hang of Greek, but with the aid of a dictionary, a 1922 edition of Smyth and Messing's *Greek Grammar*, and Google, I think I got the gist. I also scanned the relevant passage and sent it off to Professor Postmartin in Oxford.

According to Bacon, the *Prophetiae Merlini* by Geoffrey of Monmouth had originally contained a section relating to the original foundation of St Paul's in circa ad 604 and, even more interestingly, the use of bells to either signal or usher in – the translation wasn't clear – a change, or the fulfilment of a prophecy.

A bell for ringing in the changes, Martin Chorley had called the bell in the Whitechapel foundry. Or maybe the fulfilment of a prophecy? A bell made with the help of ancient stones taken from pagan and Christian religious sites. Imbued with *vestigia*, perhaps.

People had died to protect the secrets of that bell. I doubted that Chorley had it made to indulge a hitherto unreported interest in campanology.

The trouble was that I was beginning to suspect that Bacon's Greek was as bad as mine and, deciding that I had reached the limit of my Greek, I dumped it all on Professor Postmartin – who loves this sort of thing anyway.

But, to keep Nightingale happy, I read a big chunk of Geoffrey's *Historia Regum Britanniae* – the bits about Uther Pendragon and his son Arthur.

10

The Mandate of the Masses

The following Tuesday was taken up with the American first lady's visit to a school in Whitechapel. The American Secret Service were already unhappy about having their second biggest target at a largely Muslim school in London's most Muslim area. Even more so since the Home Office wouldn't let them park a couple of Abrams main battle tanks on Commercial Road. We all had to work extra hard to convince them security was tight.

The Commissioner requested on the spot Falcon coverage – just in case.

'I didn't want to ask him what contingencies he had in mind,' said Nightingale. 'I felt he might be a tad preoccupied.'

And it might have been a fun day out for all, if it hadn't been necessary to guard the bell at the foundry. Striking while everyone is distracted is Martin Chorley's signature move, so I didn't argue when Nightingale selected me for the job.

'After myself you are the most powerful practitioner we have,' he said. 'If I am to cover the first lady then it follows that you should guard the bell.'

As we did the preliminary operational planning I had

a clever idea about how we might turn the event to our advantage. Nightingale didn't like it, but he couldn't argue with my logic. Which is why Guleed has a selfie with Michelle Obama and I don't.

Martin Chorley being the dangerous criminal he was, Nightingale insisted on some additional contingency planning. Which was just as well, because just as Michelle was going peak-first lady down the road, the bell began to sing.

I'd camped out beside the bell where a work table and several tons of heavy brass wrangling tools formed an improvised barricade between me and the main gates. There I'd made myself comfortable with a coffee and a takeaway from the Café Casablanca and waited for something to happen.

I tried to concentrate on my PIP3 reading list, Professionalism in Policing Level Three being what you do after you've qualified for PIP2 – the fun never stops in the Metropolitan Police. Unfortunately 'Assessing scenes of crime for their potential to provide useful evidence' kept on slipping out of my brain. Still, I was just grappling with the best practice for determining my restricted access area when I noticed that the bell had started to softly hum.

The hum of a bell is two octaves below its nominal pitch, and is one of the partial tones that give traditionally built bells that sense of depth when they ring. It's why they ring out danger and celebration and the call to prayer and don't go *ting* the way triangles do – however big they are.

I put down the book on *Major Incident Room*

Standardised Administrative Procedures (MIRSAP) that I'd borrowed from Guleed and made sure I switched off my expensive main phone. By the time I was ready, the bell had started to sing quietly in the prime, tierce and quint partials, going in and out like a toddler playing with a wah-wah pedal.

And then Lesley was standing in the gateway.

'Please, sir,' she said, 'can we have our bell back?'

'What do you want it for anyway?' I asked.

Lesley hesitated before entering the yard. She was pausing to seem less of a threat, and also to let her eyes adjust to the lower light levels inside the foundry.

She was dressed in a nondescript blue tank top, black leggings and blue trainers. She carried no bag, or anything else that I could see, and she let her hands hang, relaxed, by her sides. The foundry yard was littered with recently cast bells and crates and Lesley was forced to take her eyes off me to pick her way between the obstacles.

It was enough of a disadvantage that I could have probably knocked her down with a sudden strike, but we'd agreed I wouldn't try. For one thing, *probably* isn't *definitely*. For another, we had other options. And, finally, we thought we might have an opportunity. Well, *I* thought we might have an opportunity – everybody else thought I was bonkers.

I stood up to mask the movement my hand made as it came to rest on the old-fashioned walkie-talkie I'd Sellotaped to the table, low down enough so it would be out of Lesley's eye line.

She stopped safely out of baton swing range and gave

me a crooked smile. She was pausing for effect, but I wasn't having that.

'Does it hurt?' I asked.

There was a fractional hesitation before she asked, 'Does what hurt?'

When she spoke, I noticed that the bell hummed in sympathy. You'd have to be listening carefully to be sure, but it was definitely there.

'When you change your face,' I said. 'Does it hurt?'

'No,' she said, but there was a twinge around the eyes that made her a liar.

'Show me?'

'No,' she said.

'I showed you mine, remember?' I said.

Back in that seaside shelter in Brightlingsea a million million years ago, when we were both on the same side. At least I hoped we were still on the same side back then. Otherwise? 'Otherwise' didn't bear thinking about.

'Peter, we don't have much time here,' said Lesley. 'Let me have the bloody bell.'

This time the bell sang loud enough to make it clear it was echoing her words.

'It's fricking eight tonnes,' I said. 'How are you even going to get it out of here?'

'Let me worry about that.'

'Why do you stay with him?' I said. 'You got your face back.'

'You think I did it for that?' asked Lesley.

'Fuck yeah, I thought you did it for that,' I said. 'I'd have done it for that.'

'Liar,' said Lesley – this time with real heat, and the bell sang loud enough for her to notice. 'Fucking liar.'

'Then why?'

I made sure I kept my left hand nice and still where it rested on the walkie-talkie. We didn't want to get premature – not now. Not now.

Lesley's lips twisted.

'You think this is a game, Peter,' she said. 'You find out there's a whole world full of weird shit, and you want to make a form for it. A form? Like you can control gods by ticking off boxes. Like you can make a procedure for dealing with monsters. You're so blind.'

'I'm just trying to do the job—'

'You don't even fucking know what the job is!' shouted Lesley, and the bell rang in sympathy. 'You used to make me sad listening to you talk about fucking engagement and fucking whatnot while the whole city turned to shit around us. Do you remember the baby, Peter? Do you even remember his fucking name?'

His name had been Harry Coopertown, and not saying it out loud hurt more than I expected – but I was so close.

'So what are you saying?' I said. 'If you can't beat them, join them?'

'Yeah. Or maybe I've got something better. You ever think of that? Did that ever even occur to you, that I might have found something not just for me – you pillock – but for everybody. Including you and, you know, your mum, and maybe even Beverley.'

'I doubt that,' I said but, actually, I didn't. Or at least I didn't doubt that she believed it. I couldn't trust the face, but her eyes were bright and confident.

'Why are you stalling me?' said Lesley. 'Everyone is busy with Mrs Obama. SCO19 and Diplomatic Protection are fully deployed elsewhere. It's just you and me, isn't it?'

Her eyes flicked left and right, and then up and to the left to the gantry which would serve as the best vantage point for a sniper on overwatch.

She didn't know – but she suspected.

'We could slope off for a pint,' I said. 'You and me. Have a chat. Sort things out.'

'It's really simple, Peter. If you hand over the bell now he won't have to make another one. Nobody else has to get hurt.'

'How many people got hurt making the first one?'

'None,' said Lesley. 'But that's because nobody got in the way.'

'I tell you what. You tell me what it's for and I'll think about it.'

I could actually feel my finger trembling as it hovered over the call tone button on the walkie-talkie.

'Okay, I'm backing off now,' said Lesley. 'Don't do anything stupid.'

'You can always call me,' I said as she backed away. 'You know that, right?'

She gave me a strange half smile and stepped out the gate.

I ripped the walkie-talkie off the table and thumbed the push to talk button.

'Anybody got eyes on?' I asked.

One of the spotters had her, and reported that she'd

been picked up by a moped, had crossed the main road and disappeared up Greatorex Street. I told everyone to maintain position just in case Martin Chorley tried to catch us off guard with an immediate follow-up.

Frank Caffrey climbed down from his position in the overhead gantry and joined me. His SA80 assault rifle was cradled in the 'ready' position. I didn't like using Caffrey's merry band of reserve Paras for operations, but Lesley had been right about the overstretch on SCO19.

And Nightingale had insisted.

'I'm not sure I approve of making a lure of yourself and casting yourself out into the water,' he'd said, when I sketched out the plan. 'I'm not sure the catch will be worth the cost.'

We'd let today's Falcon deployment 'leak' onto the police intranet over the weekend. We knew that somewhere some bent bastard was leaking operational details to Martin Chorley. DPS were monitoring the intranet in the hope they might catch him, and then we were going to turn the fucker and use him or her to feed disinformation back to Chorley.

'You should have let me take the shot,' said Caffrey, who had a very straightforward approach to these things.

'There'll be a truck somewhere nearby,' I said. 'A flatbed with its own crane.'

And it would have been stolen first thing this morning from somewhere which wouldn't notice it was gone until at least this afternoon. Martin Chorley was that methodical. But still, even he couldn't account for the human factor.

My phone rang as soon as I turned it on.

'Well?' said Nightingale. I could hear excited cheering in the background.

I remembered the way the bell had resonated when Lesley spoke, and how she'd felt it worth trying to justify herself. If not a new face and all the sociopathy she could eat, then what was Martin Chorley offering her?

Something she believed in?

Something she might want me to believe in, too?

'I think we're in with a chance,' I said.

11

Against the Dark

I n the end we broke up the bell.

Dr Conyard's lads did it with sledgehammers under his grim supervision while Nightingale watched for any supernatural funny business. It hadn't been an easy decision to destroy something so special, whatever its true purpose. We considered bringing it into the Folly for safekeeping, but even the non-classically educated among us were thinking *Trojan horse*.

I suggested the British Museum, not least because it's possible to lose just about anything in their storage area. They're still looking for a mummy that went missing in 1933 – staff believe it was stolen but Nightingale said he'd always had a sneaking suspicion that it got bored one day and walked away.

'I don't think we want to expose the museum to the risk,' he said.

There were any number of army bases and security installations we might have called, but they had even less experience with the uncanny than the British Museum. We'd also considered leaving it in place and using it as bait, but decided the risk to members of the public was too great.

So, smashed it was. And the scrap pieces transported

to the Folly to be distributed widely to randomly selected scrap metal recycling companies across the Midlands. We weren't going to take any chances with it being reassembled on the sly.

The bell sang with the first hammer and screamed with the second. And within the scream I heard a familiar laugh and the jingle of merry bells.

What do you want, you hook-nosed bastard? I asked in my head, but the third blow cracked the bell and Mister Punch fell silent. I turned away to find Nightingale watching me.

'What did you hear?' he asked.

'Mr Punch,' I said, and asked Nightingale if he hadn't heard anything. He shook his head.

Oh, me and Punch go way back, I thought. We have a *special* relationship.

Kimberley Reynolds skyped me from the States to save money and to make the NSA work for their intercept. Behind her I could see a wood veneer headboard and horrible magnolia painted walls – so I guessed she was sitting on a hotel bed. Eating doughnuts, as it turned out.

'Cleveland PD gifted them,' she said, taking a bite.

The local police being caught up in a Department of Justice investigation into their tendency to shoot people first and make up answers second. All Kimberley had to do, she said, was roll her eyes and make it clear that if it were up to her they could shoot as many people as they liked.

'I used to be a straight arrow,' she said. 'This is your bad influence.'

'What was that whole unauthorised operation in our sewers, then?'

'That,' said Kimberley, waving half a chocolate frosted doughnut at the camera, 'was me being patriotic and can-do under difficult foreign circumstances.'

'So, did you find out about our John Chapman, then?'

'Oh, you really don't want him to be *your* John Chapman,' said Reynolds. 'I had a professor like him in college.'

Kimberley's low opinion of Chapman was shared by his colleagues and most of his students. Sexually harassing his female students and failing to turn up for lectures was bad enough. But worse, according to his faculty colleagues, he was a snob and put on airs.

'Acted like he was better than them,' said Kimberley. 'Refused to socialise.'

Never invited people round to his home, not even the gullible coeds. They had all been shocked by his violent death, of course, but had managed to get on with their lives regardless.

Kimberley had interviewed a lot of the students. A few had ended up in one of several economically priced motels – never more than twice. The general consensus among those so blessed was that John Chapman had given the impression that he was enjoying the experience even less than they were.

Six months following his death, Chapman's rented apartment had been re-let and redecorated and nobody was sure where his personal effects had disappeared to. Luckily, Cleveland PD had recovered the contents of his car. Including his laptop.

'Want to guess why that was a waste of their time?' asked Kimberley.

I said I was all agog, but I wasn't surprised when it turned out that the microprocessors had inexplicably been turned to sand. As had those in the gas station pumps, the cash register, the CCTV camera and the phone recovered off Chapman's body.

'And you remember the thing I told you about when I was last over?' asked Kimberley. 'The thing with the bear.'

That had been Kimberley's first probable encounter with *vestigia*. And I knew from experience that once you knew what you were looking for, separating *vestigia* from the brain's own random background noise got easier with practice.

'You sensed something?' I asked.

She had – although she wasn't sure what it was.

'Just something,' she said.

I'd liked to have asked whether Kimberley could make it over the Pond for a bit of training. But we were still waiting for a determination from the Commissioner as to whether we could offer our newly minted *vestigia* awareness course to non-UK nationals.

Still, I trusted she had enough experience to at least know it when she felt it.

'Would there really be a trace after six months?' she asked.

I explained that concrete retained *vestigia* almost as well as stone or brick.

'But the initial incident must have been significant,' I said. 'For you to sense it over such a wide area.'

My recent experience trying to explain magic to people who really would rather it didn't exist has given me an arsenal of euphemisms. I'm particularly proud of 'initial incident' although 'subjective perception threshold' runs a close second.

'Still, there were a couple of flash drives among his effects,' said Kimberley.

USB drives can survive fairly heavy doses of magic providing they're not plugged into a powered slot at the time. I asked if any data had been recovered.

'Just a lot of unmarked essays and what looks like a TV script.'

'What's the title?' I asked, as if I didn't already know.

'*Against the Dark*,' said Kimberley. 'You interested?'

I'd never read a film script all the way through before, so I bounced off it a couple of times before I got used to the conventions. I got the distinct impression that there were two separate voices involved, one more concerned with historical accuracy than the other. Or at least it read that way. But what did I know of sixth-century London — except it didn't really exist as such. At least not inside the Roman walls. I emailed a copy to Postmartin to see what he thought of it.

While the Saxon king Sæberht and his court spoke in that strange stilted non-contracted English that indicates the writer is trying to take his period seriously, Aedan, our intrepid Irish hero, and Cyrus, his black sidekick, spoke modern vernacular, cracked wise and were generally hip and groovy.

Straight to Netflix, I thought, if it ever got made at all.

And the three people listed on the front cover were all suspiciously brown bread.

In the script itself, something was killing locals that strayed within the London walls after dark. King Sæberht believes it to be an evil spirit, Oswyn his advisor says dangerous wild animal, while Mellitus, the papal emissary, agrees with the king but might just be saying that to get him into the baptismal font. Aedan and Cyrus, with the aid of the phenomenally strong yet stupid Henric and the major babe Hilda – it actually said that in the scene directions, MAJOR BABE – track down the mysterious killer.

It went all the places I expected it to go, although the set piece in the trap-infested maze inside the abandoned Temple of Mithras probably would have been exciting with the right director. The revelation that it was, in fact, an evil spirit rather than a creature, came at page seventy-six, shortly after Cyrus, to nobody's surprise, copped it in a suitably heroic way. They trace the spirit to its lair atop the highest hill in ancient Londinium amid the ruins of the old Roman amphitheatre. There it turns out to have been created by the last of the Romans through mass human sacrifice in an attempt to repel the invading Saxons.

The revenant animates the zombified remains of both the sacrifice victims and the Roman legionaries buried conveniently nearby. There is a major boss battle at the end of which Aedan plunges a sword, sanctified by Mellitus or something like that, into the heart of the spirit after he takes over the body of Henric, thus making himself inexplicably vulnerable. He is aided by a glowing light thingy that is either the power of God (Mellitus' explanation), the spirit of Cyrus (Aedan's explanation) or Cyrus having been transformed into an angelic manifestation of God's will – Hilda's explanation.

Mellitus declares that he will build a cathedral over the cursed amphitheatre to ensure the evil spirit can never return and baptises King Sæberht on that very spot. There's a brief flash forward to the present day where it's made clear that this is, in fact, St Paul's Cathedral. The credits roll, we dance, we kiss, we schmooze, we carry on, we go home happy.

Except that John Chapman, Gabriel Tate and Richard Williams didn't – did they?

Martin Chorley was a Dark Ages enthusiast. It was possible that this script so offended him that he offed two of the writers out of sheer critical outrage. This seemed unlikely – even for a dangerously unstable psychopath like him.

More likely there was something contained in the script that he really didn't want anyone to know about. I wrote up an email for the inside inquiry team and attached the script, with the caveat that I'd refine the correlation keywords once I had the report by Postmartin.

That report arrived during practice the next morning and I read it in the Tech Cave so I could put any notes on the system direct.

'There is sign of some scholarship,' wrote Postmartin. 'Aedan is a perfectly feasible name for a 6th Century Irishman and likewise naming his companion Cyrus shows an understanding of the Hellenic character of Egypt, particularly Alexandria, at that time – the rise of

Islam and the Arab conquests of the region having not yet begun. Henric, Oswyn and Hilda are all identifiably Anglo-Saxon names and, indeed, all can be found in Bede's *A History of the English Church and People*. But also, I note, by typing 'Anglo-saxon name' into Google. Still other details in the script indicate that at least one of the authors paid more attention to historical veracity than is usual in the film industry. King Sæberht of Essex is also in Bede and is considered to be a real historical figure, as is Mellitus, who is indeed credited with the founding of St Paul's.

'The Mithraeum on the Walbrook really existed, although its excitingly labyrinthine interior is a complete invention. There isn't and has never been any evidence to suggest that a Roman amphitheatre occupied the site of St Paul's and given that a verified amphitheatre has been located under the Guildhall Museum some 600 yards to the north-east I think it unlikely there were two such even in Londinium at its most glorious.

'Why the Anglo-Saxons didn't occupy the interior of Roman London, with its defensive walls and plentiful supply of building materials, is one of the great historical mysteries. The idea of a terrible cursed revenant preventing them is as good a theory as any other. Incidentally a sword of distinctive Saxon manufacture was reportedly recovered by the famous 18th C. antiquarian Winston William Galt from a cellar in Paternoster Row so that would explain where the blessed sword went, wouldn't it?

'On an interesting side note, the Anglo-Saxons used the same metal-folding technique as the medieval

Japanese and would often create beautiful weapons that would be 'sacrificed' by throwing them into sacred streams and lakes. Some think that the legend of the Lady of the Lake could derive from this custom since any aspiring British warrior might see such deposits as a handy source of high quality weaponry.'

I thanked Postmartin by email and asked if he knew the present whereabouts of the Paternoster Sword. What with the Lady of the Lake bollocks, it sounded like the sort of thing Martin Chorley might be interested in. Then I added *Excalibur, St Paul's Cathedral* and *the Temple of Mithras* to the list of HOLMES keywords. This got me an irritable note from Sergeant Wainscrow, who pointed out that overuse of key words can be counterproductive. I said we could discuss this at the briefing on Monday morning, but of course by that time my choices had been vindicated – well, sort of.

12

The Old Man's Regatta

That year the Old Man of the River was holding his summer court at Mill End, where the Thames skirts the eastern edge of the Chilterns before dropping south to Henley and Reading. Nightingale decided that, since he had to stay in London, I'd have to represent the Folly. So I threw two mystery hampers from Molly, Beverley's overnight party bag, and Abigail into the back of the Hyundai and set off on an unseasonably grey Saturday morning.

Bev was going to travel up the Thames and meet us there.

'Got to stop off and say hello to a few people on the way,' she said.

The day was humid and overcast and the Hyundai's aircon was labouring. I tried to get clever and go up the M40 and then south at High Wycombe, but that just meant me and Abigail were sweaty and irritable on a motorway instead of an A-road.

As we started the drop into the Thames Valley proper, we could see darker clouds piling up beyond the Thames to the south. Now, I don't have Bev's intimate acquaintance with the hydrological cycle, but I thought I knew a summer thunderstorm when it's lowering at me.

'Cumulonimbus,' said Abigail, who of course knew the technical name. '"Cumulus" means a mass and "nimbus" means cloud.'

I didn't deign to answer and instead concentrated on my driving.

We whooshed through Marlow, which appeared to be composed of strange mutant detached bungalows with hipped roofs in the Dutch style, and sprawling post-war villas in the no-style-whatsoever style. Then along the course of the Thames on the A4155, which rose and fell amongst woods, villages and boutique hotels ideal for the stressed executive.

Hambleden Marina was a private marina and boat yard that sat downstream of the weir at Hambleden Lock. Beverley says you can't live on the river without coming to an accommodation with the powers that be – in this case, Father Thames.

'Not that they necessarily know that's what they're doing,' she said.

Apparently, most people thought the little rituals they performed – the occasional bottle of beer left out in a riverside garden, the champagne broken on the bow of a boat, the odd bit of bank work or rewilding done on an adjacent property – that these were harmless little superstitions. Others entered directly into a pact because the blessing of the Old Man of the River could raise wild flowers out of season and cause HSE inspectors and bank managers to let things slide until the business picks up.

Occasionally, late at night, I wonder whether this is true of Mama Thames and whether, perhaps, her blessing can make an old man kick his heroin habit and take up his trumpet again.

It is at times like that I remember the wisdom of my mother who once told me – '*As yu mek yu bed, na so yu go lehdum par nam*'. But she means it in a good way.

I figured the owner of Hambleden Marina must know what bed they're climbing into. Because when the Summer Court of Father Thames moves in, it's a little hard to ignore.

The Showmen had put in a token appearance, setting up a steam-powered merry-go-round with an authentic period automatic organ that some joker had programmed to play a medley of James Brown's and Tina Turner's greatest hits, and a couple of mini roundabouts and roller coasters to keep the kids happy. Behind them, on the field closest to the main road, were their caravans, motorhomes and horses. The marina proper was choked with boats, triple and quadruple parked in some places so that they stuck out into the channel like temporary piers. At the far end of the longest of these piers was a large boat that looked like someone had jammed an Edwardian tea pavilion onto a flat-bottomed barge and painted everything white and nautical blue. I didn't need telling that this was the heart of the Summer Court.

A red-faced white man with mutton chop whiskers, a flat cap, a string vest, braces and cor blimey trousers directed us over to the parking area at the back of the caravans. I slotted myself into a minuscule spot between a Toyota Land Cruiser and a Ford Fiesta that I'm pretty sure had once been two separate cars.

But at least by the time we'd squeezed out the car with the luggage, Beverley had turned up to help us carry it. One of the impromptu boat piers actually extended all the way out to a nameless islet that sat midstream and planks had been laid down to form a crude pontoon bridge. The little island was where the kids would pitch their tents and apparently me and Bev were going to guard the bridge, because halfway across she stopped to show off her home from home.

This turned out to be the *Pride of Putney*, a nine-metre traditional gentleman's day boat built in the 1920s, with mahogany and brass fittings. Designed to motor rich people up and down the Thames, it had been refitted so that the bench seats in the aft passenger cabin could be rearranged to make a double bed. There was no internet or other electronics, which goes some way to explaining why Bev had been so vexed with me about her erstwhile sabbatical on the upper Thames.

'Though I got used to it,' she told me later. 'Plus I quickly figured out which pubs and houses had free Wi-Fi.'

I threw my luggage into the boat and, while Bev and Abigail went to pick a site for the tent, I set off to find Oxley and pay my respects. This is important amongst the *Genii Locorum*, who like a bit of respect and are not above flooding your back garden to get it. Oxley, despite being Father Thames's right-hand river deity, usually keeps a modest establishment, a tiny house in Chertsey and an old-fashioned caravan when on the road, but this time he had the second biggest boat.

It was a flat-bottomed, flat-roofed, clapboard sided,

green painted shotgun-shack on a raft called the *Queen of the Nile*. Moored centrally so that Oxley could sit on the roof under an awning and be, if not the master of all he surveyed, then at least responsible for keeping the whole mad enterprise from flying apart. Given that we had that much in common, I probably shouldn't have been so surprised that he gave me a hug when I joined him on the roof. He was a short wiry man with long arms that I suspect could have easily lifted me above his head.

'Good timing,' he said as I sat down next to him in a deckchair with Property of Merton College stamped across the faded stripes of its canvas back. Raindrops started to splat on the awning above us as the leading edge of the storm crossed the river and hit the marina. There were shrieks as adults ran for shelter and children ran in circles – a dog started barking.

From our perch it was easy to spot Beverley and Abigail scurrying along the pontoon bridge to the *Pride of Putney*. Beverley stopped while Abigail climbed inside, looked over at Oxley's boat, spotted me, waved and then ducked inside, too.

'Is that Peter?' called Oxley's wife Isis from below.

'It is, my love,' called Oxley.

'Ask him if he wants tea.'

I said I did and then waited as Oxley was summoned down the stern ladder to help fetch it. Isis climbed up with the biscuits, which she placed on a folding table. She had an oval face, pale white skin and extraordinarily dark brown eyes. According to her and Oxley she had once been the notorious Mrs Freeman, aka Anna Maria de Burgh Coppinger, mistress and co-conspirator of the fraudulent Henry Ireland. As far as me and Postmartin could tell from the existing records, this was true. Which meant that she was supposed to have died in 1802. Which meant that it was possible that in some way she'd caught practical immortality from her husband. Something that Lady Ty didn't think was possible.

The Doctors Vaughan and Walid wanted a tissue sample.

Something I didn't think was practical.

There were only two deckchairs – Isis took her husband's and motioned me back down into mine. When Oxley made it up the ladder with the tea tray he saw how things lay and sensibly sat cross-legged at his wife's feet.

Isis gave ritual reassurance that drinking her tea and scoffing her Lidl custard creams would not bind me into perpetual servitude, and I duly ate and drank and was merry.

It began to bucket down, shrieks of annoyance and joy floating up from the marina around us.

I watched Oxley sitting in his faded blue Oasis T-shirt and frayed khaki chinos. The idea that he was born back in the ninth century seemed a little bit distant. But my biology teacher at school had been adamant that if you plucked an original *Homo sapiens sapiens* out of the Rift Valley and put him in a suit he could have walked in and taken a substitute RE class no problem.

I have a clear memory of me saying that would be a waste, since think about what he could tell us about being a caveman. But, you know, I'm not sure whether I actually did ask that or just wished I had.

Certainly I don't remember getting an answer.

Anyone who's taken statements from multiple witnesses to the same event will know how malleable memory is. And yet Oxley had been around for quite a lot of the period of my Key Stage 3 History Curriculum, and there were other Rivers who were even older.

'You're about twelve hundred years old, right?' I said.

Oxley stared at me a moment before nodding slowly.

'I should say something of that order,' he said. 'Now you come to mention it. But if it's wisdom you're after, you're asking the wrong man.'

'I was thinking more of your memory,' I said.

'Ah, well,' said Oxley. 'Memory, now – there's a tricky thing. What particular memory were you thinking of?'

'King Arthur,' I said.

'Before my time,' said Oxley.

'But was he a legend or a real king?'

'Kings were legends in those days. Or so they seemed to such poor creatures as myself. I'm not sure I could say who was king in my youth and I was quite a learned man.'

'Not even his name?'

'Do you remember who was prime minister when you were so high?'

He nodded at a small child, gender indeterminate, in blue shorts who was dancing about in the rain.

'Margaret Thatcher,' I said, and then had to think again. 'John Major.'

'Ah,' said Oxley. 'But do you truly remember that, or is that something you learnt later from a book or off the radio?'

'I remember John Major from when I was in primary school,' I said. 'But I get your point.'

'Well, that is how the past is for us,' said Oxley. 'All the historical things, the kings and other mighty bastards, the battles and coronations sort of fade. Mind you, the strangest things stick. I remember vividly being sick after being woken for matins and standing before the abbot and wishing he would shout with less force. I remember the first time I saw Isis at the Theatre Royal Drury Lane, and all I need do is close my eyes to see her again.'

'Or open them and see me in front of you,' said Isis.

'My point being that I could not for the life of me tell you the name of the king at either juncture without consulting a book,' said Oxley.

'It was Farmer George,' said Isis. 'Not long after somebody tried to shoot him in his box.'

'Painful,' I said.

'It undoubtedly would have been,' she said, and winked.

'You're not helping me here, my love,' Oxley told Isis, who laughed. 'As I was saying, my point . . .' He stopped to make sure Isis wasn't about to interrupt. 'My point being that I can't be sure whether what I know of the grand events of the past are my true memories or the same histories that you know.'

'He looks so disappointed,' said Isis.

'You're not the first gentleman wizard who came asking,' said Oxley. 'I remember one who was desperate to answer some question or other about Cromwell. Charlie Somebody, taught at Pembroke College, right keen on original sources. Couldn't help him either.'

I wondered if perhaps there was an upper limit to the capacity of the brain to retain memory. Perhaps their surplus memories manifested externally; perhaps that was the function of those strange god-ghosts like Sir William of Tyburn. It would also suggest that the *Genii Locorum* retained the same organic brain that the rest of us made do with.

I wondered if we could persuade one of them to donate their brain to science.

'There's such a thing as social history these days,' I said, and Oxley snorted.

'Ah well, but that's a difficult matter, isn't it now?' he said. 'I could tell them all about the daily life of a terrible monk, but then I'd have to reveal myself, wouldn't I? That might cause a bit of an uproar, might it not? Think of the questions!'

'Somebody should remember this stuff,' I said.

'Oh, the Old Man remembers everything,' said Oxley. 'You might say that's what makes him the Old Man.'

'So our hypothetical historian might ask him?' I asked.

'Hypothetical?' said Isis, and sipped her tea.

'Do you have a burning need to know about the past?' asked Oxley.

I said it was hypothetically possible, but Oxley shook his head slowly.

'You don't want to be asking questions of the Old Man. He asks a price, and the price is always more than what you want to pay.'

'Or I could ask him for you,' said Isis, and sipped her tea.

Oxley gave her a frown.

'Isis, my love,' he said. 'Let's not meddle too far in the affairs of wizards.'

'This isn't a wizard,' said Isis. 'This is Peter and besides, my love, it will do no harm to ask. The Old Man will either answer or he will not.'

'Or as like as not pitch you a riddle,' said Oxley. 'One that we will untangle to our cost.'

'Peter's good at riddles,' Isis told her husband, then favoured me with a bright smile. 'That, after all, is the nature of his profession.'

Oxley shrugged – conceding.

'Now, Peter, what is it you wish to know?'

'King Arthur,' I said. 'Camelot, Merlin, Excalibur – is any of it real?'

'Define real,' said Oxley.

'Real as all this is real. As you and me are real, as the Old Man is real, as Nightingale is real.'

Oxley opened his mouth – no doubt to split another hair – but his wife cut him off.

'Peter, love,' said Isis. 'Your goddess is trying to get your attention.'

The rain had slackened off and Beverley had appeared on the deck of the *Pride of Putney* and was beckoning me over.

After the rain, the day turned hot so suddenly that the grass practically steamed and some terrifyingly pale skin was suddenly exposed to direct sunlight. Although I did notice that a great deal of factor 30 and above was being slathered on children by parents and randomly concerned adults. Beverley and Abigail got straight into their swimming gear while I kept my nice lightweight summer suit on just long enough to pay my respects to Father Thames.

This involved me nodding politely and extending the respects of myself, the Folly and Nightingale to the rumpled old white man who was holding court with his cronies on the covered stern deck of his boat. Despite the old suit and the tarnished watch fob, there was no mistaking the intensity of the eyes, or the quick promise of hard work and open skies, or the smell of clean water and breath of the wind on your face.

'*Ave, Petre Grande, incantator. Di sint tecum et cum tuis,*' he said and there was a stir amongst the cronies, and a muttering – he'd never spoken to me in Latin before.

'*Tibi gratias ago, Tiberi Claudi Verica,*' I said, which is like from Chapter One of *My First Latin Primer*. Still, it got the job done and I backed out without engendering a major diplomatic incident or, worse, a major flood.

After that I stripped off, had Beverley slap the sunscreen on my back, and we headed off to do some community outreach. This involves meeting people, listening to their stories and memorising their names and faces in case you had to come back and arrest them at a later date.

Occasionally we'd catch a glimpse of Abigail in her pink, blue and red Nakimuli one-piece.

'Did you get her that?' I asked Beverley.

'Nah,' she said. 'I think Fleet did.'

'I didn't even know she knew Fleet.'

'Well, obviously she does,' said Beverley.

I watched Abigail talking to a pair of kids her own age, a boy and girl, with the sort of patchwork tans that white people get when they spend summer outdoors in a variety of different tops.

She caught us looking and waved, and her two friends turned to stare briefly before returning their complete attention to whatever Abigail was saying.

'If you're like this with your cousin,' said Beverley, 'what are you going to be like with your own children?'

'Oh, I'm going to be a tyrant,' I said.

'You're so not,' said Beverley, and took my hand. 'Their poor mother's going to have to do all the work.'

Later that evening we trooped over to an adjacent field where a circle of trestle tables had been arranged into a circle around a bonfire. I was seated next to Isis, three seats around from the Old Man himself. Beverley was on his other side, as befitted a guest of honour. As we ate I counted the sons of the Old Man and came up four short. Ash, I knew, was celebrating with Mama Thames in Wapping, but three of the heaviest hitters, Ken, Cher and Wey were notably absent.

'We sent Ken to see Sabrina and Avon,' said Oxley. 'Cher is in Herefordshire seeing the three sisters, and Wey's all the way up in Scotland making merry with the Tay.' His grin was full of mischief. 'We thought it was time to renew old friendships.'

'What brought all this on?' I asked.

'Oh, that would have been you and your good example,' said Oxley.

'Cross-community partnerships,' said Isis.

I resolved to keep my mouth shut for the rest of my

life, or at the very least around Oxley and Isis.

At some point close to midnight, when we'd all drunk way too much, the Old Man of the River stood and silence rolled out across the company, so that even the children fell quiet.

He held up a straight half pint glass filled with something amber that was definitely not beer. We all climbed to our feet and raised our own glasses. He said something in a language that I suspect hadn't been spoken widely since the Romans left Britain, and we all cheered and drained our glasses.

Once we'd sat down Oxley translated.

'Roughly,' he said, 'eat loads, drink to excess, screw your partner's brains out and be thankful the bard isn't singing.'

'You're lying about the last bit,' I said.

'How dare you,' said Oxley, and grinned.

After that, the toasts started in earnest and I couldn't leave until I'd delivered mine. I'd been warned in advance, so I'd given it some thought. When it was my turn and I stood up and called for life, liberty and peace and managed to sit down before I added a hard-boiled egg to the list.

Shortly afterwards Beverley came and rescued me by dragging me off to her boat.

'Before you're too pissed to be useful,' she said.

I was in the early stages of proving my worth when the first of the youths thundered past on the pontoon bridge. Five minutes later the next group sneaked past with exaggerated care and the giggling and clink of what sounded to me like underage drinking.

'You think it's an accident they've got their one fed moored alongside the kids' field?' said Beverley. 'They'll be sneaking and giggling past us all night.'

Later, at a fairly crucial moment, Beverley stopped moving and shushed me. I stifled a frustrated yelp with great willpower and lay perfectly still and listened.

It was more giggling and furtive movement, only this time one of the voices was far too low to be one of the teens. I was trying to work out who it might be when a woman laughed nearby – low, throaty, distinctively dirty.

'Isis?' I whispered.

I felt Beverley's suppressed laughter as a ripple along her stomach and thighs.

'Quiet,' said the man, who I was reasonably sure was Oxley. 'Or the Isaacs will get thee.'

This from a man who'd been around at the coronation of Æthelred the Unready, for all that he claimed he couldn't remember the details.

Isis said something that was probably rude and there was a slow splash, which I recognised as a water deity falling into the river. I've watched Beverley do that, the water sort of rises up to cushion the blow and she goes in with just a ripple.

'Bumptious fool,' said Isis.

I was about to shout out something, just to startle them, when Beverley kissed me and I decided that I had better things to do.

Later, as we lay there with the cabin door open to catch the breeze, we heard Abigail talking to someone, although whoever it was pitched their voice too low for us to identify. I reckoned they were outside her tent. Occasionally there was a laugh and, horrifically, the ting sound of beer cans.

After a while the conversation died down and we heard the distinctive sound of a tent door being zipped closed. What we didn't hear were any footsteps moving away.

I went to get up and check but Bev put her arm across my chest to stop me.

'Don't you dare,' she said quietly.

'Just a quick look,' I said.

'No.'

'But—'

'What do you think the Summer Court is for?'

'But I'm responsible,' I said.

'Yeah,' said Beverley. 'And so is she.'

'People say that, you know,' I said. 'But if something goes tits up suddenly everybody wants to know why the police weren't intervening at an earlier stage.'

'Relax,' said Beverley, 'She's Nightingale's apprentice and my friend. People round here would gnaw their own foot off before doing anything with Abigail that Abigail didn't want them to.'

It still took me a while to drift off.

One other thing the Summer Court was definitely for was creating a tremendous mess. But fortunately Father Thames, or more precisely Oxley, had organised a clean-up crew almost entirely composed of pale young men with hangovers. Soon the drifts of bottles, pink and blue plastic wrappers, and happily unidentifiable organic leftovers were scooped up into bin bags and dumped in an open-topped river barge that had arrived first thing that morning.

'The Old Man took the Keep Britain Tidy campaign very seriously,' said Oxley, as we supervised the hard work from deckchairs and drank coffee.

'Where's Isis?'

'Upstream with the rest of the women,' he said. 'It's customary.'

The women and girls got the morning off during the clean-up and traditionally bathed in the symbolically clean waters upstream.

'And have a picnic and gossip and all the other important mysteries of the better half. It's all to do with the female principle and that style of thing.' He caught my expression. 'This is what Isis tells me. I just keep my eye on the boys and mind my own business.'

Which was obviously the theme for the weekend.

Oxley's current mental state, caught in that transition between alcohol and caffeine, would have made it a good time to get some social history questions answered – including what the hell they did before coffee was invented – but my phone started ringing. It was Stephanopoulos.

'City of London need you to do a Falcon Assessment at a crime scene,' she said.

I asked whether it was urgent.

'As soon as pos,' said Stephanopoulos.

Nightingale was obviously busy and neither Guleed or Carey were qualified.

'I'm on my way,' I said.

I called both Bev and Abigail, but their phones went straight to voicemail

I asked Oxley to ask Beverley to bring Abigail home. Then I showered, changed and drove back to London.

And if you're the woman who, driving along the A4155 that afternoon, found herself inexplicably picking up a pair of hitchhikers and driving them all the way into London, I'm really, really sorry – I assumed Beverley would organise a lift from one of her relatives.

13

Probably Goat

Despite being the oldest part of London, the Square Mile has a faster architectural churn than anywhere else in the city. Occasionally it throws up something exciting, innovative and modern . . . but mostly it doesn't. Architects like a bit of volume, and financiers like floor space. The easiest way to maximise both is to build a cube – which is why ninety-nine per cent of all office buildings are boxes with lobbies.

The New Bloomberg building on Queen Victoria Street was going to be yet another steel-framed Metsec affair but was still half built, with plastic sheeting protecting the gaping open sides. Once the cladding and windows were in, I suspected it wasn't going to be much of an aesthetic improvement on the 1950s modernist boxes it was replacing. The site hoarding had 'Improving the Image of Construction' signs at regular intervals along its length.

Great, I thought, now can we do something about the construction itself?

It was obviously my month for wearing hard hats because the site safety officer insisted I put one on before pointing me at the temporary staircase that was bolted onto the front of the building. I nodded at the City of

London PC on guard at the bottom and made my way up.

Waiting for us at the top was a small Vietnamese woman in a City of London Police uniform with SC tags denoting that she was a special constable. This was Geneviève Nguyễn who had attended the Sorbonne and worked in Paris before being headhunted by Citigroup and moving to London. There she had discovered that any citizen of the European Economic Area could swear an oath, don a uniform and enforce the law with the same authority as their full-time colleagues.

Most of the time she stays in her expensively tailored suit and helps with fiendishly complicated fraud cases, but the City Police allow her out on the streets once in a while. She also triples up as their liaison with the Folly, and was one of the first officers to do my patented *vestigia* awareness training seminar. She didn't seem at all fazed by my wild talk of ghosts and magic – which made me really suspicious. But all she would admit to was having heard a lot of stories from her grandmother.

'Definitely a spy,' said Carey, who never knowingly left a stereotype unturned.

'What gives her away?' asked Guleed.

'It's the accent,' said Carey.

Police tape marked out the entry point for the single designated approach to the crime scene, although fortunately it was booties and gloves only – not the full noddy suit.

'What's your opinion of animal sacrifice?' asked Nguyễn as she led me further into the building.

'Well, I've got this annoying dog,' I said.

'I meant from a Falcon point of view,' said Nguyễn, who had once patiently explained to me that while she understood that the British liked a laugh, she didn't understand why we felt it necessary to inject it into every single aspect of life, no matter how inappropriate.

'Ritual sacrifices can have power,' I said. 'But usually it's something for the RSPCA.'

We went down an unfinished corridor smelling of cement dust and cut plasterboard and out into a large internal room whose newly fitted walls were a pristine white. Except for the blood spatter on every vertical surface. With some on the ceiling as well. It was definitely blood – the reek gave it away – and some of it had been sprayed with force.

It was hard to sense anything over the smell, but I got flickers of shouting and feet stamping and a rhythmic pulse like a mad rave heard from far away.

'Tell me this is animal blood,' I said.

'Yes,' said Nguyễn. 'We confirmed that this morning. That is why you're talking to me and not Major Crime.'

'We're not that far from Smithfield,' I said – the market being a good source of offal, blood, and the sort of high-spirited young people who might think flinging it about was a bit of a laugh.

I noticed that the floor was devoid of any spatter, and Nguyễn noticed me noticing.

'They put down plastic sheeting,' she said.

But hadn't covered the walls – had things got out of hand? I took a longer look at the spatter on the walls. I'm not an expert, but some of it looked like arterial spray – and there were voids. Or rather there were what

126

looked like spaces outlined by an initial spray – that of blood projected out by a beating heart – which had then been partially filled in by blood spattered later. If you squinted you could see that the voids formed the outlines of people standing against the walls when they were hit by the spray.

'Did you find anything else?' I asked.

'Not much.'

Nguyễn took me over to where the portable finds were spread out in separate bags on a sheet of white paper.

'Not much' summed it up. A couple of condom packets, a pill that had lodged in a crack at floor level and looked suspiciously like MDMA, and samples from some non-blood stains on the walls – mainly alcohol.

'Red wine,' said Nguyễn.

'Do we know what kind of animal?'

'Tentatively goat,' said Nguyễn. 'The lab will confirm it in a couple of days.'

The ravers had turned up for a party and had taken forensic countermeasures in the form of plastic sheeting on the floor and policing up condoms, bottles, cups and anything else that might contain useful DNA. Even vomit, pointed out Nguyễn, although uniforms were out searching the surrounding streets in case someone had thrown up on their way out or was careless enough to dump their rubbish nearby.

So they'd . . . What? Gathered together with booze and condoms and slaughtered a goat. I couldn't be sure, but it looked like they'd sprayed the poor thing's blood around like champagne from a winner's podium.

And then, covered with blood, they'd danced and shagged the merry night away.

Actually, it might have just been shagging since nobody had reported any loud music.

But you get *vestigia* at the site of any major live music festival, and even a little bit at your average gig. The Notting Hill Carnival generates enough potential magic that I know of at least one Russian witch who takes part in the parade just to bask in it. Football matches, Christmas shelters, village fêtes and light engineering works all generate magic – or at least enough to make Toby bark. Which is my current benchmark.

It was the forward planning and the forensic countermeasures that were dragging at my attention.

That and the goat.

'This was definitely a ritual,' I said. 'Why here?'

'It's probably the temple,' said Nguyễn. And then, off my blank look, 'The Temple of Mithras.'

'I thought it was over on Victoria Street?'

Contrary to what people think, I haven't actually memorised the location of every historically significant building in London. I did know that the temple had been discovered nearby during construction work in the mid-1950s and moved to another location for preservation. There'd been talk of moving it back, but I thought that had been kiboshed by the great financial collapse five years back.

'Bloomberg took over the project,' said Nguyễn. 'Reinstated the complete return.'

Back to its original location on the banks of the Walbrook.

'I wonder if they'll put in a labyrinth,' I said out loud, by accident.

Ritually sacrificed goats, Roman temples, bells infused with the power of ancient stones, and dead wannabe scriptwriters.

'Do you think this is one of yours?' asked Nguyễn.

'I don't know yet. Are you going to pursue the vandalism side?'

'I'm just a special. But the head of Bloomberg's London office is finishing his vacation in the Seychelles early and flying back this afternoon. So I believe some investigation is likely.'

'In that case I'll email you some names to look out for,' I said.

Back in the 'good old days' when a quarter of the map was pink and the Folly was at its height you couldn't practise magic in the UK without their permission. Sometimes the permission was implicit – if you weren't scaring the horses or curdling the milk they ignored or patronised you, especially if you were female.

But if you were a full-on Newtonian practitioner, a master of the forms and wisdoms, you had better be recognising the authority of the Society of the Wise or there were going to be consequences.

All that ended with the decimation of British and European wizardry during the Second World War, although personally I think their control might already have been slipping in the 1920s and '30s. After the war all you had to do to practise magic with impunity was not come to the attention of Britain's last official wizard.

At least until recently.

When dealing with a problem, the first thing to do is admit you have a problem. The second thing is to try and determine the scale of the problem. Now, for the last couple of years we've mainly been hunting Little Crocodiles. But in the process we've been identifying other potential practitioners and adding them to our growing database. A database that I was happy to assure the Data Protection Agency was impervious to unauthorised access on account of it being confined to old-fashioned index cards in a rather nice polished walnut filing cabinet in the upstairs magical library.

They still made me fill in my own body weight in forms.

And on one of those cards in the walnut cabinet was the name Patrick Gale – confirmed practitioner. He'd come to my attention following the death by hyperthaumaturgical necrosis of one Tony Harden – a junior colleague of his. Because neither had studied at Oxford or were on our Little Crocodiles list, or appeared as nominals in Operation Jennifer or any other Martin Chorley-related investigations, we'd kept a watching brief.

Also, Patrick Gale was a senior partner at Bock, Loupe and Stag, one of the top ten legal firms in London known collectively as 'the magic circle'. Firms like BL&S routinely swindled developing countries for fun and profit, bullied government departments and had the personal mobile numbers of media proprietors on speed dial – you don't mess with them unless you have to. Not if you want to wake up in the same career you went to bed in.

But the case that had drawn Patrick Gale to my attention had also involved the ritual sacrifice of a goat. So it had to be followed up. In policing you don't want to be explaining to the case review board why you missed that vital piece of evidence because it seemed a bit obscure and you couldn't be bothered to get off your arse. Even if in our work a case review board is pretty bloody unlikely.

So when I got back to the Folly I pulled the relevant index cards and sent the details to Nguyễn. Then I called Postmartin, who has a morbid interest in animal sacrifice.

'My interest is entirely academic and historical,' said Postmartin on the phone.

Behind him I could hear town traffic and student voices. Given it was a warm Sunday afternoon I guessed he was sitting outside the Eagle and Child enjoying a gin and tonic and pretending he was C. S. Lewis's younger, atheist, brother.

'Neither Thomas nor Abdul have ever shown any interest, beyond the practical, in ritual magic,' he said. 'Particularly if they predate the Newtonian synthesis.'

Postmartin always called it 'the Newtonian synthesis' to emphasise the fact that Newton did not so much invent magic as find the principles that underlie its practice.

'A practice that dates back millennia,' he said. 'All the way back to the dawn of Man. If not older than that.'

Postmartin favoured the 'tribal religion theory' propagated by P. J. Wickshaven, country parson, occasional wizard and amateur anthropologist. Around 1905 he wrote a treatise in which he postulated that religious rituals gained currency with early Man because they produced actually identifiable results. Furthermore, as Postmartin explained it to me, the ancient pre-Abrahamic religions maintained their effectiveness because of their essentially local nature.

'It's always Isis or Hermes of such and such a place,' he said. 'It seems entirely reasonable to me that Isis, for example, could have been a local *genius loci* who either took on the guise of the goddess or even perhaps came to embody the deity in that locality.'

Prior to Newton, Wickshaven contended, the practice of magic and that of religion were essentially indistinguishable. He'd travelled to Papua New Guinea in 1907 to find some poor lost tribe to prove his theory for him and had last been seen setting out from Port Moresby, never to return. You've got a lot of work like this in the Folly libraries – enthusiastic theories defended to the death without much in the way of corroboration. Or, as Abigail said, 'So, this is what people used to do before the internet.'

According to Wickshaven, the central figure – he called him a shaman – generates a *forma* and leads a congregation in a ritual. Even if only a couple of the attendees successfully replicate the *forma* then, presumably, that would increase the strength of the spell. And throw in an animal sacrifice?

'This ritual does seem reminiscent of the bacchanalia described in Livy or perhaps, given the sacrifice of the goat, classical Greek worship,' said Postmartin.

Sex, booze and animal sacrifice – I suppose after a

hard week flogging your slaves and inventing comic theatre you needed something to do on the weekends. I asked whether Postmartin thought this was significant.

'The London Mithraeum is thought to have been converted to the worship of Bacchus in the fourth century ad,' he said. 'Could be a coincidence.'

Only in a rational world, I thought.

'Mithras lost his lustre, did he?' I asked.

'Mithras could have been a contender,' said Postmartin. 'He was one of the big three mystery cults, along with Jesus Christ and Isis.' Then, as Postmartin had it, the Christians got the nod from Emperor Constantine and that was all she wrote for the other two gods. 'Which was a pity, because imagine world history if Europe had turned to Isis instead,' he said. 'A female priesthood would have been just the start.'

Postmartin said that there was solid evidence that there had been a Temple of Isis in London but nobody knew where it was. Not like they did with Bacchus and the Mithraeum.

'But if you do run into a candidate for it,' he said, 'you will let me know?'

So, to sum up – persons unknown had, probably, conducted a bacchanal on the exact site of what was probably London's last major temple to Bacchus, and that ceremony had produced a real magical effect – possibly intentionally.

I wasn't putting this on the whiteboard until I had some idea who the persons unknown were.

And that information was gleefully supplied the

following day by Special Constable Nguyễn.

'They were all sensible enough to leave their cars at home,' she said. 'We think most walked out of the area and then got night buses. A smaller number felt relaxed enough to summon an Uber to pick them outside the building, and one was picked up his wife in the family SUV.'

'Her name was Monika Gale. Wife of Patrick Gale.

'Boch, Loupe and Stag,' said Nguyễn. 'You guys really know how to pick your suspects. I've been asked, in my role as Folly liaison, to indicate that as far as City of London Police are concerned this is one hundred and ten per cent a Falcon case. Good luck.'

And that was that.

When dealing with the excessively rich and privileged, you've got your two basic approaches. One is to go in hard and deliberately working class. A regional accent is always a plus in this. Seawoll has been known to deploy a Mancunian dialect so impenetrable that members of Oasis would have needed subtitles, and graduate entries with double firsts from Oxford practise a credible Estuary in the mirror and drop their glottals with gay abandon when necessary.

That approach only works if the subject suffers from residual middle-class guilt – unfortunately the properly posh, the nouveau riche and senior legal professionals are rarely prey to such weaknesses. For them you have to go in obliquely and with maximum *Downton Abbey*.

Fortunately for us we have just the man.

So it was Nightingale who went striding into Patrick

Gale's workplace with his best black Dege & Skinner two piece suit, with me following behind in my serviceable tailored M&S looking like the loyal flunky I was.

Bock, Loupe and Stag occupy a large chunk of the building across from Broadgate Tower. Like that, this one was designed – as far as I could tell – by the same people who did the interior layout for Cybertron. Lots of angled struts, planes of glass and random spikes. It was, as architectural theorists like to say, a bold statement and the statement was: 'Fuck truth and beauty. We've got money and loads of it'.

'Detective Chief Inspector Nightingale to see Patrick Gale,' Nightingale said, and flashed his warrant card at the receptionist without breaking step.

Ahead was a set of security gates, like posh minimalist versions of the ticket barriers at Tube stations. I was probably the only one who noticed the tiny gesture Nightingale made with his right hand. I recognised the tight little surge which followed as a complex fifth order spell that caused the gates to lock in the open position so we could walk through.

A tall, thin Sierra Leonean man in a security guard uniform stepped up to block us.

'Step back, sir,' I said firmly.

Which he did smartly – possibly because of my impressive command voice, but more likely because his name was Obe and he was my cousin – second or third, I forget which – on my mum's side. I'd nudged him into his current job shortly after Patrick Gale came to my attention. It was down to Obe that we knew the make and model of the security barriers, how many guards would be on duty, and that Gale was currently up in his office.

Because we'd planned this as carefully as any raid on a crack house, with maps and timetables and Guleed and Carey out front and back with an arrest team just in case anybody tried to scarper. After all, you don't want to be striding resolutely into someone's office only to find they're spending a dirty weekend in Honolulu with their son's macramé tutor – do you?

Gale had an office on the sixth floor, so we risked the lift.

We emerged into an open-plan office crowded with the upmarket walnut veneer versions of drone cubicles, took a sharp left and headed down the clearway towards the big airy offices of the senior partners.

And the biggest and airiest belonged to Patrick Gale, one of the most powerful men you've never heard of.

He was a big, wide, white man with the heft that the naturally fat get when they exercise like mad in middle age. He had a good but stylistically neutral lightweight cotton suit and definitely handmade shoes. Reception had obviously had time to call up and warn him, and he'd chosen to act casual – leaning against the front of his desk with his arms folded.

He was sharp, I'll give him that. He recognised me immediately from when I interviewed him about the late Tony Harden the year before. Then I saw him clock Nightingale and a moment of utter shock crossed his face, which I reckon was him realising exactly who was in his office.

Good, I thought, you know who he is – this should make things easier.

I'll give him this, though – he didn't bluster. He kept it together enough to step up and ask us, politely, what our business was.

'Mr Gale, we're here to talk about the ritual sacrifice you took part in on the night of the twentieth at the construction site at Queen Victoria Street.'

His face went professionally blank as he considered his options.

Now, I thought, it's either going to be outraged dignity or Let's Be Civilised.

'Please,' he said, looking to retake control of his own office. 'Have a seat. Can I offer you a coffee? Tea?'

I wanted popcorn, but asking for it might have broken the mood.

Nightingale said thank you and sat down as if he was settling in to watch the rugby. I tried to follow his lead, but I suspect I was too tense for properly casual.

Patrick Gale sat down on what had to be three grands' worth of reinforced stainless steel and leather executive seating.

Bluff or denial? I wondered.

'A sacrifice?' he said.

So denial it was.

'A goat was ritually sacrificed at or around midnight at the Bloomberg construction site by person or persons unknown,' said Nightingale.

'Contrary to the Animal Welfare Act (2006),' I said.

'We believe you were intimately involved,' said Nightingale.

'And why might you think that?' asked Gale, with just a hint of smugness.

We told him about his wife's car, but he wasn't impressed.

'That's hardly a positive identification,' he said. 'I'm sure there are many reasons why my wife's car might be in the city at night. Just as there are many reasons why I might be in the vicinity. Without resorting to fanciful theories about – what was the animal you said was slaughtered?'

'Patrick,' said Nightingale, 'you need to cast off the notion that this is a matter of the law and that your superior interpretation and command of the legal niceties will see you through.'

Patrick Gale opened his mouth to speak, but Nightingale tapped a forefinger once, gently, against the arm of his chair, and no words emerged. Gale opened his mouth again, but again – nothing. The expression on his face cycled rapidly through astonishment, anger and outrage. He raised his hand, but Nightingale tapped his finger twice more and Gale's hand slapped down onto his desk top hard enough to make the keyboard jump.

'Yes,' said Nightingale. 'I can render you immobile and stop up your voice – or stop your breath, if I choose to.'

There was real fear in Patrick Gale's eyes now, and they turned to look at me – pleading.

'Follow my lead in this, Peter,' Nightingale had said when we were planning the interview. 'And do try to trust my judgement on the ethical issues this time.'

'And no doubt,' Nightingale said to Gale, 'you're thinking that what I'm doing can't possibly be legal. And, you know, I'm not sure.' He glanced at me. 'Peter?'

'You're restraining him against his will,' I said. 'It probably depends on whether you arrest him or not.'

Which was a terrible answer from a legal point of view, but in my defence I was distracted by the sheer technical difficulty of what Nightingale was doing. In many ways people, and other living creatures, are amazingly resistant to direct manipulation with magic. That's why most magical duels quickly devolve down to both parties throwing the kitchenware at each other.

But where brute force doesn't work, subtlety does. And in the practice of Newtonian magic subtlety doesn't come easy.

Just on the edge of my perception there was the tick, tick, tick of a mechanical movement, a jewelled movement, that delicately bound Patrick Gale in place and stopped the action of his larynx – or whatever the fuck kept him silent. It was a twentieth order spell at least.

'But, just as I can't prove that you attended that merry little bacchanal,' said Nightingale, 'you can't prove that I am in any way violating your rights as a suspect. The legal niceties have become irrelevant and we find ourselves making a moral choice instead.'

I felt the *formae* twist as Nightingale added another layer of complexity. And Gale's hands came together, fingers entwined over his paunch as if he was relaxing after a hard day.

'You made that choice when you took up the forms and wisdoms,' said Nightingale. 'And now you must take responsibility for that choice – don't you agree?'

Gale's face contorted and I saw his big shoulders

tense as he made a desperate attempt to separate his hands. Nightingale calmly watched him for the full ten seconds or so it took for it to become clear that escape was impossible.

Gale's shoulder's slumped and he nodded.

Nightingale snapped his fingers, a purely theatrical gesture, and Gale's hands separated as the spell was released. He wriggled his fingers a couple of times and then gave Nightingale an inquiring look, because nothing attracts the powerful quite like more power.

'Shall we start at the beginning?' said Nightingale. 'Who trained you?'

Gale hesitated, eyes flicking between us.

'I swore an oath,' he said finally. 'I was told there would be consequences if I revealed their name.'

'Well, there'll certainly be consequences if you don't,' said Nightingale.

'There's no evidence that breaking your oath has supernatural repercussions,' I added.

Beyond the obvious risk that you might have pissed off someone more powerful than you, I thought, but kept that to myself. No point cluttering up the conversation with pointless trivia.

'I learnt it from a friend of mine at Cambridge,' said Patrick Gale.

'His name?' asked Nightingale.

'John Chapman,' he said.

It's always tempting to show off your knowledge during a confrontation. But during an interview it's always better to pretend ignorance – which was why Nightingale went on to ask about John Chapman, even though Gale's answers merely confirmed the information we'd already got from the IIP.

Well, most of it anyway.

'Where did he learn magic?' asked Nightingale.

'He said he learnt it from a book,' said Gale. 'By Sir Isaac Newton, of all people.' He was sceptical.

'I think he was taught by his uncle,' he added. 'He used to let slip and mention him from time to time.'

I made a note of the uncle and tried not to sigh out loud – yet another loose thread.

'And Tony Harden?' asked Nightingale.

'John got him interested,' said Gale. 'I taught him most of what I know.'

'Did you warn him of the dangers?'

Patrick Gale blinked.

'What dangers?'

'Practising magic can damage your health,' I said.

Patrick Gale's façade cracked and he gave me a horrified look.

'You're joking,' he said.

'Nope,' I said. 'That's what killed Tony Harden.'

Gale glared.

'You told me he died of natural causes,' he said.

'He did,' I said. 'Caused naturally, by his overuse of magic.'

'Surely it should have been characterised as death by misadventure?' said Gale. 'You withheld information from the coroner's court.'

'Would you rather we had pressed for "unlawful death"?' asked Nightingale. 'As his teacher you were surely negligent in not informing him of the risks.'

'But I didn't—' Gale started, but wisely thought better of it.

'Quite,' said Nightingale. 'We may return to that point later, but first there is the matter of the Dionysian ritual you officiated at last Saturday. You did officiate, didn't you? I can't imagine you left that honour to somebody else.'

Gale nodded to show that he had, in fact, taken the role of priest in the bacchanal and I had to stop myself from asking him to verbalise it for the recording. But of course there was no recording because, legally, this was not happening.

'Have you been indulging in these revels long?' asked Nightingale.

'Since 2011,' said Gale. 'And they're not just a rave.'

He flicked his eyes at me to emphasise how different it was from the drum and bass and MDMA fuelled excesses indulged in by the urban youth of today. Chance would be a fine thing, I thought.

'We have a serious purpose,' he said.

Nightingale ignored that thread because when the suspect – I mean interviewee – wants to talk about something it's a good idea to frustrate them a little bit. That way you can get more later than they intended. Seawoll calls it the 'fuck *all* the cows' interview approach.

'Would you say they have a magical effect?' asked Nightingale.

Gale's face lost some of its habitual caution.

'Definitely,' he said. 'You could sense it lighting up the group as if it was jumping from person to person.'

He said he could feel it flowing back and forth like a wave bouncing off the edges of a swimming pool. 'Only instead of fading away, it grows stronger with every wave. Tremendous rush.'

'And the sex?' I asked.

'I've heard that's extraordinary too,' he said.

'Heard?'

'My wife,' said Gale, 'wouldn't approve. And she doesn't like to attend herself.'

'She doesn't like the goat?' I asked.

'She's a vegetarian,' he said.

'Does the sacrifice actually make a difference?' I said. 'Have you tried the ceremony without it?'

'Again,' said Gale, 'I have no doubt that it increases the mystical potency of the ritual.' His initial fright was wearing off and he was getting his bottle back. 'Have you not tried it yourselves?'

'This ceremony . . .' said Nightingale, before I could answer. 'This ceremony that you claim has a serious purpose. Might we ask what that is?'

'It keeps London from falling into riot and disorder,' said Gale. 'And I might add it seems a great deal more effective than the police in this regard.'

John Chapman had suggested as much after the summer riots in 2011.

'He thought they were suspiciously sudden,' said Gale. 'He suggested that there might be a spiritual malaise behind the violence.'

And when Chapman said 'spiritual malaise' he wasn't thinking that the youth of today should respect their elders and go to church more often. He meant a vengeful evil spirit that had plagued London since the Romans.

'And this seemed credible to you?' asked Nightingale.

'That the riots were inspired by a vengeful spirit? No – quite apart from the fact that the underclass riots on a regular basis, it wouldn't explain why the riots spread to other cities. What changed my mind was that madness in Covent Garden. I knew some of the people involved and they were not the Molotov cocktail set.'

'Quite,' said Nightingale.

They were the sort of people who have people to do their violence for them, I managed not to say. And not without some effort, I might add.

'And you've held the ritual ever since?' asked Nightingale.

Patrick Gale confirmed that they had been holding it twice a year– at the summer and winter solstices. John Chapman had suggested these would be the most effective dates. When Nightingale asked where Chapman had acquired all this esoteric knowledge, Gale told us about the Paternoster Society.

'A secret society,' he said. 'They used to meet in a house on Paternoster Row near St Paul's, until it was knocked down.'

And suddenly annoying little alarm tweets and chirps were going off in my head.

Where the pattern-welded Anglo-Saxon Excalibur candidate had been dug up. Next to the cathedral where John Chapman's script – and I was pretty certain that all the historical stuff in the script had been his – situated *its* revenant spirit.

What we desperately needed was some accurate historical sources.

I thought of Father Thames, who was old enough to remember. But when a person like Oxley cautions you about the potential cost of asking such questions it's wise to pay attention. Especially when you'd just thought of a cheaper alternative.

'Now, Mr Gale,' said Nightingale. 'We reach the question of what to do about you.'

'I'm not sure there's any legal action you can take,' said Gale, with unwise smugness.

Nightingale tapped his fingers and I felt the tick, tick, swish of a subtle little surge, and Patrick Gale sat up straight in his chair and clasped his hands together on the desk in front of him.

'Mr Gale,' said Nightingale, 'the practice of magic is hard and dangerous. Sooner or later you will overstep your bounds and suffer serious injury or death.' He smiled thinly. 'Now, I for one would be perfectly happy to let you to take the consequences of your own actions. Were it not for the fact that you have already proved yourself a danger to others.'

'In what way—' started Gale.

'You were Anthony Harden's teacher,' said Nightingale. 'And you were negligent in his training. Now he is dead. I'm afraid that I'll have to require you to place yourself under my authority for remedial training until such time as I judge you both competent and responsible enough to practise magic on your own recognisance.'

Patrick Gale was doing a good impression of a stunned kipper, but I could see the cartoon slot machine flicker behind his eyes. Nightingale was offering what the ridiculously rich always crave – a chance to be exclusive.

'Or else?' he asked.

Yes please, I thought, let's have option two.

'We take steps to prevent you practising again,' said Nightingale.

Cake or death, I thought – three guesses as to which it will be.

'What sort of schedule are we talking about?' asked Patrick Gale. 'For the training, that is.'

But me and Nightingale didn't get a chance to follow up on the mysterious Paternoster Society, or even get preliminary intelligence on the list of revellers that Patrick Gale had been pleased to supply, once Nightingale had released his hands long enough to write it down. Because we had to prepare for Operation Strong Tower – the Met's all-singing, all-dancing terrorist attack exercise. In this we were expected to use our 'special' abilities to conjure up some bangs and whistles to keep the response teams on their toes.

'Frightened, but not too frightened,' were our instructions.

It did mean, during a refs stop at the Café Rouge on Kingsway, that I got a chance to tackle Nightingale about his sudden bout of, to my mind, inappropriate inclusiveness.

'So what?' I said. 'We keep them happy with a clubhouse and a secret handshake?'

'Well,' said Nightingale, 'I hadn't thought of a handshake, but if you think it might help . . .'

'These people are not to be trusted,' I said.

'These people?'

'People with . . .' I looked over at the poshest person I've ever met and tried to think of the right word. 'Entitlement,' I said. 'They're not good at keeping promises.'

Nightingale paused with a forkful of salmon halfway to his mouth and gave me an amused look.

'Entitlement?' he said.

'You know what I mean.'

'We can always have them swear an oath,' said Nightingale. 'Something suitably restrictive and modern – like the attestation you fellows took to become constables.'

Historically, the constable's attestation mainly concerned his loyalty to the monarch. But the modern version includes a promise to be diligent, honest, respect human rights and apply the law without fear and favour. The new wording has been known to provoke hilarity amongst old lags and defence lawyers.

'Think of it as one of your community outreach programmes,' he said. 'We don't have the resources to enforce our will upon them, but perhaps we can bribe them into submission with Molly's cooking.'

'You think that'll work?'

'It has with everyone so far.'

I frowned.

'You don't approve?'

'I was thinking of the paperwork,' I said. 'Assuming that Patrick Gale is not the last stray we're going to round up, at the very least we need to develop a safety programme to ensure they don't melt their brains by accident.'

'That at least we can leave to Abdul and the irrepressible Dr Vaughan,' said Nightingale. 'Who no doubt will be delighted to extend the boundaries of their empire of information.'

'Their knowledge base,' I said.

'I believe that's what I said.'

'We can't keep this up,' I said. 'It's unsustainable.'

'Which of the many unstable aspects of our professional life are you referring to now?'

'The secrecy surrounding magic,' I said. 'Leaving aside our lack of statutory authority, and the fact that the public have no say whatsoever in our conduct of operations.'

'They do in a general sense,' said Nightingale, 'through the office of the Commissioner and, beyond him, the Home Office.'

'That is not accountability,' I said.

'Do you think the general public would make good decisions?'

'That's not the point. Sooner or later this stuff always comes back to bite you in the arse.'

'You think we should make ourselves public?' said Nightingale. 'Step out of the cupboard and into the limelight?'

'I think we need to be ready for when it happens,' I said.

'No other nation has officially acknowledged the existence of magic, Peter,' said Nightingale. 'It might be prudent to ask yourself why.'

14

Human Intelligence Assets

On the following Friday we had a meeting in the incident room of the interested principals to discuss the progress of Operation Jennifer. Seawoll wasn't happy with the progress we were making. Or, more precisely, he was even less happy than he usually was.

'We seem to be sitting around waiting for the next fucking disaster,' he said, which went into the official log as – *DCI Seawoll felt that our operational posture was too reactive.*

He wanted to go after Lesley.

'We know Chorley needs her for whatever evil bollocks he has planned,' he said. 'If we grab her he's got to be fucked – right?' *He went on to argue for a proactive intelligence-led approach going forward.*

'And we know how to find her because she's knocking off that nasty little scrote from Notting Hill,' he said.

Utilising known human intelligence assets.

Easier said than done.

We had a 'bloody expensive' surveillance team on Zachary Palmer, which he evaded every so often to slope off for what we assumed was a sly leg-over with Lesley May.

'We're going to look well stupid if he's doing something else,' said Guleed.

'A negative result is almost as good as a positive one,' said Seawoll. 'Isn't that so, Peter?'

I hate it when people listen to what I say in an inappropriate fashion.

We hadn't pushed the issue before in the hope that Zach, who was skittish – literally supernaturally skittish – would get complacent about losing his followers. The idea was that we would use a second, presumably even sneakier team, to track him after that.

'That would be me and Sahra,' said Nightingale. 'With Peter and David as perimeter and backup.'

It had to be Nightingale in case we did run into Lesley.

'I have the best chance of a clean capture,' he said. 'But I need Peter to deal with any external interference.'

'Do you think that's likely?' asked Stephanopoulos.

'It's always best to be prepared,' said Nightingale.

Unfortunately, we weren't the only ones adopting a proactive posture going forward and, before we could get the operation out of the planning stage, Martin Chorley raided the MOLA finds warehouse at their HQ in Islington.

Given the previous thefts from archaeological sites we'd guessed that MOLA was a likely target. I'd left half a dozen magic detectors around the building and warned their security, so they'd double-checked their alarms and cameras. We'd also done a discreet review of everyone who worked there, but none had a connection with Martin Chorley or the Little Crocodiles. Then we organised an alert so that CCC would call us to any incident within 400 metres of the address.

But in the end it was all over before me and Nightingale were out the garage door.

It's less than three kilometres from Russell Square to the MOLA offices. At three in the morning you can do it in less than ten minutes in the Jag with blues and twos and Nightingale driving. I spent the journey wondering, as I always do in this situation, whether it's possible to retrofit an airbag into the Jag's glove compartment.

Technically that would be an act of gross sacrilege, but it wouldn't half have been a comfort when my governor practically stood her on two wheels turning off the City Road just by the drive-through McDonald's. At least we had a couple of modern light-bars fitted either side of the windscreen so we no longer had to worry about the spinner flying off the roof on the corners.

MOLA HQ was one of a string of old warehouse/factory units built in the functional brick shithouse style made popular in the Victorian era, when the main safety criterion for an industrial building was that it didn't fall down when the steam boiler exploded. Since those happy days of light touch regulation such fripperies as fire exits and safety ladders have been added, but it still showed a stern yellow brick face both front and back.

Its recessed loading bay was guarded by a sturdy metal gate and the roll-up door to the main warehousing was solid, durable and fastened down with heavy-duty padlocks.

We were expecting devious and subtle. We weren't expecting our perpetrators to tool up with a bin lorry to wrench the gates off, a JCB to clear a way through the interior yard and smash down the roll-up door, and a fucking skip lorry to carry away just over a ton and a quarter of archaeological material.

'Lesley's behind this,' I said, as we watched forensics futilely checking for trace evidence. 'She guessed we'd be primed for subtle, and she knows we're don't have the resources to guard against this kind of direct approach.'

'Undoubtedly,' said Nightingale.

A heavy fog had rolled in just as the sun rose – the rubbish truck was a grey shadow halfway up the Eagle Wharf Road, where it had been abandoned. The heavy-duty chain was still trailing behind it, with the gate attached. Later we learned it had been stolen the previous evening in Walthamstow. There weren't any matching theft reports for the JCB, so we might have to trace that through its serial numbers. The skip lorry was nowhere to be found.

Guleed arrived with coffee and word that Stephanopoulos had turned up at the Folly and was getting people in early. She was wearing a brand new black silk bomber jacket with a white tiger and Chinese writing embroidered on the back and sleeves in white and gold, and black jeans. Not her normal work wear – I wondered if she hadn't had a chance to change.

'Were you out last night?' I asked.

'Wouldn't you like to know?' she said.

I *would* like to know, but I knew better than to ask intrusive personal questions of colleagues – especially when I also knew that Beverley would ferret out the latest gossip before the end of the week.

'Ah, Sahra, excellent,' said Nightingale when he saw her. 'I think they're ready for us to go in.'

Like the building site with the goat sacrifice, it was generally considered forensically sufficient for us to wear booties and gloves. Although Guleed obviously didn't want to risk her nice new jacket, and left it in the Jag. And not on the back seat, either – where Toby tends to ride.

'This is not what I expected from a museum,' she said, as we followed the forensically cleared path through the space where the gates had been.

The covered loading area beyond had been crowded with red plastic picking bins full of rubble and those heavy-duty white PVC buckets with safe-seal lids. Some of them had burst as they were pushed aside, to spray sand and water across the dirty cement floor.

'If you find something perishable under water,' I told Guleed when she asked, 'you temporarily keep it submerged until you can find a way to permanently store it. Otherwise it starts to decay really quickly.'

Guleed was stunned into silence by my erudition, or at least didn't ask any more questions.

As far as we could reconstruct it later, Lesley used the leading digging edge of the JCB's bucket to smash the locks at the base of the sliding inner door and then roll it up. Beyond was a high-ceilinged corridor lined with workrooms on the left and metal shelving down the right. The place had the school art room smell of wet clay and turpentine. The space was far too narrow to manoeuvre a JCB down its length, but unluckily for

MOLA the target material had all been at the loading bay end of the corridor.

Although, us being police, we all doubted it had anything to do with luck.

'We need to re-interview everyone,' said Guleed.

Somebody must have told somebody, even if they didn't know why that somebody wanted to know.

The stolen material had been stored in large containers like outsized shoeboxes made of heavy-duty brown cardboard. There was a stack of them left untouched against one wall. I looked at a couple of the labels – it was marked with a site and context number, a period P/MED and identified as HUMAN SKELETON. Most of the pile were P/MED human skeletons and I couldn't help wondering who they were and whether they'd be pleased to know that their remains had ended up in boxes in a warehouse in Islington.

'So skeletons aren't particularly magical?' asked Guleed.

'Not intrinsically so,' said Nightingale. 'It depends on context.'

What had been stolen, according to MOLA's records, was a thousand kilograms of assorted bits of masonry and approximately three hundred clay pipes excavated from a site off New Change.

'Right next to St Paul's,' I said.

'You'd better talk to the archaeologist involved,' said Nightingale. 'Sahra and I will split the interviews with the staff here between us. Carey can join us when he comes on shift.'

*

Upstairs, MOLA's offices had the same open-plan cubicle based workspace that has been the delight of code monkeys and low-level paper pushers since one time and motion consultant said to another, 'Hey, you know, I don't think we've really dehumanised these white collar drones enough'.

The big difference is that in the average office you don't walk into a cubicle area and find someone reconstructing a skeleton.

'Who's this?' I asked the tiny white woman with grey hair and pince-nez, who was holding a small bone fragment like someone with a bit of sky from a jigsaw puzzle.

'Not sure,' she said without looking up – she had an accent like a well-bred pirate. 'Found him last month.'

'Where was he?'

'Downstairs in storage,' she said distractedly. 'Mis-labelled.' She straightened suddenly. 'Aha!' she cried. 'This doesn't belong to you at all.' Then she looked at me properly. 'Can I help you?'

I told her I was looking for Robert Skene.

'He should be about somewhere,' she said. 'Are you with the police?'

I said I was, and asked what she was up to.

'It wasn't me, guv,' she said. 'He was dead when I found him – honest.'

I gave the joke the consideration it deserved.

'There's been some very good results recently extracting DNA from teeth,' she said, as she carefully placed the bone fragment down on a clean sheet of paper. 'So we've been hunting out any skulls that might have been mislaid to see what we can find.' She looked down at her nearly complete skeleton. 'I'm afraid I got a little bit distracted.'

I asked how old the body was.

'We're still waiting on the C-14 results,' she said. 'But my money's on Roman – possibly related to that lot over there.' She gestured at a row of brown cardboard boxes on a nearby work surface – each carefully labelled 'Human Skull'.

'That's a lot of heads,' I said.

'Oh, Crossrail can't sink an access shaft these days without finding skulls. We're trying to work out what these ones were doing in the Walbrook.'

'Any theories?' I asked, which got a laugh.

Apparently there were almost as many theories as skulls, but it was just possible they were victims of the Boudiccan sack of Londinium in AD 60, or possibly 61.

'Given the numbers reported killed in Tacitus,' she said, 'the bodies must have gone somewhere.'

There was a problem with that theory, in that the skulls were mostly missing their related spines and hips, arms and legs – not to mention jawbones – which did rather suggest that they'd washed down the river from further upstream. Skulls being famous for surviving trips down rivers where lesser bones do not.

I was actually getting a bit interested, but then Robert Skene arrived and it was back to work.

He was a white guy in his early thirties who spoke with a vaguely East Anglian accent, and while he was dressed office casual in jeans and a check shirt, he definitely gave the impression that big mud-encrusted boots and army surplus jackets were a plausible option. I thought, he's going to be a big fan of obscure heavy metal bands or folk music, or possibly both at the same time.

I asked about the dig where the stolen material had come from.

'St Paul's Cathedral School,' he said. 'Stage two of the One New Change development. It looked like demolition rubble, we did some test pits and some geophysics but we didn't find any structures or useful stratification and the only proper dating evidence was the clay pipes.' He shrugged. 'Our best guess is that it was rubble from the medieval phase of the cathedral that was dumped during the construction of the Wren. The pipes might have belonged to the workers.'

'That's a lot of pipes,' I said.

'Clay pipes were totally disposable in those days,' said Robert. 'They used to sell a pipe with a single charge of tobacco – smoke it and throw it.'

'So builder's rubble and fag ends?' I said.

'Pretty much.'

So I was thinking about the power of faith while I was writing up my notes.

The exact role that faith plays in imbuing supernatural entities with power has been hotly debated since Newton's day. Its importance has risen and fallen with the Folly's intellectual fashions, from the Deism of the Enlightenment to the muscular Christianity of the late Victorians, to the disillusionment and despair in the aftermath of the First World War. But not in the way you might think.

The deists, believing in a creator that had set the world in motion and then stood back to admire its work, thought faith and worship might have an impact on lesser supernatural creatures in much the same way as the wealth of nations was affected by trade. They were certain that, with the application of enough reason, the principles behind these transactions could be understood.

Those cold-shower athletic *Up, up, play the game* Victorians couldn't believe that their Lord and saviour might have to compete with the local Rivers for the favour of ordinary humanity. Their God was all powerful and existed independently of our hopes and wishes. And if their prayers had no effect then, God damn it, nobody else's did either.

Despite taking no official part in the War to End All Wars, many wizards volunteered nonetheless and nearly all lost brothers, fathers and uncles. Foxholes might breed belief, but trench systems are full of fatalistic cynics. After the war, most combatants didn't like to talk about it. But those that did were not fans of the idea that faith could move mountains – at least not literally.

Nonetheless, there is power in those old cathedrals – you can feel it through your fingers when you touch the walls. And, wherever it comes from, we all knew what Martin Chorley planned to do with it.

'Well, that's it,' said Seawoll, when we convened for the evening briefing. 'We go after Lesley.'

15

The Coop

'**D**o you think there is a God?' said Carey, apropos of fuck knows what.

We were on a stake-out. And spending a couple of hours cooped up in a car often leads to some weird conversations. But this was the first time religion had ever come up.

'You know, God,' he said. 'Creator of everything – the Bible – that kind of God.'

'Not really,' I said, and checked the mirrors to make sure we hadn't been spotted.

Not that it was likely, given that we were parked down Poplar Place which was actually round the corner from our target. We'd taken the 'last car on earth', a ten year old Rover that was fully reconditioned under the bonnet but beaten to shit on the bodywork. It moved when you wanted it to but the aircon was buggered. Which why it was always the last car anyone picked for an operation. It didn't help that it was another sweaty, overcast day, and even with the windows down Carey was suffering.

Our targets were the false houses in Bayswater that concealed not only the unsightly gash of the Circle and District Lines, but one of the hidden entrances to the clandestine tunnels that were the domain of the secret people that lived under West London. Fortunately we knew where most of the hidden entrances were. Unfortunately, so did Zachary Palmer – who was minting it as informal liaison between Crossrail and the Quiet People, as the secret folk were known, who were employed for their unique tunnelling skills.

Judging from the pattern when he evaded us, Zach used the hidden ways when he wanted to escape his surveillance team. As part of the 'arrangement' with the Quiet People the further flung of their secret entrances, not used for Crossrail, had been decommissioned. Me and Carey were stationed at the easternmost of the entrances which was still open, while Nightingale and Guleed were waiting in Notting Hill, which we figured was his most likely escape route.

'So you don't believe in God?' said Carey.

Long experience with my mother's erratic approach to Christianity has taught me to avoid this topic of conversation, but I wasn't paying attention so I just told him I didn't.

'How can you not believe in God?'

There was something in Carey's tone that made me pay attention.

'I just don't,' I said.

'But after what you've seen,' he said. 'After the shit we've seen?'

'What kind of shit?'

'You can do magic, Peter,' said Carey. 'You can shoot fireballs out of your fingers and your girlfriend is a river. That kind of shit. Like possessed BMWs and just all of it. All of that shit.'

'That's different,' I said. 'That shit is real.'

'Most people don't think it's real. They think it's all made up.'

'Like overtime,' I said, but Carey wasn't biting.

'If that's true, then why not God?'

'How does that follow?'

'Because it does.'

'No it doesn't.'

'OK, OK, maybe you just haven't met God yet,' he said and, before I could reply, my Airwave pinged.

It was Sergeant Jaget Kumar, the Folly's liaison with the British Transport Police and our man in London Underground's CCTV control room.

'You're not going to like this,' he said. 'But your target's eastbound on the District Line.'

Nightingale broke in.

'Zulu Foxtrot Two One One – go east now, see if you can get ahead of him.'

So much for secret doors, I thought, as I put the Rover in gear and peeled away with the light-bars flashing but the siren off. I considered going under the Westway at Royal Oak but decided to risk the traffic on the direct route and head up Bishop's Bridge Road. We don't speed in the Metropolitan Police, we 'make progress' where the traffic allows. Sometimes we made progress at seventy miles an hour, but not often enough to reach Edgware Road before Zach did.

'Has he ever done this before?' asked Carey, who was enjoying the breeze.

I said not.

'He knows we're following him this time,' said

Carey. 'Why else change his pattern?'

Jaget reported that Zach was off the train.

'Assume he's going east on the Hammersmith and City,' said Nightingale over the Airwave. 'And try and get to Baker Street before he does. We'll cover this end in case he doubles back.'

Fortunately Nightingale had said this early enough for me to slide off the Harrow Road and onto the Marylebone Flyover – although, as any London driver will tell you, that's not always a step up.

'He's on the eastbound platform,' said Jaget.

'Skip Baker Street,' said Nightingale. 'Go straight to King's Cross – we'll come east and cover Baker Street.'

Guleed was in for a treat if Nightingale thought he could do Notting Hill to Baker Street in under fifteen minutes.

I had to make a decision. A couple of hundred years ago the Euston Road was practically London's northern boundary. You'd clip along in your carriage with the fields and orchards of Middlesex to the north and the brand new Regency housing developments, luxury homes for the gentry – so no change there –to the south. It's a crucial east-west route and as such has been widened, turned into a dual carriageway and had underpasses and flyovers added in order to cope with the traffic volume. The result has been a road on which the motorist can while away a happy hour or so of an afternoon while admiring the limitations of sixties urban planning.

I got off it as soon as I could and went around the back of Euston Station by the secret route, known only to me and London's cabbies, and ended up approaching King's Cross down York Way. Zach hadn't got off at Baker Street, but I was seriously beginning to wonder whether he was going anywhere or was just messing us about.

'Farringdon,' said Carey. 'He could slip into the Crossrail works there and lose us.'

I relayed this via Guleed, who was making the occasional yip sound over the noise of a vintage, but beautifully maintained, inline six cylinder going flat out.

'He says stay where you are until we're in a position to cover King's Cross,' she said, and then paused while Nightingale said something indistinct in the background. 'He thinks that if he were trying to lose us he'd have made the attempt at Baker Street.'

'Where's he going?' asked Carey.

It turned out to be Liverpool Street.

As we shot down Bishopsgate I realised that the Broadgate offices of Bock, Loupe and Stag were passing on our right.

'Haven't we just been down these ends?' I said.

'It's the City,' said Carey. 'Everyone down here has their hand in everybody else's trouser pocket.'

Jaget tracked him off the train, up the escalators and out the Old Broad Street exit. By that time I'd managed to pull in by the taxi rank on Liverpool Street. Only Zach caught us by surprise by coming out our way and we had to duck down as he passed us on the other side of the street. I didn't dare back out in the car because someone was bound to honk at us and catch Zach's attention, so we threw the doors open and bundled out instead. Carey, since he's interacted with Zach the least, took the lead as he turned right down Bishopsgate.

Zach looked cheerful and suspiciously well groomed.

'He's definitely expecting to get lucky,' said Carey over his Airwave.

But where was this good fortune about to take place?

Like most of the City, Bishopsgate is in a permanent state of redevelopment. Which worked to my favour, since the scaffolding on the building next to the Church of St Botolph of the Turkish Baths gave us cover as we watched Zach cross over to the other side of the road.

We thought he was going for Houndsditch, a pedestrianised strip between Heron Tower and whatever it was they were building next door, and we hurried across to avoid getting left behind. But Zach surprised us again by veering through the revolving doors that led to Heron Tower's main lobby.

I'm not going to say anything about Heron Tower except that I'm sure the architects did their best and that the makers of Meccano probably regard it as aspirational. It's forty-six storeys high and has a couple of expensive eateries at the top, but they're served by their own lifts with a separate street entrance. Zach obviously wasn't going for those.

Carey went into the lobby while I followed cautiously ten metres behind.

Heron Tower has what the brochures call a concierge style lobby. Which is to say, just like every modern corporate building built this century, there's a reception, security and barriers to stop the unwashed from penetrating the inner fastness. Exactly like Broadgate, only this time with the largest privately owned aquarium in the UK – stocked, I like to think, with piranhas so that failing minions could be suitably punished by their superiors.

Piranhas or not, the aquarium rose like a glass wall behind the receptionists, who were all young white women, sitting in a row and dressed in identical blue uniforms.

Zach was nowhere to be seen. I suspected he was already up the escalators or heading for the main lift bank – both were the other side of the security barriers.

Carey showed the receptionist his warrant card.

'The scruffy white man who just came in,' he said. 'Where did he go?'

The receptionist, startled by his tone, hesitated, glanced at me and then, slightly panicked, to the approaching security guard. This guy was in a navy suit with an unfortunate orange tie, and was nearing us with the caution of a man on a minimum wage zero hours contract who planned to give his employers exactly what they paid for.

Carey whirled on him – he obviously hadn't enjoyed the stake-out.

'You,' he said to the security guard. 'Unless you want to be arrested for obstruction, get her to tell us where he went.'

Which they did, with speed and reproachful looks. And I noticed they knew exactly who we were talking about.

'Does anyone else go in and out of that floor?' I asked.

Not that they knew of. And the unfurnished floor was

not in common use – bought and paid for, but the client had yet to move in. Zach, who they knew as Mr Henry Hodgekins, made periodic visits and had his own pass. Later they'd furnish us with dates and descriptions and, reluctantly, financial information. But we didn't have time for that now. We did show them a picture of Lesley and asked if it rang any bells. None, they said. But this was Lesley with her new changeable face – she could go in and out all day and they might never know.

'What do you reckon?' asked Carey, flushed but pleased with himself.

'We've got to go after him,' I said.

'And if she's up there? Or something worse?'

I keyed Nightingale on my Airwave and got Guleed instead.

'We're ten minutes out,' she said.

I looked over at Carey, who shrugged and then nodded.

'We're going up,' I told her.

'Be careful,' she said.

The security guard, whose name turned out to be Mitchell, came with us to facilitate access through the barriers and guide us around the fish tank, under the escalators and into the correct lift.

It was a fast lift, but we rode up with the nagging worry that Lesley was already riding down in the adjacent shaft. The walls were glass, so we would have got a good view of her thumbing her nose as she went by. We did get a really good view south over the City proper, framed by the Gherkin and the NatWest tower and cranes rearing like flagpoles over every new development. Through the new construction I caught sight of the river, the fake blades of the Ronson and the gap where Skygarden used to be.

I couldn't quite get the angle to see St Paul's. It was a way to the west, built on the hill on the other side of the Walbrook. I wondered if that was significant.

'We should have waited,' said Carey. 'And locked down the place.'

Which is the age-old dilemma, when chasing a suspect into a big building.

'We just have to hope she doesn't know we're coming,' I said. 'You ready?'

Carey pulled his X26 from his shoulder holster and checked the charge. Following the operation in Chiswick, Seawoll had insisted that Carey and Guleed were routinely armed. Carey, who could moan about an overtime bonus, had never complained once about carrying the bulky thing.

The lift slowed, pinged and opened its doors on to the thirty-fourth floor. The lobby beyond was small, windowless and dimly lit. With its durable peach coloured carpet, neutral coloured walls and sturdy hardwood fire doors it looked temporary – a placeholder.

Mitchell the guard indicated an electronic touch lock by one of the fire doors and pulled a key card from his pocket.

'This should open it,' he said.

Carey took the card from his fingers and shushed him when he tried to protest. I gently pushed him away from the door so he wouldn't be in the line of fire or in our way, and nodded at Carey.

Carey pressed the card to the touch lock – and nothing happened.

He tried a couple more times and we both turned to glare at Mitchell, who cringed.

'It should work,' he hissed.

We pointed out, in low whispers, that it obviously didn't.

'It's supposed to open everything,' whispered Mitchell. 'For safety.'

'Well, obviously it doesn't,' said Carey.

Mitchell said if we would just give him a moment he'd fetch another card, and we let him scuttle back down in the lift.

Carey gave me an inquiring look, I nodded, and we switched off our Airwaves and our phones.

Then I blew the electromagnets that were holding the door closed.

Modern office security and fire doors are designed to fail into an unlocked position so that cubicle monkeys can make a run for it in case of a fire. Disrupt the electrical supply and you can unlock them without breaking a sweat or blowing all the microprocessors in the vicinity and accidentally triggering the sprinkler system.

But, in my defence, that only happened once and they're planning to move New Scotland Yard to a new building in any case.

There was a quiet thud as the magnets let go and I cautiously pushed the door open.

Beyond was it was wide open – at least half the thirty-fourth floor's available space, lit by the grey daylight slanting in through the glass cladding.

Zach was reclining on the red leather sofa that faced the door, a can of Red Stripe in one hand and what would turn out to be, after later examination, an enormous spliff in the other.

'You took your time,' he said before turning his head. 'I was going to spark up without you.'

Despite this, me and Carey made a cautious advance – just in case it was a trap.

'Oh, shit,' said Zach, when he realised it was us. 'And it was going to be sushi night too.' He jumped to his feet. 'What are you guys doing here?'

Carey strode forward and, before I could stop him, punched Zach in the face – hard enough to stagger him backwards.

'Where the fuck is she?' he shouted.

'How the fuck should I know?' said Zach, clutching his face and backing away towards the wide windows and their expensive view of north London.

I grabbed Carey's arm before he could hit Zach again. He shrugged off my hand but stepped back, his hands raised, palms up to show that he was finished. I was gobsmacked. You have to be a bit aggressive to be a police officer, it's the nature of the job. But I'd never seen David Carey so much as shout at a suspect before. He always said he was too lazy to hit someone.

I pointed at the brass bed that sat incongruously in an open space and told Zach to sit on it. I looked at Carey to see if he was going to be trouble, but he just shook his head.

'You watch him,' I said. 'I'll do a quick search.'

And it was a quick search, since it was standard

open-plan office floor into which what looked like a pied-à-terre's worth of furniture had been deposited. Then arranged into a wall-less imitation of a flat, with separate spaces for kitchen, bathroom, lounge and bedroom. It was creepily like a stage set or something out of a surreal episode of the original *Star Trek*.

The furniture was all high end and I suspected that if I called up the John Lewis catalogue on my phone I'd find every single item. Except maybe the trio of creepy white busts with half-formed faces that lined the top of a dresser. Wig holders, I realised.

'She used to put her masks on them,' Zach explained later.

Somebody was going to have to track the furniture in case Martin Chorley had been sloppy enough to use his own bank account to buy it. Likewise one of our forensic accountants would trace the ownership of the office space back to whatever shell company Martin Chorley had bought it with. How many of these front organisations could he have? And how many could he lose before his operation ground to a halt?

As many as he needs, I thought. Not to mention other underhand details that we haven't even thought of yet.

'Can I least finish the spliff before the handcuffs go on?' said Zach.

'Only if you give me some,' said Carey.

16

Stupidity Led

We arrested Zach for obstruction of justice but not for possession – mainly because most of the evidence was missing and Carey had become worryingly cheerful. There was definitely something up with David Carey, but I wasn't sure what to do about it – you can't talk to a senior officer without dropping your mate in the shit. And your average police, especially your average male police, don't like you insinuating that the job's getting a bit much for them.

There were probably some guidelines somewhere, but I expect they were above my pay grade.

I stayed at the open-plan flat overnight just in case Lesley was stupid enough to come back, while a couple of specialist DCs interviewed Zach for eight hours straight before coming back the next morning and doing it again for at least another six hours. If Zach told the truth at any point in the fourteen hours total, then nobody was able to prove it. The National College of Policing now use excerpts of the tapes for their advanced interview training course.

We gave up on any notion that Lesley was going to appear that morning and, around ten o'clock I went back to the Folly for a wash. As I came in the back Toby ran up, barking in what would have gone into a police notebook as 'an agitated fashion'.

'I'm going to bed,' I said. 'I don't care.'

But Toby kept up sharp little yaps in the manner of a dog who had been putting in some practice recently, and could probably keep the noise up indefinitely.

'Fine,' I said. 'Go on, then.'

Toby danced back a couple of lengths and then turned and ran up the east stairs and up another flight until we were outside one of the teaching labs on the first floor. Toby scratched on the door and I heard the unmistakably Welsh Dr Jennifer Vaughan say, 'For God's sake don't let him back in.'

Just to be safe, I knocked on the door. In the Folly you never knew what you might be walking in on.

Dr Vaughan asked who it was. I assured her it was me, and the door opened enough to reveal her face – albeit half covered by eye protectors and a filter mask. She looked down at Toby.

'Get back, fiend from hell,' she said. And then, to me, 'You can come in as long as you keep him out.'

It took a bit of effort to arrange, but once I'd got myself in I got a whiff of something that made me wish I'd stayed outside with Toby. Dr Walid and Abigail were dressed in the same style paper smocks, eye protectors and filter masks as Dr Vaughan and they were all clustered around a bench. On the bench was what I recognised as a stainless steel dissection tray.

In the tray I caught a glimpse of pink and red viscera surrounded by russet red fur, before deliberately moving away so I couldn't see any more. It had been large – dog- rather than cat-sized.

I heard Toby scrabble on the other side of the door.

'We can't tell,' said Dr Walid, 'whether he's upset over what we're doing, or thinks we've started lunch without him.'

Dr Vaughan picked up a scalpel and moved in to make another incision – Abigail leant forward to look over her shoulder.

'What is it? I asked.

'It was brought into the animal hospital in Islington,' said Dr Walid. 'But it died before it could be treated. We think it may be one of Abigail's friends.'

He looked at Abigail, who shrugged.

'What make you think that?' I asked.

'Well, he's much bigger than we would expect from an urban fox,' said Dr Vaughan as she worried something with the tip of her scalpel, 'and its brain is noticeably larger both in gross size and ratio to body mass. And, while I'll admit that I am not a veterinarian, the fact that the arrangement of the larynx resembles that of a human is a bit of a giveaway.'

'Are you sure we should be cutting it up quite so casually,' I said, 'if it's one of the talking ones?'

'We are not being casual,' said Dr Vaughan. 'This is a post mortem, not a dissection.'

'That's why Jen's doing the cutting,' said Abigail.

'Do you have a cause of death?' I asked.

'Multiple injuries caused by massive blunt force trauma,' said Dr Vaughan.

'Hit by a car,' said Abigail.

'Most likely,' said Dr Vaughan.

'Notification is going to be a bit tricky,' I said.

Not that I wanted the job of telling this fox's nearest and dearest.

'Abigail's thought of that,' said Dr Walid proudly.

Abigail held up a large brown paper forensic envelope and opened it so I could see the white towelling face cloth inside.

'I rubbed it over his fur,' she said. 'Other foxes should be able to identify him by his smell.'

'They'll probably know he's dead by the smell, too,' said Dr Walid.

'Handy. That'll save you doing that part of the notification at least,' I said, which got me stony looks from all three.

'Don't go anywhere without telling me first,' I told Abigail, and then deliberately let Toby in on my way out. I admit that was a bit petty, but in my defence I hadn't had much sleep and I was worried about Carey.

I went to my room, set my phone alarm for later that afternoon and climbed into bed.

I didn't really feel like I'd slept much when the alarm woke me, but I had my part to play in the continuing interrogation of Zachary Palmer. We'd done good cop, bad cop, patiently-trying-to-understand cop, and now we were going to try 'I'm on your side really' cop. By rights the last one should never work in a million years, but you'd be surprised. Certainly some people currently doing time have been.

I selected my wardrobe with care – jeans, trainers and my Adidas hoody of urban invisibility. Then I picked up a basket of surplus cakes from Molly, climbed into the Hyundai and headed off to Belgravia to liberate Zach the goblin boy.

'I bought you a present,' I said once he was out and we were safely in the Hyundai, and I passed over the basket.

He gave me a sour look before opening the basket and extracting a cupcake decorated with a bunny face in blue and white icing. He brandished it at me.

'Do you think this makes everything all right?' he asked, but took a bite anyway. 'It's not going to work,' he said through a mouth full of crumbs.

'Where do you want to go?' I asked.

'It's not going to work.'

'What isn't going to work?'

'You don't get all friendly, give me cake and then think I'm going to lead you to my secret hideout.'

'Do you have a secret hideout?'

'See.' Zach had a rummage in the basket to see what else he could find. 'Want something?'

I said I was trying to cut down.

'More for me,' he said.

'Lesley said that you can't stay in the same place for long. She said it was a compulsion because you're part fae.'

'That there is one of them things, isn't it?' he said.

'One of what things?'

'One of them things that is sort of true. But at the same time not really true. I like to move about, but I have stayed put once or twice – like in Notting Hill.'

Where he'd happily lived in the unfortunate James

Gallagher's flat for at least three months without moving on.

'I get restless sometimes,' he said. 'And sometimes I don't.'

Then to my surprise he snapped the basket closed, put it on his lap and folded his arms firmly over the lid.

'Maybe you should leave Lesley alone,' said Zach, after we'd sat in silence for a bit. 'It's not like there's nothing else going on, is it?'

People are often willing to tell you all sorts of secrets when they're trying to hide something from you. You should always make a mental note – it may not be your case today but you never know, it might come round later.

I asked what else was going on.

'For one thing, the Vikings have gone at Holland Park,' said Zach.

'The Vikings?'

'There used to be loads of ghosts at Holland Park.'

I said I'd never had any reports of mass ghost sightings at Holland Park and Abigail had done a really serious search the year before.

'Not on the main tube tunnels,' he said. 'The other ones. The secret ones.'

A secret bunker had been adjacent to the station during World War Two, which was now used as a private nightclub by my least favourite pair of Bev's sisters and also connected to the Quiet People's warren under Notting Hill.

'Vikings?'

'Danes maybe, Northmen certainly,' said Zach. 'Raiders from across the sea what got themselves done in by Alfred or Æthelred. One of them early kings.'

'You saw them?' I asked.

'Nah,' said Zach, 'but you could hear them, couldn't you? All screaming and yelling and lamenting.'

'And now they're gone?'

'Leaving not a single solitary moan behind.'

'You're taking the piss, aren't you?'

'On my life,' he said.

'Look,' I said, 'do you want to go home or not?'

Zach paused to give it some thought but in the end he relented – as I knew he would.

'Stanmore,' he said. 'I've got a place in Stanmore.'

We knew all about it of course – but I didn't tell him that.

I drove via Neasden to avoid the traffic and we were just crawling along the semi-detached and taxi gardened wasteland of Dudden Hill when Zach unexpectedly spilled the beans.

'They want to summon Mr Punch,' he said.

'Jesus Christ,' I said. 'Whatever for?'

Lesley had been possessed by Mr Punch, aka the restless London spirit of riot and rebellion – or possibly by the ghost of an eighteenth-century actor who thought he was Mr Punch. It had all got a bit confusing towards the end of that particular case.

'Lesley's not . . .' I started, but didn't know where to go with the question. Not still working with Mr Punch? Under his influence? Possessed?

'What do they want him for?'

'Oh,' Zach waved his hand airily. 'They're going to kill him.'

I braked sharply to avoid hitting the back of a Volvo.

'Isn't he already dead?'

'You tell me,' said Zach. 'You're the one who's met him.'

'Can he be killed?'

'Anything that's alive can be killed. But I think this is more in the way of a sacrifice. You know, for the power.'

'For the power of what?'

'He's not your ordinary ghost, is he?' said Zach. 'He's something else again.'

'I meant what do they want the power for?'

'Don't know,' said Zach. 'For something big. Old Faceless wanted to use the juice from Skygarden, but you put the kibosh on that, didn't you? He was well vexed with you, bruv, but I've got to say Lesley was impressed – I think. At least she couldn't believe you stayed in the block with the bombs.'

I can't believe I stayed in the tower that day either. Sometimes I dream I'm outside, and however hard I try I can't make myself run inside to warn the residents. Then the bombs go off and down it comes, one floor on top of the other, and above the roar of it I can hear the screams.

'It's not like I had a lot of choice, is it?' I said. And then, 'Would sacrificing Punch generate much power?'

'A raging revenant from the dawn of time? I think there might be a certain amount of wattage in that. Don't you?'

'So what does Martin Chorley need Lesley for?'

'Don't know,' said Zach. 'But I know he does because Lesley thought it was really funny in that, like, totally unfunny way that sometimes things are funny.'

'To do what, Zach?' I said. 'What the fuck does Chorley want to do?'

'Lesley never said. And, you know what? I never asked. Because it was none of my business.'

'I want you to tell Lesley that we need to meet,' I said. 'On her terms if she likes, but we've got to talk.'

Zach turned away from me and stared out his window.

'She's not going to risk seeing me again,' he said. 'Not after the shit you pulled.'

'I didn't tell her to change sides,' I said.

'You didn't exactly help her stay on yours, though,' he said. 'Did you?'

17

First Century Mandem

'Intelligence led' is one of those dire phrases that police officers feel the need to include in their operational plans. This is either because they feel senior officers might otherwise assume that they are stupidity led, or because it's an article of faith among the rank and file that everyone above superintendent has had their sense of irony surgically removed. Often the word 'proactive' is added at the front to create a kind of litany. *O lead us intelligently into the valley of the shadow of limited resources so that we might make our crime targets before the end of the Home Office reporting period – Amen.*

What intelligence led really means is trying to figure out what you're doing before you actually do it. And that means being honest about what you do and what you don't know.

And one of the things we didn't know was the true nature of Mr Punch.

You've got ghosts. Occasionally you've got ghosts which can directly affect the material world. And you've got revenant ghosts which feed on other ghosts. Then you've got *genii locorum*, the spirits of places – ranging from the playful spirit that inhabited a bookshop in Covent Garden to the Goddess of the River Thames. The distinction, as far as we can tell, lies in where they draw their power from. Ghosts get theirs from the layers of *vestigia* laid down in the material fabric of old houses or the stone geology of some rural locales.

The *genii locorum* draw their power from the locality itself – although we're still no closer to understanding where *that* power comes from. Since some of those localities include the entire watershed of the Thames above Teddington Lock you can see why we are careful to be polite around them.

Erasmus Wolfe wrote extensively about *genii locorum* in his ground-breaking and – at two thousand pages – wrist-breaking *Exotica*. He theorised that there was an upper limit to the size and power of an individual *genius loci* and, unlike many of his contemporaries, he provided some facts and figures to back himself up.

None of the really huge rivers of Europe – the Volga, the Danube or the Rhine – appeared to possess a single tutelary deity. Instead there were Rhine Maidens, plural, a French and a German Mosel, and at least ten recorded gods and goddesses of the Don.

And surely, Erasmus wrote, had the long length of the Volga possessed a single guiding spirit with loyalty to the people on its banks, Napoleon's invasion of Russia would have foundered before it began.

Or the Mississippi when the foreign invaders tooled up there, I thought, or the Congo, or the Limpopo or the Ganges or the Amazon.

That is, if you assume a power so wide in scope would even be remotely human in conception or thought. But, relatively small as they were, I wouldn't go up against either of the Thameses. And we already knew what happened to the last person who took a shot at Lady Ty.

Then there were the ghosts, or echoes or possibly past avatars, of *genii locorum* who possessed a strange half-life in the magical memory of the city.

Suddenly I had a cunning plan, but I've had too many of those in the past not to run this one past Nightingale first.

I found him in the mundane library working on a lesson plan for Abigail. He had Bassinger's *First Steps in Effective Combinations* open in front of him and was taking notes.

I know for a fact that Nightingale thinks my training has been a bit rough-and-ready. And he seems determined that, between him and Varvara, our Abigail was going to get a more thorough grounding in the basics. To do this, both her teachers were going to have to up their own basics – so I had every intention of copying Abigail's notes.

'We need the real story on Punch,' I said.

'Agreed,' said Nightingale, putting his pen down. 'Are you thinking of asking Father Thames?'

'I think we might end up paying more than we can afford,' I said. 'Oxley warned me there's always a price.'

'His sons are not going to speak on this without his permission,' said Nightingale.

Not even Ash, who could generally be induced to do just about anything for a pony and a couple of free drinks.

'I was thinking of closer to home.'

'Mama Thames's daughters are too young, surely?' said Nightingale.

'But they have long memories,' I said.

Nightingale nodded.

'You're going to pursue Sir William.'

'Who claims to have been around before the Romans,' I said. 'Which makes him the god on the spot.'

'He only seems to appear when you're *in extremis*,' said Nightingale.

The first time while I was buried underground, and later when Martin Chorley launched his abortive attack on Lady Ty.

'I think the trick is to alter your state of consciousness,' I said.

Nightingale frowned.

'I hope absinthe isn't going to play a role in this,' he said. Apparently some of the younger, more bohemian, wizards of Nightingale's youth had tried that. 'And sweat lodges and . . .' He paused to search his memory. 'Peyote.'

'Did any of it work?'

'I'm not sure they were entirely serious. Although I couldn't fault them for diligence.'

David Mellenby, Nightingale's friend and go-to guy for what passed for empiricism at the Folly, hadn't thought much of these 'experiments'.

'And in any case I'm not authorising any operation involving hallucinogens without permission from Dr Walid first.'

'Don't worry,' I said. 'What I'm proposing is going to involve some elbow grease, a bit of ritual humiliation, about four litres of bleach, one of Hugh's staffs, and the best possible bottle of wine you can prise out of Molly.'

The River Tyburn, which we must never call a repurposed storm drain if we mean to carry on walking around on two legs, splits into two branches downstream of Buckingham Palace. The northern branch flows to either side of the Palace of Westminster, marking the ancient outline of Thorney Island. The southern branch outflows just upstream of Vauxhall Bridge. Upstream the Tyburn can be pretty narrow and, let's face it, encrusted, so I wanted somewhere downstream where it's wider. The problem is if you start poking about underground near the Houses of Parliament armed guys from CTC turn up to ask you questions. This is because Counter Terrorism Command has an institutional memory that goes all the way back to Guy Fawkes.

Fortunately on the southern branch, once known as the Tachbrook, there's easy access through the manholes on Tachbrook Road. Right next to the Tachbrook Estate. Because Lady Ty may be underground, but she makes her presence felt.

So I drove down to Tachbrook with a ton of gear in the back, including my heavy-duty waders, filter mask, goggles, four litres of bleach, a plaque that I'd had made up against just this sort of need, a variety of cordless DIY tools, a bottle of 1964 Romanee Conti Grand Cru burgundy and the one present that I knew would really get her attention.

I met my Thames Water contact, Allison Conte, on the corner of Tachbrook and Churton Street, because you don't go in the sewers without asking Thames Water first, and even then they weren't happy about me going down alone.

'We're not happy about you going down alone,' said Allison, a small, wiry white woman in her thirties who claimed she had her job on account of her small size. 'Things can get tight further up,' she'd said. 'They needed someone who can fit into the two foot pipes.'

At least she couldn't fault my gear, which I'd updated, at my own expense, since my last visit to the sewers. This included an eye-watering yellow PV oversuit, a wetsuit, boots, gloves, eye protectors and a gas detector – because these days canaries are not allowed.

'I'm not going to do anything stupid,' I said as she used a metal lever to pry open the rectangular manhole cover.

I was going down a side access because, unlike the lifting shafts that run down the centre of the street, they lead to a vestibule with its own built-in ladder.

'That's not what I heard,' muttered Allison.

I pretended not to have heard *that* as I helped her set up the public safety barrier around the open manhole. Once I was down she passed me the jet wash gun and fed the hose down behind me as I moved into the drain proper.

At this point in her course the Tyburn is actually a bricked up canal. Like many of her sisters she was swallowed up by the city, first serving as an open sewer and then buried out of sight. About four metres across and three metres high, she's relatively clean but there's no getting away from the smell of old shit mixed in with the disturbingly meaty scent of old fat. Which was worse in that this far downstream it's pervasive rather than over-powering – sneaking up on you in waves when you least expect it.

Once I'd found a suitable spot I went back to the manhole and had Allison pass down the rest of my gear.

'Are you sure you don't want me down there with you?' she asked.

'If I'm not back up in two hours, come and look for me,' I said.

Allison made a sour face, but nodded.

First I used the water jet to scour the brickwork, good solid nineteenth-century London brick I noticed, with superior mortaring. Then I got out the bleach and my mum's cordless scrubber and went over it again. Then I got a brush and scrubbed like mad for an hour. In the end I had a section of tunnel that was, possibly, margin-ally cleaner than the rest.

Still, I thought, it's the thought that counts – literally.

Then, being careful to get the measurements right, I used a masonry drill to install brackets so that I could mount the plaque. I'd had it made up specially on a 'break glass in case of spiritual emergency' basis the year before and it read:

Ìya wa, òrìsà wa,
Ìya wa, tí ó ní olá
Ìya wa, tí ó ní ewà
Ìya wa títí láilái.

Which basically translated as *Our mother deity of*

bounty and beauty. Because if you're going to propitiate your actual original orisa, it's go hard or go home.

To avoid additional DIY, the plaque came with its own shelf upon which I placed a couple of vanilla scented candles I'd nicked out of Beverley's bathroom – one at each end. As my most valuable offering I hung one of my two genuine World War Two army surplus battle staffs between the candles. These had been a gift from Hugh Oswald, one of the few surviving veterans of the final battle at Ettersberg.

I took a moment to check my handiwork.

Then I pulled the cork on the 1964 burgundy and, after taking a sip to make sure it wasn't corked or something, poured a generous measure into what passed for water flowing down the central trough.

'O great Goddess of the River Tyburn, spirit of the Hanging Tree – I call on thee.'

I splashed some more in – not too much; I didn't know how long I was going to have to keep this up.

'O Lady of the Parliaments – I call on thee.'

Splash.

'O Warden of the Palace – I call on thee.'

Double splash.

'O Queen of Mayfair – I call on thee.'

'If you pour any more of that on the floor,' said a voice behind me. 'I will not be responsible for the consequences.'

I turned to find the Goddess of the River Tyburn standing behind me with her hands on her hips. She was wearing a black neoprene wetsuit with TYR on the chest. Her hair was carefully wrapped in a matching bathing cap, but her feet were bare.

'And "thee" is the singular informal,' she said. 'You shouldn't use words when you don't know what they mean.'

She held out a hand.

'Give it here,' she said, and I handed over the bottle.

She sniffed it and sighed, and with that sigh the stink of the sewer was blown away by a fresh breeze from the chalky hills of Hampstead.

'The 64 Romanee.' She gave me a reproachful look. 'This is so totally wasted on you.'

'That's why it's a gift,' I said.

Lady Ty took a sip from the bottle and swirled it around her mouth a bit before swallowing.

'You have no appreciation of its value,' she said, and paused to take a good solid swig. 'So it doesn't count as a gift.' She waved the bottle in the general direction of the plaque. 'And that borders on the ironic. If not openly mocking.'

'Not intentionally,' I said.

She gave me a sceptical look and took another couple of swigs.

'I appreciate the cleaning, though,' she said. 'The effort involved, your valuable time expended in, let's be honest, a futile gesture. Next heavy rain and this will be hip deep in shit once more.'

Another swig.

I said nothing because I knew she wasn't finished.

'It's not the intrinsic value of the gift that makes the sacrifice. It's what it's worth to you personally.'

'Well, I was going to bring Toby,' I said. 'But Molly would have objected.'

Lady Ty gave a dismissive wave with her left hand while draining the last of the bottle. When she was sure it was empty she waved it at the staff where it hung below the plaque.

'Now that is a different matter,' she said. 'Pass it over.'

She smiled when I hesitated – a wide lazy grin.

'I want it from your own hand,' she said and dropped the bottle, which bounced rather than smashed. 'Come on, chop-chop, the goddess is in.'

I lifted the staff from the shelf and, turning, went down on one knee. I held out the staff to Lady Ty as if it was a sword. She looked down at me and her smile became crooked and she shook her head.

'You've always got to push it, haven't you?' she said, and put her hand on the staff.

Her eyes closed and her mouth turned down.

'Who do you think I am – Athena?' she said, but her hand curled around the staff and she lifted it from my hands. 'Still, this is a proper gift for all that you don't appreciate its true value, either.'

As I got to my feet she shifted her grip to the end of the staff and held it upright so that the iron-shod tip rested on her shoulder.

'So what is all this in aid of?' she asked.

'I want to talk to Sir William,' I said.

'Really? What for?'

'Intelligence gathering?'

Lady Ty snorted.

'Sir William?' she said. 'He's not what you'd call plugged into the mainstream.'

'Historical witness,' I said.

'What makes you think I can help you with that? Our relationship's not what you'd call close.'

'Close enough that he put half a metre of imaginary sword through that sniper,' I said. 'You might not be on talking terms, but I reckon you're still family.'

'Where is it you think you go when you talk to him?' she asked.

'I think I stay right where I am. I think I'm tapping into the memory of the city.'

'You think too much for a policeman,' she said. 'Do you know that?'

'I get that a lot.'

'I'll bet you do.'

'Can you grant my boon or not?'

'Why not,' she said, and – as fast as an old-time preacher fleecing his flock – she leapt forward, slapped the palm of her right hand against my forehead and pushed.

Have you ever had that sensation, just as you're going to sleep, that a bomb has gone off inside your head? It's a real medical phenomena called, I kid you not, exploding head syndrome. It's what's known as a parasomnia, which is Greek for 'we don't know either'. Anyway, that's what it felt like as I pitched backwards into the black – like a big painless bomb going off in my head.

Generally speaking Exploding Head Syndrome is harmless, but should you experience the further symptoms of finding yourself talking to the avatar of a river goddess, please contact Dr Walid, who collects that sort of data as a hobby.

'Bruv!' cried William Tyburn as he dragged me to my feet and hugged me.

He smelt of kebab and wet wool and hunting and woodsmoke.

He let go of me and held me at arm's length.

'I knew you couldn't stay away.'

I was standing on the bank of a river, too narrow to be the Thames proper and choked with reeds. It was a warm overcast day and away from the water the land rose up to be crowned by a couple of thatched round-houses. Around them spread a confusion of herb gardens, drying racks, woodpiles, small animal pens and stretches where the ground had been worn away to dusty brown tracks.

On the far bank of the river the reeds gave way to trees that might have been oak and ash and alder, and all the other varieties that Beverley says would cover the lowlands of England if given half a chance.

'Welcome to Thorney Island,' said William Tyburn. 'Much better without that pseudo-Gothic monstrosity, isn't it?'

Not as monstrous as his yellow and red check trousers, I thought, although the matching red and brown check tunic had faded to the point where it no longer hurt the eyes. He had grass stains at the elbows and his front was wet with sweat. The lowly man of the soil look was undone by the torc around his neck – a thick braided coil of gold terminating in clusters of what might have been snakes, or perhaps ropes or tangles of tree roots.

'Checking the bling, right?' said Tyburn. 'Nice, isn't it? Got it totally tax free too.'

The humidity was stifling and I tried to catch my breath.

'I'd offer you a beer. But since you're not actually here that would be a bit of a waste, wouldn't it?' He grinned and stepped back and opened his arms. 'How else may I serve you, or are you stuck under another pile of rubble?'

'I was looking for some information,' I said.

'Indoor plumbing,' he said. 'It's going to be big.'

'And you wonder why no one takes you seriously.'

'Seriously enough that you're willing to pony up to have a chat.'

'What did you think of my gifts?'

He cocked his head at an angle and then shook it slowly from side to side.

'I don't know,' he said. 'But giving what it must be costing Mrs High and Mighty Muckity Muck to send you here, they must have been princely gifts indeed.'

Which was interesting – it never occurred to me that transporting me here, wherever here really was, would cost Lady Ty any effort. Something to think about later.

I still felt out of breath and tried to inhale deeply a few times to clear the feeling. As I did, I noticed a young white woman in a garish blue and red check skirt and a loose linen tunic emerge from one of the roundhouses. She paused to glance curiously at me before nodding and smiling at Tyburn. They exchanged pleasantries in a language that could have been Ancient British, or gibberish for all I knew, before she headed off over the rise in the land.

A pale young white man emerged from the same roundhouse, and gave me a similar once-over to the woman before waving a greeting to Tyburn and heading down the slope towards the river a few metres downstream of where we stood.

This man was dressed only in what were obviously his last chance trousers, the pattern faded to a light yellow and orange check and held up with a rope at his waist. He was shirtless and torcless and carried a metre-long spear over his shoulder. The tip, I noted, had a sharp point and double barbs and, judging from the whitish yellow colour, was carved from bone.

'Do they know who you are?' I asked, as we watched the young man wade into the river with his spear.

'Of course they do,' said Tyburn.

The young man took position a couple of metres out into the current with his spear held ready to strike.

'Who you really are?' I said.

'They have a much better idea of who I really am than you do.' He held up a hand for silence. 'Wait for it,' he said softly and then – 'Fish!'

The spear darted down and I saw it tremble as it struck. The young man leant on it to make sure of the kill before squatting down to pick the fish up with both hands. It took both hands because the thing was half a metre long and thrashing around vigorously. The young man wrestled it through the reeds and up the slope to dry ground, where he plonked the fish down, picked up a rock and gave it a good smack. Then again, to be on the safe side.

Once he was satisfied that the fish was thoroughly dead the young man hoisted it to his shoulder and, pausing a moment to nod respectfully at Tyburn, carried it up towards the houses.

'What, no tribute?' I asked.

'Don't be daft,' said Tyburn. 'What do I want with a bit of raw fish?'

'Really?'

'Really. I'm going to pop up later and have it when it's cooked.'

'Cushy,' I said. 'What does he get out of it?'

'He got a fish, didn't he?' Tyburn grinned. 'A big fish.'

'And you arranged that. How?'

Mysteriously,' he said. 'Have you ever considered becoming a god?'

'I don't fancy the hours.' I wondered if he was being serious.

'You get a free fish supper.'

There was a tightness in my chest that no amount of breathing seemed to help. I had to fight not to pant – soon I was going to have to fight not to panic.

'You can't catch your breath,' said Tyburn, 'because you're asphyxiating. Sooner or later Her Sewership will have to pull you out – hopefully before you go into cardiac arrest.'

'You could have told me this earlier,' I said.

He smiled and opened his mouth but I cut him off – I'd wasted enough breath already.

'Mr Punch,' I said. 'Where did he come from?' I held

up my hand. 'And if you try to tell me he has roots in the sixteenth-century Italian *commedia dell'arte* you'll be amazed at how long and painful the comeback will be.'

'Are you sure?' he said. 'It's a sad story.'

'I'm the police, Ty – they're all sad stories.'

'Imagine this geezer,' said Tyburn. 'Let's call him Cata. He's like the fifth living son of an Atrebates sub-chief, a bit weedy, raised to ride a chariot and handle a spear but you know, heart's not in the family business. Only a teen when the Romans turn up and his old man goes, "Fuck me, underfloor heating? That's the shit for me!" and they all go Roman faster than a Basildon girl in an Italian discotheque.

'Now you're thinking about the glories of Rome and all that painted stonework, but back at the start London's essentially a bridge with a shanty town attached. Not that it stayed that way with all the silver denarii flooding in to pay the legions. There's three legions, remember. That's fifteen thousand men, plus the same again in auxiliaries. And these are professional soldiers, so they like to get paid. And they like to get fed too. Anyone with a couple of acres, a plough and some manpower is going to be coining it. Hence docks and warehouses and some tasty new dwellings. Still wattle and daub, but in the modern rectangular style where you get separate bedrooms and don't have to shag in front of the rest of the family.'

'And what were you doing when all this was going on?' I asked.

'I was pretty incoherent with rage at the time,' said Tyburn, 'but this isn't about me, this is about our boy

Cata, who's sharing a Greek tutor with his brothers and learning reading, writing and rhetoric. Now, his brothers spend their lessons dreaming of their chariots and the thunder of the hooves. But Cata finds being Roman is the dog's bollocks. He loves the poetry, loves the gear, loves the not-having-to-literally-fight to maintain your position. Rest of the family, they've got the house and the togas but it's still all piss-ups, hunting and mistreating the servants.'

'So our boy hightails it up the brand new road to Londinium back when, like I said, the place is still basically a muddy field with a bridge attached to one end. Rents some land cheap, builds a house and pops down the market to buy himself a foreign wife from Alexandria. Sets himself up as a middleman between the clueless Roman importers at the docks and the dangerous barbarian-infested hinterland that is Britannia. Foreign wife speaks Latin and Greek and drops four sons and two daughters into his lap.

'Ten years later he's holding literary salons with guests from Alexandria, Ephesus and the Capital itself.'

A band was tightening around my chest but I didn't dare break the flow.

Tyburn gave me a fierce look. 'He liked being a Roman and he was good at it,' he said. 'Loyal, but not too loyal, to his patron. Generous with his largesse, diligent in his religious observance. He was a true believer in law and order and all the benefits that brings a man born without a taste for violence.

'And then one day it all came crashing down. Queen Boudicca lost her rag and led an army of seriously pissed-off Trinis and Iceni down through Camulodunum and ground the useless fucks of the Ninth into dog meat – literally, in some cases.

'Londinium is next. But Suetonius, the governor, doesn't fancy his chances so he buggers off with what troops he has and leaves the city to its fate.'

I've read my Tacitus – I knew what was coming next.

'The gentry always buggers off when London's in danger. Have you noticed that?' he said. 'One whiff of the plague, some social unrest, a bit of light bombing and the Establishment's nowhere to be found.'

Like your dad, I thought. But darkness was seeping into the corners of my eyes so I told him to get on with it.

'But our boy Cata still had faith. That the army would defend him and his family. That civilisation would save him.' Tyburn spat on the ground. 'He ended up there in the Temple of Jupiter with the rest of the schmucks when the Iceni rolled up and murdered the lot of them.

'The story is that they killed his wife and his kids in front of him to force him to reveal where he'd buried his treasure. Slowly and painfully, and one by one, because they didn't believe him when he said nothing was buried. Because he believed in truth, justice and the Roman way – so why would he need to bury anything? By the time they were working on his youngest they say he was laughing like a madman. And this started to freak them out, those big, brave Iceni child-killing warriors, so they slit his belly and left him to die.'

The pain in my chest had driven me to my knees, but it

was the waves of panic that made it hard to concentrate.

'You've met Oberon and the Old Soldiers like him,' said Tyburn. 'You know what can happen when a lot of people get slaughtered in the same place. All that life has to go somewhere.'

Sometimes, about one time in a hundred thousand, it goes into some poor sod dying slowly of something long and terminal . . . and he becomes something else. What, we haven't worked out. But something stronger, tougher and very long-lived. Only I didn't think that's what Tyburn was talking about.

There are some people who believe that if you spill enough blood you can make yourself a god. They're right, if you don't mind dying yourself. I had a horrible feeling that I knew where this story was taking me.

'So up he sprang. A thing full of hatred and mad laughter, capering through the ashes of the city. Because order did not save his children. Law did not save his wife. And, for all his faith in the gods, they did nothing.

'But London is London, because of the bridge and the river and the north and the south. And so, almost before the ashes were cool, the Romans were back with their *groma* and their *chromates* – drawing their straight lines across the world. Cata set about them – waylaying them in the dark places, whispering in the ears of the drunk and foolish, rocking the boats and kicking over amphorae full of fish guts.

'But they were a canny people, the Romans. The Greeks would have debated and written a play. His own people would have abandoned the city and made it a place of sacred fear. What do the Romans do?'

'They made him a temple,' I whispered.

'They did more than that,' said Tyburn. 'They made him a god. They were clever that way, the Romans. They could do things you modern boys can't even dream of. And they weren't afraid to slit the occasional throat to do it.'

And suddenly it all made sense: the bloody awful screenplay, the bacchanalia, that terrible unfocused rage, and the reason I was able to pin him to the bridge. Or at least pin his memory to the memory of London Bridge.

And then I thought of the skulls that the archaeologists had pulled out of the Walbrook. The ones they thought might be victims of the Boudiccan sack of Londinium. And I thought of a seemingly young woman with the sort of light brown complexion and features you might inherit if your dad was an ancient Brit and your mum was Egyptian.

Older, Beverley had said.

I used the last of my willpower to pull myself upright and face Tyburn.

'What happened to his youngest?' I asked.

'You what?'

'You said they killed his wife and kids but they were just starting on the youngest when Cata went mad,' I said. 'So what happened to the youngest?'

Sir William grabbed me by the shoulders and pulled me close so he could whisper in my ear.

'They slit her pretty little neck,' he said. 'And threw her in the Walbrook.'

He pushed me away and I fell into darkness.

*

And blinked and opened my eyes in an ambulance.

Allison Conte was riding with me and the paramedic – she didn't look happy.

'I don't care who you think you are. None of you lot are going down alone,' she said. 'Ever again.'

She'd found me in the side access alcove, sitting up against the ladder and totally out of it. She'd had to get some help and a rope to drag me out.

The paramedic wanted to know if I'd smelt or ingested anything prior to losing consciousness.

'Woodsmoke,' I said.

'Could have been carbon monoxide,' said the paramedic, because medical professionals are willing to spout total bollocks in order to maintain their air of authority. Nothing like us police, who always tell it how it is.

Generally speaking, if you've fallen unconscious for any length of time it's best to go to a hospital for blood tests and shit. So I asked them to take me to UCH. Then I called Guleed and arranged to have her pick up the Hyundai, and then go ahead to the hospital so Dr Walid could meet me in casualty. They were used to our ways there by then, and the casualty registrar didn't blink when Dr Walid ordered up a ton of phlebotomy. He's hoping to get an understanding of the biochemical consequences of my 'encounters', as he calls them. He'd have popped me in the MRI, but it was solidly booked with emergency cases that day.

Bev called me and asked if I wanted her to pick me up. But my mind felt heavy and slow, as if it was waterlogged, and I wanted time to myself. I fell asleep in one of the treatment cubicles and didn't wake up until after midnight, when the first wave of closing time casualties arrived and the unit needed their cubicle back.

I let them check my pupil reaction and blood pressure and then I walked back to the Folly.

I was walking past the quiet darkness of the park in Russell Square when the full implications of what I'd learnt sank in.

Mr Punch was a god.

And Martin Chorley wanted to sacrifice him.

18

The Tea Committee

We held a meeting of the 'Tea Committee' in the upstairs reading room. The Tea Committee consisted of me, Nightingale and other interested parties – in this case Postmartin and Dr Walid – where we thrashed out any policy involving magic. This was part of our agreement with Seawoll to avoid 'distracting' his 'normal' officers from doing their jobs properly.

'I have come to the conclusion,' Seawoll had said during one of the initial planning meetings that set up Operation Jennifer, 'that if we can't ignore it we can at least paint it pink and make it somebody else's problem.'

Dr Vaughan was off on a training course, but Abigail was allowed to be present as long as she kept her mouth shut and took notes.

We quickly reached the consensus that despite Lesley's opinion – that it would make the world a better place – we didn't think anything good was going to come of offing Mr Punch. Especially now we knew he was a god.

'Although wouldn't dealing with Punch in and of itself be a bonus?' asked Dr Walid, who'd spent a gruesome six months working with what was left of his victims the last time the little hook-nosed bastard had made his presence known.

I pointed out that, according to Bev, half the eco-logical disasters in the world occurred when people removed 'pests' or predators without thinking through the consequences.

Nightingale asked for an example, but all I could think of offhand were snakes – which if eliminated lead to a massive increase in rats. Even as I said it, I had a horrible feeling that I'd read it in a fantasy book once – possibly a comical one.

I looked over at Abigail, who tilted her head to one side in a disturbingly Molly-like way and made a note.

'You believe removing Punch might disrupt the . . .' Dr Walid paused to dredge up his medical Greek. '*Eidolonisphere*.'

Nightingale smiled.

'From *Eidolon*,' explained Postmartin. 'Greek for phantom or ghost – indeed quite apropos because it commonly refers to a phantasm or ghost that possessed the living.'

'Eidolosphere scans better,' I said. 'And I don't know what effect it will have, but in any complex system if you change one variable it can cause unpredictable effects throughout that system.'

'Quite,' said Nightingale. 'But this doesn't get us any closer to learning what Martin Chorley wants to happen.'

'We need to find a way to turn Lesley,' I said.

Nightingale sighed.

'Our last attempt in that direction hardly went well,' he said.

'Doesn't matter,' I said. 'If anyone knows what Martin

Chorley is up to, then it's going to be her.'

Nobody round the table liked the idea, but nobody could argue with the logic.

'How?' asked Dr Walid.

'I don't know,' I said. 'But perhaps when she next gets in touch with me I'll just ask for a meeting.'

'You seem very sure she'll be in touch,' said Postmartin.

'Oh, she'll be in touch,' I said. 'If only to complain about us arresting Zach.'

Nightingale gave me a long cool look, but didn't insult me by saying that I shouldn't do anything without checking with him first. After a moment he nodded gravely.

'Yes, ee should make another attempt.' He raised a finger. 'If the opportunity arises.'

Dr Walid wanted to know if there was any literature relating to the death or killing of powerful *genii locorum*. We knew of a couple of incidents for sure – the River Lugg in Herefordshire – 'Done in by Methodists', apparently. And less powerful entities who vanished after their *locus* – pond, house, or in one well-documented case, ship-of-the-line – was destroyed or disrupted.

Postmartin admitted that there was plenty of material as yet uncatalogued, both in the Folly proper and back at the 'special' stacks in Oxford.

'I believe there may be some relevant American material in the Library,' said Nightingale.

'I don't suppose you remember where?' I asked.

Nightingale frowned.

'I'm afraid not,' he said.

'That's going to be a slog.'

We all looked at Abigail, who was smiling a self-satisfied smile at her notebook.

So Postmartin returned to Oxford to rummage through his stacks while Abigail disappeared into the Magical Library, armed only with a notebook, a second-hand laptop and a look of cheerful determination.

I went back to the Outside Inquiry Office and found my in-tray full of actions that had been piling up while I'd been mucking around with metaphysics. The most urgent regarded one Camilla Turner, an archaeologist at MOLA, who had deleted her entire email archive the morning of the raid. One of the analysts in the Inside Inquiry Office had spotted this and flagged it as suspicious. Since wrangling the lost emails out of the ISP would probably involve further permission from the Home Office, it was suggested that I go and restatement Ms Turner in the hope she'd just give us permission to recover them ourselves. I wondered why I was being singled out for this job until I saw the photograph attached to her nominal file and realised that Ms Turner was the skeleton lady I'd met in the MOLA offices.

I gave MOLA a call and found that Camilla Turner hadn't turned up for work that morning, so I got her address off the Inside Inquiry Office and found myself heading for Dalston, where she had the top half of a terrace on Parkholme Road. She'd bought the place in the mid-eighties when it was half derelict and respectable people didn't live in Hackney. As an early pioneer of gentrification she was sitting on a couple of million in housing equity, which she could liberate if only she was willing to move somewhere dire – like Bromley or somewhere outside the M25. Sensibly, she'd decided to stay put.

There was a silver intercom bolted onto the wall beside the front door with, as is usual, no actual names written on the tags by the buzzers. I guessed top button, waited, pressed again, waited, and repeated a couple of times before trying the bottom.

An elderly male voice with a distinctive Caribbean accent asked me what I wanted.

I told him I was the police and that I was concerned about the welfare of his neighbour and if he could just buzz me in I wouldn't bother him any further.

The intercom cut off, then, half a minute later, I heard the front door being manually unlocked from the inside before opening about a quarter of the way to reveal an old black guy.

He was a touch shorter than me, with a cropped Afro that was mostly grey and a matching neatly trimmed beard. He was the light colour some old black guys go, with freckles across his cheeks, a strong jaw and dark suspicious eyes.

He was also strangely familiar.

'What kind of concern exactly?' he asked.

'We think she might be in danger,' I said.

'From whom?'

'Some quite serious criminals.'

'Show me your identification.'

So I got out my warrant card and held it up while he peered at it.

'How come a nice boy like you join the police?'

'I didn't join the police,' I said. 'They joined me.'

He gave this some consideration before nodding and opening the door to let me in.

Crudely carved out of the original Victorian hallway, the atrium was gloomy and overheated. The door to the ground floor flat was ajar while the second, presumably for upstairs, was firmly shut.

I asked the man if he knew whether Camilla Turner was in.

'She came in last night,' he said and then, without another word, retreated behind his own door.

I banged on Camilla's door and yelled her name – no answer.

'Ms Turner,' I called again. 'Camilla – this is Peter Grant from the police – I'm concerned for your safety. Are you in there?'

There was no answer, but I was sure I'd heard something moving on the other side.

I knocked and shouted a couple more times, just so I could write that I had at least tried that before breaking and entering.

Covertly, because I was pretty certain the neighbour was watching me through his peephole, I used an *impello* variant to shear off the latch bolt and swung the door open.

Beyond was a windowless staircase.

And halfway up sat Camilla Turner.

'Hi,' I said brightly.

Camilla stared down at me glumly.

'I knew it was a mistake deleting those emails,' she

said. 'That's how you found me, isn't it?'

I said it was, and she sighed and invited me in.

Once upstairs I gave her the caution plus two, sat her down with a cup of tea and let her incriminate herself.

The flat was pleasantly haphazard and free from the ravages of interior decoration. The collections of books that overran the other rooms had, in the living room, been constrained to a couple of antique glass-fronted bookcases. In between the bookcases, and over the genuine period fireplace, were framed sketches and watercolours, landscapes mostly, interspersed with old photographs of people, singly and in groups. The bay window overlooking the street sported that classic of 1970s interior design, the breezeblock and plank shelf with potted plants ranged across the top and stacks of magazines along the bottom.

I'd loitered in the kitchen doorway while the tea was made, but then let myself be ushered into a wing arm-chair upholstered in eye-watering orange and yellow swirls some time, judging from the worn patches on the arms, in the late eighties.

'I used to live here when it was a squat,' said Camilla. 'Then a bunch of us bought it off the landlord. And then I bought them out one by one.'

It was a vaguely plausible scenario, but it wasn't enough to stop one of our analysts going through her financial history with a nit comb. Even in the 1980s your average young archaeologist would have had diffi-culty raising capital for a house. I knew this because it's one of the things archaeologists will tell you about, at length, at the slightest provocation.

I waited until she had a soothing cup of tea in her hand to ask why she'd deleted her emails.

'I panicked,' she said. 'I heard that they'd given you access to the office intranet.'

'They' being MOLA management.

'But why did that worry you?'

'Because I told them when the New Change material was in the loading bay,' she said.

I asked who 'them' was.

'I thought . . .' she said, and sipped her tea, 'I thought it was the Paternoster Society. But of course I probably knew it wasn't. Really. Better to say it was somebody I met through the Paternoster Society.'

'Does this person have a name?'

'John Chapman,' she said.

I made a note and confirmed that the emails had come from his address.

'When did you get the last email?'

'Tuesday week,' she said. 'That would be the thirtieth.'

I didn't tell her that John Chapman had been dead for almost six months – that sort of stuff you save up if you can, the better to spook the witness later.

'What was your first contact with the . . .' I made a point of checking my notes. 'The Paternoster Society, and who are they?'

'They're a . . . Well, I thought they were a historical society,' she said. 'There are thousands of them all over the country. Ordinary people with a keen interest in history or archaeology. They've been known to conduct some very useful digs – especially these days when funding is tight.'

They'd got in touch with her back when MOLA was still part of the Museum of London proper.

'Originally they recruited me to identify their sword,' she said.

'Which sword was that?' I asked, but was already busily guessing the answer.

'An extraordinarily well-preserved Post-Roman sword that I easily identified as being of Saxon manufacture, possibly fifth or sixth century,' she said. 'Assuming it wasn't a fake of course.'

'What made you think it might be a fake?'

'When I say it was extraordinarily well preserved, I mean it was practically pristine,' she said, and held out her hands as if holding up an invisible sword for my inspection. 'I've certainly never recovered anything myself that well preserved. And it didn't help that the provenance was a bit dodgy. Dug up by an Enlightenment antiquarian – William Winston Galt.'

'Where was it found?'

As if I didn't know.

'Allegedly, during the excavation of a cellar in Paternoster Row in the eighteenth century,' she said.

'Was it genuine?' I asked. 'Could you date it?'

'Well, you can't get a C-14 date from steel and the handle had been rebound – probably in the seventeen hundreds by Galt.'

Antiquarians being notorious romantics and, with some notable exceptions, prone to embellishing their finds to suit their narrative and generally making shit up to suit themselves.

'And in any case leather is rarely used to bind hilts

until the medieval period,' said Camilla.

Fortunately our William had done a characteristically sloppy job, and some of the original handle material had been trapped underneath the new bindings. Antler in this case – from a red deer.

'I know some people at the University of York who've developed a new technique called ZooMS,' she said. 'Stands for ZooArchaeology by Mass Spectrometry. There was just enough to get a result.'

'And what was the date?'

Camilla smiled. 'Fifth century,' she said. 'I still think it's possible it was a hoax, that somebody planted the sample to give a false reading, but I think the likelihood is low.'

Which is as close as you're going to get to certainty from a modern archaeologist.

'What makes you say that?'

'I dated the leather in the later binding and got a date in the seventeen hundreds,' she said. 'So either we must posit that old William Galt somehow anticipated modern carbon dating when assembling his hoax, or that the original binding, and by extension the sword, were authentically fifth century.'

'Or both bindings were added recently using histori-cal materials,' I said.

'Well, yes. As another remote possibility – this is why context is so important.'

But it had *felt* old to Camilla.

And I wondered about that sensation.

'I expected it to get auctioned or be sold to a museum,' said Camilla, 'but John Chapman said they planned a museum of their own. An Arthurian museum, would you believe?'

This made total sense to Camilla because with the right marketing you'd hoover up a substantial portion of the fifteen million foreign tourists that visited London every year. Especially the Americans.

'I read somewhere that two thirds of Americans believe Arthur was a real historical figure,' she said. 'Extraordinarily depressing on one level, but terribly good for business.'

'So you think it's Excalibur?' I asked.

'God, no. Most likely it was forged for a high status Anglo-Saxon and then "sacrificed" in a sacred pool.'

'Once you'd dated the sword, did you continue your relationship with the Paternoster Society?' I asked.

Camilla said that she had, but not in any regular fashion. They'd invite her out for drinks occasionally. John Chapman would seek her opinion on some historical question or other – mostly relating to late antiquity or the Post-Roman period. '"Keeping up with the field," they said.'

'They?'

'Well, John mostly.'

'John Chapman?'

'That's right.'

They'd met in the Rising Sun near Smithfield Market. It was just for a friendly chat, and God knew it was a relief to talk shop with someone who wasn't going on and on about their lack of funding and the scarcity of resources.

'Archaeologists can be tiresome about such things, I'm afraid,' she said.

I nodded absently as I made a note of the pub. The Rising Sun drinking establishment exists right on the fringes of the demi-monde – not being nearly as antique or mysterious as it pretends to be. You wouldn't catch Zach in there, even if he wasn't barred. But it would be the logical watering hole for dilettante practitioners like John Chapman.

'Were you romantically involved?' I asked, which got a short little laugh.

'Nothing like that,' she said.

Which left revenge or money, and I wasn't going to bet on revenge.

'So just drinks then?' I said. 'Nothing else?'

'A free drink is a free drink,' she said. 'And he used to commission work from me.'

I asked what kind of work and she hesitated, took a deep breath and, finally, we were there.

'He wanted inside information about some of the digs.' Camilla picked up her teacup, looked at it for a moment and then put it down. 'Although I didn't understand why he couldn't wait for the reports – it's not like our work is commercially sensitive.'

'Did he seem interested in any particular topic?'

'Late Roman, Post-Roman, early Saxon – Age of Arthur stuff. I assumed he wanted it for his museum.'

'And in return?'

'A bit of a retainer.' She waved her hand dismissively. 'Five hundred quid a month.'

Six grand a year – nice.

'And you didn't get suspicious?'

'I do archaeological rescue work in the City of London.

People there drop a grand on drinks – at lunchtime. So, no, I didn't get suspicious until a bit later.'

'How much later?'

'When I arrived at work to find that someone had driven a truck into the front of the office and nicked the material I'd told John about two days beforehand.' She gave me a crooked smile. 'About then.'

One of the sacred pillars of police work is the timeline, 'when' being as important as 'who' and 'how' if you want to get a conviction. Thus the bulk of most interviews is spent nailing down, at the very least, what order events happened in, and at the very best, dates and times you can corroborate with physical evidence. So you can imagine that the police fell upon texting with cries of joy – ditto emails.

I spent some time, and a second cup of tea, getting a rough timeline off Camilla.

She'd dated the sword in 2010 and started her regular 'chats' with John Chapman in 2011, while I was still arresting drunks and chasing virtual flashers around Covent Garden. About the same time, Mr Chapman was vainly trying to persuade the top lawyers at Bock, Loupe and Stag that they needed to placate the spirit of riot and rebellion by sacrificing goats and spraying blood on each other.

John didn't get back to her until the summer of 2012 – that's when they first met at the Rising Sun and he offered her money for some 'inside information'. That had been just after Covent Garden caught fire and then flooded during an unprecedentedly posh riot. It was also about the same time Patrick Gale was persuaded to take up the mantle of the High Priest of Bacchus/ Dionysus/. . . Mr Punch?

I asked why she'd never connected the site thefts with the information she was handing over and she shrugged.

'I don't even remember those thefts being reported.' she said.

I wasn't sure I believed her, but that detail could wait.

I asked when she'd last met Chapman and she said the spring of the previous year, which accorded with our records of his departure the following June. After that they'd communicated by email.

'He said he'd got a new job that involved a lot of travelling,' she said.

I wondered if John had continued the correspondence from Cleveland prior to his death or whether somebody else had taken over immediately.

Before I called Belgravia to send someone over to pick her up, I asked about the sword.

'You said you felt something when you held the sword?'

'Felt something?'

'You said it felt old,' I said. 'Was that a powerful sensation? Did you feel anything else?

She frowned and gave it some thought.

'Yes, there was a musical tone,' she said. 'Like the sword was singing.'

19

Taming the Wild Frontier

It was while I was helping Camilla into the local IRV for transport back to Belgravia that I realised who her neighbour was. Harry Acworth – who'd played bass guitar with the Clarke-Boland Big Band and had briefly formed a trio with my dad in the late nineties. I'd have to tell my dad when I got a moment, because I was pretty sure he thought Harry was dead.

I told Camilla Turner that everything was going to be fine as long as she co-operated, and sent her off to have Stephanopoulos turn her life inside out. My main worry was that Martin Chorley might take his usual 'direct' approach to operational security, but I had some hope that he might regard Camilla as too unimportant to take the risk. Especially if we kept her stashed at Belgravia.

I got back to the Folly that evening to find that Abigail had gone to sleep on the couch in the reading room – it wasn't the first time.

She'd left her laptop open and around it a sprawl of papers. And, because I'm a nosy bastard, I sat down and had a good shufti. Judging from its position, the last thing she'd been working on was her notebook – open at a page with clusters of words written in Cyrillic.

Varvara and Nightingale had agreed, when teaching

Abigail, to stick to classical Newtonian spell notation, in Latin. But this looked suspiciously like a spell notation to me – the giveaway being фоз in Cyrillic, which I recognised as φῶς or *phos* in Greek. I thought I recognised ἐλαύνω followed by the abbreviation ел in Cyrillic – the notation for *Impello*. This was the notation that Varvara Sidorovna Tamonina had been taught during the Second World War, but following it was another notation which I didn't recognise. It looked like a doodle of ф linked by an upward curving line ел – the line representing the upwards spin you put on *lux* when combining it with *impello* to make a fireball.

Nightingale had been taught to write out in spells in full, using parentheses to indicate which *formae* were affected by which subordinate modifiers. He'd passed that system on to me.

'This way encourages clarity and precision,' he'd said, when I asked if there was a shorthand notation. 'Aim for perfection of form – speed comes later.'

He wasn't going to like this at all.

'My principal concern,' Nightingale had told me, 'is that she will run ahead of herself and put herself in danger.'

We were going to have to have the safety talk again.

I looked up to find Molly staring at me from the other side of the table. I glanced over at Abigail and saw that somebody had covered her with a red and green tartan blanket without me noticing. I looked back at Molly, who tilted her head to the left.

'Her dad's doing nights and her mum is at the hospital with her brother,' I said. 'She's going to text me when they're finished and I'll take her home.'

Molly's eyes narrowed.

'She can't live here,' I said. 'Even if it was allowed, it wouldn't be right.'

Molly gave me a reproachful look, as if that was my fault, then turned and went gliding out the door.

In among Abigail's notes I spotted the initials VGC and the sentence *Montana Territory Campaign 1877.* I had a rummage through the pile of books and found a thin, yellowing pamphlet titled *Devil River* by Robert Sharp. Along the top somebody had paper-clipped a handwritten note on good quality paper that read: *I thought you gentlemen should know how things go in the former colonies.* Signed with the initials RS.

This was probably the American material Nightingale was thinking of. I opened it up and had a look.

Robert Sharp claimed that an – unnamed – participant of the expedition had related the story to him a year after the events portrayed. I personally couldn't tell whether it was totally made up, or a heavily fictionalised account of a true story. Abigail had attached yellow Post-it Notes to strategic passages with references to proper Newtonian practice – although this was referred to in the text as 'proper knowledge', 'true magic' and on one occasion as 'white sorcery'.

The story itself purportedly followed the adventures of a group of bold gentlemen from Virginia, accompanied by scouts and experienced Indian fighters, as they sought out the legendary 'Devil' of Yellowstone River in the Montana Territory. This was somehow in revenge for the death of General George Armstrong Custer at the Battle of Little Bighorn the previous summer.

I was too knackered to get into the story or the personalities, but fortunately Abigail's Post-it Notes indicated the details we'd been looking for. The target was obviously, from the description, a *genius loci* which took the form of a *well-made Chief with a handsome countenance which belied his savage nature.*

The take-down was a classic. The gentlemen from Virginia lured out Yellowstone by formally asking for an audience and then presented him with gifts, including a red hatbox containing the *very spirit of death itself.* As soon as Yellowstone opened the box he was *struck down into a swoon* and while the rest of the company 'held off', i.e. shot the attendant locals, the leader of the Virginians – one Captain Nathanial Buford – stepped forward to deliver the coup de grâce with his pistol. He then *took great pains to recover the red box and its contents even as the fighting raged around him.*

So the sixty-four thousand dollar question – what was in the box?

The very spirit of death itself.

Again Abigail had picked out the clues. Somebody, probably Postmartin, would have to check her work, but on past form I doubted she'd missed anything. The unnamed narrator of *Devil River* was equally curious about its contents, but Captain Buford remained cagey.

On one occasion I thought to touch the box myself only to receive a severe rebuke from the Captain who called me a "D— fool!" And asked if I did not feel the evil contained within. I admitted that I had felt only a strange chill.

Buford tells the narrator that anything capable of

rendering a devil senseless would make short work of a man. But when the narrator presses him as to what that thing might be, he replies only that it is an evil brought over from a corrupt and degenerate Europe: *An infection of the old world that we have bent to God's purpose.*

'Infection' was written on the Post-it Note which marked the page.

There were two more references to infection in the book, including one that made reference to inoculation as a simile, which only proved that neither the narrator nor Captain Buford knew how inoculation worked. Or the difference between a metaphor and a simile, for that matter.

A page ripped from her notebook marked this passage and had written on it – *infection, cold, drain of power,* tactus disvitae, *vampires.*

And then, underneath:

Weaponized vampires?

I idly corrected the *z* in weaponised and then realised what I'd done.

I've been spending way too much time with librarians, I thought.

I made a note to action a scan of *Devil River* so I could send a copy to Reynolds, along with Abigail's conclusions. Also a query to Postmartin to see if he could find similar American material in the Oxford stacks.

Abigail rolled over in her sleep and said somebody's name – I think it was Simon, whoever that was – and then subsided.

Nightingale had once told me that the Germans had carried out experiments to weaponise vampirism during World War Two. Maybe they'd got the idea from the Americans. Or maybe everyone had tried it – although Nightingale denied that the British had.

And that research was probably sitting less than fifteen metres below me, hidden behind some face-hardened steel and God knew what kind of magical defences. The Black Library, the poisoned fruit of the raid on Ettersberg, with the details of the genocidal experiments carried out by the *Ahnenerbe* in an attempt to change the course of the war.

'It didn't help the fascists,' Varvara said once. 'There's nothing in there that would be any use to you.'

Still, you had to wonder.

My phone pinged – Abigail's mum was heading home from Great Ormond Street.

'Hey,' I said to Abigail. 'Wake up – time to go home.'

20

A Slave's Flattery

The next day I spent the morning going through Camilla Turner's email archive. I started by identifying as many of her contacts as possible to add to her nominal file – I did a preliminary cross-check against her colleagues at MOLA and requested that the Inside Inquiry Office run them through the PNC to see if anything nefarious popped out. Then I checked through all the messages from John Chapman's email address. There was no obvious difference in the writing style between the early emails and the ones sent after he was shot to death in Cleveland.

Then I went hunting with a variety of keyword searches: *Dark Ages* and various spellings of *sub-* and *post-Roman*, which turned up in three quarters of the emails – so no real help there. I had more luck with *Excalibur*. Here there were a couple of exchanges where Chapman was pushing the Saxon sword-in-the-lake theory. There were similar discussions around the historicity of Arthur and Merlin, but nothing about Lancelot. Presumably because he was too French.

And, probably because I was spooked by Abigail's discovery the night before, I tried 'Genius Loci' and the names of the rivers. The results were sparse and mostly related to digs located near watercourses. But one exchange caught my eye.

>I'm curious did you ever find offerings to a tutelary spirt associated with the river walbrook

Nothing that indicates a specific religious ceremony but it can be hard to separate offerings from lost items and outright rubbish.

And then, on the next exchange, 'John' makes a point of asking Camilla to keep a look out for evidence. And again in the next email he offers a bonus if she can point him in the right direction. The overture is much more blatant than previous requests and since Chapman was dead by this point I had to assume that the request was coming, directly or indirectly, from Martin Chorley.

I tagged the exchange and linked it to the prep notes for Camilla's upcoming interview. Guleed was taking it that afternoon, so she might find it a useful angle of approach. Multiple angles of approach being what we use nowadays as a replacement for proffered cigarettes and/or physical intimidation.

He liked to fling a wide net, did our Martin Chorley. From magically inclined lawyers to cash-strapped archaeologists. From predatory development firms to old-fashioned criminal gangs. But what the fuck was it all in aid of? Even Carey, who took a more results-orientated approach to policing, wanted to know that.

Kill Punch and use the released potential magic to . . . what? Take over the world? The city? The Tri-State area?

Cover all the world in a second darkness?

I finished up a couple of minor actions that mostly involved phoning confused archaeologists and asking them whether they knew a certain John Chapman or the Paternoster Society. And had anyone approached them asking for details about the London Mithraeum dig? Which netted a ton of names, including journalists and a couple of 'nutters' – the archaeologist's word not mine – who claimed to be practising Mithraists and wanted support to claim back their temple from Bloomberg.

'Good luck with that,' the archaeologist had told them. 'Let me know how it works out.'

The mystery cultists had never come back but I got their names off the archaeologist and made a note. I also got a contact address which sparked my interest because it was on Carter Lane – right next to St Paul's. So, after a couple of hours of mixed training and a shower I grabbed the Hyundai and headed for the City.

I let the City Police know I was prowling around on their patch and parked up in Dean's Court. The address turned out to be the St Paul's Youth Hostel, which sits in the Square Mile like an ideal from an earlier age. It's a surprisingly large late Victorian building which takes up almost a block just south of the cathedral. That this potential exciting new retail and office development was currently occupied by the Youth Hostel Association was probably a source of psychic pain for every right-thinking developer that walked past it.

They hung the YHA flag from a short pole over the front door just to rub in.

Inside the walls were painted all cheerful reds and

blues with sturdy modern fittings and corkboards smothered in flyers and personal messages.

At the reception desk was a cheerful Asian guy in a red sweatshirt who, once I'd made it clear I wasn't there to arrest him, or anyone else, fell over himself to be helpful. Back when I was less experienced I'd have found that behaviour suspicious but now I know it's actually how most of the public behaves when the constabulary drops unexpectedly into their lives.

He introduced me to his manager, a short white guy called Daniel, who explained that the Paternoster Society did indeed rent a section of the building known as the annexe.

'I always thought it was a strange arrangement,' he said. 'We could have used that space to expand. But every time I brought up the subject I was told that there was an "arrangement".'

He assumed that the rent was still being paid, because they hadn't been evicted, but said that the whole thing was above his pay grade. I got him to give me the name of his supervisor – presumably the person at the correct pay grade – and mentally actioned a financial search to see where the money was coming from. According to Special Constable Nguyễn, the deliberate complexity that shields businesses from investigation can backfire.

'They get so confusing that the perpetrators lose track of their own assets,' she'd said over drinks after a training session. 'All it takes is one forgotten string and you can unravel the whole scheme.'

The moral of that story being never run a game of

Hide the Lady if you can't remember where you've put the queen, because some people embrace forensic accounting as a blood sport.

The supervisor showed me around to a side door which opened to reveal a staircase going straight up two floors. The lack of a hallway was a key indicator that it had been retrofitted into the original building, but the high quality hardwood skirting board and the finished quality of the riser suggested that the refit dated from the 1930s. The energy saving bulb that dangled from a cord overhead was still warming up, so the blue painted walls looked faded and grey.

I asked the supervisor to give me the keys and stay at the bottom of the stairs.

The youth hostel, according to its website, had been built as a school for St Paul's choirboys. Which might explain the faint sense of soprano singing and nervous wee that I got when I brushed the walls of the staircase with my hand on the way up. At the top was another exterior style panelled door with a Chubb lock – fortunately one of the keys fitted, so I didn't have to cut that.

Just to be on the safe side I pushed the door open with my extendable baton and checked the threshold for tripwires, light cells and demon traps. The floor was a scuffed herringbone parquet that desperately needed polishing. The wood was a light brown and there were no obvious patterns of discolouration or stains to mark where a booby trap might go. Once I was sure the floor wasn't going to kill me, I paused in the doorway to have a look around.

It looked old, but felt off. And at first I couldn't tell

why. It was a high-ceilinged first floor room with large sash windows sealed with internal wooden shutters. I cautiously left the lights off as I crossed the shadowy room, lifted the latch and opened the first of the shutters. The furniture was antique, nineteenth century and early twentieth century walnut tables and the sort of overstuffed armchairs that littered the Folly. A series of glass-fronted bookshelves lined two walls while the remaining wall space was taken up with a random collection of prints and paintings, mostly views of St Paul's and surrounding streets and a big reproduction of Sir James Thornhill's 1712 portrait of Sir Isaac Newton. I recognised it because we have a reproduction of the same painting in the lecture room back at the Folly. The great man is wearing his own hair for a change and without his wig he looks scrawny, vexed and a dead ringer for Ian McDiarmid in *Revenge of the Sith* – just before Samuel L. Jackson rearranges his face for him. Underneath was a plaque inscribed with the words:

Gravity explains the motions of the planets, but it cannot explain who sets the planets in motion.

Which was when I realised what was troubling me. The room was like a bad copy of the Folly, done up by somebody who'd been there a couple of times and fancied the ambience.

I noticed a glass-fronted case mounted on the wall opposite the Newton portrait. It was made of dark mahogany varnished to a warm glow. The sort of thing where you might display a large fish. I looked inside. It was empty and there was a silver strip with the words *IN CASE OF BRITAIN'S GREATEST NEED – BREAK GLASS.*

Not a fish, then – a sword. And three guesses which one.

I pulled on my evidence gloves and did a quick rummage through the drawers and bookcases. There wasn't much in the way of dust; the corners had been swept regularly and there were no spiderwebs in the corners or between the bookcases and the walls. Somebody, and I doubted it was the people who thought that an Excalibur joke was funny, had cleaned the place regularly.

We did track her down later – a Romanian woman who insisted her name was Lana Stacey – but she'd had her own key and always cleaned first thing Saturday morning. She'd never met any of the members of the Paternoster Society. Neither had any of the youth hostel staff.

There were obvious gaps on the shelves where books had been removed, either singly or in groups. There was a lot of archaeology and history. Mostly what Postmartin calls the 'barbarian wave' school of historiography. I called him in Oxford and sent him some pictures – he said he would be down that afternoon. Then I contacted Nightingale and the Inside Inquiry Office in case they thought it worth sending a forensic team over. I doubted it, but you never know.

I cautiously touched the case where the sword had probably been kept.

I couldn't sense anything, but wood is terrible at retaining *vestigia*.

Geoffrey of Monmouth wrote that Arthur would return.

What if he needed a bit of help?

Was that what Martin Chorley was about?

I kept my eye on the case and phoned Isis.

'Peter,' she said when she picked up. 'What a lovely surprise. You're not phoning to cancel tomorrow, are you? Oxley would be devastated – you know how he likes to tell you his stories. Especially now that he's worn them out up here.'

'Nah, we're still on,' I said. 'Barring emergencies. I wondered whether you'd had a chance to talk to the Old Man yet?'

'Oh,' said Isis, sounding surprised. 'That. Has that become important?'

I looked over at the empty sword case and the inscription below it and said that I thought it might have done.

'I'll pop over and have a chat before we head down to meet you,' she said.

After the call I opened the shutters on one of the windows. They looked north over a courtyard and beyond that, rearing over the roofs opposite, was the white dome of St Paul's.

21

A l'ombre des jeunes rivières en crue

The next day Isis and Oxley were coming down to London for an evening performance of *La Bohème* at the Royal Opera House. We'd decided ages ago that we'd meet up for drinks beforehand and for some reason we ended up in the Punch and Judy Tavern in Covent Garden Market.

'It's amazing how little damage the fire did,' said Oxley.

The balcony ran along the middle of the west end of the market building and faced the east portico of St Paul's Church where, incidentally, I had met my first ghost. It's also famously the last resting place of many celebrated luvvies, and is thus known as the Actors' Church. Which serves to distinguish it from its larger, more famous, namesake.

'That's because Beverley here put it out,' said Isis.

'Yeah,' I said. 'The water damage was worse than the fire damage.' Beverley kicked me under the table. 'Also, this is a solid brick building. So the structure remained intact.'

Half the shops had changed, though.

Apple had taken the opportunity to put in their iBar

and the new money had scrubbed away some of the character.

Isis frowned.

'You don't mind coming here, do you?'

I assured her I didn't and explained that this was where I'd done my probation, arrested my first drunk and solved my first investigation. Kissed Beverley for the first time, too – well, that was up the road at Seven Dials, but still.

There were other memories – the ruin of Lesley's face and the realisation that I was too late. Nearly getting myself hanged on stage and Seawoll clothes-lining me in the Floral Hall Bar. And Beverley floating above me with the firelight refracting through the water before she swept it away with the wave of a hand.

And that was just the first half of the year.

Because I was, amazingly enough, off shift I managed to have my first guilt-free pint for ages. Although my phone was still on and Nightingale had told me to stay upright if at all possible.

'I don't like it, Peter,' he'd said after the morning briefing. 'It's all too complicated. Chorley has proved masterful at deceiving us in the past and I fear a great deal of what we're finding is part of an elaborate ruse. What Varvara would call a *maskirovka*.'

He wanted us to stay open-minded and alert.

And I really wanted that pint.

'Fleet was well pissed off,' said Beverley.

'As well she might be,' said Oxley.

There was an East Asian woman doing street magic in front of the portico. From the balcony I could see the way the crowd formed up around her. She was good, catching individuals' eyes, flirting with the teenagers and getting the younger kids excited by flicking her cards palm to palm like a juggler. When she did something clever you could see the surprise and excitement ripple out through the people around her.

The crowd goes one way and the thief goes the other way. They're excited, he's careful. They're relaxed, he's tense. And even if I hadn't known him by name I would have spotted him for the career pickpocket he was.

'Freddy,' I shouted down from the balcony.

He looked up. I waved. It took a moment for him to recognise me, then he looked frantically around to see if a couple of response officers were closing in on him. When he didn't spot any, he gave me a surly look.

I made a throat cutting motion and pointed south towards the Strand.

Freddy hesitated but the implication was clear – if he made me come down there and arrest him it was going to go very hard indeed. Finally he shrugged and slouched off – northwards, I noticed, the opposite of where I'd pointed.

I turned back to find the others staring at me.

'Pickpocket,' I said.

Beverley shook her head and Oxley laughed.

'Well spotted,' said Isis. 'You're not going to leave us and give chase, are you?'

I said that fortunately in these degenerate modern times such things were not necessary. Then I got my phone out and texted Inspector Neblett, my former shift commander, and let him know that our old mate

Frederick William Cotton was obviously out of prison again. Probably now planning to work Oxford Street.

I refocused as the waitress brought the second round of drinks. I had another gloriously guilt-free pint. Oxley had something called a Brewdog Vagabond Pale Ale, which came in a bottle and which he claimed never to have tasted before.

'I'm trying new things,' he said.

Including a new suit in khaki chambray that had either been tailored deliberately baggy or had once belonged to someone else. Isis was similarly smartly turned out in a burgundy floor-length dress and matching jacket with cream buttons. I did mention that the opera had got a lot more informal since they last attended, which didn't seem to bother Isis at all.

'Well, I dress to please myself,' said Isis, and clinked glasses with Beverley.

'And I dress to please my love,' said Oxley.

They all looked at me.

'I dress to project an aura of confident authority,' I said.

'Not to please your goddess?' said Oxley.

'We much prefer the pair of you as nature intended,' said Isis.

'In which case,' said Oxley, putting down his drink, 'your wish is my command.'

He started stripping off his jacket and was only stopped when Isis grabbed his hand.

'Don't you dare,' she said.

'Are they not as fickle as the wind?' said Oxley. 'And as changeable as the sea.'

'I'm not going anywhere near that, mate,' I said, and Isis asked Beverley what she planned to do with her degree.

'I've still got another year,' said Beverley.

Down in the Piazza the street magician had given way to a small white man in a shabby suit and a top hat. I felt a moment of unease until he pulled out a yellow balloon and started comically failing to make an animal out of it. He did his patter in a broad West Country accent that had nothing to do with the skeleton army or the cruel streets of nineteenth-century London.

'I was thinking of going into flood management,' said Beverley.

'Isn't that cheating?' asked Isis.

'I like to think of it more as offering a unique insight.'

'The insight being that they pay you money and you don't flood their back gardens?' said Isis.

Beverley denied the extortion aspect, although she admitted that she might end up having to extract some promises from her sisters if she did work in the lower Thames.

'Which reminds me,' said Isis. 'When are Nicky and Brent coming up to visit?'

'Are you sure you want them back?' I asked. 'After what happened last time?'

Oxley waved away any problems.

'After all,' he said. 'Who hasn't capsized a boat when they were young?'

'And I was asked to ask if Abigail might come up before school starts again,' said Isis. 'We'd love to have her for a week or two.'

I thought of all that chatting late at night and the sound of the tent zipping up.

'Asked by who?' I asked.

'See how he bristles?' said Oxley. 'Ever vigilant of his sister's honour.'

'Not my sister,' I said, which the others seemed to find hilarious.

I said I'd check with her parents, but I already knew they'd say yes. They were horribly trusting, and worse, held me responsible. My dad said that this would be a good preview of life with my own children, but what he thought he might know about it I don't know.

Oxley asked if we were eating and Beverley did the honours – summoning up a startled looking white guy in a blue pinstripe shirt, who I sincerely hoped was bar staff and not some random member of the public. We've talked about the ethics of this, but she does like to show off in front of her country cousins.

Anyway, whoever the guy was, fish and chips and steak and ale pie arrived pretty damn quick. Oxley turned out to be a surprisingly dainty eater and at one point Beverley nudged me and told me to stop embarrassing her in public. But, I mean, if you can't eat battered cod with your fingers, how should you eat it?

'Patience,' said Isis. 'It only took me a couple of hundred years to stop my darling from farting at the table.'

I pointed out that Beverley had her own bad habits, such as leaving her wetsuits lying around the living room.

'While still wet,' I said. 'Not to mention that time you

climbed into bed in the middle of the night still wearing it.'

'I was going out again in a minute,' said Beverley. 'I didn't want all the hassle of putting it back on.' Not even after she'd kissed me awake.

Isis and Oxley, who both made a point of swimming unabashedly naked, gave me an interested look, which I ignored. My dad says that a gentleman never tells and my mum says *nor tel me business to other person* despite being quite happy to tell my business to a non-trivial proportion of London's Sierra Leonean population. I decided it was time to change the subject, so I asked Isis if she'd had a chance to ask Father Thames about King Arthur.

'Ha,' said Isis. 'Yes, I did. Although I think I should have listened to my husband.'

'I warned you it would be a pretty riddle,' said Oxley.

'I couldn't speak to its beauty, but it was in Latin.' Isis asked me if I was sure I wanted to hear it. 'Often times the answer is not worth the question.'

'Nice,' said Beverley. 'I'll remember that one.'

'I'll take the risk,' I said.

'*Dicito praeconi lucis*,' said Isis.

'*lucis*' I recognised but '*praeconi*' I didn't know.

'Something of the morning?' I asked.

'Herald,' said Oxley. 'Herald of the morning – that's you, by the way.'

'I thought I was a starling,' I said.

'*And* the herald of the morning,' said Isis.

'I thought the herald of the dawn was the rooster.'

'Do you want to hear the rest or not?'

'Sorry.'

'Dicito praeconi lucis,' she said. *'Si pontem ad urbem servandam dissolvet, praemium suum exilium erit.'*

'Should I *dissolvo* the bridge?'

Even as I said it, I remembered the feel of the ghost spear in my hand, the feel of the impact as I drove it through the chest of Punch and pinned him to the decking of the first London Bridge.

A ghost spear, a dream Punch, a memory of London's past.

Praemium suum exilium erit.

His reward will be exile.

'Peter?' said Beverley – they were all staring at me.

'I don't fancy exile,' I said.

'That's your actual prophecy, that is,' said Oxley. 'You'd better watch out.'

Because when you find the hand of destiny on your shoulder, the proper London response is to deny you're the one she's looking for.

'What, me, guv?' I said.

22

What You Were Supposed to Do

You don't have to tell a police officer that life can go sideways with no warning. But knowing this is one thing, and getting a phone call from Lesley while I was halfway through a smoked kipper is another.

'Shut up, Peter, and listen,' she said – which was harsh, given I hadn't said anything yet.

'Go,' I said.

'Martin's going to do something stupid. He's going to run an experimental sacrifice.'

'Jesus Christ, Lesley, you've—' I began, but Lesley talked right over me.

'I don't know who the subject's going to be,' she said. 'But he said that the city had enough rivers already and nobody was going to miss one.'

I went cold at that.

'Anything else?' I asked.

'Just that,' said Lesley.

'Was he playing you?'

'Do me a favour,' she said, and cut the call.

It's just as well that Nightingale insists that we all dress for breakfast, because we were down the stairs and out the back into the Portakabin in under sixty seconds.

Nightingale called Oxley and I called Beverley first and Lady Ty second.

'How credible is this?' she asked.

'Credible,' I said. 'Can you alert everyone else?'

She said she would, and then get back to me with the dispositions.

After I put the phone down I called Stephanopoulos and alerted her, then Jaget Kumar at BTP and finally, because it had been a contact with Lesley, DI William Pollock at the DPS.

Once we were sure everyone had been warned, we went back upstairs to finish our breakfast.

'There's no point rushing around on an empty stomach,' said Nightingale.

Well, he finished *his* breakfast . . . I wasn't hungry any more.

'This could be another trap,' he said, tucking his napkin back into his collar.

I said I didn't think so – if only because the clues to a trap would have to be clearer.

'Another distraction, then?'

'Maybe,' I said, and sat down.

There was still some toast so I buttered a bit and had that, because it was either toast or my fingernails.

The last time Martin Chorley had gone after one of the Rivers, his assassin had got a metre of metaphysical steel through his chest and Chorley himself had been swept away by a bijou urban tsunami.

And that was when Lady Ty hadn't known he was coming.

I almost wanted him to have another go, because it

would save us a lot of time and effort if someone – say, Fleet – were to vigorously defend herself to the point of saving the criminal justice system a ton of paperwork.

But then I remembered the Yellowstone and the weaponised vampirism and the dead John Chapman's sudden interest in the Walbrook. I called Beverley on my mobile.

'Hi, babes,' she said. 'Suddenly we're all at Mum's.'

'Is anybody covering Walbrook?' I asked.

I heard her asking about – in the background the football, 'Prisoner' by the Weeknd, and an all-comers junior Rivers shouting contest were attempting to drown each other out. While she was doing that I walked back up to my room and dug out my undercover Metvest. This is just an ordinary Metvest, only with a beige pocketless nylon cover instead of the blue one that goes with the uniform. Wearing it makes you about as inconspicuous as a silver Astra parked outside a youth centre, but I've come to find the sensation of wearing a rigid plastic tank top strangely comforting.

Down the phone I could hear Brent threatening to flood the living room unless she got the next go on the games console, and I was quite curious to see if she'd follow through, but Beverley came back on line to tell me that no one had thought to check on Walbrook.

'She never has anything to do with us,' she said.

It was Guleed's day off so I scooped up Carey from the breakfast room, and while he was digging up *his* Metvest I went to confer with Nightingale in the incident room.

'At the very least you can warn her,' said Nightingale.

'Sahra's on her way in. Once she's here we'll head over to St Paul's and use that as a staging post.'

'You think the cathedral is important?' I asked.

Nightingale tapped the point on the whiteboard where arrows from John Chapman and the Paternoster Society converged on a crude picture of the dome of St Paul's.

'It keeps coming up in the investigation,' he said. 'However, more germane to today's operation is that it's a good central location. From there I'll be in a position to support you and David or deploy somewhere else should the need arise.'

'What's to stop him going up the river, or somewhere else entirely?' I asked.

'Word, as they say, is out,' said Nightingale. 'Lady Ty and Oxley have been using their national contacts and even small fry like your friend Chester are now covered. And all his behaviour in the last year has centred around the City in one way or another.' He tapped the whiteboard again and frowned.

'Yes,' he said. 'Walbrook – I'll feel better when you're there.'

I made sure we had a couple of screamers in the nondescript Rover before we pulled out. Then I interpreted Nightingale's impatience as assigning an A Grade to the shout, stuck on the blues and twos as we cleared the gates and were doing a brisk, but totally within guidelines, forty mph before I hit Theobalds Road.

'Is there something I should know?' asked Carey, as he braced himself against the dash.

I explained as best as I could while swerving around

deaf commuters and suicidal white van drivers, although I left out the metaphysics and concentrated on the policing.

'We think Chorley might try and off one of Lady Ty's sisters,' I said.

'Is that the one with the pub in Shoreditch?' asked Carey, showing that he did actually stay awake in the briefings – he must have been the only one below the rank of inspector who did.

'That's the one,' I said.

'If that's the case, why are we going and not Nightingale?'

Definitely staying awake during the briefings.

'Because . . .' I started, and then paused to say a little prayer as we crossed the course of the Fleet at Farringdon. 'Because we don't know for sure.'

I didn't need to tell anyone as well briefed as Carey that Chorley loved a bit of bait and switch.

'Oh, I get it,' he said with surprising cheerfulness. 'We're the canaries.'

There's no avoiding the Old Street Roundabout, so I powered up Clerkenwell Road and hoped for the best. Which turned out to be quite good, except for an ancient Ford Fiesta who couldn't seem to get the hang of how roundabouts worked, and swerved right across our path. Carey swore and wrote down the vehicle index.

Then we accelerated up the eastern half of Old Street, then down Rivington Street, which, in case you don't know, turns into a one-way street going the other way. But I felt my cause was just, so down the wrong way we went. And luckily only one poor sod was driving the right way. He panicked, swerved and, we discovered later, managed to hit one of the bollards placed on Rivington Street for just that purpose. We squeaked past and went right on Curtain Road.

By now India 99 was overhead and was reporting anything untoward and Nightingale was mobile. I switched off the lights and siren and gently turned into New Inn Yard. Ahead we could see the railway bridge and the faded pub sign.

As we got closer I couldn't spot any suspicious activity.

'I don't see anything,' said Carey, and reported that to Nightingale, who said in which case he was going to proceed to St Paul's as we'd planned.

As we pulled up, Carey said that after my driving he was owed a drink. I was just about to say he wanted to be cautious about any pint he drank in that particular pub . . . except that suddenly everything got rather confusing.

As we reconstructed events later, Martin Chorley had obviously got hold of the Virginia Gentlemen's playbook of total bastardness and started on page one. His packaged evil in a can arrived at the Goat and Crocodile with the regular weekly beer delivery. This was a surprise, not least because I was amazed to find that the Goat and Crocodile had enough customers to justify a regular weekly delivery in the first place.

All Martin had to do was wait outside until he was sure Walbrook had been incapacitated before moving in. He'd obviously learnt his lesson from his abortive attack on Lady Ty, because he came mob-handed just in case things didn't go strictly to plan. Which of course they didn't, because me and Carey turned up at just that point.

The first we knew of it was when the front façade of the Goat and Crocodile came screaming across the street and into the side of our car. All I'm going to say is that it was a good thing it wasn't the Jag.

For a moment I thought it was just us getting closer to the pub, but then my brain registered that the angles were all wrong – and in any case we'd practically stopped. I knew right then that the only suspect who could throw a wall like that was Chorley, and that he must be in the pub. I also knew, in a strange coldly amused way, that that information was totally useless. I think I gave the mental command to my body to duck – but before any useful muscle groups moved, the front of the pub hit the side of my car.

As I said, after that things got confusing.

Suddenly the airbag was as big as an elephant but I'm swinging sideways against my seatbelt as the car flips over. I hear Carey swearing and I'm thinking that thank God the pub was made out of piece-of-shit cement sections and not bricks. I'm also thinking that if he's smart Martin Chorley's not going to wait for the car to stop moving before hitting us with his follow-up.

I had thought we were going to roll over, but the roof slammed into the good solid Victorian brick of the railway arch and my head whiplashed in the other direction as the car bounced back onto its wheels. Despite the ringing in my ears, I had my belt off and the door open before the suspension had settled, and I rolled out. I staggered to my feet with a screamer in my left hand

and my right extended and my shield up.

Ahead of me the Goat was missing its front façade and the interior was blown to matchwood. Bizarrely, only the solid antique bar remained standing – but it was on fire. I couldn't see any hostile movement and, more importantly, no casualties. Careful to keep my shield up and angled towards the pub, I threw the screamer down the street and turned and ducked down to see if Carey was all right. The passenger door was open and the seat was empty.

'David?' I called.

'Get under cover, you pillock,' he shouted back from behind the car.

It seemed a sensible idea, so I dashed around the back and into the gap between it and the archway. Carey was tucked in there with his back against the car, his face grey and his feet against the wall.

'Are you all right?' I asked as I joined him.

'No,' he said. 'I'm fucking not.'

'What's wrong?'

'I'm fed up.'

I grinned with relief.

'It's not fucking funny,' he said.

I said I'd go and assess the situation if he checked for casualties in the pub.

Carey gave a pained grunt and then said, 'After you.'

I checked my Airwave and found, amazingly, that it was still working. I told Stephanopoulos, who was currently running the op from Belgravia, about my plan. She told me to be careful and that Nightingale was less than five minutes out. I seriously considered just staying where I was but then I heard a van start up. I shuffled to the end of the car and had a look around the back, just in time to see a genuine antique Mark I Transit van resprayed in Prussian blue pull out from behind the ruins of the Goat and Crocodile and make a ponderous turn to the east on New Inn Yard.

I knew from my last visit that fifty metres further east New Inn Yard hit Anning Street. The south turn was a cul-de-sac and beyond the crossing New Inn Yard became bicycle only and was blocked off by a trio of cast-iron bollards. The only way the transit van could go was north up Anning Sreet, and Stephanopoulos had just told me the Incident Response Vehicle had blocked that route off.

Leaving Carey to check the pub, I took off up the street after the van, which was gunning its short-arse two-litre V4. An old-fashioned engine in a carefully chosen old-fashioned van with no chip-controlled fuel injection that a slightly desperate young Detective Constable could disable with magic. Chorley, the bastard, had probably chosen it for just that reason.

I was wondering if I could fireball the rear tyres, but tyres are difficult – small, hard to hit, and if you do burst them you've turned the vehicle into a couple of tons of random destruction.

I gained ground as the van slowed and I expected it to go left and be blocked by the approaching IRV, but instead it ploughed forward onto the cycle track. Something black and solid and about a metre long flew up and over the van – tumbling lazily to crash into the road behind it. I recognised it as the sort of solid metal bollard councils use to block traffic from cycle lanes and pedestrianised streets. The van practically stopped while Chorley dealt with the two remaining bollards. As the second thudded into the tarmac I got close enough to fling a handful of fireballs at the left rear tyre – all of which bloody missed. Although I think I got someone's attention, because the third bollard came scything right at me at head height. I dropped and heard it bounce on the roadway behind me with a strange hollow *boing* sound.

The van lurched forward even as I was getting to my feet and I thought it was going to get away when it suddenly ground to a halt again. Later we determined that the back axle had caught on a spur of concrete created when one of the bollards was ripped up.

The van's left rear door opened and I caught sight of Martin Chorley crouched in the back, and behind him a young woman slumped against the van wall, arms extended forward as if chained at the wrist, a look of agony on her face. It was Walbrook.

Chorley leant to out to see what his van was caught on. I was tempted to throw everything I had at him while he wasn't looking, but I couldn't risk it with a hostage just behind him.

Still, I was gaining enough to be wondering what the hell I was going to do when I got there. I'm getting better at magic, but Chorley was in the Nightingale-weight class. And although he'd promised Lesley he wouldn't kill me, there were many unpleasant things he might do short of that.

Setting my clothes on fire for a starter.

Chorley gave me a disgusted look and waved his hand. I flinched but I wasn't the target. Instead, the back of the van lifted half a metre off the ground and the whole thing lurched forward half a length before the rear dropped back onto its wheels.

Chorley gave a mocking salute, the rear doors closed and the van accelerated away. There was supposed to be another bollard where the cycle path met Shoreditch High Street but it seemed to have vanished in the excitement. Bizarrely, the van driver signalled before turning left. As it disappeared I saw half a dozen pedestrians hugging the wall, including a cycle courier.

The courier, a young black guy in blue and red lycra, stared at me in incomprehension as I bore down on him frantically waving my warrant card and yelling, 'Police, police, I need your bike!'

He shifted his grip on the handlebars and for a moment I thought he was going to fight me for it, but then he stepped back to hold it at arm's length and give me unimpeded access.

Thank God the bike was a hybrid, not a racer, and didn't have toecaps, because I didn't have time for adjustments as I grabbed it and launched myself after the van. I think I might have said thank you but I can't remember.

Ahead, the van had done a classic dash and stop, getting a hundred metres up the road before being blocked by a 149 bus going north and a lorry coming south. I saw it give an uncertain wiggle as the driver looked for a way around. I could hear India 99 overhead, which meant that Seawoll, Stephanopoulos and probably half the Met were watching the van in real time.

I wondered what they thought of yours truly, pedalling madly up behind it.

And where did Chorley think he was going? He must have known that once we had air support and assets with eyeballs on him there wasn't any getting away. I started to worry about India 99. Chorley had form trying to shoot down helicopters, and I know for a fact that Nightingale downed a couple of planes during World War Two.

I leant forward and stepped hard on the pedals, hoping to catch up when the van hit the inevitable traffic jam further up the road. As I did so, there was a ripping sound and I felt both shoulders of my jacket go loose and start to slip down my arms – I'd managed to tear the back of my jacket. As I struggled to flap the sleeve off my left arm, an IRV screamed past me with sirens and lights on. I learnt later that they were responding to a different shout and that CCC hadn't alerted them in time to reroute. Chorley obviously didn't know that, because I glanced up just in time to see the IRV's bonnet go fluttering into the air and a dirty yellow ball of fire erupt from its engine.

They don't let you drive an IRV until you know how to crash it safely and the vehicle went into a textbook emergency stop. I swerved around it and held my breath as I passed through the curtain of oily smoke coming off the engine. I felt the heat on my face and smelt smoke as I risked a quick look back to make sure the response officers had managed to bale. They had, and one of them even had a fire extinguisher on the go.

Collateral damage, I realised suddenly. That was how Chorley was going to ditch us. Create enough mayhem to make us draw back, and then shift to a second vehicle. He might even have minions already cruising in for a pickup.

His next logical step would be to pick off a bus or something equally high value.

My Airwave was totally dusted, but I had to assume that Nightingale was on his way.

Which meant all I had to do was distract Chorley for long enough for that to happen.

I think it's important to state that what happened next was totally an accident and I really do not recommend it to anyone in a similar situation. I'd got within three metres of the van, and the angle was wrong to hit the tyres so I used an *impello* variant to pull the bloody doors off.

Not an easy thing to do when you're pedalling your guts out, I might add.

I reckoned this would distract Chorley from any notions about creating general mayhem and focus his attention on me, although admittedly I didn't have a plan of what to do when he did. I can't be expected to think of everything, can I?

As the doors clanged onto the tarmac on either side of me I tried to accelerate, anticipating that the van would speed up – only for the driver to slam the brakes on. I just might have been able to swerve to the left or right, but I didn't think of it at the time. Instead I have a very clear memory of the interior of the van growing suddenly closer as my front wheel hit the rear bumper and I went over the handlebars and into the back.

The side door was half open and Martin Chorley was crouched beside it. He'd obviously been in the process of opening it when I'd ripped the back doors off, and had half turned to see what the hell was going on. He was dressed for an afternoon's gardening at his place in the country, jeans, open neck shirt, tweed sports jacket with elbow patches. I shall treasure the look of dismayed surprise on his face as he found me flying towards him until my dying day. Which almost turned out to be thirty seconds later.

Walbrook was still flattened against the side wall, but now I could see that she was wrapped in chains that were fastened to a cargo rack mounted behind her. Her wrists were chained together and attached by a short length to a purple and white octagonal Quality Street sweet tin, sealed with gaffer tape and wrapped like a Christmas present with a thin bicycle chain. The whole assemblage was attached by a thicker chain to an eyelet welded to the roof.

Her clothes were torn and her eyes were closed, and she was breathing hard, as if in pain.

There was no partition, so I could see through to the driver – although all I got was the sense that he was white and had grey hair in a number two trim – before I smacked face down on the cold metal floor of the van. Chorley came for me and I grabbed the chain attaching the tin to the ceiling to pull myself up.

It was like grabbing a steam pipe. Pain, followed by a shocking numbness.

I screamed and yanked my hand away, which ironically

meant that the vicious kick Chorley had aimed at my head went whooshing past my ear. I tried to grab his leg while he was off balance, but he scuttled back out of reach.

'Vampires?' I shouted as I got to my feet. 'Really?'

'Just a little bit of one,' said Chorley.

He balled his fist – I felt his spell assemble like the flat of a blade running up the skin of my face. But he never got a chance to release it, because the driver threw the van into a sharp left turn that threw me and Chorley into the right side of the van. Chorley hadn't seen it coming, but I'd spotted the pair of TSG Sprinter vans skidding into a makeshift roadblock on the road ahead. So while Chorley was flailing around I did my best to kick him out of the half-open side door.

My foot definitely connected with something soft and dangly, because I heard Chorley grunt. But he managed to hold onto the door frame and, before I could follow up, the van straightened and we both went flying the other way. We ended up against the storage rack with Walbrook between us. My arm brushed the family-sized tin of vampire and that was enough to numb it from elbow to wrist.

We'd spent quite a lot of time discussing what I was going to do if I found myself face to face with Chorley. Nightingale said it was like fighting a man with a knife. Get inside his reach and trap the weapon.

'Don't bother with magic,' he'd said. 'Get in close and strike at his head. You want him dazed and confused.'

He didn't say what to do if there was a civilian hostage between us.

I dropped back and kicked the tin of vampire at him. I was pleased to discover that the patented acid-resistant soles of my Doc Martens were also vampire resistant. The tin, just as I'd planned, swung like a church censer and smacked Chorley in the face. He shrieked and fell back.

I hit the chain that bound Walbrook to the vampire tin with the hottest thing I had. There was a spark, but I could feel the power being sucked away. I heard a thump, and the tin jiggled as if whatever was inside had moved of its own accord.

There was a moment's pause during which me and Chorley both looked first at the tin and then at each other. Then I threw a left at his face. He instinctively raised his arm to block, which was what I was waiting for – I grabbed his wrist with my right hand and threw myself out the back of the lorry.

Stephanopoulos wouldn't have forced the van down a side road if they weren't planning to contain it. Since I couldn't separate Walbrook from the vampire tin, I needed to get Chorley away from both so somebody else could get in there with the bolt cutters. It was a brilliant plan with only one drawback – it involved jumping out the back of a moving van.

This is going to hurt, I thought, and probably break things.

Only it didn't, because something I can only describe as a cushion of air got between me and the cobbles. Not enough to stop it hurting and ripping my trousers to shit – although at least the Metvest kept the worst of the road rash off my back.

Unfortunately, the same was true of Chorley. Although I did try and belt him one as he rolled away from me. I'd thought he'd done the air cushion himself, but I'd been close enough to sense any *formae*, and there hadn't been none.

I looked back at the van just in time to see all four wheels fly off at the same time. They went straight to the side with just a tiny bit of upward angle to stop them scraping the tarmac. Momentum carried them bouncing down the street, but the van fell onto its axles and ground to a halt in a bright shower of sparks.

Both me and Chorley knew only one person who could work with that kind of precision, and while Chorley was looking around desperately for Nightingale, I hammered him with an *impello-palma* combination that should have sent him screaming across the road.

Without even looking at me, Chorley threw up a hand and my own spell bounced back to smack me in the face. I got a taste of my own *signare* even as I was knocked off my knees and rolled into the gutter. I tried to get to my feet and slammed my head hard against an anti-parking bollard.

My ears were ringing and my sight was blurred, but not enough so I couldn't see Chorley turning to give me his full attention. But suddenly he was sucked backwards off his feet and through an arched window in the office building opposite.

Then I heard footsteps coming up the road and Nightingale barked:

'On your feet, Grant.'

And I was up before the command had consciously

registered. Nightingale had put himself between me and the broken window.

'Secure the van,' Nightingale ordered, and suddenly he was surrounded by a globe of rippling air. I didn't see what happened next, because I had my orders.

I ran towards the van, sitting on its axles at a crossroad. I could see Walbrook was still in the back, chained to the big fun tin of quality badness, but the driver had climbed out and was lurching towards me.

He was a big white man, dressed in the traditional garb of the working villain – black cargo trousers, navy blue sweatshirt and donkey jacket, all of it bought from jumble sales and charity shops the better to be discarded when the job's done. He had a big square face, no neck, and arms about the same size as my thighs.

He frowned at me and shook his head.

My extendable baton was back with the flipped car, as was my pepper spray and my speedcuffs. Some backup would have been nice about then, but we'd all agreed the tactics in advance.

It's the calculus of magical combat. Masters fight masters while the apprentices secure the objective.

I flicked a water bomb into his face – a nice cold one, thanks to a trick Varvara taught me – and followed up by kicking him in the bollocks. He gave me a puzzled look and then fell flat on his face. It turned out later that he'd been suffering from a concussion, probably picked up when the wheels came off the van, so it's probably just as well I hadn't smacked him on the bonce with a baton.

I would have paused to put him in the recovery position, but his boss chose that moment to emerge from the courtyard beside the office and fling a quarter of a ton of metal bars – the remnants of the courtyard gate – at Nightingale. The bars twisted as they flew until they formed a whirling mass like the blades of a turbine two metres across.

Despite being within charging distance of Chorley, I didn't dare engage. He might be concentrating on Nightingale, but I thought it was better to hop back in the van on the basis that what the eye can't see the mad supernatural psychopath can't hit.

Walbrook's eyes were open by then, and she pointedly stared at me and then at the purple tin of doom. Chorley had a knack for being insanely over-prepared, and it didn't surprise me to find that he'd stashed a bolt cutter in a toolbox behind the front seats. Moving carefully to avoid the tin, I cut the chain around Walbrook's wrist and it had barely hit the floor when she dived over the front seat.

'Stay down,' I said, and cut the chain holding the tin to the ceiling.

It dropped with an ominous clonk, as if it was much heavier than it had any right to be. I checked out the back and found Martin Chorley staring at me with an expression that was perversely similar to one my mum used to use.

'What the hell did you do that for?' he said.

The tin did a little jump for emphasis, as if something were bouncing up and down inside.

I swung the bolt cutters like a golf club and whacked the vampire tin in his general direction. Typically he did an elegant pivot out of the way, but before he could complete his turn his clothes turned white with frost and I saw the hair on his head actually freeze. I assumed this was Nightingale proving that I wasn't the only one who'd been getting tips off Varvara. I'd have loved to have stood around and watched but, still having my orders, I followed Walbrook over the back of the front seat and out the passenger door.

I found Walbrook furiously pulling the last of her chains off.

'Where is he?' she said when she saw me. 'I'm going to have him.'

Behind me there was a sudden furnace blast of heat and I saw orange flames reflected in the shop windows behind Walbrook. I ran forward and bore her down to the ground as the van behind me exploded. If that was Chorley getting rid of his frostbite, then it was certainly overkill.

A bit of van – I learnt later it was a panel torn off the side – wiffled overhead and smashed the windows of the YCN gallery. Walbrook rolled me off – not angrily, but firmly, and we both cautiously got to our feet.

The van was missing from the chassis up and coils of dark smoke were rising from its blackened engine block. Through the smoke I could see Nightingale dragging the – hopefully unconscious – body of Chorley's goon away from the fire. He was using his left arm while keeping his right free for action. I did a scan for damage and while there was smouldering debris over a wide area and plentiful broken windows, none of the buildings were on fire.

I spotted the tin of quality vampire five metres up the road.

There was no sign of Martin Chorley.

I asked Walbrook if she could put the fire out.

She grimaced at me, then sighed and gave a little contemptuous wave with her left hand. I felt a weird sucking sensation from the remains of the van and a wind briefly rushed past my head. A small cloud formed over the van like a time-lapse weather sequence and it proceeded to bucket down for five minutes.

'Nice,' I said.

'Haven't done that in a long time,' said Walbrook. 'Where's the Nightingale going?'

He was sprinting up Rivington Place. Which, I decided, showed a touching faith in my ability to control the scene.

It doesn't stop there, of course, with the villain getting away and you looking stupid. I was already talking to Stephanopoulos on my back-up back-up burner phone before Nightingale was out of sight. Chorley went through the back wall of the old Shoreditch Town Hall, but Nightingale had to break off pursuit when he spotted some civilian casualties and had to stop and look after them. No doubt this was what Chorley was counting on.

Later, as we reconstructed it from CCTV and eyewitness accounts, he calmly stepped out the front of the town hall and flagged down a random Nissan Micra and was driven away. When we traced the driver via his vehicle's index he had no memory of picking up a strange man at all, and grew quite distressed when we showed him the footage. Thus Chorley was out of the area before we even had a perimeter established.

The rest of the emergency service circus arrived at our smouldering van less than a minute later. Seawoll, who never passes up a good shouting opportunity, turned up in the first wave, leaving me with only two immediate problems:

What to do with our bumper fun tin of vampire; and how to stop Walbrook walking off before I had a chance to interview her.

Fortunately Frank Caffrey turned up with the bomb squad, whereupon they performed what Caffrey was careful to explain was not a controlled explosion.

'You use a controlled explosion to disrupt a device's detonator,' he said. 'This is more like a contained incineration.'

This involved a big box made of composite armour and surrounded by sandbags into which I, since I stupidly volunteered, used a big pair of tongs to drop the tin. Even with the gloves provided, I felt the horrible not-real cold of the *tactus disvitae* creeping up through my hands. Needless to say, I was pretty fucking swift. The tin rattled as I swung it over the box, getting frantic just before I dropped it.

Was there some sentience there? I wondered. It certainly seemed to sense its fate.

The phosphorus charge had already been laid. It was just a question of plonking on a lid, adding more sandbags, and retiring to a safe distance. Caffrey gave the nod, the bomb squad pressed the button and there was a slightly disappointing *wumph* sound. A couple of seconds later, wisps of smoke rose from the edges of the box.

Caffrey said we had to wait at least half an hour to

make sure it was cooked, so I went back to see if Walbrook would talk to me. There was a slight delay as I was set upon by militant paramedics, who insisted on dressing the various scrapes I'd forgotten about until they reminded me.

So, stinging with antiseptic, I found Walbrook up the road with Guleed in the back of Franco's Takeaway, which had, by strange good fortune, been allowed to stay open despite being just inside our public exclusion zone.

'Funny how that worked out,' said Guleed around a mouthful of pasta salad.

'You OK?' I asked Walbrook, whose brush with vampirism hadn't seemed to dent her appetite none. She nodded and continued to fork spaghetti into her mouth.

'How's David?' asked Guleed, and I realised I had no idea where Carey was.

'Don't know,' I said. 'I'll check in a minute.'

I wanted to get a statement from Walbrook, but I realised that my notebook was in my jacket pocket left, probably, somewhere down Shoreditch High Street. I asked if I could borrow Guleed's, but she gave me a funny look.

So funny that I started laughing uncontrollably. When I couldn't stop myself I clamped my hand over my mouth and went outside. The thing about having a stress reaction is that, even when you know you're having a stress reaction, that knowledge doesn't seem to do you any good. I found a doorway across the road where a parked police Sprinter van blocked the view from the rest of the street.

I leant against the door and let myself slip down until I was sitting with my back to it. I closed my eyes and focused on my breathing until the giggles stopped. The edge of my Metvest was digging into my armpit, so I unfastened it and pulled it off. Underneath, my nice blue pinstripe shirt was soaked with sweat and ripped at the elbow. Probably beyond even Molly's skills.

I closed my eyes again and focused on my breathing. One thing learning magic does teach you is finding your centre, or at least making an educated stab at its location. There was a smell like burnt hair and ground nutmeg and a sensation like wind blowing through the trees. And the coppery taste of blood in my mouth which, on later examination, turned out to be actual blood from where I'd split my lip. There was nothing coherent, nothing I recognised as a *vestigium* – it was all just random neurons firing in my brain.

I felt that if I wanted to, I could probably get up and walk around and make a good impression.

'Peter?'

I looked up to find Guleed looking down at me.

'I've called Dr Walid,' she said. 'He's coming down to collect you.'

'Not UCH again,' I said.

Guleed was unsympathetic – she pointed out that it was policy that any officer involved in a serious Falcon incident where they may have been exposed to hazardous materials or practices was required to undergo an evaluation by an appropriately trained medical professional.

I groaned and said I didn't want to go.

'You probably shouldn't have written that policy, then,' she said. 'Should you?'

'What about Nightingale and Carey?' I asked, because misery loves company.

'Carey already went in an ambulance. Nightingale is waiting around on the off-chance Chorley pops up again. Plus he's an inspector and gets to do what he likes.'

'And we need to get a statement from Walbrook,' I said.

'I can do that,' she said. 'Besides, I'm the one with a notebook.'

Bits of my back, arm and leg had woken up to the fact that my hysterical moment had passed and that rational attendance to their needs might be forthcoming if only they could get my attention.

'Do me a favour,' I said. 'And make sure you ask whether King Arthur and Merlin were real people.'

'King Arthur?'

'Just make sure you ask.'

Guleed shrugged.

'If you think it's important,' she said, and reached down to help me up.

23

The Long Weekend

'I want you to take the weekend off,' said Dr Walid.

'But it's only Thursday afternoon,' I said.

'Then take a long weekend off,' said Dr Walid.

But I cheated and went to the briefing on Friday morning.

'I thought you had the weekend off?' asked Guleed as I sat down beside her. 'I wish I did.'

David Carey didn't make an appearance – obviously he'd been given the same instructions I had. Only he'd been sensible enough to follow them. Stephanopoulos gave an after-action report on our attempted godnapping/deicide/behaviour likely to cause a breach of the peace.

I had a strange fancy that my head was made out of rubber and that words were bouncing off them. From what meaning I caught as they boinged past I gathered that, while we'd utterly failed to catch Martin Chorley, we'd managed to thwart – Stephanopoulos actually used the word *thwart* – his plans. And that was always going to be a good thing. The various analysts reported their progress chipping away at his financial empire, and Nightingale explained what to look for in a vampire infestation. Me and Guleed knew this bit off by heart, so engaged in a bit of competitive doodling while we waited for him to finish.

'Go see your parents,' Nightingale told me as soon as the briefing broke up. 'They're worried about you.'

'What makes you say that?' I asked.

'Because your mother phoned me this morning and told me so,' he said.

So home I went, where my mum promptly made me go out shopping with her down Ridley Road market so I could carry the bags back, including a massive tin of palm oil. I told her you can get palm oil just about anywhere these days, but she claims that Ridley Road is the only place you can get authentic Sierra Leonean palm oil. Shopping with my mum in Dalston is never fast, because every five metres there's an aunty or an uncle or cousin or old friend. There will be stopping and chatting and asking after people. Plus she made me get a haircut in the barber off Kingsland High Street where they'd cut my hair from the age of five onwards and had, as far as I could tell, never changed the décor in that whole time.

It was also probably the same guy asking whether I was still police and telling me that he'd heard crime was going down and didn't that mean I'd be out of a job, but not to worry: he could have me trained up in no time. Finally – a respectable career.

Since my mum was watching, I got it shorn short but with a nice even fade on both sides. Outside, my head felt far less rubbery and way more naked, so I treated Mum to tea and cake in a Kurdish bakery before dragging a month's worth of food home. Since I'd carried most of it, I stayed for dinner, where my dad talked about an offer he'd got to record a vinyl exclusive and what did I think.

I thought I might want to run some checks on the characters making the offer. But what I said was that it sounded brilliant. And I asked whether it was going to make any money. My dad actually looked a bit puzzled at the concept, but judging from my mum's expression she had that side of the business in hand.

Bev turned up while I was doing the washing up and insisted on being fed, which meant I had to do two sets of washing up while she and Mum had a conversation pitched too low for me to hear. Not that I was trying that hard to eavesdrop, honest.

Afterwards we sat on the sofa and cracked open some of the emergency Red Stripe Mum keeps stashed behind the rice barrel. Because just for once there was no live football on anywhere in the world, we watched *Twenty Moments That Rocked Talent Shows*, but Mum and Dad went to bed just before Susan Boyle blew Simon Cowell's socks off. Once they were safely out of the way we lay down on the sofa, muted the TV and listened to the rain. There was a lightning flash and I used Bev's heartbeat to time the delay before the thunder – she has a very steady heartbeat.

Nine beats, three kilometres, a loud crash somewhere to the north.

The council had replaced the windows since I'd left home. In the old days heavy rain used to seep in around the edges and mess up Mum's DIY. Now it just bounced off the double glazing. There was nothing they could do about the thickness of the interior walls, though, so we could clearly hear Stan Getz's 'Moonlight in Vermont' coming from my parents' room.

'That's nice,' said Beverley. 'Does your dad always play music before sleeping?'

'That's the arrangement with the Claus Ogerman strings,' I said. 'That's not what my parents sleep to.'

It took a couple of seconds to sink in, and then Beverley wriggled around in my arms so that she could stare me in the face.

'No,' she said.

'According to my mum that's what my dad was playing when she walked into the old 606 Club in 1983,' I said. 'So that's been their tune ever since.'

Beverley sniggered and wriggled around again to lay her head against my shoulder.

'That's so sweet,' she said.

There was another blue-white flash, a longer interval – maybe ten seconds. The thunder was further away. We listened as the strings fell away and Getz played a final phrase, wrapping it all up with a neat little ribbon.

'You were probably conceived to this,' said Beverley.

'You had to go there, didn't you?'

'Yes.' Beverley kissed the back of my hand. 'Yes, I did.'

And as the thunderstorm grumbled off to the north we both, amazingly, fell asleep.

We woke up the next morning in my old room – which was a bit of a surprise, since I have no memory of waking up and shifting all the boxes and spare suitcases full of clothes from where my mum stacked them on my bed and onto the floor. Thank God the sheets and duvet covers were clean, if a bit musty with non-use.

I watched as Beverley, in just her knickers and a yellow T-shirt liberated from one of the boxes, peered cautiously through a crack in the door before risking a dash to the toilet. Then I checked the messages on my phone, of which the most pertinent was from Dr Walid and read: *You are officially on a sick day: do not come in to work.*

It sounded like good advice to me, so when Beverley climbed back into bed I asked what she wanted to do.

'Pretty much this,' she said. 'But in a bigger bed.'

So after breakfast we drove across the river to her house where, Sod's Law being what it is, we ended up on Wimbledon Common helping Maksim plant reed beds along Beverley's course. Well, I helped Maksim while Beverley spent time poking at the riverbank and muttering about flow rates. Then we had a cheeky Nando's on Hill Rise near the bridge along with most of Richmond, who then followed us to the local Odeon to watch Allison Carter play against type as a single mother trying to balance her responsibilities to her children and her career as a highly paid assassin. We both agreed that her inability to control her fourteen year old goth daughter was hilariously white and neither of us would have got away with talking back to our mothers that way. Then we met up for drinks with some of Bev's old school friends on the riverside terrace at the White Cross, and finally an Uber home and bed.

And then we stayed mainly in bed for the whole next day.

I left my phone on in case Lesley tried to get in touch. But nothing. I wondered if Chorley knew he'd been grassed up and whether I should find a way to let him know. Would that be enough of a wedge to break up the team? I decided I wanted to discuss it with Nightingale first – at the very least.

Early Monday morning Seawoll texted me and said he wanted to see me and Guleed in his office at Belgravia first thing.

'I'm afraid I have bad news,' he said once we were seated. 'David Carey is taking indefinite medical leave.'

'I didn't think he was that hurt,' I said.

Seawoll held up a hand to stop me.

'The problem is not his physical injuries. David has been diagnosed as suffering from acute stress and is undergoing a psychiatric evaluation. I wanted you both to know before the official announcement.'

'Where is he?' I asked. 'Can we see him?'

'No,' said Seawoll. 'He has specifically requested that neither of you visit him.'

He squinted at us and took a deep breath before asking how we were.

We both said we were fine, of course. Now, coppering is famously stressful and equally famous for its macho working-class disregard for the realities of mental health. So naturally Seawoll didn't believe a word of it.

'I've seen this happen before,' he said. 'In cases involving the Special Assessment Unit back before we called it that.'

'What did you call it, sir?' I asked.

'We didn't fucking call it anything, Peter. We tried

very hard not to talk about it at all. But the thing is that this job is hard enough,' he caught my eye and then Guleed's. 'As you both know full well. But at least all the shit you get in the day-to-day is familiar. You get used to it – you learn how to cope. It's part of the job. But this . . . supernatural shit is different. Ordinary coppers don't get any training for it. They don't know what to do with cursed safes, possessed cars or magic bells. And that causes them stress.'

I wondered about the cursed safe. It wasn't a case I'd worked on. But I decided this was not the time to ask about it.

'A sense of powerlessness can seriously exacerbate stress,' said Seawoll. 'Especially for individuals who are burdened with the expectations of a wider community that assume they'll master any potential crisis.' He looked straight at me again. 'They fucking want us to look like we sodding know what we're doing. And you might know what you're doing, although I doubt it. We sure as shit don't. Not even Nightingale knows what he's doing half the time.'

He sighed again, his big shoulders rising and falling in exaggerated despair.

'It's simple. I need to know that you two are going to look out for each other,' he said. 'And I don't mean physically – that goes without saying. There's far too much macho bullshit in this job and I expect you two to rise above it. Is that understood?'

We both said it was.

Seawoll turned his attention back to me – because obviously I'm cursed.

'I want you to include a mental health component in your stage two discussion document,' he said. 'I want it incorporated into the Falcon risk assessment matrix.'

'Stage three,' I said. 'Stage two has already been distributed and I don't have any experience with mental health issues, so I'm not competent to draw up such guidelines. Neither are Dr Walid and Dr Vaughan.'

Seawoll gave me a long-suffering look.

'I know a couple of specialists. They've done work with combat-related PTSD and the like. If that's acceptable to you.'

'Yes, sir,' I said. 'Subject to approval by Chief Inspector Nightingale.'

'Yes, obviously,' said Seawoll. 'Now fuck off. You're making me tired and it's only eight in the morning.'

Me and Guleed just about made it to the door before Seawoll spoke again.

'And let's be careful out there,' he said.

'You're unbelievable,' said Guleed once we were safely out the back on Ebury Square, where I'd left the surviving unmarked Hyundai. The glittering aftermath of Thursday night's thunderstorm was long gone and we were back to sweaty and overcast.

Guleed said that since I'd totalled the old Rover she had to have the Hyundai, because she was actioned to check out some scrap merchants in Enfield as part of the hunt for Chorley's second bell. She did at least offer to drop me off at the Folly first.

'Even though it's out of my way,' she said.

I got my revenge by asking about Michael Cheung, on the pretext that a senior officer had asked me to keep a close eye on her emotional stability.

'We're dating, if you must know,' she said.

'Dating?'

'Yeah. Dating, Peter. That's when you go out to social events with someone and get to know them rather than just diving in and shagging the first river you meet.'

'So you've been doing that since last October?' I said.

'Maybe.'

'That's like eight months,' I said.

'I don't like to move fast.'

'You're so totally shagging him,' I said.

'Fuck off, Peter,' she said. But she was smiling when she said it.

'Just remember I'm keeping my eye on you.'

'Don't you worry about me. I'm not the one that jumps out of moving vehicles.'

'It made sense at the time,' I said.

'Only to you.'

I got into the Folly just in time for Stephanopoulos to hold the briefing. It was the usual stuff, but some of the reconstruction of events surrounding the kidnap at the Goat and Crocodile was interesting. I'd only seen one van and one henchman, but it turned out there'd been at least two decoy vans, three relay vans to transfer into, and half a dozen Essex boys recruited for the one job. All of which had gone for nothing, because I hadn't even seen the decoys and thus chased the right van. Afterwards Nightingale used the incident as an exemplar of why you shouldn't make your operations over-complex.

'Always try to match your strengths to his weakness,' he said.

I was tempted to ask what our strengths actually were, but that probably would have been a cue for more practice and I do, eventually, learn from my mistakes.

With Guleed out checking scrapyards, I ended up working through a couple of Carey's actions. As I started phoning a list of foundries in the Midlands I couldn't help wonder whether I shouldn't have spotted that he was in distress. He'd said he wasn't happy and uncharacteristically smacked Zach . . . but that could have been general grumpiness. It was all very well telling people to look out for each other, but what were we supposed to look for? I added *Check Seawoll's guidelines include stress awareness training* into my medium-term action file. Just under *Buy modern Latin textbooks*.

A bit after lunch I got a call from Special Police Constable Geneviève Nguyễn, who said she once again had something she wanted me to look at.

'Not another goat?' I said, but she said no and gave me an address.

Amen Court – within spitting distance of St Paul's Cathedral.

Surprise! I thought sourly.

Nguyễn, in plain clothes this time, met me on Warwick Lane, which was blocked off by an unmarked Sprinter van, and led me to Amen Court. Just across the avenue, I noticed, was Paternoster Square and the huge stainless steel sculpture nicknamed 'The Zipper'. Beyond that, hidden behind the gleaming Portland stone façades of the new buildings, was St Paul's Cathedral.

At the entrance to the court was a scrupulously polite sign by the entrance that said in white letters on black:

**NOT OPEN
TO THE PUBLIC
PLEASE RESPECT THE PRIVACY
OF THE PEOPLE WHO LIVE HERE**

On seeing that, my first thought was that someone obviously hadn't respected their privacy and my second thought was to wonder just who *did* live in the rather tasty terraces beyond the sign.

'Used to be housing for church officials,' said Nguyễn. 'And they're still owned by the cathedral. Now it's all commercial.'

The narrow alleyway continued until it opened up into the court proper, now a garden space overlooking what would have been really nice, if expensive, places to live if they hadn't been converted into offices.

The court was bounded on the west by a high brick wall built of what looked like Regency or early Victorian brick. This was a famous wall – a last remnant of the infamous Newgate Prison. Behind it ran Dead Man's Walk, along which the condemned, some of them actually even guilty, were led to the gallows.

More police tape had staked out a section of the wall a good five or six metres wide. Forensics had come and gone, but I recognised the late-night kebab smell of burnt offerings.

'A cage full of rats,' said Nguyễn. 'Very fast fire,

273

hot enough to partially melt the cage – no sign of an accelerant.'

'Anything written on the wall?'

'No, but there's a standard pentagram scratched into the ground around the cage,' said Nguyễn. 'I'm hoping this is not another influential group of lawyers, because I believe that would be a problem.'

'So am I,' I said as I pulled on my evidence gloves.

The rats were a pathetic burnt heap, so it was impossible to tell whether they were feral or pet whites. I really didn't want to touch them, but I was getting flashes of something while I was half a metre away and I needed to know what.

Growling, snarling, fear, misery and the taste of blood. The smell of sweat and resignation, of floral scent and old rope. And the shape and slink of an animal as it slunk on its belly to oblivion.

'Not the Black Dog again,' I said.

There is a legend that in the reign of Henry II a poor scholar was thrown into Newgate for the crime of sorcery. The prison had been undergoing one of its periodic efficiency drives, with savings being largely taken from the catering budget. The prisoners, driven mad by hunger, fell upon the young milk-fed scholar with glee and, presumably, some sort of condiment. The scholar was said to have uttered a terrible curse and thereby given rise to a hideous black dog which, one by one, hunted down and devoured all those who had tasted of the young man's flesh. Even those who had been released and scattered to the four corners of the land.

'Medical students?' said Nguyễn.

Everybody knew about the Black Dog. Especially, for some historical reason or other, the trainee doctors at Barts Hospital, which is located not far to the north. And they, being the future health professionals that they are, love to carry out macabre rituals at the wall. Usually involving bits stolen from the pathology lab and a lot of magical symbology cribbed off the internet.

But not animal sacrifice. And not with such a workaday pentagram.

'Are you going to handle the usual?' I asked – meaning CCTV checks and door to door.

'Nightingale will have to work his charm on my inspector,' said Nguyễn. 'If he says yes, then we shall see what we can find. Do you think it's important?'

'I don't know, Geneviève. You know how it is. You never know what's important until it's important.'

On that basis, I stuck around for a bit to do an initial *vestigia* survey around the crime scene just in case there were some lurking hotspots. But by the afternoon I hadn't found anything, so I hopped on a number 8 bus in the hope of missing the worst of the rush hour.

The bus was stop-starting just past Chancery Lane when my phone rang.

'What's up?' said Lesley.

24

A Fine Distinction

'I'm not in the mood for this shit today,' I said wearily and hung up.

The phone rang again, as I thought it might, and I already had my backup phone out and was texting the 'Help, Lesley has called me,' code to the Folly. They would try to trace the call, but we knew from bitter experience that Lesley had access to a ton of different ways to spoof that.

Before I answered I plugged my earbuds into the phone.

'Yeah?' she said, 'Why are you in a strop then?'

'Why do you care?'

With the earbuds in I could hear the background noise that her phone picked up. I heard cars and bigger vehicles, street sounds – she was definitely in a city. I had a feeling she was close, but of course she could have been in Manchester or somewhere equally exotic.

'Because I worry about you,' she said.

There – a loud car horn behind Lesley and an instant later I heard the same horn in the distance – east up High Holborn. I twisted in my seat to look up the street towards Chancery Lane, but I couldn't see her amongst the traffic and the crowds.

'Yeah, why's that?' I asked.

Or it could have been a completely different horn.

'Because you never think of yourself,' she said.

The ambience changed. She was now indoors, maybe. I heard the distinctive swish-chunk of a bus door closing. On a bus now – damn – no more helpful car horns.

'I'm more worried about you than about me,' I said.

'Why's that?'

'Because you're working for a mad fucker.'

'I prefer working *with*,' said Lesley.

'I think working without would be better.'

'Can we have a talk?' asked Lesley. 'Like, in person – without your mob interrupting.'

I felt a surge of excitement and I'll admit a little bit of glee. I'd been right.

I looked out the window and spotted a likely venue.

'You know that Wetherspoon's on High Holborn?' I said.

'The one opposite the Sainsbury's?'

'Meet me there in ten minutes,' I said.

'Copy that,' she said and hung up.

I jumped down the stairs, flashed my warrant card at the driver and got him to open the doors for me. It wasn't like it wasn't much of a hassle for him since we were barely moving anyway.

The Penderel's Oak was your typical Wetherspoon's pub, its interior a strange theme-park recreation of the old-fashioned British pub caught in a frozen moment between wood-panelled, tie-dyed carpeted 1970s and the rise of cream coloured gastropub. Beverley's sister Effra, who has a degree in fine arts and considers herself a style guru, calls them the apotheosis of British pub culture.

I ordered a couple of pints of John Smith's and picked a table near the back with limited sight of the windows and away from the fire exits. While I waited I texted where I was to the Folly and got a sideways smiley face in confirmation. Lesley must be close, but they'd still have to wait until I confirmed her arrival.

Which was before I'd even finished sitting down. Looking back later, I realised she'd probably been on the bus with me. I did catch the tail end of a strange fluttery *vestigium* like a bloodhound shaking its jowls, which I guessed meant she'd walked in with somebody else's face.

She sat down, grabbed her pint and took a gulp.

'Needed that,' she said, putting the glass down. 'Is Walbrook safe?'

'Yes she is,' I said. 'Thank you. Does he know you tipped us off?'

'Of course he does. I told him I wasn't happy, so he can't be surprised I took steps.'

'He's a very understanding boss.'

'Like I said, he's not my boss.'

'Working *with*,' I said. 'I remember. So since when do you care for supernatural folk?'

I've always cared, they're all people,' she said. 'Except for the ones that are not. And anyway you've got to have some standards, haven't you?'

I thought of the woman we found without a face in the dripping woods outside Crawley, the drug dealer who got laminated to a tree, and all the others who got between Martin Chorley and whatever mad scheme he had in mind. But maybe it was the same old story. You're not that bothered about the people dying far away to make your trainers, but you don't like it when they die on your doorstep.

'So, you can't use my tip-off to drive a wedge,' she said.

'What makes you think I'd do that?'

'Because it's twisty and clever. I'm vexed with you for hiding that side from me. You see, I know you can do the job now, Peter.'

'I'm glad you think so,' I said. 'You didn't used to.'

Lesley smiled.

'I was willing to be convinced,' she said. 'And you are full of surprises.'

'So you reckon I can do the job now?'

'That's what I said, didn't I?'

But, I thought, I no longer trust the things you say – do I?

'But that's not your problem is it?' she said, and sipped her beer.

'So now I've got a new problem?'

'When we first met you always wanted to go clubbing,' she said. 'You were the one that wanted to catch a film, watch TV, go out for a curry.'

'Not just me,' I said. 'Especially the curry thing.'

'Yeah, maybe not the curry thing,' she said. 'But that's not my point.'

'You have a point? I thought we were just chatting – now you've got a point?'

'When was the last time you took leave?' she said.

'See? You've got to think about it – it's that rare a thing. You must have accumulated a shitload of holiday time.'

'Not as much as you'd think,' I said.

'I want you to take some time off.'

'Chance would be a fine thing.'

'Yeah,' said Lesley. 'This is that chance.'

'For how long?' I asked, but Lesley wasn't going to fall for that.

'Until things have settled down,' she said. 'You'll know when that happens.'

'You think killing Punch is going to settle things down?' I said, and shouldn't have.

Because now Lesley knew that I knew. But sometimes you've got to push to win.

'You always were good at working stuff out,' she said. 'Not always exactly quick, but you get there in the end, don't you?'

'So what's it all in aid of?' I asked. 'What does Marty want?'

'He wants to make the world a better place.'

'How?'

Lesley's eyes were suddenly cold.

'Well,' she said, 'killing Punch would be a good start.'

'What if getting rid of Punch fucks everything up?'

'Like what?'

'Like the city. Maybe he's part of the ecosystem – maybe he's necessary.'

Lesley pinched her own cheek and pulled – it stretched a little bit further than was normal.

'Talk to me about fucking Punch,' she said. 'I dare you. The cunt was in my head for months, Peter, fucking with my mind. I don't care if the whole fucking city falls into a hole. Nobody does. Not really. At least nobody outside the M25.'

'That's a bit harsh,' I said. 'What's the city ever done to you?'

'You don't get it, Peter,' she said. 'London sucks.'

'Fuck off.'

'Fucking does – London sucks. Sucks the rest of the country dry. You want to get ahead, you have to go to London. You want to get away – go to fucking London. All the jobs, all the money goes to London. The rest of the country gets the leftovers, the bits that London doesn't want.'

'Like the DVLA,' I said.

'Exactly.'

'And the BBC, of course.'

'Not the important bit,' she said, and checked her watch. 'Out of time.' She got up and started pulling on her coat. 'Any longer and people are going to start looking for you.'

'I didn't call anyone,' I said.

'More fool you, then.' She turned to go. 'Take the holiday, Peter,' she said over her shoulder. 'And don't follow me out.'

I waited until I was sure she couldn't see me and then scrambled after her – keeping low so the crowd would shield me if she looked back. Dusk had fallen while we talked and I burst out the front door into the warm half-light of Holborn. I looked left and right, but no sign of Lesley or even a stranger with Lesley's walk.

To the left was Holborn Station, but I didn't think she'd

risk the CCTV coverage on the Underground. Where would she go? Down the back streets and into Lincoln's Inn, maybe? I was pulling my phone out when an IRV, a silver Astra with Battenberg squares, pulled up with no lights and no siren. The uniform inside leant over and called my name.

'Yeah?'

'Get in,' he said. 'They're setting up a perimeter.'

I got in, but even while I was pulling on the seatbelt I was wondering who 'they' were since I hadn't called it in when Lesley arrived. Nightingale wouldn't have me tracked – right?

I went to click the seat belt in, but an arm wrapped around my chest from behind and I smelt beer and clean hair – Lesley. Something bit into my neck and I heard her tell the driver to cut the lights. Contrary to the films, no safe sedative will put you out instantly. But whatever Lesley had jabbed me with was filling up the corners of my mind with beer flavoured milkshake. I stopped trying to dislodge Lesley's arm and flailed at the driver. I had some mad idea that if I could distract him we might crash, or at least draw attention to the car. It might have worked. I don't know, because the milkshake was foaming over my eyes and my last thought was that Nightingale was going to be disappointed and Beverley was going to be really pissed off.

25

An Alarming Lack
of Cocktail Parties

I woke up in darkness and, judging from the smell of my own breath, wearing a cloth hood. I was lying on my side on a metal surface with my legs fastened and my arms tied behind my back. There was something yielding that was supporting my head, carefully placed to avoid positional asphyxiation. Which was just as well, since I was definitely not feeling well. Like I said . . . nothing that sedates you that fast is remotely safe.

Even with a hood on, I was unmistakably in the back of Sprinter or a Transit van. I was a bit short of clues otherwise. I tried counting turns as I was thrown from side to side, but lost track and all I could smell was the inside of the hood. I doubted I was going to be recreating this journey with the help of a preternaturally perceptive blind person and a deceptively cheerful flock of geese. I suppose it could have been worse – I could have been head down in a barrel.

I've never been that good at judging time without an external reference. Dr Walid thinks it's because I'm outwardly orientated and always looking to establish my position within the wider environment. He thinks that might be why I'm good at *vestigia*. But, given that his data pool consists of five people, I'm not giving that theory much weight. Whatever, I think it was about half an hour from when I regained consciousness to the van coming to a halt.

I heard the back doors creak open and was seriously considering lashing out with my feet when hands grabbed my legs and dragged me out. They were strong, whoever it was, strong enough to effortlessly lift me and sling me over their shoulder. And it wasn't a wide shoulder either, and bony enough to dig into my stomach. What with the aftermath of the sedative, the hood and the jogging up and down, they were all sodding lucky they didn't have to wash that hood afterwards.

Then I was lowered, with surprising care, into a chair with my wrists behind the seat back. The ridiculously strong hands kept me from moving while somebody else fixed what felt suspiciously like alligator clamps to my left index finger and the top of my right sock.

I heard Chorley ask whether things were ready and Lesley say they were. I felt the tape securing the neck of the hood being ripped off, followed by the hood proper. I squinted in the sudden light.

I was in a large, high-ceilinged room with a row of tall metal-framed windows with small panes. The walls were whitewashed brick with rounded edges along the windowsills and doorways. Interwar Art Deco industrial, I guessed, a former school or office, not so common a design that I couldn't trace it later.

Chorley was perched on a chair in front of me, elbows on his knees, leaning forward intently but not, unluckily, close enough for me to bite his nose. He was dressed office casual in tan slacks and a light blue pinstripe shirt, top button undone – no tie.

I knew it was futile but I conjured up a shield to cut the ties on my hands. Before I even had the *forma* lined up my body gave an involuntary jump – a thudding shock and then pain.

'Don't,' said Lesley from behind me.

I recognised the set-up – it came straight out of Nightingale's wartime guide to holding practitioner POWs.

'What have you got that plugged into?' I asked. 'The mains?'

'As it happens, yes,' said Lesley. 'We couldn't find a car battery.'

'Now we've established that we've taken adequate precautions,' said Chorley, 'perhaps we can get down to business?'

'You've kidnapped a police officer,' I said. 'The last time that happened Nightingale hunted the perpetrators down like dogs – and I mean literally like dogs – from horseback.'

'Tell me about it,' said Chorley. 'I personally wanted you dead. I had some talent lined up to shoot you as you came out of your mother's flat.'

You want to be calm and in control and insouciant in the face of danger. But I was thinking of the 'talent' and my mum and dad and for a moment I was paralysed by the conflicting waves of fear and rage. I could feel my face burning and my hands flex – Lesley gave me a little cautionary shock.

I didn't snarl – *Stay away from my family* – because I felt we could take the horrific and protracted vengeance speech as read. Still, I'd have to take the threat to my parents more seriously in the future.

If I lived long enough.

'I wouldn't worry about your parents,' said Chorley. 'I'm not foolish enough to think that would slow you down for a moment, and it is unnecessary in any case. Short of killing you, this is by far the most elegant solution.'

'Why not kill me?' I asked, because I'm stupid that way.

'You know why not,' he snapped. 'Your friend Lesley has an unwarranted soft spot for you. Although I'm beginning to see that you could well have a place in our new tomorrow. That's why I let her have one last go at persuading you to stand down – which is why you're still alive now. Despite our little contretemps the other day.'

'Oh, that,' I said.

'Yes, that,' said Chorley.

And because you never know your luck, I asked him where he got the vampire bits from.

'You'd be surprised what you can buy on the dark web these days,' said Chorley. 'And what shadows lie behind the shadows you think you know.'

'Really?' I said. 'What shadows are those?'

'Lesley is right about you in one way. You are persistent. I'm not about to breach my own operational security. And besides,' he gave me a bright smile, 'most of it will be irrelevant soon.'

'What, you mean when the sleeper awakes and leads a jihad to conquer the known universe,' I said.

'Very funny,' said Chorley.

'What was that about?' asked Lesley.

'Sorry, wrong power fantasy,' I said. 'I mean when Arthur wakes and rides out with his chosen knights to . . . What, exactly? Storm Buckingham Palace? What are you expecting to happen?'

'I'm not sure what you think you know, Peter,' said Chorley, frowning.

'I know you're obsessed with the Dark Ages and with Arthur,' I said. 'And I know you think you've got hold of Excalibur. And I know you murdered John Chapman and probably Gabriel Tate to keep the details quiet.'

'Actually,' said Chorley, 'the first I knew about John and Gabriel's deaths was when Lesley read your report on it and told me. Sorry – nothing to do with me.'

His mobile rang then – the jingling factory-set tune – and he pulled it out, glanced at the screen, and grimaced.

'Sorry,' he said, getting up. 'I've got to take this. Back in a mo.'

I waited until I was certain he was out of the room before asking for a cup of tea.

'Later,' she said. 'If you're good.'

'You know he's a plastic toy short of a happy meal – right?'

'What?' she said. 'Because he believes in magic?'

'Because he plans to bring back King Arthur. The Once and Future King. You know, the one that was totally made up by a bunch of Welsh Nationalists and romantic Frenchmen.'

I heard Lesley laugh behind me.

'Yeah,' I said. 'I've done a bit of reading on the subject.'

'I bet that helped you with your PIP2 qualifications.'

'Still passed,' I said, because Lesley always did know how to sidetrack me.

'Not Arthur,' she said suddenly. 'We don't need a man with a sword, do we?'

'What do we need?'

'We need the power behind the legend. The brains, the magic. You should like this. This is your kind of stuff.'

Oh shit, I thought. And suddenly I could see it. Chorley was a man who liked to walk in the shadows and stand beside the throne – not Arthur. Never Arthur. Not the king of Camelot.

But its architect,

'Do me a favour,' I said wearily.

'That's exactly what I've been trying to do from the start.'

'There never was a Merlin,' I said.

'Yeah?' said Lesley. 'And you know that because?'

'Because people have spent the last hundred years looking for him,' I said. 'And he's nowhere to be found.'

I heard the scrape of chair legs on cement and Lesley walked out in front of me. She was carrying a silver and black metal button box of the kind used to operate heavy industrial equipment, which trailed a braided blue cable behind it. I didn't need to ask where that went.

Still, my chair didn't seem to be fastened down. And with Lesley now in front of me I reckoned that if her attention wavered I could yank myself free of the clips before she could react. That's why the operator is supposed to stay behind the prisoner.

Lesley must have caught my attitude, because she frowned and wiggled the button box at me.

'Regarding Merlin,' she said, 'absence of evidence is not evidence of absence.'

'And children's books are not evidence of shit,' I said. 'Or both of us would have gone to Hogwarts.'

'I don't get it, Peter. We've both met people . . .' she put a deliberately alien stress on the word *people*, 'who are thousands of years old. People hidden beneath the streets. And you're shagging a river, for Christ's sake. We do spells. I mean, what do you find intrinsically unlikely about Merlin being a real person?'

'What if he's Welsh?'

'What if he is?'

'Then he's hardly likely to give you back the England you want, is he?'

'He's not going to give us anything,' she said. 'He's going to help us make Britain a better place.'

'Better how?'

'Just better,' she said, the corners of her mouth drawing downwards. 'Nicer, cleaner, *better*!' She shouted the last word and then paused to get control. 'Not the shithole it is now.'

'Something we can all be proud of,' said Chorley, coming back into the room.

He nodded at Lesley, who retreated back out of my sight – the button box cable swishing behind her like an angry tail.

Chorley beckoned to someone else behind me.

'Come over here, Foxglove,' he said. 'I want to introduce you properly.'

I twisted my head to track a pale white woman stepping hesitantly into view.

I'd never met a more obvious fae who wasn't riding a unicorn. She was impossibly tall and slender, with elongated arms that emerged from a loose brown sleeveless smock and ended in long-fingered hands. She had supermodel legs in black leggings that ended at the ankles to expose dainty pink feet. Her face was long and oval, with a small mouth and chin, prominent cheekbones and big hazel eyes. Her hair was a cascade of gleaming black down her back.

She shyly stopped beside Chorley and did a little nod and dip in my direction.

'Foxglove,' said Chorley. 'This is Peter Grant, who will be staying with you for a while.'

'Hi,' I said, as brightly as a man tied to a chair can.

I might have gone for a bit of charm, except Foxglove stepped forward and, with no real discernible effort, lifted me up and threw me over her shoulder. This explained the painfully thin shoulder from earlier, I thought – where was this one when I was carrying ten tons of shopping back from Ridley Road market?

She carried me quickly out of the room and, I think, down a corridor and into another room. I was hoping I'd become detached from the pain-making machine but Lesley was nippily following us and kept giving me low-level shocks every fifteen seconds or so to keep me off balance. Mostly, all I could see was Foxglove's hair but I caught glimpses of more cream coloured 1930s brick, a corridor, a double door and then we were out into an echoing space full of natural light.

Finally Foxglove plonked me down, seized my shoulders and turned me to face forward. We were in a large room – a workshop with high walls and a dirty glass skylight roof. The floor was bare cement with no visible furniture and at my feet lay an ominous dark round hole three metres across.

'I made this especially for you, Peter,' said Martin Chorley. So he'd followed us, too. 'To keep you safe and sound until the work is finished.'

I looked down the hole – all I could see was a circular stretch of vinyl matting at least five metres down. It didn't look very safe to me.

'And afterwards, when we're all eating dung for dinner,' I said, 'you don't think I'm going to come looking for payback?'

I felt strong fingers break the ties on my feet and then my wrists.

'Not particularly,' he said. 'I know your type, Peter. You believe in law and order, and soon there will be a new order.'

'And I'll just knuckle under, is that it?'

I yelped as Lesley gave me a final shock before disconnecting the crocodile clips. I turned to find Foxglove blocking any attack on Chorley. Beside him Lesley was methodically wrapping the control cable around the button box.

'Knuckle under?' he said. 'I expect you to be my champion – a paladin for justice. We'll get you a suit of armour and you can wear Lesley's favour on your lance.'

'It's all a lie,' I said. 'There never was a King Arthur

or a Camelot – Geoffrey of Monmouth made him up out of old stories.'

I reckoned a dive to the side to get away from the hole and then I'd worry about what happened next.

'We shall see,' said Chorley, and Foxglove pushed me into the hole.

26

Of the Captivity of Peter

Five metres is a leg-breaking drop. And that's the good option. You're supposed to relax and roll on impact – which is easier said than done when you're screaming for your mum. Not that I was screaming for my mum – didn't have time. My landing was fast and surprisingly soft, followed by a bounce that almost pitched me on my head and killed me that way. I managed to get my hands out in front of my face and ended up lying across a low padded wall like something from a children's playground. I rolled over, spotted Chorley's face staring down at me and threw a fireball at it.

Nothing happened.

I gave it another couple of goes, but for some reason I couldn't get a grasp on the *formae* – they kept slipping away like a common word you know you know but can't remember.

'As I said,' said Chorley with a grin, 'especially made for you.'

I tried once more – just for luck – and Chorley shook his head sadly and withdrew.

I got up and looked around. I was in a circular underground cell eight metres wide at the base, with walls that went straight up for two metres before narrowing

293

to form a dome with the entrance at its centre. Because of my misspent youth playing role-playing games I recognised it instantly as an oubliette – a place where you left people who you wanted to forget.

Though it was a very clean example of the type. With whitewashed walls, two futon beds, one on each side, a toilet, a shower and a sink.

The bedding on one futon bed was neatly folded up at the end while the other was loosely made up, the duvet clean but rumpled in the traditional manner of someone in too much of a hurry to make their own bed.

I wondered who that might be and whether they would be pleased to have a cellmate.

I noticed there were no tables, chairs, fridges or televisions.

No light fittings either – all the light came in through the entrance above.

I checked the shower but it consisted of an old-fashioned *Psycho*-style head cemented at an angle into the wall. Likewise, the sink and the toilet had all been designed with the minimum exposed piping. I flushed and twisted taps and found it all worked. There was a single shelf of white laminated chipboard above the sink with two lidless plastic takeaway trays, each with a toothbrush, toothpaste and a squeeze tube stolen from a hotel with *The Best Shower Gel You Will Ever Steal* printed on the side. I assumed that the box with the toothbrush still in its packaging was mine.

No moisturising cream, I noticed – not even some cocoa butter.

And not much in the way of entertainment.

'Can't I at least get Wi-Fi?' I shouted up.

There was movement above and I jumped back as a hardback book fluttered down from the hole to land in front of me. Cautiously, just in case something heavy was about to join it, I grabbed the book and retreated back towards the unused futon. When I was sure nothing else was forthcoming I had a look. It was old, but not an antique. A 1977 first edition of Tolkien's *The Silmarillion*. And it might have been worth something if still had its dust jacket, and hadn't been covered with finger marks and coffee rings and had its page corners turned down to mark the reader's position. According to the stamp on the inside cover it had once belonged to Macclesfield Library.

Which is the closest library to Alderley Edge, where Martin Chorley grew up. Which meant it was likely that he'd half-inched it as a boy. I wondered if there were any useful notes in the margin. I retreated until my back was against the wall, then stood still and listened until I was pretty sure nobody was watching before sitting down and starting to read.

Who I was sharing my oubliette with became clear five pages in when Foxglove jumped down – landing on the drop mat elegantly with a slight bend at the knees. She had a courier's bag around her shoulders, which she unslung and threw in my direction before loping over to what I now realised was her bed.

I didn't have a chance to move, but the bag dropped into my lap. Inside was a white towelling bathrobe of the kind regularly stolen from four star hotels, a packet of Marks and Spencer's boxers and a pair of plain blue cotton T-shirts. I had a good rummage but couldn't find any receipts or other identification.

I looked up to find Foxglove sitting cross-legged on her bed and glaring at me.

I gave her a friendly smile.

'So when's dinner then?' I asked.

Her eyes narrowed further.

'Being kidnapped makes me hungry,' I said.

She tried glaring again, but you'd think people would have figured out that I'm pretty immune to that now.

Foxglove sprang off the bed, jumped onto the drop mat and, as if it were a trampoline, shot up and out of the oubliette.

That was definitely magical, I thought. So I got up and tried a range of spells including the snapdragon, whose only purpose was to make a loud noise to scare off wild animals.

Nothing – the *formae* just wouldn't catch. But I was starting to recognise the sensation. It was the same feeling I had when I couldn't do magic in fairyland. I wondered if the oubliette was also part of an intrusion by fairyland into our world. That would explain why Foxglove could leap about and maybe also why she slept down there.

I went back to my book.

Since I was stuck there I'd decided to see if I could get all the way through 'The Music of the Ainur', the first bit of *The Silmarillion* and something I've never managed to do before. Tolkien and my dad had weirdly convergent ideas about the musical nature of the universe, although my dad would probably have been more forgiving of Melkor's improvisation. You know, providing it didn't step on his solo.

During the draggy passages I calculated what might be happening while I was tucked into my personal tertiary subspace manifold.

They knew that I'd encountered Lesley, and where, so there'd be no mucking about or down period while everyone wondered where I was. Say an hour, tops, to pull the CCTV at Wetherspoon's and Holborn, and confirm that I'd got into a fake police car.

Or was it a real one? We knew Chorley and Lesley had contacts in the Met.

If it was real then snatching me would have blown his cover – good. I hope they threw the bastard to the wild Seawoll. That'd learn him.

A kidnapped police officer, even one as accident-prone as me, is always a priority case. So no more than a couple of hours with ANPR and CCTV to track the police car, fake or otherwise, and work out where the switch to a van took place. The big variable was how long it would take them to identify the van. And I guessed the answer to that, given the operation had been planned by Lesley, was probably never.

So what next?

Zach would have been brought in again. Fuck, everyone on the Little Crocodiles list who Seawoll and Stephanopoulos even thought might be worth a tug would be tugged. That would include Patrick Gale and Camilla Turner. And they wouldn't be interviewed in the ABE suites, either. Nightingale would be out with Guleed, putting the frighteners on the demi-monde.

And a whole web of contacts and arrangements that we'd painstakingly built up over the last couple of years would be strained to breaking point.

I wondered what Beverley was doing, and hoped it didn't involve major property damage.

So I reckoned I was on my own. All I had to do was escape from a trap devised by the most devious fucker I'd ever met and a woman who once caught an entire gang selling counterfeit Gucci bags while on her coffee break. A woman who knew me better than I knew myself.

Or at least thought she did.

I let the words on the page blur out and let myself sense my surroundings. Assuming I really was in a bubble of fairyland, or more like an interface where the bubble intersected with the real world, then it must be the bubble that interfered with the *formae* I needed to create to produce a magical effect.

And if it had an effect on something I created, then it stood to reason that I should be able to detect that effect, the way the fingers can feel the rough surface of the board through the chalk.

We really were going to have to come up with some terminology one of these days. I supposed we could leave it to Abigail, if we didn't mind having the basic magical particle called the Wicked and possessed with the qualities of positive or negative charge, pro and anti-ship and bae.

There. I felt a ripple above me like a raindrop in a puddle – looked up and saw Foxglove drop onto the landing mat with her arms full of flimsy white takeaway bags.

I jumped up and stepped forward.

There was a flicker of movement and suddenly I was slammed back against the wall with Foxglove's face centimetres from my own and an ominously cold line across my throat. I was close enough to see little flecks of silver and gold that surrounded her pupils. Later I would speculate that those colours were unlikely to have been produced by the melanin concentration in her iris or Tyndall scattering in her stroma. But at that precise moment I was a bit more worried about what I assumed was a knife at my throat.

Behind her on the landing mat the white takeaway bags were still bouncing.

Without moving my head I glanced down to confirm that she was holding something to my throat with her right arm while pinning me to the wall with her left. I seriously doubted it was a paintbrush.

I looked back up at Foxglove who, when she was sure she had my full attention, stepped back and raised her knife for my inspection. It had a wickedly curved blade of white stone shading to a translucent pink at the edges – agate, I learnt later. I didn't even know you could chip and polish a stone to such a beautiful, smooth and, above all, sharp edge.

Foxglove gave me a meaningful look and tilted her head to one side.

'Never even occurred to me,' I said.

Foxglove looked sceptical but backed away, the knife vanishing under her smock.

'And you've made a mess,' I said, straightening my collar to hide the tremor in my hands.

One of the white bags had split and was leaking orange coloured sweet and sour sauce onto the landing mat. Foxglove frowned at me as if it was my fault.

'I'll clean it up, shall I?' I said, and she skipped back to give me room.

Fortunately it was just the sauce. The rest of the generic plastic food containers had stayed sealed. I surreptitiously checked for receipts or any other identification but there was none.

Foxglove approached with a roll of kitchen roll held out as a peace offering.

'Thank you,' I said, and finished cleaning up, dumped the rubbish into one of the plastic bags and held it out to Foxglove for disposal. She gave it, and then me, a suspicious look.

'There's no bin down here,' I said. 'So you've got to get rid of it.'

After a while I put it down on the mat, took what looked to be half the food and retreated to my bed. Foxglove took her half and retreated to hers. In addition to what was left of the tub of sweet and sour sauce I had pork balls and egg fried rice but no, I noticed, cutlery. I looked across the oubliette at Foxglove, who saw and raised her eyebrow.

'I know a knife and fork are out of the question,' I said. 'But what about a spoon?'

In answer she opened her rice tray and stuck her face in it and methodically ate the whole lot without coming up for air. Towards the end I could see her long tongue through the semi-transparent sides of the tray, snaking around to get the last bits. When it was all done she looked straight at me with a triumphant smile.

There were bits of rice stuck to her face so I ripped a couple of sheets off the kitchen roll and, cautiously, crossed the floor to hand them over. She took them graciously enough and wiped her face. I went back to my bed and ate with my fingers.

Afterwards I packed up the rubbish in the last plastic bag and left it pointedly in the middle of the landing mat. Then I washed my hands, unwrapped the toothbrush and cleaned my teeth. Foxglove sat cross-legged on her bed and watched me with interest while picking the occasional sliver of food out of her teeth with her fingernail.

The daylight coming in through the hole began to fade.

At this time of year sunset was around nine o'clock, which meant it had been at least twenty-four hours since I'd been taken.

'I'm having a wee,' I said. 'You better not be looking.'

She shrugged and lay down on her futon – I chose to believe that she kept her eyes averted and thank God it was just a wee.

She was under her duvet by the time I'd washed my hands so I got under mine before it was too dark to see. I lay there with my eyes closed and tried to feel the changes in the *vestigia* around me. I thought for a moment, while I was drifting off, that I felt a bubble rhythmically expand and contract as if it were breathing.

But that might just have been my own breath.

27

An Unlikely Premise for a Sitcom

I'm an only child so I've never been that comfortable sharing a room. It took me a while to get used to sharing a bed with Beverley. Mind you, Bev is a very active sleeper and, if she's not trying to snuggle me off one side of the bed, she talks in her sleep. One night I swear she was reciting the Shipping Forecast – Sole, Fastnet, Lundy, Irish Sea. And giggling after every one. She seemed to find the prospect of *Thames: gales imminent* particularly funny. When I asked her about it in the morning she insisted that I'd dreamt the whole thing up.

I woke up that first morning in the oubliette feeling sticky in my clothes and decided that I was going to have to ablute and perform bodily functions whether Foxglove was watching or not. Fortunately she seemed just as keen on my cleanliness as I was, or at least that's how interpreted her pointing emphatically at the shower before leaping up and out of our cosy little home.

And that became the pattern for the days that followed.

After my shower she dropped in with breakfast – pitta breads stuffed with cold falafel and a limp salad. More takeaway, so I was definitely within range of a Chinese and kebab place – which narrowed my location down, I calculated, to somewhere in the UK.

Or possibly the Costa del Sol, although I think I might have noticed a flight.

Foxglove bounced out of the hole with the rubbish and when she didn't return after half an hour I sat down and picked up *The Silmarillion* again.

I lasted about an hour before the naming of the Valar drove me to exercise.

One advantage of training in a gym that was last updated in 1939 is that I've learnt to do without equipment. You can give yourself a good workout in an hour if you push it, but I broke it up into twenty minute chunks to stretch it through the day.

Once in a while I'd have a go at creating a *forma*, because you never know. But they all sputtered out without catching. Even *lux*, which I can normally reliably do while standing on my head.

Foxglove returned at lunch with bread, cheese, some loose tomatoes and a bottle of beer, and again later in the evening with half a roast chicken, chips and salad – probably from the same place the falafel had come from. She watched me eat and then left me alone until it was dark.

This time I wasn't knackered from a long day of being kidnapped, so it was much harder to sleep. Still, in the quiet darkness I did my breathing and slowly tried to feel out the parameters of the bubble that held me. I think it rained that night because I could hear drops splattering on the skylights far above the entrance and got 'May It Be' by Enya stuck on an endless loop in my head. But I also sensed a ripple as Foxglove dropped through the entrance and onto the landing mat. She stared at me for a long moment and then slipped silently over to her own bed.

The next day after breakfast – this time a selection of Kellogg's Nutri-Grain breakfast bars and a bottle of Lucozade Zero Pink Lemonade – Foxglove reappeared with a basket full of clean bedding, which she dumped in front of me. She stripped her own bed and stood around tapping her foot until I got the message and stripped mine. Then she vaulted away with the basket full of used linen. While she was gone I made both our beds, being particularly careful to do a good job on Foxglove's. I had a thorough look round while I was doing it, but the thing about futons is that they're a bit short of hiding places – I suspected that was the point.

Lunch that day was a steak slice, grated carrot and sultana salad in a clear plastic box, an iced bun. Somebody – I suspect Lesley – had taken care to remove any identifying bags or receipts but I know Greggs when I'm eating it. Another point on the triangulation should I ever get out – especially since the steak slice was still oven warm.

After the food delivery Foxglove cautiously approached her bed and examined my handiwork. Finding it acceptable, she turned and gave me a polite little nod and a quizzical tilt of her head.

'It's not like I have anything else to do with my time,' I said, and waved the remains of my iced bun at her. 'I like this stuff. Can we have this again for dinner?'

Foxglove stared at my iced bun for a moment, then shrugged and departed, leaving me alone with Thingol the terminally lost and the rest of the slightly dim-witted Elves of the years before the First Age.

Dinner was late and while I waited I noticed that the bubble definitely faded a bit when Foxglove wasn't there. Half of magic is recognising the reality behind all the mental noise of everyday life. And once you've noticed something it's easier to spot it again.

Allowing for confirmation bias, of course.

When it finally arrived, dinner was shish kebab in a pitta and chips and a can of Dr Pepper. So that was all the food groups covered, then. Foxglove made a point of daintily eating her meat one chunk at a time, but she seemed a bit puzzled about what to do with the salad.

That evening I did extra exercise in the hope of wearing myself out, and then I had a shower even though Foxglove was still in the oubliette. She didn't seem to mind, but I caught her giving me a speculative look while I was drying myself off.

That night I amused myself by seeing if I could recount the whole of *The Emperor's New Groove* from memory, and when I laughed out loud for the third time Foxglove slapped the side of her futon to get my attention and hissed.

'Why do we even have that lever?' I asked her, but then shut up because I knew from experience with Molly that that particular style of hissing was a bad sign.

So of course then I couldn't sleep, because I worried she was going sneak over and murder me in my bed.

Another morning in the armpit of paradise, more breakfast bars and a bottle of Perrier.

'These,' I told Foxglove when she handed over the

food, 'are not nearly as good for you as the packaging pretends they are. And would it kill you to give me some caffeine?'

To be honest, I was shocked to find that by Day Five I was beginning to run out of Blitz spirit. It's hard to maintain the requisite levels of Cockney cheer when sleeping on a futon and going without coffee. However, I was cheered immensely when the washing basket made a reappearance, dropping down from the entrance hole like a beacon of hope.

Before Foxglove could reappear I stripped the bedding off both our futons and dumped it in the basket. While I worked I sang a medley of late teens Grime hits with the occasional impromptu percussion accompaniment and finishing with as much of 'Too Many Man' as I could remember. It did kind of peter out a bit when I turned round to find Foxglove standing right behind me.

I jumped. She smiled, but the joke was on her.

She accepted the dirty laundry from me and jumped out without checking it was all there. I've found that if you voluntarily take on a chore somebody else doesn't want to do, they don't check the results too closely – in case they have to do it again themselves. Once I was sure she was safely gone I pulled the sheet I'd nicked from her bed, folded it into a rectangle and hid it inside my nice fresh duvet cover. I didn't know how I was going to escape, but I was pretty certain that access to ye olde knotted sheet rope would be a good start.

If they had cameras then I was stuffed. But I was willing to bet they didn't work in fairyland, either.

*

That afternoon, as I came to terms with the twin burdens of cold falafel for lunch and Fëanor's staggering denseness re: Morgoth's intentions, Foxglove dropped down with a large artist's sketchpad and an empty Heinz beans tin full of sticks of charcoal. She sat cross-legged on her bed and began to draw.

I sat on my bed with my back against the wall and pretended to read *The Silmarillion*. She kept giving me sly looks over the top of her pad. We were both playing the game of pretend indifference – I had no intention of trying to win, but I had to wait long enough for it to be convincing.

I gave it ten minutes.

'Are you any good?' I asked.

She gave me an inquiring look, as if she wasn't sure what I was talking about.

'At drawing,' I said. 'Are you any good? I'm famously bad at drawing. Life-changingly bad, in fact.'

Her eyes narrowed – perhaps she thought I was taking the piss.

'Can I have a look?'

Foxglove tilted her pad against her chest to hide it and suddenly I realised that the loose top she was wearing was a linen artist's smock – in fact, all she needed was a beret and the cliché would have been complete.

I thought of Molly and her Edwardian maid's outfit and wondered if the costume was significant. Noted fairy botherer Charles Kingsley argued that many of the true fae *take particular care to array themselves in the garb that most closely represents their nature.*

Not a maid, and not a warrior queen of the Stone Age but what – an artist?

I tried hard not to smile because I know about artists. Well, musicians really. But same difference.

'Seriously,' I said. 'It can't be as bad as my work.'

She gave me a suspicious look which I returned with as much sincerity as I could muster.

She came to a decision and leapt to her feet. Flipping her pad shut, she took two steps and flew up the shaft and out of sight.

I sighed and went back to my book, in which Morgoth nicked the eponymous jewels and had away with them back to Angbad. Sorry mate, I thought, not my jurisdiction. Did you have them insured? Whereupon Fëanor gets a crime number and a leaflet about being on guard against theft and the wiles of the personification of evil.

Like I said, I think I was wearing a little bit thin at that point.

Supper was pizza, which arrived in a Pizza Express box along with garlic bread and a two-litre bottle of Coca-Cola. Caffeine at last, I thought, and saved half the bottle for breakfast. While I ate Foxglove sketched me from across the room and, to my surprise, showed me her work after I'd cleared up. She was good – having caught me in a few bold charcoal strokes. I must have looked impressed because she gave a little hiss of pleasure and turned pink.

I let her pose me for more work, because in a kidnapping situation you're supposed to take every opportunity to bond with your captors. The theory being the more they relate to you as a person the harder it is for them to casually off you when the time comes.

The light from above turned rainy grey and we could hear heavy drops bouncing off the glass roof far above. As it grew dark, Foxglove kept going until I was fairly certain that she was drawing from memory.

I used to think that being forced to attend one of my mum's family's christenings was most the boring thing I'd ever done – now I know better.

Posing also turned out to be surprisingly tiring and I think I fell asleep almost as soon as I got into bed.

Apart from delivering breakfast and lunch, Foxglove left me alone for most of the day. That at least allowed me to confirm that without her presence the bubble definitely weakened. Not enough that I could actually do a spell, but enough to explain why she had to sleep down in the oubliette with me.

I wondered if Molly could have the same effect. If she did, that would allow us to make truly magic-proof cells in the Folly. Then the main obstacle to locking up practitioners like Martin Chorley would be making the Folly PACE compatible – custody sergeant and everything.

Still, I'd got the impression that Foxglove had already slept in the oubliette before I'd arrived. Perhaps she was more comfortable sleeping in her little bubble. Which begged the question – would Molly be more comfortable sleeping in the same? Which, of course, led to one of those three in the morning thoughts – what if she already was? I knew she had her lair in the front part of the basement where Nightingale pointedly never intruded, and I'd always followed his lead. She could have been spending her nights in Narnia for all we knew.

After supper – kebab again, which at least meant I got to have Foxglove's leftover pitta and salad – she brought out her sketchpad and charcoals and looked at me expectantly.

I clowned a bit to see if I could make her laugh, trying various heroic poses which backfired when she insisted that I stay fixed in my impression of Anteros, god of requited love, as depicted by Alfred Gilbert's statue in Piccadilly Circus. Which meant standing on one foot while leaning forward and pulling an imaginary bow and arrow.

I lasted all of five minutes before falling over, which caused Foxglove to make the short hissing sound that I recognised as laughter. She motioned for me to take up the pose again, but I refused and she had to make do with Peter Grant heroically massaging his ankle.

Foxglove kept it up until the light began to dim.

'Do you like working for Chorley?' I asked, as she packed away her work.

Her head tilted as if considering the question.

'I mean, does he pay well?'

There was a short hissing sound again.

'So why work for him?'

The mouth turned down and she pressed her wrists together and held them out as if they were handcuffed or bound with invisible rope.

'You're a prisoner?' I asked.

The mouth turned mournful.

'Not prisoner,' I asked. 'Slave?'

Foxglove's head drooped and her hands, still invisibly bound, dropped into her lap.

'How?'

Without looking up, Foxglove shrugged and slid under her duvet and went to sleep.

I wished I could.

'Hi, Peter,' said Lesley. 'You awake down there?'

It was after lunch the next day and Lesley, sensibly, didn't come down to join me. Instead she stood at the edge of the hole and called down.

I folded over my page to mark it and sauntered over to look up at her.

'What are you doing here?'

'I thought I'd pop in see how you're doing,' she said.

'Fine,' I said. 'Although I'm finding Thingol a bit of a prat to be honest.'

'Who's Thingol when he's at home?'

'Guy in a book,' I said. 'What have you been up to?'

'This and that,' she said.

'Aiding and abetting?'

'Before, after and during the fact,' she said. 'Just like everybody else – if they're honest.'

'Slavery's a new one for you, though, isn't it?'

'Slavery?'

'Yeah,' I said. 'I know you've been out of the police business for a while but they passed a whole new anti-slavery law this year. Specifically includes people that sit by and let it happen.'

'Who the fuck do you think is a slave?'

'Foxglove thinks she is.'

'Bollocks.'

'No, straight up,' I said, 'Told me so herself.'

'She can walk out of here whenever she likes,' said Lesley.

'But she doesn't, does she? Why do you think that is?'

'How should I know? And in what way is that different from Molly?'

I know a losing argument when I'm having it, so I changed the subject.

'Are you going to come down?' I said. 'I'm getting a crick in my neck here.'

She grinned, the old grin, the one I remembered.

'That would be stupid of me, wouldn't it? But don't worry, you're not going to be down there much longer. Job's nearly done.'

'Lesley,' I said, 'there's no Merlin for you to bring back, no Arthur waiting for England's greatest need and that sword is not fucking Excalibur. You're just going to fuck things up for people.'

'People is already fucked up,' said Lesley. 'And maybe instead of moaning, Peter, maybe you should help and make things better. That reminds me—'

She reached out of sight and pulled out a white and blue Tesco bag, which she dangled over the hole.

'Watch out. It's heavy,' she said, and dropped it.

I should have let it hit the floor. But you can take caution too far, plus it was heavy and there was a glass clink as it landed in my arms.

'Check you later,' said Lesley, and was gone.

Inside the bag was a mega packet of Doritos, three packets of salt and vinegar crisps, a jar of Tesco's own brand hot salsa dip and a bottle of Bacardi. Crumpled in the bottom of the bag was the receipt – I smoothed it out. Lesley had been shopping in the Covent Garden branch of Tesco. Unless I'd been the victim of a spectacular bit of misdirection I doubted we could be anywhere near central London – not with all this expensive empty space. Still, I noted the time and date of purchase and tucked it into my shoe for safe keeping.

When Foxglove dropped back in, half an hour later, I asked her for some glasses and she fetched me some plastic tumblers, the flimsy thin-walled kind that are difficult to fashion into a shiv.

I offered her some of the Bacardi but she sniffed the tumbler and handed it back. She did try the Doritos and the dip which, much to my amusement, she found too spicy. I think I must have overdone the Bacardi, though, because I told her some stories about my work – although I steered clear of anything involving Chorley or the fae. I don't think she understood the haunted BMWs or the sentient mould, but she seemed to find the incident at Kew Gardens hilarious. Everyone seems to find that case funny, except for me – and the custodians at Kew, of course.

I woke up the next morning with that floppy buzz you get when you drink enough to get fuzzy but not enough to get a hangover.

I also had a cold feeling in my stomach.

Job's nearly done, Lesley had said.

I needed out of the oubliette and fast.

28

I am Curious (Batman)

It started with me taking my shirt off so that Foxglove could get a good look at my rippling shoulder muscles, elegantly shaped biceps and my almost six pack. Not for the reason you might be thinking, because a) I ain't that conceited and b) I've learnt that the fae don't think like that.

But artists like the challenge of the naked human form – or at least that's what Oberon and Effra tell me. And they're from South London, so they should know. We also started straight after lunch, which was unusual and slightly worrying. I'd got the impression that Foxglove was off doing chores most of the day but now she seemed to have a lot of free time. I feared that one phase of Chorley's operation was winding down in preparation for Punch Day.

I waited for a natural break in the rhythm of her work before asking how she came to be working for Martin Chorley.

Foxglove gave me a long stare, as if weighing whether I was serious, and then she made an elegant swooping motion with her left hand which ended with her fingers resting high on her chest. Her eyes locked with mine.

'Yes, I want to know,' I said.

So Foxglove started to tell me. It took ages to get the story out, and even after independently corroborating some of it there are parts where I'm not sure I interpreted her meaning correctly. I did suggest that she draw pictures, but either she didn't understand the concept or she didn't want to remember things that way.

The gist was that she had been traded by her queen for something valuable – Foxglove didn't know what – to a strange man. The trade took place near the sea and definitely not in London. There'd been a group of them and at least two had been separated from the group immediately. Then they'd been put in a box on wheels drawn by horses – a carriage or a cart – and taken somewhere underground.

'Where we are now?' I asked.

Foxglove shook her head.

It got confused after that, but I think decades went by while Foxglove and her sisters worked in some capacity for their 'owner'. I still haven't discovered what work they were doing, but I think during that time Foxglove was taught to paint and draw. But not, I noticed, to read or write.

There was a break while Foxglove fetched supper, one of those incredibly greasy almost-but-not-quite KFC fried chicken buckets, which we divided up on paper plates and ate together sitting on the landing mat. Foxglove ate her chicken bones and all, happily crunching up the denuded drumsticks as if they were breadsticks. I offered her mine, which seemed to please her.

Afterwards we stayed on the mat drinking generic lemonade while Foxglove continued with her sad, sad story.

After some years they were put in a metal box, possibly a van this time, and taken to another place where they were put to work cleaning – I recognised some serious mop action in the mime show – and doing a weird strut while holding something aloft with one hand. When Foxglove mimed handing out drinks I realised she was waitressing. And when she demonstrated a smile of fake enticement I knew, with a sick feeling, which club she was waitressing in.

Albert Woodville-Gentle, Faceless Man the first, had owned a club in Soho in the 1960s and '70s. Within its gilt and red velvet embrace he'd offered his exclusive clientele the exotic delights of people altered by magic to conform to their fantasies. There were real cat-girls and cat-boys, and other things that Nightingale has made a point of keeping from me. The place became known as the Strip Club of Doctor Moreau until Stephanopoulos threatened dire consequences if we didn't drop the term.

Albert Woodville-Gentle was crippled in a magical duel in 1979 and finally died just after Christmas 2012 – a lucky escape for him. since I'm almost certain Nightingale had *plans*.

Which left the question of what had become of Foxglove and her 'sisters', of which two were left, after Woodville-Gentle was gone. The answer is: somebody put them in a pit, not unlike the one I was in, and left them in it for, I estimate, about fifteen years. They survived by luring rats and insects into the hole for food and licking moisture off the walls.

Foxglove was shocked by my reaction and so, frankly,

was I. Us police are supposed to be tough, but there are limits. I hid my eyes with my hand and we both spent a long time staring at the ground.

We stayed that way as the light faded and we both climbed into our respective beds.

One day, I thought, I will find whoever it was put you in that pit.

And then what will I do?

Prosecute them for false imprisonment and/or attempted murder?

Make sure they were branded as sex offenders, that was for certain.

Having started her tale, Foxglove couldn't wait to continue, even as I was having my breakfast the next morning. I was less ready. I had an inkling about what was coming next.

Then the darkness lifted and they were rescued.

'Who by?' I asked.

Foxglove made a gesture as if elegantly placing a mask upon her face. The same gesture she'd used to describe Albert Woodville-Gentle. This would be the Faceless Man mark two – Martin Chorley. He was their new master, and a much kinder master he proved. There were soft beds and good food and clean clothes and, best of all, he not only let Foxglove paint but encouraged her to do so.

She disappeared after lunch and returned with a plastic bucket stuffed with art supplies. Then she proudly showed me her museum-quality oils and acrylics and a truly astonishing range of brushes kept in a series of baked beans tins, round-tipped and pointed, sable or bristle haired depending on style.

More than that, she went on to tell me, on some nights Chorley would lead her out of the club and to big houses where rows and rows of paintings hung.

Foxglove fetched some of the copies she'd made, all stored in a genuine brown leather A1 sized art case that was probably older then my dad and definitely better maintained.

Most of her pictures were portraits and mythological scenes, of the diaphanous dress and cherub school of slipping one past a disapproving censor. My limited art knowledge pegged the majority as post-Renaissance to Victorian. One I did recognise was of a white woman in a blue dress drawing a magic circle around herself while a brazier belches a column of white smoke into the sky. *The Magic Circle* by John William Waterhouse, which I'd stumbled across while researching Martin Chorley's taste in art. It stuck in my mind because of the subject's flagrant health and safety violation. As any competent practitioner will tell you, you always complete your protective circle *before* you start your workings.

The steel blue of the sorceress's dress was brighter than I remembered from the original and the belt sash a deeper, richer burgundy. The crows that watched her were the same midnight black as her hair.

Perhaps, I thought, this is what the painting looked like when Waterhouse turned it out in the 1880s – before the years dimmed its canvas.

Now, my brushes with fine art have mostly involved magic pots and guilt-ridden Old Soldiers, but I seriously doubted that Martin Chorley had been encouraging Foxglove's hobby out of the goodness of his heart.

I reckoned that when I got out there were going to prove to be some serious gaps in some famous collections.

If I got out.

I told Foxglove, truthfully, that her painting was beautiful and she beamed.

Then her head cocked to one side – as if she were listening.

'Who is it?' I asked.

Foxglove snatched her work from my hands and, springing over to her bed, stuffed them and the art case under her mattress. She turned to glare at me and put her hand across her mouth.

'Not a word,' I said. 'I promise.'

'Foxglove,' called a voice from above – Chorley. 'Where are you?' He sounded like an adult trying to restrain their impatience with a child. 'Chop-chop. All hands on deck.'

Foxglove jumped up. And for the first time I got a sense of how she was doing it – the ripple in the fabric of the bubble that propelled her upwards as if it were coughing her up.

'Don't get too comfortable with him,' I heard Chorley say. 'He eats your kind for breakfast.'

I heard footsteps moving away and waited in silence – listening.

There was the occasional echo of a door slamming in the distance, Somebody, I think it might have been Lesley, very clearly shouted – 'Fuck shit bugger!'

Followed by a metallic crash and a deep resonant chime whose harmonics actually caused the fairy bubble to resonate around me.

It was the bell. Something was happening, and it was happening soon.

Or maybe not, because Foxglove was on time with supper, which was a set of disappointing ham sandwiches of the type you bought from garage shops. I ate them wistfully, thinking of Molly and daydreaming of coffee while Foxglove hopped impatiently from foot to foot. She was obviously dying to show me something but wanted my full attention.

I forwent the final sandwich – it wasn't much of a sacrifice.

From her art case Foxglove drew an A4 sized ring-bound sketchpad. It had seen some use – one of the corners had been blunted by a hard impact, and the cover was smudged with fingerprints where Foxglove had handled it while drawing.

The first picture was of a young woman with eyes slotted like a cat's and ears that rose to a tufted point. The style was what they call in posh art circles hyper-realism – Foxglove had lovingly captured the luxurious fur that covered face, head and shoulders. She looked like really good cosplay but I didn't think she was somebody having fun on the weekend. And Foxglove had captured a haunted look in her eyes.

I must have grunted something suitably encouraging, because Foxglove cheerfully flipped the pad to reveal another young woman drawn in the same hyperrealistic style. A pale, high-cheekboned face with a cascade of long black hair, and the disturbing turn of the mouth as if hiding too many teeth. Somebody I recognised, although I hadn't known her long. And most of the time I had known her she'd been trying to kill me. It was the Pale Lady that I'd chased into the Trocadero Centre, who'd hit me so hard I thought I'd felt my ribs creak. Who I'd knocked over a balcony five storeys up and who'd fallen to her death in complete silence.

'Very fine,' I said. 'Who is she?'

Foxglove touched the sketch with two fingers and then transferred them to her chest about where everyone thinks the heart is located. My own heart hurt. There's no other word for it. And suddenly I felt sick.

'Your friend,' I said, and Foxglove nodded.

She flipped the pad to show me another familiar face. Also someone I'd met quite briefly while, coincidentally, they were trying to kill me. It was the nanny from Richard Williams's house. Again Foxglove touched first the picture and then her heart.

When me and Lesley were doing our probation at Charing Cross nick our duty inspector was Francis Neblett. He was a proper old-fashioned copper, not like what the public thinks is old-fashioned, which is all TV bollocks, but so upright and steeped in the Peelian Principles that if you sliced him in half you'd have found BOBBY running all the way through him like a stick of rock.

He once told me that the problem was not that criminals were evil but that most of them were pathetic – in the proper sense of the word. *Arousing pity, especially through vulnerability or sadness.* Recently I'd learnt the Greek root: *pathetos – liable to suffer.*

'You've got to feel sorry for them,' he said.

And you didn't have to be in the job long to see what he meant. The addicts, the runaways, the men who were fine unless they had a couple of drinks. The ex-squaddies who'd seen too much. The sad fuckers who just didn't have a clue how to make the world work for them, or had started so beaten down they barely learnt to walk upright. The people who shoplifted toilet paper or food or treats for their kids.

'This is a trap,' he'd said. 'You're not a social worker or a doctor. If people really wanted these problems solved there'd be more social workers and doctors.'

I'd asked what we were supposed to do.

'You can't fix their problems, Peter,' he'd said. 'Most of the time you can't even steer them in the right direction. But you can do the job without making things worse.'

I looked at the sketches and back at Foxglove's expectant face.

What would Lesley do? I wondered.

She'd lie, or at least mislead – imply that she knew exactly where Foxglove's sisters were and if only Foxglove helped her escape they could be reunited.

You're in a hole, Peter, Lesley would say, there's nothing helpful you can do for anyone until you're out of the hole, is there? Escape first. Then you'll be able to be all compassionate and thoughtful.

But I'm not Lesley or Nightingale, or even Neblett, am I?

'I know them,' I said. 'But I'm afraid they're both dead.'

It took a moment to register and then her eyes widened and her lips parted in dismay. She took an involuntary step backwards and clutched the sketchpad to her chest. I tentatively held out my hand but she flinched back, her face suddenly broken in its grief. She half turned and took a couple of steps towards her bed. I took a step to follow, but she threw up her hand to stop me.

I stayed where I was and watched as, bent over in pain, Foxglove stumbled back to her bed and lay down curled around her sketchpad, face towards the wall. Not knowing what else to do, I retreated to my bed and sat down to watch over her.

The light began to dim and I called out her name, but even to me my voice sounded flat, dull and unhelpful.

I became aware of a smell of dampness and mildew and old brick. The smell of cellars – the smell, I realised, that the oubliette should have had from the start. Once I thought to look, I sensed the bubble beginning to fray.

I called Foxglove's name but she didn't respond.

This was my chance, I realised. Quickly I pulled the sheet I'd nicked and stripped the second one off the mattress. Then I pulled off the duvet cover and ripped it apart at the seams so that I ended up with two separate sheets. You're supposed to tear the sheets into strips and braid them to make a proper rope, but I didn't think I had that much time. So I knotted them in the traditional cartoon fashion and hoped for the best.

I conjured a werelight and this time the *forma* stuck – a bit hesitantly, but I could feel the fairy bubble shivering and failing. It looked like magic was back on the options menu.

You can't lift yourself with *impello*. Nobody knows why. You also can't hold on to something or wear a harness attached to something and lift that with *impello*. Once, Nightingale had discovered me experimenting and he gave me a couple of notebooks which detailed the numerous ways the wizards of the Folly had tried to get round this limitation. Many of the contraptions in the notebook looked like something Dastardly and Muttley would pilot, and provided a good laugh, if not any actual hope that I was going to fly any time soon.

But I didn't need to fly. I just needed to fix one end of my bedsheet rope to the lip of the hole firmly enough for me to climb it. And I had just the spell for that. All I needed was something separate and robust enough that I could use to pin the top of the rope to the brickwork. I picked up my copy of *The Silmarillion* – that would do nicely.

I took rope and book to the landing pad and tried another werelight – this time it burnt brightly – the bubble was almost gone. I extinguished the light and concentrated.

Then I threw my copy of *The Silmarillion* upwards and used *impello* to guide it and *scindere* to stick it upright on the edge of the hole. I'd fashioned a noose at one end of the rope and reckoned it should be a simple matter to throw it up and over the book as if it were a mooring bollard.

I looked back at Foxglove, who was a dim shape in the darkness.

'I'm going to get help,' I said.

I got the noose around *The Silmarillion* on the third try and put my whole weight on it as a test. Totally solid – which did surprise me a little bit.

I looked back again at Foxglove, who still hadn't moved. Just to be on the safe side I went back to check.

She was completely still and I couldn't hear any breathing. I cautiously touched her neck – the skin was cool and I couldn't find a pulse.

I was CPR qualified but I'd never had to do it for real and even if I did, it's a temporary measure to maintain oxygen supply to the brain until help arrived. But if I didn't escape help wouldn't arrive.

Common sense said I should scarper. But as anyone will tell you, me and common sense have always had an open relationship. And anyway I was remembering Simone and her sisters when I found them quiet and cool amongst the shadows of the Café de Paris.

Duty of care and all that.

You can't do CPR on a mattress, so I grabbed Foxglove's arm and dragged her off the bed. I rolled her onto her back, and as I did that I saw a definite flicker of expression. I pushed her sketchbook downwards and out of the way so I could put my ear to her chest. There it was. A heartbeat, clear but slow.

Whatever ailed Foxglove, it was clearly psychosomatic. And the speculation about how it worked so quickly would give Doctors Vaughan and Walid months of fun. If I could just bring them a live subject.

'We need you, Foxglove,' I said. 'For science.'

She was still clutching the sketchbook to her stomach.

If Foxglove was literally dying of despair then the answer was obvious.

'Foxglove,' I said, 'you know the two friends who were separated from you at the beginning? I think I know where one of them is.'

I was actually expecting a pause, but instead Foxglove's eyes flew open. Her face was a pale oval in the darkness, registering surprise and anger.

I heard a slithering sound from the entrance followed by a thump as my copy of *The Silmarillion* hit the landing mat.

'Bollocks,' I said.

Then Foxglove was on her feet so fast I was thrown onto my back. I swear she trailed a weird luminescent wake behind her as she ran to the centre of the oubliette and jumped away.

I stayed on my back because I couldn't think of a good reason to get up. Although it wasn't totally dark, I noticed the entrance hole was a disc of slightly lighter tone among the blackness.

When I was in primary school I had a general education teacher called Miss Bosworth, who thought I was slow. She was very nice about it, was Miss Bosworth – she just made sure she explained everything to me very clearly and made a point of not asking me to do anything particularly difficult. I thought she was great, and she was probably my first love if you don't count my Lego Space Station Zenon kit.

I remember overhearing her telling my mum that while I was a lovely boy, if a bit boisterous, she probably shouldn't hold out much hope for an academic career. I don't remember what my mum said. But looking back I can't help notice that was the last parent-teacher conference they ever had.

I don't actually remember what Miss Bosworth looked like any more. I think she must have been white and had brown hair, but that's it. The Space Station Zenon kit, on the other hand, came with three minifigs, several 1×8 plates and the forty-five degree sloping pieces and canopy that allowed you to make really cool hypersonic jet planes. I like to think it's still out there in Sierra Leone somewhere, being used to make dreams and inconvenience parents in the middle of the night.

If she stays away long enough, I thought, the bubble will collapse again.

I pulled myself to my feet and cautiously felt my way over to the landing mat. But before I could recover my makeshift rope and copy of *The Silmarillion*, Foxglove jumped down, grabbed me around the waist and jumped out again.

29

One Does Not Simply Walk Into The Folly

We were in the big workshop space with the glazed ceiling I'd had a glimpse of before being pushed into the hole. The last of the daylight had seeped out of the sky and there was only reflected light pollution to illuminate walls and shadows. Foxglove's face was almost luminous and random fairy sparkles clung to her sleeves and hair.

I was about to ask her which way was out when she jumped back down into the oubliette.

'What are you doing?' I hissed after her – keeping it low in case random minions were still on site.

I could hear Foxglove moving about and I was that close to dangling over the edge to look for her when she jumped back up, clutching her art case and giving me a defiant look.

'Fine,' I whispered. 'Which way out?'

Foxglove pointed, a pale shape in the darkness, down the length of the workshop. Then, realising that, unlike her, I couldn't see anything, she took my hand and led me off. Once I got close to the far end I could see a door. It was locked, so I popped out the lock with the imaginatively titled *clausurafrange* spell. Beyond was a small courtyard surrounded by high brick walls with broken glass embedded at the top.

There was another exterior-style door at the other end, but when I headed towards it Foxglove wouldn't follow. She hovered in the doorway with her eyes fixed firmly on the ground.

'Just a little bit further,' I said. 'And we're away for ever.'

She gave me a lopsided smile, hoisted her art case over her head as if to keep off the rain, and let me take her hand and lead her to the door. Which was also locked, but not for long.

There was an access road on the other side. Lined by high garden walls on the left and the dark square bulks of early 1980s light engineering units on the right. Ahead there was a traffic barrier and a main road. I trotted towards it, pulling Foxglove behind me. She was making little distressed hissing sounds and still holding the art case above her head, but she easily kept up with me.

A wise man once said that when fleeing it was always important to focus on 'away' rather than worrying about what was behind you. It's sage advice, as demonstrated by the way I nearly got myself creamed by a number 45 bus while checking over my shoulder for pursuit.

I stopped to orientate myself and spotted a street sign – Coldharbour Lane. I'd been in bloody Brixton the whole time. Effra was going to be pissed off when she found out, but at least I now knew where I was.

Foxglove had a painful grip on my arm and her face buried in my shoulder, as if she couldn't bear to look. My warrant card was long gone and I couldn't be sure that Lesley or Chorley or minions weren't right behind us. I wanted off the street, but didn't want to put a random homeowner in danger. Instead we ran left towards the train station.

After less than a hundred metres Foxglove was showing signs of serious distress and I felt her stumble a couple of times, but we'd reached the shopping parade by then and fortunately the Nisa Local was still open. A nervous black girl of about fifteen who was manning the tills gave us a weary look of disgust as we rushed in. Then got all confused when I told her I was a police officer and that I needed to use a phone.

'You have to ask the manager,' she said.

'I know you're carrying one,' I said. 'Hand it over.'

She mumbled something about not being supposed to carry them on the shop floor but handed over her HTC OnePlus 2. I retreated with Foxglove into the corner where we'd be hidden by the shelves and called Guleed. I probably should have called CCC first, but I didn't want to take the chance that Chorley still had access to a leak.

Foxglove, who seemed much less panicky now she had a roof over her head, was staring with fascination at the dental health section we were hiding behind. She took down a packet of mint floss and sniffed it.

'Behave,' I said.

Guleed picked up and I told her where I was, and where Chorley's lair was, and let her get on with it. She said she'd pick me up personally. Which I took to mean she was worried about leaks, too.

A thin, overworked, middle-aged white woman appeared at the end of the aisle and nervously asked if we were really police. I said that I was, in my brightest reassuring-the-public voice and handed back the phone.

'This is a witness. I'm afraid there's been a serious incident, but there's no need to worry. My colleagues will be here soon.'

'Can I help?' she asked

I told her we were fine – only to discover that Foxglove had been squirting hand sanitiser on the floor behind me. The woman smiled madly and backed off – no doubt to dial 999 as soon as she thought we couldn't hear her.

Foxglove showed me an air freshener and gave me a quizzical look.

'Later,' I said, and made her put it back.

Guleed arrived three minutes later, coming through the front door with her extendable baton in her hand – at which point the manager ran off and locked herself in the staff loos.

Guleed put it away when she saw us, and looked me up and down, then peered around me to smile at Foxglove, who was using me as a shield.

'Nightingale's setting up a perimeter,' she said. 'And who's this?'

'This is Foxglove,' I said. 'Foxglove, this is Sahra – a friend of mine.'

Foxglove reached around me to shake Guleed's hand.

'Nightingale wants to know if it's safe to breach,' said Guleed.

I said I didn't know, but anyway we had to put

Foxglove somewhere before we could raid my former prison. Since the only safe place I could think of was the Folly, that meant Nightingale had to tool over to the Nisa Local to inspect her first. He arrived just before the area manager did and Sahra had to escort him to see the manager.

When the cop cars come screaming to a halt outside a bank robbery, the bit the films don't show is the two hours of us milling about as we all sort out who's going to do what to who and under what legislation.

And that's not counting the risk assessment.

I felt Foxglove tremble at Nightingale's approach, but he was careful and patient and we all got through the introductions without anyone biting anyone. I briefed him on what I knew about the layout of what had indeed turned out to be a former factory and on my best guess of the likelihood of booby traps (high) or minions (low). We had two options – raid the premises immediately or wait to see if Chorley and Lesley returned.

'I definitely heard them moving a second bell,' I said.

'The longer we wait, the greater the risk of squandering this advantage you've bought us,' said Nightingale immediately. 'I'll lead the raid in now to deal with any booby traps. Sahra will come in behind me with her team to make any necessary arrests and secure for a search.' He looked at me and then at Foxglove – tilting his head slightly to the side. 'You can accompany Foxglove back to the Folly and stay with her.'

We couldn't risk leaving a former associate of Chorley unsupervised – not least because we didn't know how Molly would react.

'Dr Walid will meet you there,' said Nightingale. 'Any questions?'

'Sahra has a team now?' I asked, and glared at Guleed, who gave me a smug smile.

Nightingale shook his head. 'Off you go, Peter. I'll let you know as soon as the area's secure.'

Me and Foxglove rode home to the Folly in the back of a pool car. Foxglove spent the journey staring excitedly out the window although she flat out refused to put on her seatbelt.

For obvious reasons, I didn't want Foxglove's arrival at the Folly to be through the tradesman's entrance. So I had the pool car drop us off at the Russell Square entrance. Then I took her hand and led her inside. I hesitated in the lobby to see whether the famous 'defences' had any objection to Foxglove, who had immediately been drawn to the statue of Isaac Newton.

Nothing zapped anybody, so obviously the 'defences' weren't against the likes of Foxglove. What *had* those, justifiably paranoid, wartime wizards been worried about?

There was nobody in the visitors' lounge or even the atrium. The police staff would have headed home so I supposed everyone one else was out raiding chez captivity.

I called out for Molly.

'I've brought someone to see you,' I said.

There was a terrible crash and I turned to see Molly sweeping towards us, having dropped her tray on the tiles behind her – a milk jug on its second bounce and leaving a spray of white behind it.

Before I could move, Foxglove ducked around me and rushed to meet Molly. They both stopped suddenly, facing each other, centimetres apart. Molly's hand rose as if to touch Foxglove's face and hesitated. But Foxglove seized it with her own and pressed it to her cheek. Molly's face crumpled into an agonised shape and I thought I saw tears before she buried it in Foxglove's shoulder.

Then, with astonishing speed, they swept away out through the servants' door by the east staircase.

That's one problem down, I thought. Time to call Bev.

Only then Dr Walid arrived and did, fairly unobtrusively, medical things to me right there in the atrium before declaring that I seemed fine. But if I felt dizzy, fatigued or nauseous I was to let him know immediately. I said, while guiding him firmly towards the front door, that of course I would. But what I was really looking forward to was my bed. Thank you for your concern.

'And likewise if you have any psychological symptoms,' he said, which made me pause.

'What kind of symptoms?' I asked.

'Recurrent memories, flashbacks, upsetting dreams, avoidance, negative feelings, emotional numbness and memory problems,' he said.

I informed him that if any of that happened he'd be the first person I'd call, which mollified him enough to get him out the door.

'Don't forget to call your parents,' he said, as I practically closed the door in his face.

So I called my parents on the Folly landline and got my mum's voicemail, thank God. I left a brief reassuring message and was about to finally call Beverley when

I heard Toby bark and found him sitting beside me with his lead in his mouth.

'Five minutes tops,' I said, but in the end the walk was more like fifteen.

Then I phoned Beverley.

'Where are you?' she asked.

I told her and asked where she was.

'Outside the back door,' she said.

'Why didn't you come in?'

'You know why,' she said.

So I ran to the back and found her waiting for me in her emergency work jeans and the purple sweatshirt she wears when everything else is in the wash. She grabbed me and kissed me and we snogged on the doorstop like we were both fifteen and had disapproving parents. She tasted of liquorice and seawater and that first ever rum and Coke I'd sneaked, courtesy of an older cousin, at a christening.

'Are you sure you can't come in?' I asked during a break.

'No,' she said. 'But I've been camping in your Tech Cave since you went missing.'

So I followed her up the spiral staircase to find that she hadn't been so distressed that she hadn't brought in an inflatable mattress and nicked bedding from Molly to cover it. Any of my stuff that had got in the way had been pushed to the sides and then covered with a layer of discarded underwear.

I didn't care. I was so pleased to see her I didn't even think of tidying up until the next morning.

30

Skulking for Cheese Puffs

There was no sign of Molly, or breakfast, the next morning. So me and Guleed picked up something on the drive down to Coldharbour Lane. Nightingale had stayed overnight to supervise the POLSA team and to step in, in the event of demon traps or vengeful spirits – and to deal with the curious foxes.

'Abigail's big talking ones,' said Guleed.

The 'factory' as we were now calling it was, like most of London's vestigial industrial capacity, built beside railway tracks. It had been put up in the 1930s complete with its own goods sidings to supply raw materials. Once freight had shifted firmly to motor vehicles in the 1950s the sidings went derelict before being redeveloped as an industrial park in the 1980s.

Since London's railway tracks have long served as conduits for its urban wildlife, it didn't surprise me the foxes were taking an interest. I asked if Nightingale had taken a statement.

'They might have spotted something,' I said.

'Abigail's doing that this afternoon,' said Guleed. 'I think you'll find it's on your action list.'

The place was smaller than I remembered it, consisting of two workshops, a loading bay, a row of rooms that included the one I'd been in when they de-hooded me, two obvious storerooms, one with the sort of sad kitchen seen in every small office, shop and workshop in the country. Once I'd had a look in the fridge I was glad they'd been feeding me takeaway.

'Yeah,' said Guleed when I slammed the fridge door shut. 'Nightingale thought there might be something alive in there.'

I thought of the Quality Street tin of vampire and really hoped their biocontainment had been somewhere else.

Someone had put a ladder down into the oubliette so that forensics could have a good rummage. I didn't go down, but the mildew and damp smell was strong – had Foxglove's bubble of faerie somehow inhibited decay? Or had it just masked it, like perfume over sweat?

One of the forensic techs asked if I wanted anything brought up.

'Just any clothes and art you find down there,' I said.

Foxglove would get her drawings back, although I did hear a rumour that a particularly fine but unfinished sketch of me imitating the centrepiece statue of Piccadilly Circus found its way into the Charing Cross canteen.

I made a point of bagging any art materials I found and labelling them as evidence to be shipped to the Folly.

What we didn't find was a bell or any vehicles in the loading bay.

All the businesses in the industrial estate had CCTV, but by an amazing coincidence none of them covered

337

the access road. The camera positioned at the street entrance to the estate had perfect coverage of both the access road and Coldharbour Lane. It had already been digitally copied and farmed out to teams at Charing Cross and the Folly. Meanwhile house-to-house teams were confirming what traffic movements belonged to the other businesses on the estate, even as our forensic accountants investigated to see if they were connected to Martin Chorley in some way. Guleed estimated that at least eighty people were now working directly off this one scene.

'I can't help worrying that this might be the entire purpose,' said Nightingale.

'He's tricky, isn't he?' I said.

'Worse,' said Nightingale. 'He builds his plans with multiple redundancy. Had you not escaped then we would be deprived of a major asset. But since you did, we're forced to expend matériel chasing leads.'

'That's to our advantage though, isn't it?' I said. 'We have personnel and an overtime budget.'

'Not an unlimited budget. Not for this level of operational tempo.'

I pointed out that Chorley must have a deadline too.

'Why else grab me?' I said. 'And Lesley practically said as much.'

'Yes,' said Nightingale. 'I'm not sure that's much comfort.'

What was comforting was that one of the CCTV teams had managed to identify the Sprinter van that been used to deliver me to the factory. It was clearly visible turning off the lane at one in the morning and then departing two hours later, sporting different plates. Between then and my escape a total of twenty-eight separate vehicles had come and gone the same way. All but a couple had been traced, their owners interviewed and their current whereabouts ascertained.

The lack of bell disturbed me.

'The bell was in there,' I said.

'Well, it didn't go out the front,' said Guleed. 'And we haven't found a back door yet.'

'Let's see what the Fox Whisperer finds out,' I said.

One of the police staff dropped off Abigail before lunch and we pushed our way through some scrub down to where a fence marked the border of the railway tracks. We stopped there and Abigail extracted a Tupperware box from her shoulder bag and opened it. Inside were genuine Molly-baked cheese puffs.

I asked whether Molly was cooking again, but Abigail said no.

'I keep a stash of these in the fridge just in case,' she said.

'So what now?' I asked, making a sly grab which got my hand slapped.

'On past form, anything from thirty seconds to five minutes,' she said, 'With an average arrival time of around two minutes.'

It was less than sixty seconds later that a large dog fox strolled up with the 'Yeah, what?' of a creature who's figured out that they don't allow hunting dog packs in built-up areas.

'Wotcha, Abi.' Its voice was breathy but surprisingly deep and cockney.

339

'All right,' said Abigail.

'Is that a cheese puff?' said the fox, sidling closer.

'What do you think?' asked Abigail.

'Is there any chance of that becoming *my* cheese puff?' he said.

'Don't know,' said Abigail. 'It depends on whether you're going to be helpful or not, don't it?'

The fox bobbed his head.

'How can I be of service?' he said.

'Who's been watching this place?' she asked, and I thought – what the fuck?

'Don't know what you're talking about,' said the fox. 'Honest.'

Abigail folded her arms and tapped her feet.

'All right,' said the fox. 'Here's my problem, right. If I bring you the one who might have been keeping an eye on this place, then they're going to be rewarded with a cheese puff – yes?'

'Possibly,' said Abigail.

'But what of I, the one which facilitated this engagement without whom no information would be exchanged,' said the fox. 'What reward for myself?'

'I might give you a cheese puff,' said Abigail.

Reaching into the box, she produced a cheese puff and handed it to me. The fox watched me intently as I took a bite – it was delicious.

'Cheddar with a hint of thyme,' I said. 'Also, crumbled bacon.'

The fox gave a low whine.

'Might give me one?' he said. 'How might "might" become "will"?'

Abigail took out another cheese puff, took a bite and waved the remainder around for emphasis.

'That depends upon how long me and this one have to spend waiting for you,' she said.

'I see,' said the fox, turning and vanishing back into the undergrowth.

I eyed up the remaining cheese puffs.

'Do you think he's going to be long?' I asked.

'Nah,' said Abigail. 'The watcher will be his mate – he knew what we were after, but by talking to us first they get two bites of the cherry, don't they?'

'That's sly,' I said.

'That's foxes, isn't it?'

The fox came back with his mate, a vixen with a particularly long face. They sat on their haunches side by side.

'Hello,' said the vixen. 'Let's have it then.' Her voice had a higher register but seemed just as cockney.

'Have what?' asked Abigail.

'The cheese puff,' said the vixen.

'Let's get your report first,' said Abigail. 'Then we'll talk baked goods.'

'This is a bit of an impasse, isn't it? Because I'm not about to cough up what I've got without something upfront,' said the vixen.

Abigail removed another cheese puff, broke it in half and threw one bit to each fox. They caught them neatly out of the air and ate them in a single bite. Long tongues emerged to lick the crumbs off their muzzles.

'Now,' said Abigail. 'Your report.'

The report was oddly full of jargon. The foxes spoke

of being covert and not wanting to risk being blown by being too obvious while they maintained eyes on the opposition assets. Some of it was incomprehensible: *mouse-time*, *first* and *second dark* all related to times of day, and Abigail had to translate. Still, since the vixen had watched with great interest as me and Foxglove had run down the access road in our rush for freedom and a local convenience, we had a fixed point to work our timings around.

Two big smelly metal boxes had left the factory the previous mouse-time, which Abigail translated as early evening. Two vans which had not registered on the CCTV camera that covered the entrance from Coldharbour Lane.

I backtracked a bit and asked questions in various different ways, but the vixen was better than most people, better than most trained professionals in fact. I let them have the rest of the cheese puffs. Abigail disapproved.

'You shouldn't spoil them,' she said after we'd watched them disappear into the undergrowth.

'Watchers?' I asked as we walked back to the factory. 'Assets, reports, covert? Is there something you want to tell me?'

'It's not me,' said Abigail. 'They think they're spies.'

'Working for who?'

'They won't say. I'm not sure there is anyone. I think it's part of the process that made them big and smart.'

We didn't see Molly for two whole days and everybody had to make do with takeaway until she resurfaced. Well, except for the second day when I cooked jollof rice, groundnut chicken, stock fish, palava sauce – with way too much palm oil – and fried plantain. Admittedly, I did have my mum to help. And I did have to physically restrain her from putting a year's supply of pepper in the soup. We compromised and had a pot of what she called properly seasoned Tola sauce, which proved surprisingly popular with some of the analysts. One white guy kept coming back despite the fact that he'd turned bright pink and was damp with sweat.

'I know it's killing me,' he said. 'But it just tastes that good.'

Stephanopoulos filled her plate with a blithe disregard for thermodynamics and later asked my mum for the recipe for groundnut chicken.

Even while turning pink, the CCTV teams managed to establish that the footage from the entrance camera had been doctored – presumably to hide the departure of the two vans the vixen had seen. One of them, probably, carrying the new bell.

But even Chorley couldn't get to every camera on Coldharbour Lane. And by suppertime the day after we'd fed the foxes, we had the colour, make and index of both vans. Not that we expected the indexes to remain the same – in fact we were working on the assumption they'd be changed. The City of London Police and CTC had spent a great deal of the last thirty years waiting for the next big truck bomb – be it IRA, IRA classic, various varieties of cryptofascists or jihadists – and they had systems for finding vans with dodgy numbers.

Nightingale insisted that me and Guleed got as much rest as we could.

'Whatever happens next,' he said, 'is likely to be the final operation of the campaign. I need you two to be fully combat-fit, as it were.'

I always worry when Nightingale goes all *Band of Brothers* on us, which is one of the reasons I took up feeding the multitudes as a distraction. Still, at least after a worrying silence from Molly we got reassurance that Foxglove was settling in.

On some nights the full moon rises above the skylight and floods the atrium with cold light. On those nights Molly turns all the electric lights off, including the Emergency Exit signs, even though I've told her she's not supposed to, and glides around the atrium and the balconies in weird random patterns. I'd got so used to it that I could walk down from my room to the kitchen, looking for a snack, without paying any attention to the silent shadow that darts here and there – always in the periphery of my sight.

The first such moonlit night after Foxglove joined us I was out in search of a nightcap when I realised that Nightingale was standing on the upper balcony. Silently he beckoned me over and pointed down to the atrium floor.

Below I saw Molly flit across the tiles, her hair streaming out behind her like a shadow. Behind her came a second figure, Foxglove, dressed in a loose silk shift that looked blood red in the moonlight. In her right hand she trailed a long ribbon of white fabric. Then Molly turned, grabbed Foxglove around the waist, and swept her around in a circle – the white fabric looping around them as they spun in place. I don't how long we watched them dance, silent but for the swoosh of their clothes and Foxglove's streamer, but when they finally vanished into shadows I heard Nightingale sigh.

'Here's a comforting thought for you, Peter,' he said. 'However long you may live, the world will never lose its ability to surprise you with its beauty.'

And the next morning there was kippers and jam and coffee and toast and everything was all right in the world.

For about six hours at least.

31

The Winkle Garden

There once were railway sidings that ran right under Smithfield Market, allowing tons of animal carcasses to be shipped into the cold stores prior to dismemberment, distribution and, ultimately, dinner. In the 1960s they were closed by the same people who gave us streets in the sky, the urban motorway and myriad buildings that architects have spent the last forty years trying to blame on somebody else.

The sidings became an underground car park, but in an ironic twist their entrance is an elegant spiral ramp that winds its way around a small circular park. The park itself was built by the Victorians on a site made famous as an execution ground for such celebrities as William Wallace, Wat Tyler and a couple of hundred Protestants who got on the wrong side of Queen Mary. According to the Folly's records, the area had been *pacificatus* as part of the process of building the original railway, the ramp and the park. The dispersal of all that negative energy was capped off with a bronze statue of 'Peace' by John Birnie Philip, which the Sons of Weyland had, apparently, had a hand in.

'Does it say in what way?' I asked.

'Nope,' said Abigail, who was back in the library at the

Folly digging up references in real time.

I was sitting on a bench in the courtyard in the Church of St Bartholomew-the-Less, peering through the railings out at West Smithfield in the hope of catching sight of Martin Chorley and/or associates. I was there because parked halfway down the spiral ramp was one of the vans last seen leaving Martin Chorley's factory. Spotted by one of the car park attendants, who called it in because the number plate 'looked iffy', which set off a flag at CCC, which filtered quickly over to Operation Jennifer, which didn't so much spring into action as lurch sideways like a startled crab.

This is totally normal police behaviour, by the way, and nothing to be alarmed about.

Ranks and chain of command are all very well for administration, but when the wheels come off and the world is going fruit-metaphor-of-your choice, then the plod on the spot needs to know who's in charge of what. That's why we have the Gold, Silver and Bronze Incident Management Procedure (page 560, *Blackstone's Police Operational Handbook*, Second Edition). Seawoll was Gold, which meant he was stuck in the Portakabin back at the Folly. Because this was a Falcon incident Nightingale was Silver and, theoretically, should have also been in a control room somewhere – like that was going to happen – while Stephanopoulos was Bronze (public safety) and I was Bronze (Falcon containment).

'The Victorians did a lot of this *pacificatus* stuff,' said Abigail. 'And not just in London either.'

And was it just the unquiet dead? I wondered, thinking of the god of the Yellowstone River. Or had the wizards of the Folly gone forth like the loyal sons of the British Empire they were and done a bit of *pacificatus* in the dominions?

I thought you gentlemen should know how things go in the former colonies, the letter from America had said.

'Peter?' said Stephanopoulos over the Airwave. 'See anything?'

I couldn't see the van from my position, but I did have a good view of the roads around the park. Sandwiched between Smithfield Market to the north and Barts Hospital to the south, both providing ample cover to bring up van-loads of backup, the car park was tactically a terrible choice for Chorley to get caught in. Stephanopoulos already had spotters on the roofs and the upper floors of the buildings all around and two whole serials of TSG lounging around in the courtyard behind the hospital museum. This particular lot had worked with us before and had taken to wearing a sprig of mistletoe on their Metvests, presumably because a bulb of garlic would look stupid. TSG officers spend a lot of time waiting around in the backs of Sprinter vans and so are prone to violent practical jokes and moments of whimsy. Seawoll had suggested celery, but nobody but me got the joke.

I replied to Stephanopoulos. 'Nothing from here.'

I listened while Nightingale and the rest of the spotters reported in from their various positions around the perimeter. Nightingale, I knew, was in Smithfield Market with Guleed comfortably ensconced in the Butcher's Hook pub on the east side.

'What's the target, do you think?' asked Seawoll.

'St Paul's at a guess,' said Nightingale. 'Possibly the site of the Mithraeum.'

The cathedral was half a kilometre to the south and the Bloomberg building site was further to the east and twice as far.

'He certainly likes the Square Mile,' said Guleed.

She was right. The Rising Sun, where Camilla Turner met the late John Chapman, was just around the corner, and beyond that was the Barbican, where Faceless Man senior had been stashed for all those years. Behind me on the other side of the hospital was Little Britain, where Martin Chorley had his think tank.

'Everyone's in position,' said Stephanopoulos. 'What now?'

'If we're lucky the fucker will show his face and Thomas can twat him,' said Seawoll.

'We're not exactly covert,' said Stephanopoulos. 'We've got a couple of hours before we're all over Facebook.'

'If that,' said Guleed.

'The longer we wait the more we pass tactical advantage to Chorley,' said Nightingale. 'And I think we've all had quite enough of that.'

'The bell is the key,' I said. 'We half-inch the bell and Chorley's stuffed.'

'There were two vans,' said Stephanopoulos. 'How do we know the bell's in that one?'

'Or not already in place somewhere,' said Nightingale – unhelpfully in my opinion.

'Somebody's going to have to have a look, aren't they?' said Stephanopoulos.

It was a difficult decision. Chorley knew me, Guleed

and Nightingale on sight and there was no way we were going to risk some poor non-Falcon qualified copper. In the end Stephanopoulos nicked a green London Ambulance service jacket from one of the nearby ambulance crews and got ready to do the walk past herself.

'And what if you meet Lesley?' I asked.

'Then that will be one less problem to worry about, won't it?' she said.

'Make sure she fucking wears her Metvest,' said Gold leader when we outlined the plan.

Stephanopoulos, who claimed to have stashed her Metvest in her wife's henhouse the day she made inspector, nonetheless promised not to get stabbed. I donned my magic hoody and dashed around through the hospital grounds so I could loiter suspiciously on the corner of Little Britain and keep the entrance ramp in view.

It was a bright day with scattered clouds and the air was still and warm. Stephanopoulos wore the jacket over one shoulder to sell the illusion, and to disguise the fact that it was too small for her. And to hide the X26 taser she was carrying in her left hand.

I still couldn't see the van but I knew its exact position halfway down the ramp. I reckoned if I vaulted the safety rail further up, where the drop was less than a metre, I could get there in less than twenty seconds.

'I'm approaching the van,' said Stephanopoulos.

I've been told that in the old days undercover officers had to try and disguise the fact that they were using a radio. But now you just wear headphones and carry a phone in your hand. This explains why the next thing she said was, 'Just as long as we don't have asparagus again.' A pause. 'Because I hate asparagus.'

'I've always said you were wasted on the police,' said Seawoll.

'I'm having a look through the front window,' said Stephanopoulos in a low voice. 'I can see something in the back and she's sitting low on her suspension.' And then much louder, 'How many times do I have to tell you: the goat is not allowed in the house.'

Nightingale told me to saunter up the entrance to the ramp while he went to the top of the pedestrian access stairs on the other side of the park, so he could cover Stephanopoulos' exit.

I was halfway across the road when a spotter reported that a mint coloured Fiesta was heading up Long Lane and was indicating for a left turn – meaning it might be heading for the car park. I said I'd keep an eye out.

I was almost across when Stephanopoulos said, 'Oh shit. Chorley just came out of the underground bit.'

There was a bit of loud breathing and then Stephanopoulos said she was hidden behind a different van but she could probably get a shot with her taser as Chorley went past.

'I wouldn't advise it,' said Nightingale.

'Wait for him to pass and get the fuck out of the way,' said Seawoll.

'Peter,' said Nightingale, 'turn the car away.'

I looked over and saw the Fiesta, mint coloured as advertised, turning out of Long Lane and making an obvious beeline for the entrance at the top of the ramp. I stepped quickly out in front of it and held up my hand in that gesture all police hope is authoritative enough to halt over a tonne of moving metal.

The trick is to always be ready to dive out of the way.

The driver was a white woman in her mid-twenties; white blouse, lightweight navy suit jacket, brown hair.

I made a friendly fending-off gesture, but the woman's expression gave her away.

I'd know that look of exasperation anywhere – even when it's not on the right face.

'Lesley's in the Fiesta,' I said over the Airwave.

She'd been slowing to negotiate the ramp, but as soon as she saw me Lesley floored it. I threw a car killer into the bonnet and the engine died. But she had too much momentum and I had to vault the safety rail to avoid getting run down.

'Pillock!' I heard her shouting as she went past.

I made what they call a tactical assessment.

I could see the van a third of the way around and down the ramp. Because the ramp formed almost a complete circle I had sight of Nightingale to my right as he went for the pedestrian staircase less than forty metres away. I watched as he jumped over the railing and dropped down onto one of the landings below. I decided that my job, as usual, was Lesley, and took after the Fiesta as it rolled down the ramp.

The ramp was built for carriages and drays drawn by huge Clydesdale draught horses, and so was cobbled for traction and maximum tripping and leg-breaking potential. Still, I went flat out on the basis that I really didn't want to be tag-teamed by Lesley and Chorley together.

I was good enough by then to throw car killers about

without sanding my Airwave, so I was still online to hear one of the spotters yell something unintelligible and Seawoll order the containment teams to set up a safety perimeter. This was the appropriate Falcon response plan in action – the TSG keeps the public out of harm's way while we lucky few go toe to toe with the Faceless Man.

And not forgetting his sidekick – the mutable Lesley.

The Fiesta pulled up by the van and Lesley tumbled out, still wearing her fake face.

She pulled her hand back into a fist when she saw me, but I was already casting a nice reliable *impello palma* even as I closed the distance between us. The spell knocked her on her back, but she rolled, did something that I didn't recognise, and a viciously bright flash in front of my face blinded me. I went crashing down to the cobbles. All I could see was a bruise-coloured blotch in front of my eyes. But, figuring that lying on the cobbles was not conducive to my health, I scrambled off to my right where I knew there were parked cars. After banging my face on somebody's hatchback, I found the gap between cars and slotted myself in.

I crouched down with my back to a wheel arch and blinked, trying to clear my vision.

It's the ultraviolet content of a bright light that damages your retinas – I just had to hope Lesley had her flashbulb *lux* variant tuned to the lower wavelengths. Meanwhile I found I could follow the magic part of the fight through the echoes of the combatants' *formae*.

There was the tick-tock precision of Nightingale doing something complicated, followed by a whispering crash like cymbals when his spell hit home. Chorley was a series of painful razor strops speeding up until it was like a buzz saw meeting metal. Somewhere out in the real world I heard real metal tearing and sirens in the distance.

And then there was Lesley with a little bit of tick-tock, some razor strop, and a strange cry like a seagull that I was beginning to recognise as uniquely her own.

Now, it would be really useful if I could use all these lovely sense impressions to get a sense of distance. But some hours spent wearing a blindfold while Abigail and Nightingale set spells off around me had proved you couldn't. At least I couldn't. At least not yet.

Still, the beauty of being stuck on a down ramp with nice solid Victorian brick walls on either side was that there was a limited number of directions Lesley could be coming from. When I sensed her gearing up to cast her next spell – some difficult *impello*-based procedure – I lobbed a glitter bomb in her general direction.

This was one of Varvara's wartime spells as translated by Abigail – *Ledyanaya Bomba* in Russian, but we call it a glitter bomb because of the way light sparkles off the ice crystals that form around the epicentre.

I distinctly heard Lesley say 'fuck' not five metres away, and then I felt the wave of cold air roll over me. The sight in my left eye was mostly purple but my right was almost clear – obviously I'd been squinting. I risked a look.

Everything around the van was bright and sparkly, like a bright winter's day after a frost. I saw a blurry figure who was probably Lesley turn away from me and start to run down the ramp, only to slip over and fall down hard with a yelp.

I wasn't going to get a better invitation than that, so I rolled out of my hiding place and charged down the slope with my shield up for good measure. Which is just as well, as I ran straight into Chorley coming the other way. I was half blind and he was looking over his shoulder – it was one of them meeting engagements that military theorists suggest you should never ever do if you can help it. He didn't spot me until we were less than three metres apart. He tried to turn away, but slipped and went down on one knee with an audible crack. It looked really painful, but not as painful as I was planning to make it.

Lesley was to his right, trying to get to her feet. She was trying to wrench something out of her jacket pocket, and making a mess of both actions. I couldn't pass up a shot at Chorley, so I tried to body-slam him with my shield.

I'm not sure, but I think he sort of picked up my shield and used it and my momentum to throw me over his head. Certainly for me there was a confused moment where everything was upside down, a painful impact on my back, and then I slid down the icy cobbles for a couple of metres.

I rolled over in time to see Chorley turn his full attention on me, with a look in his eyes that said I'd just reached the end of the rope he'd been giving me.

Then he fell twitching to the floor – I knew that twitch. I've suffered it myself. There were wires trailing from his back to the yellow X26 taser in Stephanopoulos' hand, and she kept pumping the juice just as instructed by the big bumper manual of how to deal with criminal practitioners.

Lesley was still trying to get something free of her jacket, and I scrambled up to stop her. But before I could get to my feet she had a compact semi-automatic pistol in her hand, which she pointed at Stephanopoulos.

'Drop the fucking taser,' she shouted.

Stephanopoulos signalled me to hold back.

'Or what?' she asked Lesley.

'Don't test me,' said Lesley. 'I'm having a very trying day.'

'For God's sake, just shoot her,' said Chorley, and then wriggled a bit as the current hit him again. 'Or Peter. Or fucking somebody.'

I thought it might be quite handy if Nightingale were to turn up about then.

'If you're going to shoot, then shoot,' said Stephanopoulos.

So Lesley shot her in the leg – which, looking back, was probably the sensible thing to do. If you were Lesley.

Stephanopoulos fell over sideways as her left leg gave way. She tried to keep hold of the taser, but Chorley had taken advantage of the distraction to pull the barbs out. I was already surging forward when Lesley turned the gun on me.

'Plan B,' said Chorley as he got up and headed for the van.

'Copy that,' said Lesley, keeping the gun on me.

Stephanopoulos had dragged herself behind a parked car but I could hear her swearing.

There was the sound of shooting behind me and I instinctively crouched down. At first I thought Seawoll had escalated up to an armed response once Stephanopoulos had been shot. But the gunshots didn't sound right. Chorley was in the van by then and had it started. I jumped to the side as it pulled out and turned, not up-slope as I expected, but down towards the underground car park. The curve of the ramp meant I couldn't see the actual entrance, but there was no mistaking the bark of shotguns firing from that direction. Suddenly a white man dressed in dark military trousers and a navy bomber jacket flew backwards into view and landed on the roof of a parked car. Chorley had obviously been out recruiting in Essex again. Even as he bounced onto the bonnet he held tight to a pump-action shotgun. But before he could recover, the shotgun was wrenched out of his hands and sent flying all the way up and over the safety railing to West Smithfield Road fifteen metres above.

That explained what had delayed Nightingale.

I turned back to find Lesley had gone, so I ran over to find Stephanopoulos lying on her back with her leg elevated and her belt in place as a tourniquet. She gave me a look of annoyed exasperation.

'Get down there and help Nightingale,' she said.

I hesitated.

'Ambulance is on its way,' she said. 'Go.'

I went down the ramp with my shield up and rounded the curve to find Nightingale finishing off a couple of wannabe hard men by knocking them down, stripping off their weapons with *impello* and throwing them up and out of reach in the direction of Smithfield Market.

As the guns went up, somebody unseen above threw down a couple of pairs of speedcuffs. Nightingale grabbed one and threw me the other – together we cuffed the pair and left them for the follow-up team.

I wanted at least to ask them their names, but Nightingale said we had to hurry.

'He's gone to ground,' he said. 'But he won't stay there long.'

There were two vehicle and one pedestrian entrances into the underground. We took up position by a blue and white painted wooden office extension where we could cover the vehicle access. Behind us TSG officers in public order gear collected up our suspects while others guided one of their Sprinter vans to reverse so that it blocked the door to the pedestrian footpath.

'Who were those guys?'

I indicated the two men as they were led away. Both their faces had a waxy sheen and they averted their eyes as they passed Nightingale.

'Another one of Chorley's distractions,' he said. 'They had a hostage. I had to resolve that before I could give chase.'

'Yes but where do you think they came from? And what did you do to them?'

'Irrelevant,' said Nightingale, 'And less than they deserved.'

We inspected the situation. Two eight-metre high Victorian brick arches marked the entrance to separate 'in' and 'out' tunnels, also from the original Victorian build. They both ran straight for twenty metres before veering left and out of sight.

There was another 'operational pause' while we checked that Stephanopoulos was being taken care of, that the other pedestrian access points had been locked down, and that Lesley May was nowhere to be found.

'Chorley is our priority,' said Seawoll. And there wasn't any arguing with that.

'Two tunnels,' said Nightingale. 'And, beyond that, two floors of parking.'

'He could drill his way up into Smithfield,' I said. 'He's good enough.'

'But not before I could stop him,' said Nightingale.

'Two tunnels,' I said. 'One each?'

'No,' said Nightingale. 'This time we want the odds to be in our favour.'

We brought down the other TSG van and used that to block the entrance to the out tunnel. As Nightingale said, it didn't need to be impenetrable. It just had to slow Chorley down enough for us to catch up with him.

I borrowed a taser and holster and stripped off my hoody.

'Ready?' asked Nightingale.

'No,' I said. 'Not really.'

'Good man,' said Nightingale. 'Off we go.'

We went single file up the tunnel, clinging to the left-hand wall so Chorley wouldn't see us coming. We paused when we reached the turn and Nightingale crouched down to peer around the corner.

'I can see the ramp,' he said. 'Do you think he's on the upper or lower level?'

I said I hadn't got a clue.

'I have an idea,' he said. 'I want you to conjure one of your experimental werelights – the one that flies erratically like a bumblebee.'

'That's why we call it a bumblebee,' I said. 'It's not really very good for anything yet.'

I'd been trying to develop a self-guiding fireball, but so far all I've managed is one that ricochets unpredictably.

'It will do for our purposes. And when you conjure it see if you can imbue it with . . .' He hesitated. 'Some of your essence.'

'My essence?'

'Your personality,' he said.

I gave it a go. The basis is your bog-standard *lux-impello* combination – the complications come in the various modifiers you add to the principal *formae*. I opened my hand and an orangey-red sphere the size of a golf ball immediately shot back down the tunnel the way we'd come.

'Ah,' said Nightingale.

'It always does that,' I said. 'Wait a second.'

The bumblebee came racing back past us and shot into the car park, making the low hum which is the other reason we call it the bumblebee. It also made a distinctive squealing sound when it bounced off walls or cars. I hoped I'd made it low-powered enough not to dust the electronics of every vehicle in the place.

After it zig-zagged down the ramp into the lower level, Nightingale had me conjure another and see if I couldn't pitch it onto the upper level. I got it first time and soon we could hear the second bumblebee bouncing off walls.

Then we heard the bell – a low shimmering tone that I didn't think had anything to do with actual sound waves. Then the sound of an engine starting up, which definitely did.

'Flushed him, by God,' said Nightingale.

The engine revved, not a particularly big one by the sound – one of the two-and-a-bit-litre diesels that Ford plonked into the older Transits.

'That's the van,' I said.

There was a squeal of tyres and the engine noise got louder.

'He's going to try to bolt,' said Nightingale. 'Stay behind me – I'll deal with any magic while you stop the van.'

We shuffled forward so that Nightingale could get a better look around the corner. The engine noise was randomly reflecting off the flat concrete surfaces of the garage, but it was definitely getting closer.

There was suddenly a sharp taste of copper in my mouth.

'Here he comes,' said Nightingale.

Something hit Nightingale's shield and spun away to gouge chunks off the brickwork around us. I saw the van grab some air as it came over the lip of the ramp and got my spell ready, but a wave of roiling dust swept past it and over us, blotting everything out. Real dust, I realised, when I breathed it in – I fumbled the spell. Not that I had a target.

We heard the van roar down the second tunnel on our

right – the one blocked by the TSG van. I hoped nobody had sneaked back in it for a kip.

'Come on!' yelled Nightingale.

We ran through the brown billows of settling dust and followed the van down the tunnel. But we'd barely made it past the turn when the dusty air turned orange and yellow and a wave of heat and sound smacked us in the face.

We stopped – the van was completely on fire from front to back, flames and smoke pouring out of the open back door. I could just see the silhouette of the bell inside. We advanced as close as we dared – because modern vans don't explode like that without help.

I activated a phone and called Seawoll, who'd already heard about the explosion.

'Did anyone come out of the tunnel?' I asked.

'No,' said Seawoll. 'Chorley?'

I looked at Nightingale, who shrugged.

'We think he was in the van,' I said.

'I fucking hope so,' said Seawoll.

32

What Remains

Burnt beyond recognition.

No one was buying that, not even when the dental records confirmed his identity.

'We're sending a team to check they haven't been tampered with,' said Seawoll at the morning briefing.

DNA tests were ongoing in three separate labs using several different reference samples, including that of his late daughter. Two to three days for confirmation one way or the other.

And Lesley was still out there.

'Assuming this is a fake-out,' I said, 'he must know we'll confirm it's not him pretty quickly. He must be planning to do something soon.'

'But what?' said Seawoll. 'We have his second bloody bell.'

Which was already on its way to the Whitechapel foundry to face the hammer.

'What if there's a third bell?' asked Guleed.

Seawoll fixed her with a stern disciplinary look that wasn't fooling me for a second.

'Then you'd probably better find out where he made it,' he said.

I said that I wished she hadn't said that, and got a proper stern look for my pains.

'There was no sign of the sword,' said Seawoll. 'Now I'm not a scholar of the Arthurian legendarium but I'm pretty fucking certain that Excalibur comes into it bleeding somewhere. So Guleed finds the bell.' He glared at me again for good measure. 'You see if you can narrow down the target.'

He looked at Nightingale, who nodded his approval.

'Good,' he said. 'Let's get on with it, then.'

Strangely enough, they don't cover metaphysics at Hendon. But fortunately they do at Oxford, and Postmartin had spent a lifetime reading about the point where the meta meets the physical. He was also, conveniently, currently staying at the Folly. He said this was to keep abreast of developments in Operation Jennifer, but I suspected it was so he could scope out our latest house guest. I'd certainly caught Foxglove showing him her portfolio after he bribed her with two hundred quid's worth of Polychromos artists' pencils – whatever they were.

Luckily I managed to drag him away before Foxglove convinced him to strip off and pose for her. We convened in the upstairs reading room, where a frighteningly cheerful Molly brought us tea and cakes.

'So, where do we think Martin Chorley plans to make his sacrifice?' said Nightingale.

'St Paul's Cathedral remains the obvious choice,' said Postmartin. 'Given what we know of the history of Mr Punch, the next highest probability, I would say, is the true location of the Temple of Mithras. Why else would he have John Chapman encourage his banker friends to conduct their bacchanalia there?'

'That's assuming Punch is the determining factor,' said Nightingale.

'Our problem,' I said, 'is that Martin Chorley isn't concerned with evidence – it's the truth of the heart, isn't it? Now that I've had a chance to chat to him, I think he really believes in it.'

'Believes in what?' asked Postmartin.

'All of it,' I said. 'Arthur, Camelot, a British golden age, or at least the modern equivalent.'

'A romantic,' said Nightingale. 'The most dangerous people on earth.'

'For all we know he could be looking for Arthur back up at Alderley Edge,' I said.

'In Cheshire?' asked Nightingale. 'Whatever for?'

'There's a rather fine children's book set there,' said Postmartin. '*The Weirdstone of Brisingamen*, and a sequel too – *The Moon of Gomrath*.'

'No,' said Nightingale. 'We should not confuse a mistaken belief with a general incredulity. He may be no true scholar but it seems to me he has always followed the forms. The places that interest him will be those that present him with the most respectable "evidence".'

'If we're talking Arthur, then it's quite a long list,' said Postmartin. 'The hill fort at Cadbury. Camlann, which is in the Welsh sources. Badon Hill likewise. Tintagel and Glastonbury, if we stretch the scholarship somewhat.'

'All out of London, I notice,' said Nightingale. 'We can at least ask the local constabulary to keep an eye on the places we can identify.' He looked at Postmartin. 'If you had to pick your most likely target, which would it be?'

'Oh, Glastonbury,' said Postmartin. 'Without a doubt. If you're a romantic then the Isle of Avalon is always going to appeal.'

'I don't like splitting our forces,' said Nightingale. 'But I can reach Glastonbury in just over two hours, give the area the once-over and be back by nightfall.' He looked at me. 'I'd like you to kit up and be on immediate standby. If Chorley makes his move in London, God forbid, I want you to get in and disrupt him. I think we've eliminated most of his mundane assets, so just do what you do best and frustrate the hell out of him.'

I understood the logic. We already had St Paul's covered, ditto the Bloomberg building. Seawoll had booked up a couple more vans' worth of TSG and I'd noticed a couple of Frank Caffrey's 'associates' in the breakfast room that morning. It would be just like Chorley to wait until we were fixed on London and then make his move out in the country. Postmartin would already be working on a potential target list and no doubt having enormous fun in the process. Meanwhile Nightingale was the only one of us with a chance of going up against Chorley without backup, so it had to be him that went.

I still didn't like it. But what are you going to do?

To my surprise, I found Seawoll downstairs, sitting in one of the overstuffed chairs in the atrium, the remains of an elaborate morning tea spread out on an occasional table beside him. He beckoned me over and I asked why he wasn't at Belgravia nick.

'I'm keeping a bloody eye on you lot,' he said. 'Plus

this is closer to the City and that's where the action is. Which reminds me . . .'

He pulled out an envelope and shook it under my nose – coins jingled inside. Not that there were many coins. It seemed to be mostly full of tenners.

'Whip-round for Miriam,' he said.

I handed over a tenner and asked how she was.

'Serious, but not life-threatening. No bones were broken and the bullet went straight through so she should make a full recovery.' He tucked the envelope back in his jacket pocket. 'I can't remember the last time a detective inspector got themselves shot. Do you think our Lesley went for non-lethal on purpose?'

I said I thought she had, and Seawoll nodded grimly.

'You've been right all along. Whatever our Lesley's reasons for going to the dark side she still thinks she's straight. That's why she's protecting you and went for the leg shot with Miriam. There's still a little bit of the old Lesley in there.' Seawoll jabbed a finger at me. 'You must not hesitate to use that against her. I want this business finished, Peter. I want you to promise me that if you have to go hard to get the job done, that's what you'll do.'

I nodded, which seemed to satisfy him.

Go hard, I thought as I headed for my room. What did that even mean in this context?

Kitting up consisted of me climbing into a pair of jeans, my public order boots, utility belt and keeping my Metvest with me at all times. I considered borrowing a taser. But you know, despite Stephanopoulos' good example, I'd never had that much luck with them.

I ended up in the atrium trying to finish the copy of *The Silmarillion* I'd downloaded onto my phone. Fuck all else happened, except that Foxglove turned up and did some preliminary sketches for the now famous *Hither Came Peter, the Librarian* which is currently hanging in the National Portrait Gallery.

Around five o'clock I took Toby out for a walk and then I did paperwork until seven.

Go hard – but I felt soft, mushy, as if I was walking around on a thick carpet of pink polyurethane foam. I wanted to cross the river and climb into what I realised I now thought of as *our* bed – mine and Bev's. Instead I let Seawoll know where I was and lay down fully dressed in my room upstairs.

It was dark when I was woken up by Nightingale's call from Glastonbury.

'He's definitely been here sometime in the past,' he said. 'He bought a farmhouse nearby and he's practised magic in St Michael's Tower at the top of the hill – I recognised his *signare*.'

'Recently?' I asked.

'Hard to say,' said Nightingale.

It always was with *vestigia*, which faded or were retained according to a complex set of interactions with material, environment and source, and whether something supernatural had been subsisting off them. Nightingale had sensed no trace of Lesley's *signare*, so the magic could have happened any time in the last twenty years.

'He might have regarded it as his country retreat,' I said.

'Quite. I've checked for booby traps and handed it over to the local boys. Alexander is sending a search team tomorrow.'

He asked after Stephanopoulos and I passed on the assurances that Dr Walid had given me. I asked if he was heading back tonight and he said he was.

'Anything else to report?' he asked.

'A creeping sense of existential dread,' I said. 'Apart from that I'm good.'

'Chin up, Peter. He's on his last legs – I can feel it.'

Once Nightingale had rung off I called Guleed, who'd been arriving as a nasty surprise to bell foundries and metal casting companies from Dudley to Wolverhampton all that day.

She said she'd been just about to phone.

'I was right,' she said. 'There's another bell.'

My mum's done a lot of shit jobs – literally, in the case of that gig she had cleaning the toilets of that gym in Bloomsbury – but I've never seen her hesitate. During the period of my life I like to refer to as 'that year when I fucked around doing sod all useful' I used to supplement the dole by tagging along on cleaning gigs. She'd been taking me to work since I was seven, whenever she couldn't get a babysitter and my dad was too stoned to be reliable. This particular time I was getting the going rate, such as it was, and I was expected to work for it.

You should have seen those men's loos – I don't know what they were eating but I remember walking in one time to find that some poor unfortunate had pebble-dashed the walls of a stall to thigh height. I kid you not. The gym staff had taken one look, sealed the stall off with yellow and black hazard tape and left it for the overnight cleaners. I really didn't want to go in there.

'Why are you wasting time?' my mum had said. 'You are here to do a job and it's not going to go away on its own.'

So in I went clutching my Domestos and my spray bottle of generic own-brand surface cleaner and got on with it. Pausing a couple of times to throw up while I did.

Sometimes you've got to go hard to get the job done.

Although not always in the way that people are expecting.

Parking in the City of London is always a nightmare even with a warrant card, so I got Caffrey to drive me to London Bridge in his van and drop me off in the middle.

'Are you going to be all right?' he asked.

'Don't worry. It's just magic stuff,' I said. 'I'll get a cab back.'

The sun was long gone by the time I got there and sky was overcast. Beyond Tower Bridge the sawn-off blocks of Canada Water were ochre silhouettes against a murky orange sky. The Thames was in flood and HMS *Belfast* rode high. I could smell salt water and petrol fumes and the onset of rain. When I put my hands on the railings I got a shock of static electricity.

And I heard a thin, high-pitched giggle.

'You want to watch it, bruv,' I said. 'There's some people who want you dead.'

The giggle grew into a howl of laughter that I was amazed they weren't hearing as far away as Canary Wharf.

'Or deader than you are already.'

The merriment got a bit grimmer, but no less manic then before.

'They already had a go at your little girl,' I said, and the laughter stopped.

So the Lord of Misrule is a hypocrite just like everyone else – *quelle surprise*.

Then Punch spoke, but not with the rasp I was used to. This time softly and sadly.

'Of all the girls that are so smart,
There's none like pretty Polly:
She is the darling of my heart,
She is so plump and jolly.'

Plump and jolly, I thought, like a child.

I hauled myself up and sat on the railing with my legs dangling over the parapet – trying to make it look as casual as possible.

'It looks likes you and me have got a beef with the same people,' I said.

Punch laughed – this time it sounded rueful and ironic.

'Why don't we see if we can sort this out?' I said.

And that's when we came to our agreement. Although at the time I couldn't be sure I'd done what I thought I'd done. Practical metaphysics being a pretty uncertain process, especially when you're dealing with a hysterical psychotic like our Mr Punch.

I was brought back to reality when my phone rang – it was Beverley.

'What are you doing up there?' she asked.

I looked down and saw Beverley three storeys below me, standing hip deep in the water in that impossible way she and her sisters do. She held a phone in one hand and waved with the other.

'I'm communing with the numinous,' I said.

'You can do that when you get home,' she said. 'Which is going to be when, exactly?'

'If I jumped, would you catch me?'

'No. But I might fish you out afterwards. Get off the railing, babes. You're making me nervous.'

The rain started in earnest, big summer drops coming straight down and slapping my hands where they rested on the cool metal of the railing.

I sighed and climbed down and onto the pavement.

Even from a distance I could see Beverley's shoulders relaxing and I realised that she'd been genuinely worried I'd jump. I considered explaining what I'd been up to, but I was worried that might make me sound even crazier. Even to Bev, who once rescued me from fairyland.

'And when you do come home, bring some of your mum's chicken,' said Beverley. 'I know you've got some stashed in the fridge.'

'No probs,' I said.

She told me that she loved me and to call her when I got off duty – whenever that might be.

There's always a bit in a TV series where the detective or whatever has a final revelation that solves the case. You get the close-up on House or Poirot as the light of comprehension dawns in their eyes – usually accompanied by a soft but insistent musical cue.

I didn't get a musical cue or a close-up, so I didn't know I'd just solved the case until it was much too late. I just remembered that Lesley had been shopping around the Covent Garden area, so I decided to catch a cab there and have a look round before returning to the Folly.

That's how I found myself standing out of the rain in the fake portico on the west side of the Covent Garden Piazza, wondering if the ghosts were ever going to come back. Which was why I put my hand against one of the pillars and felt for their *vestigia* and got, very faintly, the ringing tone of the bell.

All right, I'll admit – that was a musical cue.

I called Seawoll on his personal number and that's something I've never done before.

He must have clocked my ID on his phone because he said 'Oh fuck,' without preamble and then, 'This can't be fucking good.'

'It's the bloody Actors' Church,' I said. 'It's been the Actors' Church all along.'

All that shit about the Temple of Mithras and St Paul's had been a distraction. I told him where I was, and what I'd learnt.

'Nightingale is at least an hour away,' he said. 'And Guleed is unavailable. So what we'll do is this: I'll put in a perimeter, nice and quiet like, while you, very carefully, ascertain the full extent of the shit we've landed in.'

'It's a plan,' I said.

'It's a bloody cock-up, is what it is,' said Seawoll. 'And

can I make it clear that when I say very carefully I mean *very fucking carefully*. I'm all for courageous action, in moderation, Peter. But you have an alarming tendency towards heroics. I do not want to be getting the justified hairy eyeball from your mum at any memorial service other than my own. Is that clear?'

'Crystal, guv,' I said.

'However, should you spot a window of opportunity to deploy your undoubted talents at bolloxing things up for Chorley et al, feel free to proceed. But carefully.'

'Yes, guv.'

'Off you go.'

When the fourth Earl of Bedford hired Inigo Jones to build him an Italianate piazza on land that Henry VIII had 'appropriated' from the local convent, for some reason the 7th Earl decreed that a church be built, on the cheap, on the west side of the square. Since the business end of an Anglican church is supposed to be at the east end of the nave, the portico that sticks out into the square is a fake, as is the door in its centre. The main entrance is at the west end, opening into the old cemetery, now a pleasant urban garden enclosed by the tall former houses that are now all shops and offices. The main entrance is on the far side of the park, on Bedford Lane. But you can climb over the spiky fence on the piazza providing you are both careful and very stupid.

Or slightly desperate. Like me.

I made my way past the sunken steps and pressed myself to the wall so I could peer around the corner. The west end of the church is plainer than the east, being all brick and square doors and lacking those fake classical flourishes that no Renaissance landowner could live without. It still has a pediment, though, this one with a ridiculously wide lower cornice that jutted out like a particularly unsafe balcony.

Parked on the flagstones was a vintage white Ford Transit van, back doors open to show emptiness. I texted Seawoll what I was seeing and, as I pressed *Send*, I felt a magic detonation from the opposite side of the church. Sand, gravel and a couple of half bricks bounced off the pediment and onto the roof of the van.

'Try it now,' said Chorley – I judged he was standing on the left side of the cornice.

'That did it,' said Lesley, more muffled – so probably inside.

I texted Seawoll that the crime was ongoing and I was moving to disrupt – TOO LATE, GOING IN.

The main doors were unlocked and I slipped into the narthex, which is the fancy term for that bit of a church with the collection box and the pamphlets and souvenir stand. This being the Actors' Church, there was a lot of stuff you could buy. There were also two staircases going up – one to the belfry on the left and one to the belfry on the right.

I didn't have to pause long before I heard a thump and someone swearing up on the left. I went up the stairs as quietly as I could, pushed through the door at the top and nearly got the drop on both of them.

If only the bloody bell hadn't started humming.

The Punch-summoning bell was larger than the church bell it was replacing, so Chorley had had to knock a big hole in the wall to get it into position. It hung from the original headstock while the original bell perched precariously on the landing.

Lesley was holding the sword occasionally known as Excalibur, while Chorley stood out in the rain on the cornice.

He saw me first.

'Ah, Peter,' he said. 'Why am I not surprised?'

'So much for Plan B,' said Lesley.

They were both dressed in boiler suits and blue nylon cagoules, all the better to pass as council workers or contractors.

I was going to say something clever, but Lesley put the point of Excalibur against my chest and pushed gently so that I was forced out onto the cornice with Chorley. The rain had eased off a bit, but the cement was slick. There was no safety rail and the courtyard was a good twelve metres straight down. There was a clock with a blue face in the middle of the pediment and in the distance I heard a roll of thunder – all we were missing was a DeLorean.

'Do you believe in fate, Peter?' asked Chorley.

'No,' I said.

'Neither do I,' he said. 'And yet despite all our efforts to the contrary – here we are.'

Lesley climbed out to join us. I caught her eye. She'd transferred the sword to her left hand and in her right was the compact semi-automatic she'd used to shoot Stephanopoulos. She held it pointed down by her side with her finger safely outside the trigger guard as Caffrey had taught us both.

'There's no—' I said, but Chorley cut me off with a bark of laughter.

'No Arthur, no Merlin, no one sword,' he said. 'It's all dull old socio-economic forces acting on an undifferentiated mass of semi-evolved primates.'

'Sorry,' I said.

'Is he right?' asked Lesley.

'Why don't you ring the bell, and we'll find out?' said Chorley.

'Am I right, Marty?' I said. 'I think I am.'

'You're a bright boy, Peter,' said Chorley. 'I've always thought so. But you've never understood the limitations of your own viewpoint. It doesn't matter whether there was an actual Round Table, a king, a sword, a mighty magician. Because we can make it so.'

'And how do we do that?' I asked, because Chorley liked the sound of his own voice and so did I – especially when I was playing for time.

'Magic is about man reshaping reality itself,' he said. 'That's what the *formae* do, that's what a spell is. A tool to reshape the universe.'

'And you think you can just wish Merlin into existence?' I asked.

'No.' Chorley gave me a disturbingly confident grin. 'I think we can change existence so that Merlin is real. Given enough magic – enough juice, so to speak.'

'Wow. I didn't realise we were going to have to section you – I was hoping for a trial.'

But I was wondering whether he was right. There were definitely moments when I suspected that Beverley somehow warped the world into a more congenial shape around her. But she was a goddess, and did things beyond mortal ken. And anyway, if it were that easy Lady Ty's husband would be ageless and her daughter slightly less gullible.

'Martin,' said Lesley, pocketing her pistol, 'he's stalling.'

'Of course he is,' said Chorley. 'Are you ready?'

Lesley transferred the sword to her right hand.

'Lesley, this is insane,' I said. 'He's talking bollocks.'

Lesley ignored me and caught Chorley's eye.

'I do this and, whatever else, Punch dies?'

'Dead as a doornail,' said Chorley.

'Good enough for me,' said Lesley and swung the sword.

As I told the subsequent inquiry, I wasn't sure what I thought I was doing, but I wanted to try and disrupt Chorley's insane bit of ritual. Given that Lesley was armed with a sword, and Chorley wasn't, my choice was obvious. While Lesley was swinging I tensed. And as she hit the bell I threw myself at Chorley.

There was a flash that had nothing to do with reflected photons, and a beautiful sound.

The sword is a singing sword, I thought, as the chime struck me like a wave of freezing water. My shoulder struck Chorley just below the armpit and he staggered. I was counting on him being more centred, but he must have been distracted by the beauty of the chime. Because he went over backwards, off the side of the cornice.

And me with him.

I've got to stop doing this, I thought, as I fell into the rainy black.

A much shorter distance than I was expecting. And onto mud, not flagstones.

I'd lost my grip on Chorley, so I rolled away on general principle. But not fast enough to avoid getting a kick in the head. I rolled some more but managed to hit a tree – and that's when I knew where I was.

'I don't have time for this,' said Chorley. Of course he didn't. Because we were still falling and sooner or later real gravity was going to forcefully introduce us to the real flagstones of real London. 'Deal with him,' he said.

Not liking the sound of that, I used the tree trunk to pull myself up.

I was standing in light woodland, in dim grey light, morning or evening – I couldn't tell – with a light drizzle and mist. Three metres in front of me was a short white man in a yellow buff coat, matching trousers and big floppy cavalry boots. He wore a breastplate over his coat and I just had time to register the pistol he was pointing at me when there was a click, a hiss, a loud bang and a cloud of smoke. Nothing else happened.

Matchlock pistol – effective range five metres in ideal conditions. Which these weren't.

My cavalier didn't seem at all surprised at the miss. He calmly stuffed the pistol in his belt, and pulled out a rather fine cavalry sabre with a basket hilt and an effective range of whatever it got close to.

Weirdly, my Metvest would have served quite well if only I could have persuaded him not to stick me in the face, or the arms or the groin – particularly not the groin.

I considered surrendering, but settled for ducking behind the tree.

The man gave me an annoyed grimace, like a builder who's just been asked to do a bit of extra finishing up, and stepped forward. I could see in my head what was going to happen next. He'd feint one way and then stab me with the point when I moved the other way. The trunk of the tree suddenly seemed very small.

I was about to leg it in the other direction, on the basis I wasn't the one wearing the metal armour, when a high-pitched ululation from nearby interrupted us both. My poor cavalier had just enough time to grumpily turn to face in the right direction when a javelin whistled out of nowhere and pierced his throat. He staggered a step backwards and then fell with a look of profound irritation on his face.

I was expecting Tyburn, but instead got a much younger white guy, tall and lithe, with blond hair spiked up with grease and blue swirls on his face and naked chest. A golden torc gleamed at his neck and a cape made of dozens of beaver pelts stitched together hung rakishly off his shoulders.

Before I had a chance to speak he closed the distance between us, grabbed me and kissed me on the lips. Proper snog too, with tongue and everything. Not only was it not terrible as kisses go, it was also strangely familiar.

'Beverley,' I said when we broke for air. 'What the fuck is going on?'

'War has come to London,' he said and then, after a pause, added, 'Again.'

'Chorley is heading for the bridge,' I said – looking around to get my bearings. 'And I have to stop him.'

I was standing on high ground three hundred metres north of the ancient Thames, about where St Paul's Church was standing in the real world. The landscape had a strange unreal quality and was shrouded in a weird mist, as if I were playing a video game with a short draw distance.

I was still falling.

None of this was real.

But I've learnt that just because something isn't real doesn't mean it's not important.

I could look east at the wide and winding course of the river and see Londinium as a vague smudge. No walls, though – too early for them. The bridge was still there – laid low over pontoons to the first of the islands that made up Southwark. I thought something glittered on the central span.

To my south was the road, curving east before dropping down into the Fleet valley to that bridge and up again into Londinium.

'Come on,' I said. 'The road.'

'Whatever you say, babes,' he said and, grabbing my hand, starting running.

Fuck me, but these ancient rivers were fit. It was all I could do to keep up and I didn't have any imaginary breath left to speak. This close to the city, the road was the proper full Roman – three metres of cambered gravel with big drainage ditches either side. The Fleet was about a kilometre ahead and I could actually see Chorley on the road, halfway there. But he was walking – limping, in fact – and I reckoned I could take him.

But Beverley wouldn't let go of my hand.

'Hold up, babes,' he said.

There was a bestial howl from across the river and something black and doglike bounded down to the bank. Behind it thundered a couple of hundred men on horses, all in variations of the cuirass and long coat worn by my dead friend with the matchlock pistol.

That would be the Black Dog of Newgate, I thought, and the cavaliers might be riding the missing horses from Brentford.

To the right of the river crossing appeared, as if spawning into a video game, a couple of thousand burly men in mail and armour made of small plates of metal. They carried round shields, spears and axes and swords. On their heads were helmets that most definitely didn't have horns on them.

'So that's where the Holland Park Vikings went,' I said. 'Mr Chorley has been a busy, busy man.'

Had he known there'd be a confrontation? Or was it just his usual planning in depth? I decided that would be one of the many things we would have a conversation about by and by.

And, if the unreconstructed Lego merchants weren't enough, another mass came boiling out of the indistinct wattle and daub rectangles of Roman London. This was a rabble dressed from every period in London's history – stout men in doublet and hose, crooked bravos in puffy shorts and jackets with slashed sleeves to show the silk shirts below. There were top hats and bowlers, swords and muskets and clubs and pikes. From this levy *en masse* came an ugly, hate-filled muttering.

I've faced groups like this at closing time. Drunk,

angry people spoiling for a fight. You can talk down most Saturday night wastemen but there's always a hard core who don't think it's a proper night out if someone doesn't get hurt.

Among them rode men on horses, singly or in groups of three or four. They were straight-backed and arrogant and stank of money. I'd faced these too, but not as often – the likes of me didn't get to feel their collars very often.

'Who the fuck are they?' I asked.

'That's the gentry and their servants,' said blond Beverley. 'All the liars, hypocrites, exploiters, dog-bastards, wankers, janissaries, Monday men, cat-ranchers and people who fly-tip in protected waterways.'

'There's a lot of them,' I said.

'What can I say?' said Beverley. 'It's London, isn't it?'

I couldn't do the calculation in my head, but I was pretty sure that falling twelve metres at 9.8 m/s² meant I was going to hit the flagstones in just over a second. And whatever the real time/weirdo memory of London ratio was, I didn't think I had time to hang about.

I didn't need to fight them all. I just had to reach Chorley before he got to the bridge.

'Let's go,' I said, but Beverley put his hand on my arm to stop me.

'Wait,' he said. 'Got reinforcements coming.'

I heard them before they arrived. It was like a thousand pots and pans being rhythmically rattled against each other. And through the soles of my feet the stamp-stamp-stamp of thousands of hobnailed sandals hitting the ground in unison.

But trotting out of the arbitrary draw distance came

a pair of shaggy ponies, manes plaited and beribboned in yellow and green, drawing a wickerwork chariot with big wheels. Standing in the forward driving position was the first Tyburn, this time smartly dressed in a metal lorica, segmented skirt and deep red cloak. The only thing he was missing was a helmet with a horse-hair plume.

He did a flash little stop and swerve so that the open back of the chariot was towards me.

'Up you get,' he said, and pulled me into the chariot. 'Here they come.'

I looked to the west just in time for an entire bloody Roman legion to come jogging into view. Rank after rank, by the cohort and the numbers, but with no standard raised – no eagle.

The smell of blood rolled off them and, weirdly, olive oil.

They came to a halt in a clatter of iron.

'Fuck me,' I said. 'I'm in an episode of *Game of Thrones.*'

33

The Sacrifice of Gaius C. Pulcinella Considered as a Deleted Scene from The Lord of the Rings

'Useless fucks of the Ninth!' shouted Tyburn, and the legion muttered – a rolling sound like distant thunder. 'You failed this city once.' Jeers, catcalls, and I didn't need any Latin to recognise that tone. 'But the gods have given you a second chance.'

The legion fell silent – which was scarier than when they were making a noise.

'And this time you're going to get the job done!' shouted Tyburn.

There were mutters and sporadic cheers.

'Right?'

A cheer started in the cohort directly in front of us. It was taken up by those on either side and proceeded to roll outward and then back, finally to peter out as Tyburn held up his fist.

'Right!'

Five thousand men cheered and stamped their feet in unison; the ponies shied and pulled away. Tyburn didn't try and stop them. I looked back at Beverley, who blew me a kiss before running out to the flank with a javelin ready in his hand.

The Romans liked to outsource their cavalry, but every legion had a small contingent of its own. Small wiry men in mail on horses the size of Shetland ponies – their saddles looked ridiculous, with absurdly high cantles and no stirrups. But the points of their spears glittered in the sunlight.

As the chariot picked up speed down the road they formed up around us as an escort.

Up ahead Chorley had limped onto the bridge across the Fleet and looked back to find us bearing down in all our righteous fury. I saw him shout something and gesture and a brace of Norsemen barred the way.

'Take this,' said Fleet, and handed me a spear. I handed it back.

'I'm not using that,' I said. 'Haven't you got something a bit less lethal?'

'I'll see what I can do,' he said.

The Norsemen formed a line and braced their shields.

'Time to earn your triple pay, boys!' yelled Tyburn as the chariot went down the slope towards the bridge, picking up speed as it went.

The Roman cavalry surged ahead. There was a flurry of movement and then they wheeled away to the left and right. Straight ahead men at the centre of the shield wall were staggering backwards, or sitting down coughing up blood, with spears through important parts of their anatomy.

I could hear the screaming even over the mad thundering of our horses, but the line looked unbroken and we were going to hit it any second.

'Hold on!' yelled Tyburn.

Whooping, he vaulted over the edge of the chariot and ran along the pole until he was standing upright on the yoke between the heads of his horses, one javelin poised to throw, another in his left hand ready to go.

With another high-pitched yell he threw both spears, one after another. Two Norsemen directly ahead fell away and the rest looked at Tyburn's face and scattered. The shield wall broke and the chariot ploughed through.

As we did, Tyburn dropped down on the yoke and scooped something off the ground as the chariot passed over it. Then he popped back up and ran lightly along the pole to join me in the chariot. He passed me a round Norse shield.

'That better?' he asked.

I took the shield – it was heavier than the riot shield I'd trained with, made with wood bound with a metal rim and a centre grip within the boss. It was well balanced, nicely made, but probably not supposed to be wielded as a primary weapon.

We thundered across the bridge and the horses only slowed a little as they climbed out of the valley of the Fleet into Ludgate Hill, or at least what would be Ludgate Hill when there was a gate for it to be named after.

A shanty town with a bridge attached Tyburn had called early Londinium. But, even worse, it was spread out so thin that it was practically the countryside. Only the fort to the north had any stonework. Everything wattle and daub and thatch – half of them being the traditional British roundhouse.

The roads, though, were wide and well maintained, and fanned out from the point where the bridge met

387

the high ground like a net cast to catch an island. And ahead on Watling Street I saw Chorley halfway to the bridge already.

'We'll have him in no time,' said Tyburn, just as something huge and dog-shaped leapt out of nowhere and killed the chariot's left-hand horse.

The chariot pitched forward like an unexpected pole-vaulter and I think Tyburn threw me clear, because I have a definite memory of tumbling along the muddy verge, stopping and looking back in time to see a wheel scything into the thatch of a nearby roundhouse. The remaining horse was screaming and Tyburn was yelling as he wrestled with the Black Dog of Newgate Prison. I grabbed my shield that was, miraculously, nearby and legged it after Chorley.

If this turns out to be cyclical, I thought, I'm going to have serious words with whoever's in charge.

It was less than a kilometre from Ludgate Hill to the north end of London Bridge.

I was younger and fitter than Chorley, but he had a head start and the occasional friend who tried to kill me. I wasn't sure what death in the realm of memory would entail – probably nothing permanent. It wasn't going to be this very short gentleman with a leather jacket and a switchblade that killed me. It was going to be the sudden transfer of energy from potential into kinetic.

But I wasn't so sure about the matter that I didn't hit Leather Jacket very hard in the face with my shield and then stamp on his knife wrist, just to be on the safe side. Ditto for the posh guy on a horse, who obviously hadn't done any cavalry training or he wouldn't have pulled up beside me and tried to use a riding crop. I like to think the horse was quite relieved to be rid of him. He went into the Walbrook – the muddy creek, that is, not the conspicuously absent goddess.

I had a good view of the bridge by then. A classic bit of Roman military engineering, a wooden roadbed laid over a series of pontoons. It would rise and fall with the tides.

There was nobody on it apart from Martin Chorley.

When I saw this I stopped running and walked the rest of the way. Obviously today was my day.

Chorley glowered at me as he watched me approach.

'Where is Punch?' Chorley asked me when I reached him.

'He's behind you,' I said, and when he turned to look I punched him in the face.

His head snapped to the side and he staggered and gave me a look of hurt outrage. A look I've seen so many times on the street, or in an interview room or the magistrates' court. The one on the face of every bully that ever got what was coming to them and counted it unfair, an outrage – You can't do this to me. I know my rights.

'You let him go?' he said.

I said that I had.

'Why?' Chorley seemed sincerely perplexed.

'He thought I was the lesser of two evils,' said Punch suddenly beside us.

Not the moon-faced Italian puppet but the youngest son of an Atrebates sub-chief – black haired, square faced, dressed in the blood-stained remains of his fashionable Roman tunic, ripped across the front to show the horrid gaping wound in his belly. He was a sad sight, but his eyes were full of a screaming and dangerous mirth.

'More fool him,' he shrieked, and seized Chorley by the throat and lifted him off his feet.

I jumped forward but Punch casually backhanded me so hard I landed on my back more than a metre away.

'We had a deal,' I shouted.

'I don't bargain,' screamed Punch as I got to my feet.

'Father,' said a woman.

Still holding Chorley aloft, Punch turned to look at his daughter as she walked across the bridge towards us. She seemed taller, thinner and darker, and wore a sheath of white linen from armpit to ankle. From her shoulders trailed a shawl of implausibly gauzy material that streamed a couple of metres behind her in a non-existent wind.

Light blazed from the circlet around her head.

Isis of the Walbrook, I thought, you kept that quiet, girl, didn't you?

Punch turned to his daughter, his face stricken, mouth drawn down in pain.

'Never like that,' he said. 'You promised.'

The light faded, the gauzy shawl slipped from Walbrook's shoulders and went fluttering over the dark gleaming river. She became shorter, stockier and lighter until she was the women I'd met in the pub a month ago, complete with orange capri pants and purple scorpion T-shirt.

'Come on, Dad,' she said. 'Put the little man down.'

'Don't want to,' said Punch petulantly. 'Why should I?'

'Because my boy there is going to deal with him,' she said, glancing at me. 'And I owe him. And I pays my debts.'

'Shan't,' said Punch.

'Drop him!' said Walbrook sharply, and Punch let go and Chorley fell to the floor.

Punch dropped to his knees, grasped his daughter around her waist and pulled her tightly to him. His face was buried in her hair, tears streamed from his eyes, and he mumbled continuously something that sounded like Italian but was probably Latin.

Ack, I thought. Melodrama.

Walbrook turned to me and said, 'You still here?'

And then I was falling through the rain again.

Then we hit. But not the flagstones.

We hit something white and cold that buckled under the impact. Softer than cement, but still hard enough to rattle my brain. And I didn't have a chance to do anything useful before we rolled off the roof of the Transit van and fell the last metre and a half. This time we hit stone and it was even more painful than I was expecting.

The whole of my left side from shoulder to knee went numb, in that worrying numb-now pain-later way of a major injury, and the air was literally knocked out of my body. I was trying to breathe in but it felt as if my lungs were paralysed. Then I coughed. It hurt, then I breathed in – it was wonderful.

I rolled onto my back and looked up through the gently falling rain to see Lesley frowning down at me from the cornice. Then she vanished and I realised I had about twenty seconds while she ran down the steps.

And she'd still have that pistol, wouldn't she?

The flagstones were slick, so getting up was hard work. And I didn't like the way my knee hurt. My only consolation was that Martin Chorley was moaning and wasn't moving any faster than I was. I got to my feet while Chorley was still on his hands and knees. Grabbing him struck me as being too complicated an action and I did consider falling on him, but decided to caution him instead.

I got as far as 'Anything you say might be' when he flung out his hand and tried to *impello* me into the far wall of the cemetery. Fortunately he was in pain and I was ready with a shield – even so, I skidded back on my heels from the force of it. At which point Lesley came out of the main doors and, without hesitating, ran up to Chorley and kicked him in the stomach.

'He's not dead!' she screamed. 'You fucking fucker! You didn't kill him!'

This time the *impello* hit home, but on Lesley not me, and she went sprawling onto her back. Chorley took the opportunity to climb to his feet.

'That's hardly my fault!' he shouted. 'You can blame your fucking boyfriend.'

The rain was getting heavier and was dribbling into my eyes, but Nightingale has made me train in worse weather. I wondered if Chorley had ever practised in the rain – somehow I didn't think so.

Lesley got to her feet and that's how we found ourselves recreating the stand-off scene from *The Good, the Bad and the Ugly*, only wetter, closer together, and in central London.

I caught Lesley's eye for a fraction of a fraction of a second and tilted my head at Chorley. He didn't catch the gesture, but was hesitating because he didn't know which one of us to attack first.

We jumped, as we had jumped belligerent drunks every bloody weekend for two whole years. I went high, she went low, and we had the fucking Faceless Man face down on the ground and wearing my speedcuffs before you could say 'properly authorised restraint technique'.

Then we both hauled him to his feet and looked at each other, and sniggered.

Chorley started to react but I jerked the speedcuffs up in the approved manner and broke his chain of concentration.

'What now?' asked Lesley.

'You turn supergrass, don't you?' I said.

'You're not serious?' she said.

'I asked the CPS to draw up the paperwork ages ago.'

Chorley moved again and this time I stuck my finger in his ear and wriggled it to disrupt any spell formation. This I knew from conducting experiments with Nicky's enthusiastic help. The trick is to keep changing the method of disruption – it didn't hurt that Chorley was dazed and in pain after the fall.

Still, backup couldn't arrive fast enough – I was listening for sirens.

'I'm not talking about me,' she said, and pulled Chorley's nose. 'You can't be serious about arresting him.'

'That's the job,' I said.

'He'll escape,' she said, which reminded me to tweak the cuffs again.

393

'We've got plans,' I said. 'And brand new holding cells.'

'Oh shit,' said Lesley.

'And thanks to you I may even have a—'

Lesley pulled out her pistol and shot Martin Chorley in the head.

I flinched as something that was not rain splashed my face and as, with no more than a rustle of his clothing, Chorley flopped bonelessly to the ground. I looked back at Lesley, who had taken a step backwards so she could point the gun at my face without it being within arm's reach.

'Check his pulse,' she said.

Slowly I squatted down and fumbled in the wet collar of Martin Chorley's coat. I felt his neck for a pulse. Nothing. Not really surprising, given there was an entry wound where his right eye should have been.

'Is he dead?' asked Lesley. The rain was running down her face, but her aim was steady.

I stood and the barrel of the gun followed me up.

'What now?' I asked. 'Am I next?'

Lesley laughed. It surprised me – I think it surprised her too.

'You pillock,' she said. 'I did this for you. If you'd helped we could have done it nice and clean and nobody would have been the wiser. Do you think anyone wanted a trial? Do you really think you could have kept him banged up in Belmarsh without him escaping?'

'That's not the point—'

'That is the point,' she said firmly, and because she still had a gun on me I didn't push the matter. 'And now an avalanche of shit is going to land on your head. If you're still in the job in a year I will be totally gob-smacked.' She paused and shrugged. 'Although if you want I could shoot you in your leg – make your statement look a bit better.'

'I think I'll forgo the maiming,' I said. 'If it's all the same to you.'

'Yeah, OK,' said Lesley. 'Besides, Bev would be well vexed if I sent you back with a hole.'

Instead, she made me unlock the cuffs on Martin Chorley and cuff myself to him – using my right wrist. Then she took the key.

'So what about you?' I asked, because every minute talking to me raised the likelihood Nightingale would catch up with us.

'Oh, I'm getting the fuck out of here,' she said. 'And you really don't want to come after me.'

She made me lie down next to the corpse with my hands clasped behind my head. Because of the cuffs Martin Chorley's cold hand kept on brushing up against my wrist.

The rain fell heavily enough on the cobbles to mask Lesley's footsteps, but I'm pretty certain she was gone thirty seconds later.

I probably could have sprung up, snapped the speed-cuffs and given chase, but I had nothing left. So I lay on the cobbles and waited for someone else to clean up the mess.

34

Gardening Leave

They suspended me. They had to. Martin Chorley had died in my custody, wearing my cuffs and shot by a former colleague of mine. And this time I was plucked from the warm familiar surroundings of the Department of Professional Standards and into the cold embrace of the IPCC. I went to interviews with my Federation rep by my side and gave minimalist answers to their questions with an air of helpful bafflement. I didn't think they'd charge me especially since, apart from anything else, I got the impression they had more corrupt fish than me to fry.

Still, these internal investigations take months and I was advised to start thinking of it as a long paid sabbatical.

Because the Folly was officially a police station, I had to move out and move in with Beverley full time. Which at least, I thought, would be a respite from Latin, Greek and practical thaumaturgy. Alas, Nightingale proved perfectly capable of driving across the river and worse, had mastered the dark art of skyping. I blamed Abigail for the latter, although she denied everything.

I also had to get myself my own car, although I did suggest that I might borrow the Ferrari – which caused

Nightingale to spontaneously burst out laughing. I eyed up some second-hand BMWs and a Mercedes, but I didn't have the cash. In the end Beverley bought me a bright orange Ford Focus as an early birthday present.

'And you have to keep this one intact,' she said. 'Because it's a present.'

It could have been worse. It could have been a Kia.

Abigail went back to school, but alternated on the weekend between taking classes with Nightingale at the Folly and with me at Beverley's. She also passed on the gossip in exchange for some of my illicit magical research.

I was, finally, invited up to have dinner up chez Stephanopoulos to meet 'her indoors', who turned out to be a round-faced white woman called Pam who taught Strategic Management at the University of Middlesex. There was indeed a chicken coop in the back garden and a newly furnished nursery about which they asked me for no advice whatsoever.

Stephanopoulos was walking with a stick and expected to be back at work before I was.

Strangely, despite my conspicuous absence from operational policing, London was spared a plague of headless horsemen or psychotic gnomes. Although Nightingale and Frank Caffrey dealt with a vampire nest in Neasden. Curiously, these vampires turned out to be infected rats. Which meant not only was I spared any ethical qualms, but also Dr Vaughan got some tissue samples.

'I hope you're taking precautions,' I said, while undergoing my monthly physical.

'Do you think that's really necessary?' asked Dr Vaughan.

'Yes, absolutely,' I said.

'And there was I about to set them up as a conversation piece on my coffee table,' she said. 'But at least I'll get to use some of that biohazard training that I took especially.'

'You're losing weight,' said Dr Walid.

'And missing Molly,' I said.

Although, according to Abigail, she wasn't missing me.

'I think she smiled the other day,' she said. 'And Foxglove is painting the kitchen.'

'What colour?'

'Henri Rousseau,' said Abigail. 'And what are you planning to do about Foxglove?'

There are legal provisions that allow victims of trafficking to claim *discretionary leave to remain* or asylum status, but they're bureaucratic and stressful and frankly designed to deter people from trying. Worse still, the screening centre in Croydon would be bound to ask difficult questions, like – *Where exactly are you from originally?* So I called in a favour from Lady Ty, who was always having her wicked way with the Home Office.

'What favour exactly,' said Lady Ty, 'do you think you're calling in?'

'I'm not calling it in,' I said. 'I'm giving you a chance to pay it forward.'

'And I'm going to do this thing . . . because?'

'Because then I'll owe you a favour.'

'Because that worked out so well last time,' she said.

'Like it or not, Ty, you're going to be working with me in the future,' I said.

'I thought you were suspended?'

'Me or someone like me.'

'Peter,' said Lady Ty, 'every morning I wake up and give thanks that there's nobody else like you.'

'So you'll put the fix in, right?'

'Yeah, yeah, yeah,' she said. 'Whatever.'

There was no way that we were allowing Patrick Gale and his fellow practitioners the run of the Folly, so we agreed that their training would take place in a neutral location. I'd wanted to stick them in the community rooms at my parents' flats but Nightingale vetoed that on security grounds.

'There's no point keeping them at arm's length,' he said, 'if we give them your parents' address.'

So we ended up renting space from the Talacre Community Sports Centre down the road. But before they got a sniff of training we made them swear an oath and, more importantly, sign a non-disclosure agreement three centimetres thick. This gave Patrick Gale pause, but when we made it clear that the agreement wasn't up for negotiation he and his friends signed.

There were six of them – three were lawyers, two worked in HR, and one was Patrick's Executive Assistant. We started by marching them over to UCH, where Dr Walid put their heads in an MRI and Dr Vaughan spent a merry twenty minutes showing them her highly educational brain collection. Once they'd been suitably apprised of the dangers Nightingale assessed them for basic magical competency.

'As I thought likely,' he said. 'None of them had progressed far beyond the *lux* forma and its many variations.'

We'd agreed that we wanted to keep this curriculum as non-lethal as possible, so Nightingale had dredged up his own memories of his first year at Casterbrook's school for future wizards.

'By necessity your education has had to be somewhat martial,' he said. 'I found it quite satisfying to teach the beginning *formae* in a more relaxed fashion. I might even consider teaching full time when I retire.'

'Let's not get ahead of ourselves,' I said.

'Quite,' said Nightingale.

There was a report in the *Evening Standard* that two figures dressed as Ninjas had been seen running across the rooftops of Soho, waving swords and doing gravity-defying leaps and bounds from building to building. Online speculation was that this was some kind of elaborate prank carried out in the Japanese style and sooner or later the result would appear on YouTube complete with badly translated subtitles.

'Was that you?' I asked Guleed and Michael Cheung when we were out on a double date at the Number Four Restaurant on the Hertford Road.

'That's an operational matter,' she said. 'And I am strictly forbidden to talk to you about that stuff.'

I personally was reassured to know that Guleed was

out on the cobbles, showing her face and creating order out of chaos. I did make time to ask Nightingale about the 'agreement' with Chinatown.

'There really is nothing mysterious about it,' he said. 'By the 1970s a large number of Chinese were setting up businesses around Gerrard Street. I knew from my experiences in America that this would quickly acquire what you would call a distinct ethnic identity.'

This, he surmised, would include their own structures and hierarchies because nothing says persistence likefour thousand years of continuous civilisation.

'I went and talked to some influential business people and made a bit of a demonstration.' Nightingale made a sharp downward gesture with his hand that I've learnt to associate with his more showier bits of magic. 'Said I was agreeable to a meeting to get things sorted out and let them formulate their own response. A couple of days later I received a hand-delivered invitation at the Folly.'

'Had you told them about the Folly?'

'No.'

'So they . . .' I left the implication hanging.

'Yes,' he said. 'Precisely. So that evening I sat down for a perfectly splendid meal with some very distinguished gentlemen who introduced me to a young man called Simon Wong, who said that, should I be agreeable, he would take responsibility for maintaining the peace within Chinatown.'

'Did he have a sword?'

'Yes,' said Nightingale. 'Although he didn't have a card identifying himself as a legendary swordsman.

That seems a more modern form of whimsy. I sensed that the sword was important, though, in a mythic or symbolic sense.'

'In what way?'

'I was rather hoping that one day Sahra could tell us.'

'You're such a romantic,' I said.

'Merely an interested observer. And as such I need to ask you a personal question.'

'Ask away,' I said, but only because I couldn't see a convenient window I could dive out of.

'Have you talked to anyone about your experiences?' he said.

'I'm considering it,' I said.

'May I suggest you do more than that? After I came back from the war I found it very useful to talk things through.'

There was quite a long silence as I waited for more – in vain, as it happened.

'I'll do that then,' I said.

'Jolly good,' said Nightingale.

So I got someone to talk to. A very nice old lady psychiatrist that Postmartin knew, called Valerie Green. Her father had been a famous psychiatrist in Vienna and her mother had been a famous singer. He'd been Jewish and she'd been Sinti – both had fetched up in London in 1938. Valerie had been born after the war and had gone into her father's profession.

'Couldn't sing, darling,' she said.

Postmartin hinted strongly that one of her parents had been a practitioner of some kind, although Valerie wouldn't say which one. It did mean that I could tell her everything without being immediately committed, and I suspect that David Carey was another client of hers. But of course she wouldn't say.

All this meant that I was now expected to reveal my innermost thoughts to at least three people. Although, to be fair, I don't think Toby was that interested.

Nightingale had been right – it was useful.

As was the magic training, the Latin, the Greek, teaching Abigail, and writing the ever-expanding Folly Expansion document – now incorporating the lessons learnt from Operation Jennifer.

The principal one being that we needed to maintain a complement of at least six new practitioners, and that was only counting the ones that were also police officers.

All of this helped keep my mind off the possibility of being dismissed or, more likely, being quietly given the option to retire with full benefits or else.

'Would it be so bad if it was or else?' asked Beverley one afternoon in late August.

'You mean apart from the public disgrace and the loss of my pension?'

We were in her big tub at her house, having spent the morning strenuously avoiding any possible physical exertion. Beverley's head was leaning comfortably against my chest and she was occasionally persuading the water to warm itself up.

'Yeah, apart from that,' she said.

'I haven't finished,' I said.

'Finished what?'

'Any of it. The magic, the policing, the reorganisation—' I stopped when Beverley shook with suppressed laughter.

'The reorganisation,' she wheezed.

'It's important,' I said.

'The reorganisation,' she said, and sighed. 'Would you quit if I asked you to?'

'Truthfully?'

'Of course truthfully,' she said. 'Always truthfully.'

'I don't know,' I said. 'Do you want me to quit?'

'Truthfully?'

'Yeah.'

'I don't know,' she said.

'What's brought all this on?'

'Ah yes,' she said. 'There's something you need to know.'

She took my hand and firmly placed it on her belly – it was smooth and warm.

And then, as they say, the penny dropped.

'No,' I said.

'Yes,' said Beverley.

'But what about your degree?'

'It doesn't actually cause your brains to dribble out of your ears,' she said.

I had a good feel, but her stomach felt the same shape as before – at least I think it did.

'Stop it,' said Beverley. 'That tickles.'

'Mum will be pleased,' I said.

'So will mine.'

'Tyburn's going to be well pissed off, though.'

'Bonus,' said Beverley, and wriggled round to kiss me.

HISTORICAL AND TECHNICAL NOTES

The Whitechapel Bell Foundry was a real place up until April 2017, when it left London to be replaced, no doubt, by a boutique hotel, some luxury flats and a coffee shop. All the workers described in this book are 100% made up and any resemblance to any real person living or dead is completely coincidental.

The London Mithraeum has been returned to its original location, thanks to Bloomberg, and is now open to the public. I've visited and it's worth a look, although I prefer to think of it as the Temple of Bacchus – a deity who seems much more in keeping with the spirit of London than grumpy old Mithras. I also find it a comforting to think that somewhere in the City under all that money and modernist concrete is a Temple of Isis – unless it's under St Paul's, that is.

The skulls in the Walbrook are now thought to have been washed there by occasional floods from graveyards outside the Roman city boundaries, rather than being the victims of Boudicca's sack of Londinium. This probably won't be the last time Peter jumps to a conclusion based on evidence that is later disproved.

ACKNOWLEDGEMENTS

I'd like to thank my colleagues Andrew and James who have to listen to the plots of these books long before they make any kind of coherent sense. Also a thanks to John my agent and Jon, Gillian, Stevie, Jen, Paul S, Paul H and the rest of the gang at Orion. Steve for the meticulous copyedit. Anne and Liz who run my life and Joel who keeps the books. Last but not least all those professionals who patiently answered really obvious questions about policing – Bob Hunter; biology – Lucy Stewart; sewer maintenance – Vincent Minney; archaeology – Amy Reid and everyone else at MOLA: and not least lots of extra Latin from Penelope and Paul of the Classics Department of Leeds University.

Help us make the next generation of readers

We – both author and publisher – hope you enjoyed this book. We believe that you can become a reader at any time in your life, but we'd love your help to give the next generation a head start.

Did you know that 9% of children don't have a book of their own in their home, rising to 13% in disadvantaged families*? We'd like to try to change that by asking you to consider the role you could play in helping to build readers of the future.

We'd love you to think of sharing, borrowing, reading, buying or talking about a book with a child in your life and spreading the love of reading. We want to make sure the next generation continue to have access to books, wherever they come from.

And if you would like to consider donating to charities that help fund literacy projects, find out more at www.literacytrust.org.uk and www.booktrust.org.uk.

Thank you.

*As reported by the National Literacy Trust